GRR

KT-433-884

BOOKS BY E L JAMES

Fifty Shades of Grey

Fifty Shades Darker

Fifty Shades Freed

Grey

GREY

E L JAMES

arrow books

1 3 5 7 9 10 8 6 4 2

Arrow Books
20 Vauxhall Bridge Road
London SW1V 2SA

Arrow Books is part of the Penguin Random House group of companies
whose addresses can be found at global.penguinrandomhouse.com.

First published in Great Britain by Arrow Books in 2015

www.randomhouse.co.uk

A CIP catalogue record for this book is available from the British Library.

ISBN 9781784753252

Book design by Claudia Martinez
Cover design by Sqicedragon and Megan Wilson

Printed and bound by CPI Group (UK) Ltd, Croydon, CR0 4YY

MIX
Paper from
responsible sources
FSC® C018179
FSC
www.fsc.org

Penguin Random House is committed to a sustainable future
for our business, our readers and our planet. This book is made
from Forest Stewardship Council® certified paper.

*This book is dedicated to those readers who asked . . .
and asked . . . and asked . . . and asked for this.*

Thank you for all that you've done for me.

You rock my world every day.

ACKNOWLEDGMENTS

Thanks to:

Anne Messitte for her guidance, good humor, and belief in me. For her generosity with her time and for her unstinting effort to untangle my prose, I am forever indebted.

Tony Chirico and Russell Perreault for always looking out for me, and the fabulous production editorial and design team who saw this book across the finish line: Amy Brosey, Lydia Buechler, Katherine Hourigan, Andy Hughes, Claudia Martinez, and Megan Wilson.

Niall Leonard for his love, support, and guidance, and for being the only man who can really, really make me laugh.

Valerie Hoskins, my agent, without whom I'd still be working in TV. Thank you for everything.

Kathleen Blandino, Ruth Clampett, and Belinda Willis: thanks for the pre-read.

The Lost Girls for their precious friendship and the therapy.

The Bunker Babes for their constant wit, wisdom, support, and friendship.

The FP ladies for help with my Americanisms.

Peter Branston for his help with SFBT.

Brian Brunetti for his guidance in flying a helicopter.

Professor Dawn Carusi for help in navigating the U.S. higher education system.

Professor Chris Collins for an education in soil science.

Dr. Raina Sluder for her insights into behavioral health.

And last but by no means least, my children. I love you more than words can ever say. You bring such joy to my life and to those around you. You are beautiful, funny, bright, compassionate young men, and I could not be more proud of you.

GREY

MONDAY, MAY 9, 2011

I have three cars. They go fast across the floor. So fast. One is red. One is green. One is yellow. I like the green one. It's the best. Mommy likes them, too. I like when Mommy plays with the cars and me. The red is her best. Today she sits on the couch staring at the wall. The green car flies into the rug. The red car follows. Then the yellow. Crash! But Mommy doesn't see. I do it again. Crash! But Mommy doesn't see. I aim the green car at her feet. But the green car goes under the couch. I can't reach it. My hand is too big for the gap. Mommy doesn't see. I want my green car. But Mommy stays on the couch staring at the wall. *Mommy. My car.* She doesn't hear me. *Mommy.* I pull her hand and she lies back and closes her eyes. *Not now, Maggot. Not now,* she says. My green car stays under the couch. It's always under the couch. I can see it. But I can't reach it. My green car is fuzzy. Covered in gray fur and dirt. I want it back. But I can't reach it. I can never reach it. My green car is lost. Lost. And I can never play with it again.

I open my eyes and my dream fades in the early-morning light. *What the hell was that about?* I grasp at the fragments as they recede, but fail to catch any of them.

Dismissing it, like I do most mornings, I climb out of bed and find some newly laundered sweats in my walk-in closet. Outside, a leaden sky promises rain, and I'm not in the mood to be rained on during my run today. I head upstairs to my gym, switch on the TV for the morning business news, and step onto the treadmill.

My thoughts stray to the day. I've nothing but meetings, though I'm seeing my personal trainer later for a workout at my office—Bastille is always a welcome challenge.

Maybe I should call Elena?

Yeah. Maybe. We can do dinner later this week.

I stop the treadmill, breathless, and head down to the shower to start another monotonous day.

"TOMORROW," I MUTTER, DISMISSING Claude Bastille as he stands at the threshold of my office.

"Golf, this week, Grey." Bastille grins with easy arrogance, knowing that his victory on the golf course is assured.

I scowl at him as he turns and leaves. His parting words rub salt into my wounds because, despite my heroic attempts during our workout today, my personal trainer has kicked my ass. Bastille is the only one who can beat me, and now he wants another pound of flesh on the golf course. I detest golf, but so much business is done on the fairways, I have to endure his lessons there, too . . . and though I hate to admit it, playing against Bastille does improve my game.

As I stare out the window at the Seattle skyline, the familiar ennui seeps unwelcome into my consciousness. My mood is as flat and gray as the weather. My days are blending together with no distinction, and I need some kind of diversion. I've worked all weekend, and now, in the continued confines of my office, I'm restless. I shouldn't feel this way, not after several bouts with Bastille. But I do.

I frown. The sobering truth is that the only thing to capture my interest recently has been my decision to send two freighters of cargo to Sudan. This reminds me—Ros is supposed to come back to me with numbers and logistics. *What the hell is keeping her?* I check my schedule and reach for the phone.

Damn. I have to endure an interview with the persistent Miss Kavanagh for the WSU student newspaper. *Why the hell did I agree to this?* I loathe interviews—inane questions from ill-informed, envious people intent on probing my private life. *And she's a student.* The phone buzzes.

"Yes," I snap at Andrea, as if she's to blame. At least I can keep this interview short.

"Miss Anastasia Steele is here to see you, Mr. Grey."

"Steele? I was expecting Katherine Kavanagh."

"It's Miss Anastasia Steele who's here, sir."

I hate the unexpected. "Show her in."

Well, well . . . Miss Kavanagh is unavailable. I know her father, Eamon, the owner of Kavanagh Media. We've done business together, and he seems like a shrewd operator and a rational human being. This interview is a favor to him—one that I mean to cash in on later when it suits me. And I have to admit I was vaguely curious about his daughter, interested to see if the apple has fallen far from the tree.

A commotion at the door brings me to my feet as a whirl of long chestnut hair, pale limbs, and brown boots dives headfirst into my office. Repressing my natural annoyance at such clumsiness, I hurry over to the girl who has landed on her hands and knees on the floor. Clasping slim shoulders, I help her to her feet.

Clear, embarrassed eyes meet mine and halt me in my tracks. They are the most extraordinary color, powder blue, and guileless, and for one awful moment, I think she can see right through me and I'm left . . . exposed. The thought is unnerving, so I dismiss it immediately.

She has a small, sweet face that is blushing now, an innocent pale rose. I wonder briefly if all her skin is like that—flawless—and what it would look like pink and warmed from the bite of a cane.

Damn.

I stop my wayward thoughts, alarmed at their direction. *What the hell are you thinking, Grey?* This girl is much too young. She gapes at me, and I resist rolling my eyes. *Yeah, yeah, baby, it's just a face, and it's only skin deep.* I need to dispel that admiring look from those eyes but let's have some fun in the process!

"Miss Kavanagh. I'm Christian Grey. Are you all right? Would you like to sit?"

There's that blush again. In command once more, I study her. She's quite attractive—slight, pale, with a mane of dark hair barely contained by a hair tie.

A brunette.

Yeah, she's attractive. I extend my hand as she stutters the beginning of a mortified apology and places her hand in mine. Her skin is cool and soft, but her handshake surprisingly firm.

"Miss Kavanagh is indisposed, so she sent me. I hope you don't mind, Mr. Grey." Her voice is quiet with a hesitant musicality, and she blinks erratically, long lashes fluttering.

Unable to keep the amusement from my voice as I recall her less-than-elegant entrance into my office, I ask who she is.

"Anastasia Steele. I'm studying English literature with Kate, um . . . Katherine . . . um . . . Miss Kavanagh, at WSU Vancouver."

A *bashful, bookish type, eh?* She looks it: poorly dressed, her slight frame hidden beneath a shapeless sweater, an A-line brown skirt, and utilitarian boots. *Does she have any sense of style at all?* She looks nervously around my office—everywhere but at me, I note, with amused irony.

How can this young woman be a journalist? She doesn't have an assertive bone in her body. She's flustered, meek . . . submissive. Bemused at my inappropriate thoughts, I shake my head and wonder if first impressions are reliable. Muttering some platitude, I ask her to sit, then notice her discerning gaze appraising my office paintings. Before I can stop myself, I find I'm explaining them. "A local artist. Trouton."

"They're lovely. Raising the ordinary to extraordinary," she says dreamily, lost in the exquisite, fine artistry of Trouton's work. Her profile is delicate—an upturned nose, soft, full lips—and in her words she has captured my sentiments exactly. *Raising the ordinary to extraordinary.* It's a keen observation. Miss Steele is bright.

I agree and watch, fascinated, as that flush creeps slowly over her skin once more. As I sit down opposite her, I try to bridle my thoughts. She fishes some crumpled sheets of paper and a digital recorder out of her large bag. She's all thumbs, dropping the damned thing twice on my Bauhaus coffee table. It's obvious she's never done this before, but for some reason I can't fathom, I find it amusing. Under normal circumstances her maladroitness would irritate the hell out of me, but now I hide my smile beneath my index finger and resist the urge to set it up for her myself.

As she fumbles and grows more and more flustered, it occurs to me that I could refine her motor skills with the aid of a riding crop. Adeptly used, it can bring even the most skittish to heel. The errant thought makes me shift in my chair. She peeks up at me and bites down on her full bottom lip.

Fuck! How did I not notice how inviting that mouth is?

"S-Sorry, I'm not used to this."

I can tell, baby, but right now I don't give a damn because I can't take my eyes off your mouth.

"Take all the time you need, Miss Steele." I need another moment to marshal my wayward thoughts.

Grey . . . stop this, now.

"Do you mind if I record your answers?" she asks, her face candid and expectant.

I want to laugh. "After you've taken so much trouble to set up the recorder, you ask me now?"

She blinks, her eyes large and lost for a moment, and I'm overcome by an unfamiliar twinge of guilt.

Stop being such a shit, Grey. "No, I don't mind." I don't want to be responsible for that look.

"Did Kate, I mean, Miss Kavanagh, explain what the interview was for?"

"Yes, to appear in the graduation issue of the student newspaper, as I shall be giving the commencement address at this year's graduation ceremony." Why the hell I've agreed to do *that*, I don't know. Sam in PR tells me that WSU's environmental sciences department needs the publicity in order to attract additional funding to match the grant I've given them, and Sam will go to any lengths for media exposure.

Miss Steele blinks once more, as if this is news to her—and she looks disapproving. Hasn't she done any background work for this interview? She should know this. The thought cools my blood. It's . . . displeasing, not what I expect from someone who's imposing on my time.

"Good. I have some questions, Mr. Grey." She tucks a lock of hair behind her ear, distracting me from my annoyance.

"I thought you might," I say dryly. Let's make her squirm. Obligingly, she does, then pulls herself upright and squares her small shoulders. She means business. Leaning forward, she presses the start button on the recorder and frowns as she glances down at her crumpled notes.

"You're very young to have amassed such an empire. To what do you owe your success?"

Surely she can do better than this. What a dull question. Not one iota of originality. It's disappointing. I trot out my usual response about having exceptional people working for me. People I trust, insofar as I trust anyone, and pay well—blah, blah, blah . . . But Miss Steele, the simple fact is, I'm brilliant at what I do. For me it's like falling off a log. Buying ailing, mismanaged companies and fixing them, keeping some or, if they're really broken, stripping their assets and selling them off to the highest bidder. It's simply a question of knowing the difference between the two, and invariably it comes down to the people in charge. To succeed in business you need good people, and I can judge a person, better than most.

"Maybe you're just lucky," she says quietly.

Lucky? A frisson of annoyance runs through me. *Lucky?* How dare she? She looks unassuming and quiet, but this question? No one has ever suggested that I was lucky. Hard work, bringing people with me, keeping a close watch on them, and second-guessing them if I need to, and if they aren't up to the task, ditching them. *That's what I do, and I do it well. It's nothing to do with luck! Well, to hell with that.* Flaunting my erudition, I quote the words of Andrew Carnegie, my favorite industrialist. "The growth and development of people is the highest calling of leadership."

"You sound like a control freak," she says, and she's perfectly serious.

What the hell? Maybe she *can* see through me.

"Control" is my middle name, sweetheart.

I glare at her, hoping to intimidate her. "Oh, I exercise control in all things, Miss Steele." And I'd like to exercise it over you, right here, right now.

That attractive blush steals across her face, and she bites that lip again. I ramble on, trying to distract myself from her mouth.

"Besides, immense power is acquired by assuring yourself, in your secret reveries, that you were born to control things."

"Do you feel that you have immense power?" she asks in a soft, soothing voice, but she arches a delicate brow with a look that conveys her censure. Is she deliberately trying to goad me? Is it her questions, her attitude, or the fact that I find her attractive that's pissing me off? My annoyance grows.

"I employ over forty thousand people. That gives me a certain sense of responsibility—power, if you will. If I were to decide I was no longer interested in the telecommunications business and sell, twenty thousand people would struggle to make their mortgage payments after a month or so."

Her mouth pops open at my response. That's more like it. *Suck it up, baby.* I feel my equilibrium returning.

"Don't you have a board to answer to?"

"I own my company. I don't have to answer to a board." She should know this.

"And do you have any interests outside your work?" she continues hastily, correctly gauging my reaction. She knows I'm pissed, and for some inexplicable reason this pleases me.

"I have varied interests, Miss Steele. Very varied." Images of her in assorted positions in my playroom flash through my mind: shackled on the cross, spread-eagled on the four-poster, splayed over the whipping bench. And behold—there's that blush again. It's like a defense mechanism.

"But if you work so hard, what do you do to chill out?"

"Chill out?" Those words out of her smart mouth sound odd but amusing. Besides, when do I get time to chill out? She has no idea what I do. But she looks at me again with those ingenuous big eyes, and to my surprise I find myself considering her question. *What do I do to chill out?* Sailing, flying, fucking . . . testing the limits of attractive brunettes like her, and bringing them to heel . . . The thought makes me shift in my seat, but I answer her smoothly, omitting a few favorite hobbies.

"You invest in manufacturing. Why, specifically?"

"I like to build things. I like to know how things work: what makes things tick, how to construct and deconstruct. And I have a love of ships. What can I say?" They transport food around the planet.

"That sounds like your heart talking, rather than logic and facts."

Heart? Me? Oh no, baby.

My heart was savaged beyond recognition a long time ago. "Possibly. Though there are people who'd say I don't have a heart."

"Why would they say that?"

"Because they know me well." I give her a wry smile. In fact, no one knows me that well, except maybe Elena. I wonder what she would make of little Miss Steele here. The girl is a mass of contradictions: shy, awkward, obviously bright, and arousing as hell.

Yes, okay, I admit it. I find her alluring.

She recites the next question by rote. "Would your friends say you're easy to get to know?"

"I'm a very private person. I go a long way to protect my privacy. I don't often give interviews." Doing what I do, living the life I've chosen, I need my privacy.

"Why did you agree to do this one?"

"Because I'm a benefactor of the university, and for all intents and purposes, I couldn't get Miss Kavanagh off my back. She badgered and badgered my PR people, and I admire that kind of tenacity." But I'm glad it's you who turned up and not her.

"You also invest in farming technologies. Why are you interested in this area?"

"We can't eat money, Miss Steele, and there are too many people on this planet who don't have enough food." I stare at her, poker-faced.

"That sounds very philanthropic. Is that something you feel passionately about? Feeding the world's poor?" She regards me with a puzzled look, as if I'm a conundrum, but there's no way I want her seeing into my dark soul. This is not an area open to discussion. *Move it along, Grey.*

"It's shrewd business," I mutter, feigning boredom, and I imagine fucking that mouth to distract myself from all thoughts of hunger. Yes, her mouth needs training, and I imagine her on her knees before me. Now, that thought is appealing.

She recites her next question, dragging me away from my fantasy. "Do you have a philosophy? If so, what is it?"

"I don't have a philosophy as such. Maybe a guiding principle—Carnegie's: 'A man who acquires the ability to take full possession of his own mind may take possession of anything else to which he is justly entitled.' I'm very singular, driven. I like control—of myself and those around me."

"So you want to possess things?"

Yes, baby. You, for one. I frown, startled by the thought.

"I want to deserve to possess them, but yes, bottom line, I do."

"You sound like the ultimate consumer." Her voice is tinged with disapproval, pissing me off again.

"I am."

She sounds like a rich kid who's had all she ever wanted, but as I take a closer look at her clothes—she's dressed in clothes from some cheap store like Old Navy or H&M—I know that isn't it. She hasn't grown up in an affluent household.

I could really take care of you.

Where the hell did that thought come from?

Although, now that I consider it, I do need a new sub. It's been, what—two months since Susannah? And here I am, salivating over this woman. I try an agreeable smile. Nothing wrong with consumption—after all, it drives what's left of the American economy.

"You were adopted. How much do you think that's shaped the way you are?"

What does this have to do with the price of oil? What a ridiculous question. If I'd stayed with the crack whore, I'd probably be dead. I blow her off with a non-answer, trying to keep my voice level, but she pushes me, demanding to know how old I was when I was adopted.

Shut her down, Grey!

My tone goes cold. "That's a matter of public record, Miss Steele."

She should know this, too. Now she looks contrite as she tucks an escaped strand of hair behind her ear. *Good.*

"You've had to sacrifice family life for your work."

"That's not a question," I snap.

She startles, clearly embarrassed, but she has the grace to apologize and she rephrases the question: "Have you had to sacrifice family life for your work?"

What do I want with a family? "I have a family. I have a brother, a sister, and two loving parents. I'm not interested in extending my family beyond that."

"Are you gay, Mr. Grey?"

What the hell!

I cannot believe she's said that out loud! Ironically, the question even my own family will not ask. How dare she! I have a sudden urge to drag her out of her seat, bend her over my knee, spank her, and then fuck her over my desk with her hands tied behind her back. That would answer her ridiculous question. I take a deep calming breath. To my vindictive delight, she appears to be mortified by her own question.

"No, Anastasia, I'm not." I raise my eyebrows, but keep my expression impassive. *Anastasia.* It's a lovely name. I like the way my tongue rolls around it.

"I apologize. It's, um . . . written here." She's at it again with the hair behind the ear. Obviously it's a nervous habit.

Are these not her questions? I ask her, and she pales. Damn, she really is attractive, in an understated sort of way.

"Er . . . no. Kate—Miss Kavanagh—she compiled the questions."

"Are you colleagues on the student paper?"

"No. She's my roommate."

No wonder she's all over the place. I scratch my chin, debating whether or not to give her a really hard time.

"Did you volunteer to do this interview?" I ask, and I'm rewarded with her submissive look: she's nervous about my reaction. I like the effect I have on her.

"I was drafted. She's not well." Her voice is soft.

"That explains a great deal."

There's a knock at the door, and Andrea appears.

"Mr. Grey, forgive me for interrupting, but your next meeting is in two minutes."

"We're not finished here, Andrea. Please cancel my next meeting."

Andrea gapes at me, looking confused. I stare at her. *Out! Now!* I'm busy with little Miss Steele here.

"Very well, Mr. Grey," she says, recovering quickly, and turning on her heel, she leaves us.

I turn my attention back to the intriguing, frustrating creature on my couch. "Where were we, Miss Steele?"

"Please, don't let me keep you from anything."

Oh no, baby. It's my turn now. I want to know if there are any secrets to uncover behind that lovely face.

"I want to know about you. I think that's only fair." As I lean back and press my fingers to my lips, her eyes flick to my mouth and she swallows. *Oh yes—the usual effect.* And it is gratifying to know she isn't completely oblivious of my charms.

"There's not much to know," she says, her blush returning.

I'm intimidating her. "What are your plans after you graduate?"

"I haven't made any plans, Mr. Grey. I just need to get through my final exams."

"We run an excellent internship program here."

What possessed me ever to say that? It's against the rules, Grey. Never fuck the staff . . . But you're not fucking this girl.

She looks surprised, and her teeth sink into that lip again. Why is that so arousing?

"Oh. I'll bear that in mind," she replies. "Though I'm not sure I'd fit in here."

"Why do you say that?" I ask. *What's wrong with my company?*

"It's obvious, isn't it?"

"Not to me." I'm confounded by her response. She's flustered again as she reaches for the recorder.

Shit, she's going. Mentally I run through my schedule for that afternoon—there is nothing that won't keep. "Would you like me to show you around?"

"I'm sure you're far too busy, Mr. Grey, and I do have a long drive."

"You're driving back to Vancouver?" I glance out the window. It's one hell of a drive, and it's raining. She shouldn't be driving in this weather, but I can't forbid her. The thought irritates me. "Well, you'd better drive carefully." My voice is sterner than I intend. She fumbles with the recorder. She wants out of my office, and to my surprise, I don't want her to go.

"Did you get everything you need?" I ask in a transparent effort to prolong her stay.

"Yes, sir," she says quietly. Her response floors me—the way those words sound, coming out of that smart mouth—and briefly I imagine that mouth at my beck and call.

"Thank you for the interview, Mr. Grey."

"The pleasure's been all mine," I respond—truthfully, because I haven't been this fascinated by anyone for a while. The thought is unsettling. She stands and I extend my hand, eager to touch her.

"Until we meet again, Miss Steele." My voice is low as she places her hand in mine. Yes, I want to flog and fuck this girl in my playroom. Have her bound and wanting . . . needing me, trusting me. I swallow.

It ain't going to happen, Grey.

"Mr. Grey." She nods and withdraws her hand quickly, too quickly.

I can't let her go like this. It's obvious she's desperate to leave. It's irritating, but inspiration hits me as I open my office door.

"Just ensuring you make it through the door," I quip.

Her lips form a hard line. "That's very considerate, Mr. Grey," she snaps.

Miss Steele bites back! I grin behind her as she exits, and follow her out. Both Andrea and Olivia look up in shock. *Yeah, yeah. I'm just seeing the girl out.*

"Did you have a coat?" I ask.

"A jacket."

I give Olivia a pointed look and she immediately leaps up to retrieve a navy jacket, passing it to me with her usual simpering expression. Christ, Olivia is annoying—mooning over me all the time.

Hmm. The jacket is worn and cheap. Miss Anastasia Steele should be better dressed. I hold it up for her, and as I pull it over her slim shoulders, I touch the skin at the base of her neck. She stills at the contact and pales.

Yes! She is affected by me. The knowledge is immensely pleasing. Strolling over to the elevator, I press the call button while she stands fidgeting beside me.

Oh, I could stop your fidgeting, baby.

The doors open and she scurries in, then turns to face me. She's more than attractive. I would go as far as to say she's beautiful.

"Anastasia," I say, in good-bye.

"Christian," she answers, her voice soft. And the elevator doors close, leaving my name hanging in the air between us, sounding odd and unfamiliar, but sexy as hell.

I need to know more about this girl.

"Andrea," I bark as I return to my office. "Get me Welch on the line, now."

As I sit at my desk and wait for the call, I look at the paintings on the wall of my office, and Miss Steele's words drift back to me.

"*Raising the ordinary to extraordinary.*" She could so easily have been describing herself.

My phone buzzes. "I have Mr. Welch on the line for you."

"Put him through."

"Yes, sir."

"Welch, I need a background check."

ANASTASIA ROSE STEELE

DOB:	Sept. 10, 1989, Montesano, WA
Address:	1114 SW Green Street, Apartment 7, Haven Heights, Vancouver, WA 98888
Mobile No:	360-959-4352
Social Security No:	987-65-4320
Bank:	Wells Fargo Bank, Vancouver, WA: Acct. No.: 309361: $683.16 balance
Occupation:	Undergraduate Student WSU Vancouver College of Arts and Sciences English Major
GPA:	4.0
Prior Education:	Montesano Jr. Sr. High School
SAT Score:	2150
Employment:	Clayton's Hardware Store, NW Vancouver Drive, Portland, OR (part-time)
Father:	Franklin A. Lambert, DOB: Sept. 1, 1969, Deceased Sept. 11, 1989
Mother:	Carla May Wilks Adams, DOB: July 18, 1970 m. Frank Lambert March 1, 1989, widowed Sept. 11, 1989 m. Raymond Steele June 6, 1990, divorced July 12, 2006 m. Stephen M. Morton Aug. 16, 2006, divorced Jan. 31, 2007 m. Bob Adams April 6, 2009
Political Affiliations:	None Found
Religious Affiliations:	None Found
Sexual Orientation:	Not Known
Relationships:	None Indicated at Present

I pore over the executive summary for the hundredth time since I received it two days ago, looking for some insight into the enigmatic Miss Anastasia Rose Steele. I cannot get the damned woman out of my mind, and it's seriously beginning to piss me off. This past week, during particularly dull meetings, I've found myself replaying the interview in my head. Her fumbling fingers on the recorder, the way she tucked her hair behind her ear, the lip biting. Yes. The lip biting gets me every time.

And now here I am, parked outside Clayton's, a mom-and-pop hardware store on the outskirts of Portland where she works.

You're a fool, Grey. Why are you here?

I knew it would lead to this. All week . . . I knew I'd have to see her again. I'd known it since she uttered my name in the elevator. I'd tried to resist. I'd waited five days, five tedious days, to see if I'd forget about her.

And I don't do waiting. I hate waiting . . . for anything.

I've never pursued a woman before. The women I've had understood what I expected of them. My fear now is that Miss Steele is just too young and that she won't be interested in what I have to offer. *Will she?* Will she even make a good submissive? I shake my head. So here I am, an ass, sitting in a suburban parking lot in a dreary part of Portland.

Her background check has produced nothing remarkable— except the last fact, which has been at the forefront of my mind. It's the reason I'm here. *Why no boyfriend, Miss Steele?* Sexual orientation unknown—perhaps she's gay. I snort, thinking that unlikely. I recall the question she asked during the interview, her acute embarrassment, the way her skin flushed a pale rose . . . I've been suffering from these lascivious thoughts since I met her.

That's why you're here.

I'm itching to see her again—those blue eyes have haunted me, even in my dreams. I haven't mentioned her to Flynn, and I'm glad because I'm now behaving like a stalker. *Perhaps I should let him know.* No. I don't want him hounding me about his latest solution-based-therapy shit. I just need a distraction, and right now the only distraction I want is the one working as a salesclerk in a hardware store.

You've come all this way. Let's see if little Miss Steele is as appealing as you remember.

Showtime, Grey.

A bell chimes a flat electronic note as I walk into the store. It's much bigger than it looks from the outside, and although it's almost lunchtime the place is quiet, for a Saturday. There are aisles and aisles of the usual junk you'd expect. I'd forgotten the possibilities that a hardware store could present to someone like me. I mainly shop online for my needs, but while I'm here, maybe I'll stock up on a few items: Velcro, split rings—*Yeah.* I'll find the delectable Miss Steele and have some fun.

It takes me all of three seconds to spot her. She's hunched over the counter, staring intently at a computer screen and picking at her lunch—a bagel. Absentmindedly, she wipes a crumb from the corner of her lips and into her mouth and sucks on her finger. My cock twitches in response.

What am I, fourteen?

My body's reaction is irritating. Maybe this will stop if I fetter, fuck, and flog her . . . and not necessarily in that order. *Yeah. That's what I need.*

She is thoroughly absorbed by her task, and it gives me an opportunity to study her. Salacious thoughts aside, she's attractive, seriously attractive. I've remembered her well.

She looks up and freezes. It's as unnerving as the first time I met her. She pins me with a discerning stare—shocked, I think—and I don't know if this is a good response or a bad response.

"Miss Steele. What a pleasant surprise."

"Mr. Grey," she says, breathy and flustered. *Ah, a good response.*

"I was in the area. I need to stock up on a few things. It's a pleasure to see you again." *A real pleasure.* She's dressed in a tight T-shirt and jeans, not the shapeless shit she was wearing earlier this week. She's all long legs, narrow waist, and perfect tits. Her lips are still parted in surprise, and I have to resist the urge to tip her chin up and close her mouth. I've flown from Seattle just to see you, and the way you look right now, it was really worth the journey.

"Ana. My name's Ana. What can I help you with, Mr. Grey?" She takes a deep breath, squares her shoulders like she did in the interview, and gives me a fake smile that I'm sure she reserves for customers.

Game on, Miss Steele.

"There are a few items I need. To start with, I'd like some cable ties."

My request catches her off guard; she looks stunned.

Oh, this is going to be fun. You'd be amazed what I can do with a few cable ties, baby.

"We stock various lengths. Shall I show you?" she says, finding her voice.

"Please. Lead the way."

She steps out from behind the counter and gestures toward one of the aisles. She's wearing chucks. Idly I wonder what she'd look like in skyscraper heels. Louboutins . . . nothing but Louboutins.

"They're with the electrical goods, aisle eight." Her voice wavers and she blushes . . .

She *is* affected by me. Hope blooms in my chest.

She's not gay, then. I smirk.

"After you." I hold my hand out for her to lead the way. Letting her walk ahead gives me the space and time to admire her fantastic ass. Her long, thick ponytail keeps time like a metronome to the gentle sway of her hips. She really is the whole package: sweet, polite, and beautiful, with all the physical attributes I value in a submissive. But the million-dollar question is, could she be a submissive? She probably knows nothing of the lifestyle—my lifestyle—but I very much want to introduce her to it. *You are getting way ahead of yourself on this deal, Grey.*

"Are you in Portland on business?" she asks, interrupting my thoughts. Her voice is high; she's feigning disinterest. It makes me want to laugh. Women rarely make me laugh.

"I was visiting the WSU farming division. It's based in Vancouver," I lie. *Actually, I'm here to see you, Miss Steele.*

Her face falls, and I feel like a shit.

"I'm currently funding some research there in crop rotation and soil science." That, at least, is true.

"All part of your feed-the-world plan?" She arches a brow, amused.

"Something like that," I mutter. *Is she laughing at me?* Oh, I'd love to put a stop to that if she is. But how to start? Maybe with dinner, rather than the usual interview . . . now, that would be novel: taking a prospect out to dinner.

We arrive at the cable ties, which are arranged in an assortment of lengths and colors. Absentmindedly, my fingers trace over the packets. *I could just ask her out for dinner.* Like on a date? Would she accept? When I glance at her she's examining her knotted fingers. She can't look at me . . . this is promising. I select the longer ties. They are more flexible, after all, as they can accommodate two ankles and two wrists at once.

"These will do."

"Is there anything else?" she says quickly—either she's being super-attentive or she wants to get me out of the store, I don't know which.

"I'd like some masking tape."

"Are you redecorating?"

"No, not redecorating." *Oh, if you only knew . . .*

"This way," she says. "Masking tape is in the decorating aisle." *Come on, Grey. You don't have much time. Engage her in some conversation.* "Have you worked here long?" Of course, I already know the answer. Unlike some people, I do my research. For some reason she's embarrassed. Christ, this girl is shy. I don't have a hope in hell. She turns quickly and walks down the aisle toward the section labeled *Decorating.* I follow her eagerly, like a puppy.

"Four years," she mumbles as we reach the masking tape. She bends down and grasps two rolls, each a different width.

"I'll take that one." The wider tape is much more effective as a gag. As she passes it to me, the tips of our fingers touch, briefly. It resonates in my groin. *Damn!*

She pales. "Anything else?" Her voice is soft and husky.

*Christ, I'm having the same effect on her that she has on me.
Maybe . . .*

"Some rope, I think."

"This way." She scoots up the aisle, giving me another chance
to appreciate her fine ass.

"What sort were you after? We have synthetic and natural filament rope . . . twine . . . cable cord . . ."

Shit—stop. I groan inwardly, trying to chase away the image of
her suspended from the ceiling in my playroom.

"I'll take five yards of the natural filament rope, please." It's
coarser and chafes more if you struggle against it . . . my rope of
choice.

A tremor runs through her fingers, but she measures out five
yards like a pro. Pulling a utility knife from her right pocket, she
cuts the rope in one swift gesture, coils it neatly, and ties it off with
a slipknot. Impressive.

"Were you a Girl Scout?"

"Organized group activities aren't really my thing, Mr. Grey."

"What is your thing, Anastasia?" Her pupils dilate as I stare.
Yes!

"Books," she answers.

"What kind of books?"

"Oh, you know. The usual. The classics. British literature,
mainly."

British literature? The Brontës and Austen, I bet. All those
romantic hearts-and-flowers types.

That's not good.

"Anything else you need?"

"I don't know. What else would you recommend?" I want to
see her reaction.

"For a do-it-yourselfer?" she asks, surprised.

I want to hoot with laughter. *Oh, baby, DIY is not my thing.* I
nod, stifling my mirth. Her eyes flick down my body and I tense.
She's checking me out!

"Coveralls," she blurts out.

It's the most unexpected thing I've heard her say since the "Are you gay?" question.

"You wouldn't want to ruin your clothing." She gestures to my jeans.

I can't resist. "I could always take them off."

"Um." She flushes beet red and stares down.

I put her out of her misery. "I'll take some coveralls. Heaven forbid I should ruin any clothing." Without a word, she turns and walks briskly up the aisle, and I follow in her enticing wake.

"Do you need anything else?" she says, sounding breathless as she hands me a pair of blue coveralls. She's mortified, eyes still cast down. *Christ, she does things to me.*

"How's the article coming along?" I ask, in the hope she might relax a little.

She looks up and gives me a brief relieved smile.

Finally.

"I'm not writing it, Katherine is. Miss Kavanagh. My room-mate, she's the writer. She's very happy with it. She's the editor of the newspaper, and she was devastated that she couldn't do the interview in person."

It's the longest sentence she's uttered since we first met, and she's talking about someone else, not herself. *Interesting.*

Before I can comment, she adds, "Her only concern is that she doesn't have any original photographs of you."

The tenacious Miss Kavanagh wants photographs. Publicity stills, eh? I can do that. It will allow me to spend time with the delectable Miss Steele.

"What sort of photographs does she want?"

She gazes at me for a moment, then shakes her head, perplexed, not knowing what to say.

"Well, I'm around. Tomorrow, perhaps . . ." I can stay in Portland. Work from a hotel. A room at The Heathman, perhaps. I'll need Taylor to come down, bring my laptop and some clothes. Or Elliot—unless he's screwing around, which is his usual MO over the weekend.

"You'd be willing to do a photo shoot?" She cannot contain her surprise.

I give her a brief nod. *Yeah, I want to spend more time with you . . .*

Steady, Grey.

"Kate will be delighted—if we can find a photographer." She smiles and her face lights up like a cloudless dawn. She's breath-taking.

"Let me know about tomorrow." I pull my wallet from my jeans. "My card. It has my cell number on it. You'll need to call before ten in the morning." And if she doesn't, I'll head on back to Seattle and forget about this stupid venture.

The thought depresses me.

"Okay." She continues to grin.

"Ana!" We both turn as a young man dressed in casual designer gear appears at the far end of the aisle. His eyes are all over Miss Anastasia Steele. *Who the hell is this prick?*

"Er, excuse me for a moment, Mr. Grey." She walks toward him, and the asshole engulfs her in a gorilla-like hug. My blood runs cold. It's a primal response.

Get your fucking paws off her.

I fist my hands and am only slightly mollified when she doesn't return his hug.

They fall into a whispered conversation. Maybe Welch's facts were wrong. Maybe this guy is her boyfriend. He looks the right age, and he can't take his greedy little eyes off her. He holds her for a moment at arm's length, examining her, then stands with his arm resting on her shoulder. It seems like a casual gesture, but I know he's staking a claim and telling me to back off. She seems embar-rassed, shifting from foot to foot.

Shit. I should go. I've overplayed my hand. She's with this guy. Then she says something else to him and moves out of his reach, touching his arm, not his hand, shrugging him off. It's clear they aren't close.

Good.

"Er . . . Paul, this is Christian Grey. Mr. Grey, this is Paul Clayton. His brother owns the place." She gives me an odd look that I don't understand and continues, "I've known Paul ever since I've worked here, though we don't see each other that often. He's back from Princeton, where he's studying business administration." She's babbling, giving me a long explanation and telling me they're not together, I think. The boss's brother, not a boyfriend. I'm relieved, but the extent of the relief I feel is unexpected, and it makes me frown. *This woman has really gotten under my skin.*

"Mr. Clayton." My tone is deliberately clipped.

"Mr. Grey." His handshake is limp, like his hair. *Asshole.* "Wait up—not *the* Christian Grey? Of Grey Enterprises Holdings?"

Yeah, that's me, you prick.

In a heartbeat I watch him morph from territorial to obsequious.

"Wow—is there anything I can get you?"

"Anastasia has it covered, Mr. Clayton. She's been very attentive." *Now fuck off.*

"Cool," he gushes, all white teeth and deferential. "Catch you later, Ana."

"Sure, Paul," she says, and he ambles off to the back of the store. I watch him disappear.

"Anything else, Mr. Grey?"

"Just these items," I mutter. *Shit,* I'm out of time, and I still don't know if I'm going to see her again. I have to know whether there's a hope in hell she might consider what I have in mind. How can I ask her? Am I ready to take on a submissive who knows nothing? She's going to need substantial training. Closing my eyes, I imagine the interesting possibilities this presents . . . getting there is going to be half the fun. Will she even be up for this? Or do I have it all wrong?

She walks back to the cashier's counter and rings up my purchases, all the while keeping her eyes on the register.

Look at me, damn it! I want to see her face again and gauge what she's thinking.

Finally she raises her head. "That will be forty-three dollars, please."

Is that all?

"Would you like a bag?" she asks, as I pass her my AmEx.

"Please, Anastasia." Her name—a beautiful name for a beautiful girl—flows smoothly over my tongue.

She packs the items briskly. This is it. I have to go.

"You'll call me if you want me to do the photo shoot?"

She nods as she hands back my charge card.

"Good. Until tomorrow, perhaps." I can't just leave. I have to let her know I'm interested. "Oh—and Anastasia, I'm glad Miss Kavanagh couldn't do the interview." She looks surprised and flattered.

This is good.

I sling the bag over my shoulder and exit the store.

Yes, against my better judgment, I want her. Now I have to wait . . . fucking wait . . . again. Utilizing willpower that would make Elena proud, I keep my eyes ahead as I take my cell out of my pocket and climb into the rental car. I'm deliberately not looking back at her. I'm not. I'm not. My eyes flick to the rearview mirror, where I can see the shop door, but all I see is the quaint storefront. She's not in the window, staring out at me.

It's disappointing.

I press 1 on speed dial and Taylor answers before the phone has a chance to ring.

"Mr. Grey," he says.

"Make reservations at The Heathman; I'm staying in Portland this weekend, and can you bring down the SUV, my computer, and the paperwork beneath it, and a change or two of clothes."

"Yes, sir. And *Charlie Tango*?"

"Have Joe move her to PDX."

"Will do, sir. I'll be with you in about three and a half hours."

I hang up and start the car. So I have a few hours in Portland while I wait to see if this girl is interested in me. What to do? Time for a hike, I think. Maybe I can walk this strange hunger out of my system.

IT'S BEEN FIVE HOURS with no phone call from the delectable Miss Steele. What the hell was I thinking? I watch the street from the window of my suite at The Heathman. I loathe waiting. I always have. The weather, now cloudy, held for my hike through Forest Park, but the walk has done nothing to cure my agitation. I'm annoyed at her for not phoning, but mostly I'm angry with myself. I'm a fool for being here. What a waste of time it's been chasing this woman. When have I ever chased a woman?

Grey, get a grip.

Sighing, I check my phone once again in the hope that I've just missed her call, but there's nothing. At least Taylor has arrived and I have all my shit. I have Barney's report on his department's graphene tests to read and I can work in peace.

Peace? I haven't known peace since Miss Steele fell into my office.

WHEN I GLANCE UP, dusk has shrouded my suite in gray shadows. The prospect of a night alone again is depressing. While I contemplate what to do my phone vibrates against the polished wood of the desk and an unknown but vaguely familiar number with a Washington area code flashes on the screen. Suddenly my heart is pumping as if I've run ten miles.

Is it her?

I answer.

"Er . . . Mr. Grey? It's Anastasia Steele."

My face erupts in a shit-eating grin. *Well, well.* A breathy, nervous, soft-spoken Miss Steele. My evening is looking up.

"Miss Steele. How nice to hear from you." I hear her breath hitch and the sound travels directly to my groin.

Great. I'm affecting her. Like she's affecting me.

"Um—we'd like to go ahead with the photo shoot for the article. Tomorrow, if that's okay. Where would be convenient for you, sir?"

In my room. Just you, me, and the cable ties.

"I'm staying at The Heathman in Portland. Shall we say nine thirty tomorrow morning?"

"Okay, we'll see you there," she gushes, unable to hide the relief and delight in her voice.

"I look forward to it, Miss Steele." I hang up before she senses my excitement and how pleased I am. Leaning back in my chair, I gaze at the darkening skyline and run both my hands through my hair.

How the hell am I going to close this deal?

SUNDAY, MAY 15, 2011

With Moby blasting in my ears I run down Southwest Salmon Street toward the Willamette River. It's 6:30 in the morning and I'm trying to clear my head. Last night I dreamed of her. Blue eyes, breathy voice . . . her sentences ending with "sir" as she knelt before me. Since I've met her, my dreams have been a welcome change from the occasional nightmare. I wonder what Flynn would make of that. The thought is disconcerting, so I ignore it and concentrate on pushing my body to its limits along the bank of the Willamette. As my feet pound the walkway, sunshine breaks through the clouds and it gives me hope.

TWO HOURS LATER AS I jog back to the hotel I pass a coffee shop. Maybe I should take her for coffee.

Like a date?

Well. No. Not a date. I laugh at the ridiculous thought. Just a chat—an interview of sorts. Then I can find out a little more about this enigmatic woman and if she's interested, or if I'm on a wild-goose chase. I'm alone in the elevator as I stretch out. Finishing my stretches in my hotel suite, I'm centered and calm for the first time since I arrived in Portland. Breakfast has been delivered and I'm famished. It's not a feeling I tolerate—ever. Sitting down to breakfast in my sweats, I decide to eat before I shower.

THERE'S A BRISK KNOCK on the door. I open it and Taylor stands on the threshold.

"Good morning, Mr. Grey."

"Morning. They ready for me?"

"Yes, sir. They're set up in room 601."

"I'll be right down." I close the door and tuck my shirt into my gray pants. My hair is wet from my shower, but I don't give a shit. One glance at the louche fucker in the mirror and I exit to follow Taylor to the elevator.

Room 601 is crowded with people, lights, and camera boxes, but I spot her immediately. She's standing to the side. Her hair is loose: a lush, glossy mane that falls beneath her breasts. She's wearing tight jeans and chucks with a short-sleeved navy jacket and a white T-shirt beneath. Are jeans and chucks her signature look? While not very convenient, they do flatter her shapely legs. Her eyes, disarming as ever, widen as I approach.

"Miss Steele, we meet again." She takes my extended hand and for a moment I want to squeeze hers and raise it to my lips.

Don't be absurd, Grey.

She turns her delicious pink and waves in the direction of her friend, who is standing too close, waiting for my attention.

"Mr. Grey, this is Katherine Kavanagh," she says. With reluctance I release her and turn to the persistent Miss Kavanagh. She's tall, striking, and well groomed, like her father, but she has her mother's eyes, and I have her to thank for my introduction to the delightful Miss Steele. That thought makes me feel a little more benevolent toward her.

"The tenacious Miss Kavanagh. How do you do? I trust you're feeling better? Anastasia said you were unwell last week."

"I'm fine, thank you, Mr. Grey."

She has a firm, confident handshake, and I doubt she's ever faced a day of hardship in her privileged life. I wonder why these women are friends. They have nothing in common.

"Thank you for taking the time to do this," Katherine says.

"It's a pleasure," I reply, and glance at Anastasia, who rewards me with her telltale flush.

Is it just me who makes her blush? The thought pleases me.

"This is José Rodriguez, our photographer," Anastasia says, and her face lights up as she introduces him.

Shit. Is this the boyfriend?

Rodriguez blooms under Ana's sweet smile.

Are they fucking?

"Mr. Grey." Rodriguez gives me a dark look as we shake hands. It's a warning. He's telling me to back off. He likes her. He likes her a lot.

Well, game on, kid.

"Mr. Rodriguez, where would you like me?" My tone is a challenge, and he hears it, but Katherine intervenes and waves me toward a chair. Ah. She likes to be in charge. The thought amuses me as I sit. Another young man who appears to be working with Rodriguez switches on the lights, and momentarily I'm blinded.

Hell!

As the glare recedes I search out the lovely Miss Steele. She's standing at the back of the room, observing the proceedings. Does she always shy away like this? Maybe that's why she and Kavanagh are friends; she's content to be in the background and let Katherine take center stage.

Hmm . . . a natural submissive.

The photographer appears professional enough and absorbed in the job he's been assigned to do. I regard Miss Steele as she watches both of us. Our eyes meet; hers are honest and innocent, and for a moment I reconsider my plan. But then she bites her lip and my breath catches in my throat.

Back down, Anastasia. I will her to stop staring, and as if she can hear me, she's the first to look away.

Good girl.

Katherine asks me to stand as Rodriguez continues to take snaps. Then we're done and this is my chance.

"Thank you again, Mr. Grey." Katherine surges forward and shakes my hand, followed by the photographer, who regards me with ill-concealed disapproval. His antagonism makes me smile.

Oh, man . . . you have no idea.

"I look forward to reading the article, Miss Kavanagh," I say, giving her a brief polite nod. It's Ana I want to talk to. "Will you walk with me, Miss Steele?" I ask, when I reach her by the door.

"Sure," she says with surprise.

Seize the day, Grey.

I mutter some platitude to those still in the room and usher her out the door, wanting to put some distance between her and Rodriguez. In the corridor she stands fiddling with her hair, then her fingers, as Taylor follows me out.

"I'll call you, Taylor," I say, and when he's almost out of earshot I ask Ana to join me for coffee, my breath held for her response.

Her long lashes flicker over her eyes. "I have to drive everyone home," she says with dismay.

"Taylor," I call after him, making her jump. I must make her nervous and I don't know if this is good or bad. And she can't stop fidgeting. Thinking about all the ways I could make her stop is distracting.

"Are they based at the university?" She nods and I ask Taylor to take her friends home.

"There. Now can you join me for coffee?"

"Um—Mr. Grey, er—this really . . ." She stops.

Shit. It's a "no." I'm going to lose this deal. She looks directly at me, eyes bright. "Look, Taylor doesn't have to drive them home. I'll swap vehicles with Kate, if you give me a moment."

My relief is tangible and I grin.

I have a date!

Opening the door, I let her back into the room as Taylor conceals his puzzled look.

"Can you grab my jacket, Taylor?"

"Certainly, sir."

He turns on his heel, his lips twitching as he heads up the corridor. I watch him with narrowed eyes as he disappears into the elevator while I lean against the wall and wait for Miss Steele.

What the hell am I going to say to her?

"How would you like to be my submissive?"

No. Steady, Grey. Let's take this one stage at a time.

Taylor is back within a couple of minutes, holding my jacket.

"Will that be all, sir?"

"Yes. Thanks."

He gives it to me and leaves me standing like an idiot in the corridor.

How long is Anastasia going to be? I check my watch. She must be negotiating the car swap with Katherine. Or she's talking to Rodriguez, explaining that she's just going for coffee to placate me and keep me sweet for the article. My thoughts darken. Maybe she's kissing him good-bye.

Damn.

She emerges a moment later, and I'm pleased. She doesn't look like she's just been kissed.

"Okay," she says with resolve. "Let's do coffee." But her reddening cheeks somewhat undermine her effort to look confident.

"After you, Miss Steele." I conceal my delight as she falls into step ahead of me. As I catch up with her my curiosity is piqued about her relationship with Katherine, specifically their compatibility. I ask her how long they've known each other.

"Since our freshman year. She's a good friend." Her voice is full of warmth. Ana is clearly devoted. She came all the way to Seattle to interview me when Katherine was ill, and I find myself hoping that Miss Kavanagh treats her with the same loyalty and respect.

At the elevators I press the call button and almost immediately the doors open. A couple in a passionate embrace spring apart, embarrassed to be caught. Ignoring them, we step into the elevator, but I catch Anastasia's impish smile.

As we travel to the first floor the atmosphere is thick with unfulfilled desire. And I don't know if it's emanating from the couple behind us or from me.

Yes. I want her. Will she want what I have to offer?

I'm relieved when the doors open again and I take her hand, which is cool and not clammy as expected. Perhaps I don't affect her as much as I'd like. The thought is disheartening.

In our wake we hear embarrassed giggling from the couple.

"What is it about elevators?" I mutter. And I have to admit there's something wholesome and naïve about their giggling that's totally charming. Miss Steele seems that innocent, just like them, and as we walk onto the street I question my motives again.

She's too young. She's too inexperienced, but, damn, I like the feel of her hand in mine.

In the coffee shop I direct her to find a table and ask what she wants to drink. She stutters through her order: English Breakfast tea—hot water, bag on the side. That's a new one to me.

"No coffee?"

"I'm not keen on coffee."

"Okay, bag-out tea. Sugar?"

"No thanks," she says, staring down at her fingers.

"Anything to eat?"

"No thank you." She shakes her head and tosses her hair over her shoulder, highlighting glints of auburn.

I have to wait in line while the two matronly women behind the counter exchange inane pleasantries with *all* their customers. It's frustrating and keeping me from my objective: Anastasia.

"Hey, handsome, what can I get you?" the older woman asks with a twinkle in her eye. *It's just a pretty face, sweetheart.*

"I'll have a coffee with steamed milk. English Breakfast tea. Teabag on the side. And a blueberry muffin."

Anastasia might change her mind and eat.

"You visiting Portland?"

"Yes."

"The weekend?"

"Yes."

"The weather sure has picked up today."

"Yes."

"I hope you get out to enjoy some sunshine."

Please stop talking to me and hurry the fuck up.

"Yes," I hiss through my teeth and glance over at Ana, who quickly looks away.

She's watching me. Is she checking me out?

A bubble of hope swells in my chest.

"There you go." The woman winks and places the drinks on my tray. "Pay at the register, honey, and you have a nice day, now."

I manage a cordial response. "Thank you."

At the table Anastasia is staring at her fingers, reflecting on heaven knows what.

Me?

"Penny for your thoughts?" I ask.

She jumps and turns red as I set out her tea and my coffee. She sits mute and mortified. Why? Does she really not want to be here?

"Your thoughts?" I ask again, and she fidgets with the teabag.

"This is my favorite tea," she says, and I revise my mental note that it's Twinings English Breakfast tea she likes. I watch her dunk the teabag in the teapot. It's an elaborate and messy spectacle. She fishes it out almost immediately and places the used teabag on her saucer. My mouth is twitching with my amusement. As she tells me she likes her tea weak and black, for a moment I think she's describing what she likes in a man.

Get a grip, Grey. She's talking about tea.

Enough of this preamble; it's time for some due diligence in this deal. "Is he your boyfriend?"

Her brows knit together, forming a small *v* above her nose.

"Who?"

This is a good response.

"The photographer. José Rodriguez."

She laughs. At me.

At me!

And I don't know if it's from relief or if she thinks I'm funny. It's annoying. I can't get her measure. Does she like me or not? She tells me he's just a friend.

Oh, sweetheart, he wants to be more than a friend.

"Why did you think he was my boyfriend?" she asks.

"The way you smiled at him, and he at you." *You have no idea, do you?* The boy is smitten.

"He's more like family," she says.

Okay, so the lust is one-sided, and for a moment I wonder if she realizes how lovely she is. She eyes the blueberry muffin as I peel back the paper, and for a moment I imagine her on her knees beside me as I feed her, a morsel at a time. The thought is diverting—and arousing. "Do you want some?" I ask.

She shakes her head. "No thanks." Her voice is hesitant and

she stares once more at her hands. Why is she so jittery? Maybe because of me?

"And the boy I met yesterday, at the store. He's not your boyfriend?"

"No. Paul's just a friend. I told you yesterday." She frowns again as if she's confused, and crosses her arms in defense. She doesn't like being asked about these boys. I remember how uncomfortable she seemed when the kid at the store put his arm around her, staking his claim. "Why do you ask?" she adds.

"You seem nervous around men."

Her eyes widen. They really are beautiful, the color of the ocean at Cabo, the bluest of blue seas. I should take her there.

What? Where did that come from?

"I find you intimidating," she says, and looks down, fidgeting once more with her fingers. On the one hand she's so submissive, but on the other she's . . . challenging.

"You should find me intimidating."

Yeah. She should. There aren't many people brave enough to tell me that I intimidate them. She's honest, and I tell her so—but when she averts her eyes, I don't know what she's thinking. It's frustrating. Does she like me? Or is she tolerating this meeting to keep Kavanagh's interview on track? Which is it?

"You're a mystery, Miss Steele."

"There's nothing mysterious about me."

"I think you're very self-contained." Like any good submissive. "Except when you blush, of course, which is often. I just wish I knew what you were blushing about." *There.* That will goad her into a response. Popping a small piece of the blueberry muffin into my mouth, I await her reply.

"Do you always make such personal observations?"

That's not that personal, is it? "I hadn't realized I was. Have I offended you?"

"No."

"Good."

"But you're very high-handed."

"I'm used to getting my own way, Anastasia. In all things."

"I don't doubt it," she mutters, and then wants to know why I haven't asked her to call me by my first name.

What?

And I remember her leaving my office in the elevator—and how my name sounded coming out of her smart mouth. Has she seen through me? Is she deliberately antagonizing me? I tell her that no one calls me Christian, except my family . . .

I don't even know if it's my real name.

Don't go there, Grey.

I change the subject. I want to know about her.

"Are you an only child?"

Her eyelashes flutter several times before she answers that she is.

"Tell me about your parents."

She rolls her eyes and I have to fight the compulsion to scold her.

"My mom lives in Georgia with her new husband, Bob. My stepdad lives in Montesano."

Of course I know all this from Welch's background check, but it's important to hear it from her. Her lips soften with a fond smile when she mentions her stepdad.

"Your father?" I ask.

"My father died when I was a baby."

For a moment I'm catapulted into my nightmares, looking at a prostrate body on a grimy floor. "I'm sorry," I mutter.

"I don't remember him," she says, dragging me back to the now. Her expression is clear and bright, and I know that Raymond Steele has been a good father to this girl. Her mother's relationship with her, on the other hand—that remains to be seen.

"And your mother remarried?"

Her laugh is bitter. "You could say that." But she doesn't elaborate. She's one of the few women I've met who can sit in silence. Which is great, but not what I want at the moment.

"You're not giving much away, are you?"

"Neither are you," she parries.

Oh, Miss Steele. Game on.

And it's with great pleasure and a smirk that I remind her that she's interviewed me already. "I can recollect some quite probing questions."

Yes. You asked me if I was gay.

My statement has the desired effect and she's embarrassed. She starts babbling about herself and a few details hit home. Her mother is an incurable romantic. I suppose someone on her fourth marriage is embracing hope over experience. Is she like her mother? I can't bring myself to ask her. If she says she is—then I have no hope. And I don't want this interview to end. I'm enjoying myself too much.

I ask about her stepfather and she confirms my hunch. It's obvious she loves him. Her face is luminous when she talks about him: his job (he's a carpenter), his hobbies (he likes European soccer and fishing). She preferred to live with him when her mom married the third time.

Interesting.

She straightens her shoulders. "Tell me about *your* parents," she demands, in an attempt to divert the conversation from her family. I don't like talking about mine, so I give her the bare details.

"My dad's a lawyer, my mom is a pediatrician. They live in Seattle."

"What do your siblings do?"

She wants to go there? I give her the short answer that Elliot works in construction and Mia is at cooking school in Paris.

She listens, rapt. "I hear Paris is lovely," she says with a dreamy expression.

"It's beautiful. Have you been?"

"I've never left mainland USA." The cadence in her voice falls, tinged with regret. I could take her there.

"Would you like to go?"

First Cabo, now Paris? Get a grip, Grey.

"To Paris? Of course. But it's England that I'd really like to visit."

Her face brightens with excitement. Miss Steele wants to travel. But why England? I ask her.

"It's the home of Shakespeare, Austen, the Brontë sisters, Thomas Hardy. I'd like to see the places that inspired those people to write such wonderful books." It's obvious this is her first love.

Books.

She said as much in Clayton's yesterday. That means I'm competing with Darcy, Rochester, and Angel Clare: impossible romantic heroes. Here's the proof I needed. She's an incurable romantic, like her mother—and this isn't going to work. To add insult to injury, she looks at her watch. She's done.

I've blown this deal.

"I'd better go. I have to study," she says.

I offer to walk her back to her friend's car, which means I'll have the walk back to the hotel to make my case.

But should I?

"Thank you for the tea, Mr. Grey," she says.

"You're welcome, Anastasia. It's my pleasure." As I say the words I realize that the last twenty minutes have been . . . enjoyable. Giving her my most dazzling smile, guaranteed to disarm, I offer her my hand. "Come," I say. She takes my hand, and as we walk back to The Heathman I can't shake how agreeable her hand feels in mine.

Maybe this could work.

"Do you always wear jeans?" I ask.

"Mostly," she says, and it's two strikes against her: incurable romantic who only wears jeans . . . I like my women in skirts. I like them accessible.

"Do you have a girlfriend?" she asks out of the blue, and it's the third strike. I'm out of this fledgling deal. She wants romance, and I can't offer her that.

"No, Anastasia. I don't do the girlfriend thing."

Stricken with a frown, she turns abruptly and stumbles into the road.

"Shit, Ana!" I shout, tugging her toward me to stop her from falling in the path of an idiot cyclist who's flying the wrong way up the street. All of a sudden she's in my arms clutching my biceps, staring up at me. Her eyes are startled, and for the first time I notice a darker ring of blue circling her irises; they're beautiful, more beautiful this close. Her pupils dilate and I know I could fall into her gaze and never return. She takes a deep breath.

"Are you okay?" My voice sounds alien and distant, and I realize she's touching me and I don't care. My fingers caress her cheek. Her skin is soft and smooth, and as I brush my thumb against her lower lip, my breath catches in my throat. Her body is pressed against mine, and the feel of her breasts and her heat through my shirt is arousing. She has a fresh, wholesome fragrance that reminds me of my grandfather's apple orchard. Closing my eyes, I inhale, committing her scent to memory. When I open them she's still staring at me, entreating me, begging me, her eyes on my mouth.

Shit. She wants me to kiss her.

And I want to. Just once. Her lips are parted, ready, waiting. Her mouth felt welcoming beneath my thumb.

No. No. No. Don't do this, Grey.

She's not the girl for you.

She wants hearts and flowers, and you don't do that shit.

I close my eyes to blot her out and fight the temptation, and when I open them again, my decision is made. "Anastasia," I whisper, "you should steer clear of me. I'm not the man for you."

The little *v* forms between her brows, and I think she's stopped breathing.

"Breathe, Anastasia, breathe." I have to let her go before I do something stupid, but I'm surprised at my reluctance. I want to hold her for a moment longer. "I'm going to stand you up and let you go." I step back and she releases her hold on me, yet weirdly, I don't feel any relief. I slide my hands to her shoulders to ensure she can stand. Her expression clouds with humiliation. She's mortified by my rebuff.

Hell. I didn't mean to hurt you.

"I've got this," she says, disappointment ringing in her clipped tone. She's formal and distant, but she doesn't move out of my hold. "Thank you," she adds.

"For what?"

"For saving me."

And I want to tell her that I'm saving her from me . . . that it's a noble gesture, but that's not what she wants to hear. "That idiot was riding the wrong way. I'm glad I was here. I shudder to think what could have happened to you." Now it's me that's babbling, and I still can't let her go. I offer to sit with her in the hotel, knowing it's a ploy to prolong my time with her, and only then do I release her.

She shakes her head, her back ramrod stiff, and wraps her arms around herself in a protective gesture. A moment later she bolts across the street and I have to hurry to keep up with her.

When we reach the hotel, she turns and faces me once more, composed. "Thanks for the tea and doing the photo shoot." She regards me dispassionately and regret flares in my gut.

"Anastasia . . . I . . ." I can't think what to say, except that I'm sorry.

"What, Christian?" she snaps.

Whoa. She's mad at me, pouring all the contempt she can into each syllable of my name. It's novel. And she's leaving. And I don't want her to go. "Good luck with your exams."

Her eyes flash with hurt and indignation. "Thanks," she mutters, disdain in her tone. "Good-bye, Mr. Grey." She turns away and strides up the street toward the underground garage. I watch her go, hoping that she'll give me a second look, but she doesn't. She disappears into the building, leaving in her wake a trace of regret, the memory of her beautiful blue eyes, and the scent of an apple orchard in the fall.

THURSDAY, MAY 19, 2011

No! My scream bounces off the bedroom walls and wakes me from my nightmare. I'm smothered in sweat, with the stench of stale beer, cigarettes, and poverty in my nostrils and a lingering dread of drunken violence. Sitting up, I put my head in my hands as I try to calm my escalated heart rate and erratic breathing. It's been the same for the last four nights. Glancing at the clock, I see it's 3:00 a.m.

I have two major meetings tomorrow . . . today . . . and I need a clear head and some sleep. *Damn it, what I'd give for a good night's sleep.* And I have a round of fucking golf with Bastille. I should cancel the golf; the thought of playing and losing darkens my already bleak mood.

Clambering out of bed, I wander down the corridor and into the kitchen. There, I fill a glass with water and catch sight of myself, dressed only in pajama pants, reflected in the glass wall at the other side of the room. I turn away in disgust.

You turned her down.

She wanted you.

And you turned her down.

It was for her own good.

This has needled me for days now. Her beautiful face appears in my mind without warning, taunting me. If my shrink was back from his vacation in England I could call him. His psychobabble shit would stop me feeling this lousy.

Grey, she was just a pretty girl.

Perhaps I need a distraction; a new sub, maybe. It's been too long since Susannah. I contemplate calling Elena in the morning.

She always finds suitable candidates for me. But the truth is, I don't want anyone new.

I want Ana.

Her disappointment, her wounded indignation, and her contempt remain with me. She walked away without a backward glance. Perhaps I raised her hopes by asking her out for coffee, only to disappoint her.

Maybe I should find some way to apologize, then I can forget about this whole sorry episode and get the girl out of my head. Leaving the glass in the sink for my housekeeper to wash, I trudge back to bed.

THE RADIO ALARM JOLTS to life at 5:45 as I'm staring at the ceiling. I haven't slept and I'm exhausted.

Fuck! This is ridiculous.

The program on the radio is a welcome distraction until the second news item. It's about the sale of a rare manuscript: an unfinished novel by Jane Austen called *The Watsons* that's being auctioned in London.

"Books," she said.

Christ. Even the news reminds me of little Miss Bookworm.

She's an incurable romantic who loves the English classics. But then so do I, but for different reasons. I don't have any Jane Austen first editions, or Brontës, for that matter . . . but I do have two Thomas Hardys.

Of course! This is it! This is what I can do.

Moments later I'm in my library with *Jude the Obscure* and a boxed set of *Tess of the d'Urbervilles* in its three volumes laid out on the billiard table in front of me. Both are bleak books, with tragic themes. Hardy had a dark, twisted soul.

Like me.

I shake off the thought and examine the books. Even though *Jude* is in better condition, it's no contest. In *Jude* there is no redemption, so I'll send her *Tess*, with a suitable quote. I know it's not the most romantic book, considering the evils that befall the heroine, but she has a brief taste of romantic love in the bucolic idyll that is the English countryside. And Tess does exact revenge on the man who wronged her.

But that's not the point. Ana mentioned Hardy as a favorite and I'm sure she's never seen, let alone owned, a first edition.

"You sound like the ultimate consumer." Her judgmental retort from the interview comes back to haunt me. Yes. I like to possess things, things that will rise in value, like first editions.

Feeling calmer and more composed, and a little pleased with myself, I head back into my closet and change into my running gear.

IN THE BACK OF the car I leaf through book one of the *Tess* first edition, looking for a quote, and at the same time wonder when Ana's last exam will take place. I read the book years ago and have a hazy recollection of the plot. Fiction was my sanctuary when I was a teenager. My mother always marveled that I read; Elliot not so much. I craved the escape that fiction provided. He didn't need an escape.

"Mr. Grey," Taylor interrupts. "We're here, sir." He climbs out of the car and opens my door. "I'll be outside at two o'clock to take you to your golf game."

I nod and head into Grey House, the books tucked under my arm. The young receptionist greets me with a flirtatious wave.

Every day . . . Like a cheesy tune on repeat.

Ignoring her, I make my way to the elevator that will take me straight to my floor.

"Good morning, Mr. Grey," Barry on security greets me as he presses the button to summon the elevator.

"How's your son, Barry?"

"Better, sir."

"I'm glad to hear it."

I step into the elevator and it shoots up to the twentieth floor. Andrea is on hand to greet me.

"Good morning, Mr. Grey. Ros wants to see you to discuss the Darfur project. Barney would like a few minutes—"

I hold my hand up to silence her. "Forget those for now. Get me Welch on the line and find out when Flynn is back from vacation. Once I've spoken to Welch we can pick up the day's schedule."

"Yes, sir."

"And I need a double espresso. Get Olivia to make it for me."

But looking around I notice that Olivia is absent. It's a relief. The girl is always mooning over me and it's fucking irritating.

"Would you like milk, sir?" Andrea asks.

Good girl. I give her a smile.

"Not today." I do like to keep them guessing how I take my coffee.

"Very good, Mr. Grey." She looks pleased with herself, which she should be. She's the best PA I've had.

Three minutes later she has Welch on the line.

"Welch?"

"Mr. Grey."

"The background check you did for me last week. Anastasia Steele. Studying at WSU."

"Yes, sir. I remember."

"I'd like you to find out when her last final exam takes place and let me know as a matter of priority."

"Very good, sir. Anything else?"

"No, that will be all." I hang up and stare at the books on my desk. I need to find a quote.

ROS, MY NUMBER TWO and my chief operating officer, is in full flow. "We're getting clearance from the Sudanese authorities to put the shipments into Port Sudan. But our contacts on the ground are hesitant about the road journey to Darfur. They're doing a risk assessment to see how viable it is." Logistics must be tough; her normal sunny disposition is absent.

"We could always air-drop."

"Christian, the expense of an airdrop—"

"I know. Let's see what our NGO friends come back with."

"Okay," she says and sighs. "I'm also waiting for the all-clear from the State Department."

I roll my eyes. Fucking red tape. "If we have to grease some palms—or get Senator Blandino to intervene—let me know."

"So the next topic is where to site the new plant. You know the tax breaks in Detroit are huge. I sent you a summary."

"I know. But God, does it have to be Detroit?"

"I don't know what you have against the place. It meets our criteria."

"Okay, get Bill to check out potential brownfield sites. And let's do one more site search to see if any other municipality would offer more favorable terms."

"Bill has already sent Ruth out there to meet with the Detroit Brownfield Redevelopment Authority, who couldn't be more accommodating, but I'll ask Bill to do a final check."

My phone buzzes.

"Yes," I growl at Andrea—she knows I hate being interrupted in a meeting.

"I have Welch for you."

My watch says 11:30. That was quick. "Put him through."

I signal for Ros to stay.

"Mr. Grey?"

"Welch. What news?"

"Miss Steele's last exam is tomorrow, May twentieth."

Damn. I don't have long.

"Great. That's all I need to know." I hang up.

"Ros, bear with me one moment."

I pick up the phone. Andrea answers immediately.

"Andrea, I need a blank notecard to write a message within the next hour," I say, and hang up. "Right, Ros, where were we?"

AT 12:30 OLIVIA SHUFFLES into my office with lunch. She's a tall, willowy girl with a pretty face. Sadly, it's always misdirected at me with longing. She's carrying a tray with what I hope is something edible. After a busy morning, I'm starving. She trembles as she puts it on my desk.

Tuna salad. Okay. She hasn't fucked this up for once.

She also places three different white cards, all different sizes, with corresponding envelopes on my desk.

"Great," I mutter. *Now go.* She scuttles out.

I take one bite of tuna to assuage my hunger, then reach for my pen. I've chosen a quote. A warning. I made the correct choice, walking away from her. Not all men are romantic heroes. I'll take the word "men-folk" out. She'll understand.

> *Why didn't you tell me there was danger? Why didn't you*
> *warn me? Ladies know what to guard against, because*
> *they read novels that tell them of these tricks . . .*

I slip the card into the envelope provided and on it write Ana's address, which is ingrained in my memory from Welch's background check. I buzz Andrea.

"Yes, Mr. Grey."

"Can you come in, please?"

"Yes, sir."

She appears at my door a moment later. "Mr. Grey?"

"Take these, package them, and courier them to Anastasia Steele, the girl who interviewed me last week. Here's her address."

"Right away, Mr. Grey."

"They have to arrive by tomorrow at the latest."

"Yes, sir. Will that be all?"

"No. Find me a set of replacements."

"For these books?"

"Yes. First editions. Get Olivia on it."

"What books are these?"

"*Tess of the d'Urbervilles.*"

"Yes, sir." She gives me a rare smile and leaves my office.

Why is she smiling?

She never smiles. Dismissing the thought, I wonder if that will be the last I see of the books, and I have to acknowledge that deep down I hope not.

I've slept well for the first time in five days. Maybe I'm feeling the closure I had hoped for, now that I've sent those books to Anastasia. As I shave, the asshole in the mirror stares back at me with cool, gray eyes.

Liar.

Fuck.

Okay. Okay. I'm hoping she'll call. She has my number.

Mrs. Jones looks up when I walk into the kitchen.

"Good morning, Mr. Grey."

"Morning, Gail."

"What would you like for breakfast?"

"I'll have an omelet. Thank you." I sit at the kitchen counter as she prepares my food and leaf through *The Wall Street Journal* and *The New York Times*, then I pore over *The Seattle Times*. While I'm lost in the papers my phone buzzes.

It's Elliot. What the hell does my big brother want?

"Elliot?"

"Dude. I need to get out of Seattle this weekend. This chick is all over my junk and I've got to get away."

"Your junk?"

"Yeah. You would know if you had any."

I ignore his jibe, and then a devious thought occurs to me. "How about hiking around Portland. We could go this afternoon. Stay down there. Come home Sunday."

"Sounds cool. In the chopper, or do you want to drive?"

"It's a helicopter, Elliot, and I'll drive us down. Come by the office at lunchtime and we'll head out."

"Thanks, bro. I owe you." Elliot hangs up.

Elliot has always had a problem containing himself. As do the women he associates with: whoever the unfortunate girl is, she's just another in a long, long line of his casual liaisons.

"Mr. Grey. What would you like to do for food this weekend?"

"Just prepare something light and leave it in the fridge. I may be back on Saturday."

Or I may not.

She didn't give you a second glance, Grey.

Having spent a great deal of my working life managing others' expectations, I should be better at managing my own.

ELLIOT SLEEPS MOST OF the way to Portland. Poor fucker must be fried. Working and fucking: that's Elliot's raison d'être. He sprawls out in the passenger seat and snores.

Some company he's going to be.

It'll be after three when we arrive in Portland, so I call Andrea on the hands-free.

"Mr. Grey," she answers in two rings.

"Can you have two mountain bikes delivered to The Heathman?"

"For what time, sir?"

"Three."

"The bikes are for you and your brother?"

"Yes."

"Your brother is about six-two?"

"Yes."

"I'll get on it right away."

"Great." I hang up, then call Taylor.

"Mr. Grey," he answers on one ring.

"What time will you be here?"

"I'll check in around nine o'clock tonight."

"Will you bring the R8?"

"With pleasure, sir." Taylor is a car fanatic, too.

"Good." I end the call and turn up the music. Let's see if Elliot can sleep through The Verve.

As we cruise down I-5 my excitement mounts.

Have the books been delivered yet? I'm tempted to call Andrea
again, but I know I've left her with a ton of work. Besides, I don't
want to give my staff an excuse to gossip. I don't normally do this
kind of shit.

Why did you send them in the first place?

Because I want to see her again.

We pass the exit for Vancouver and I wonder if she's finished
her exam.

"Hey, man, where we at?" Elliot blurts.

"Behold, he wakes," I mutter. "We're nearly there. We're going
mountain biking."

"We are?"

"Yes."

"Cool. Remember when Dad used to take us?"

"Yep." I shake my head at the memory. My father is a polymath,
a real renaissance man: academic, sporting, at ease in the city,
more at ease in the great outdoors. He'd embraced three adopted
kids . . . and I'm the one who didn't live up to his expectations.

But before I hit adolescence we had a bond. He'd been my
hero. He used to love taking us camping and doing all the outdoor
pursuits I now enjoy: sailing, kayaking, biking, we did it all.

Puberty ruined all that for me.

"I figured if we were arriving mid-afternoon, we wouldn't have
time for a hike."

"Good thinking."

"So who are you running from?"

"Man, I'm a love-'em-and-leave-'em type. You know that. No
strings. I don't know, chicks find out you run your own business
and they start getting crazy ideas." He gives me a sideways look.
"You've got the right idea keeping your dick to yourself."

"I don't think we're discussing my dick, we're discussing yours,
and who's been on the sharp end of it recently."

Elliot snickers. "I've lost count. Anyway, enough of me. How's
the stimulating world of commerce and high finance?"

"You really want to know?" I shoot him a glance.

"Nah," he bleats and I laugh at his apathy and lack of eloquence.

"How's the business?" I ask.

"You checking on your investment?"

"Always." It's my job.

"Well, we broke ground on the Spokani Eden project last week and it's on schedule, but then it's only been a week." He shrugs. Beneath his somewhat casual exterior my brother is an eco-warrior. His passion for sustainable living makes for some heated Sunday dinner conversations with the family, and his latest project is an eco-friendly development of low-cost housing north of Seattle.

"I'm hoping to install that new gray-water system I was telling you about. It will mean all the homes will reduce their water usage and their bills by twenty-five percent."

"Impressive."

"I hope so."

We drive in silence into downtown Portland and just as we're pulling into the underground garage at The Heathman—the last place I saw her—Elliot mutters, "You know we're missing the Mariners game this evening."

"Maybe you can have a night in front of the TV. Give your dick a rest and watch baseball."

"Sounds like a plan."

KEEPING UP WITH ELLIOT is a challenge. He tears down the trail with the same devil-may-fucking-care attitude he applies to most situations. Elliot knows no fear—it's why I admire him. But riding at this pace I have no chance to appreciate our surroundings. I'm vaguely aware of the lush greenery flashing past me, but my eyes are on the trail, trying to avoid the potholes.

By the end of the ride we're both filthy and exhausted.

"That was the most fun I've had with my clothes on in a while," Elliot says as we hand the bikes over to the bellboy at The Heathman.

"Yeah," I mutter, and then recall holding Anastasia when I

saved her from the cyclist. Her warmth, her breasts pressed against me, her scent invading my senses.

I had my clothes on then . . . "Yeah," I murmur again.

We check our phones in the elevator as we head up to the top floor.

I have e-mails, a couple of texts from Elena asking what I'm doing this weekend, but no missed calls from Anastasia. It's just before 7:00—she must have received the books by now. The thought depresses me: I've come all the way to Portland on a wild-goose chase again.

"Man, that chick has called me five times and sent me four texts. Doesn't she know how desperate she comes across?" Elliot whines.

"Maybe she's pregnant."

Elliot pales and I laugh.

"Not funny, hotshot," he grumbles. "Besides, I haven't known her that long. Or that often."

AFTER A QUICK SHOWER I join Elliot in his suite and we sit down to watch the rest of the Mariners game against the San Diego Padres. We order up steak, salad, fries, and a couple of beers, and I sit back to enjoy the game in Elliot's easy company. I've resigned myself to the fact that Anastasia's not going to call. The Mariners are in the lead and it looks like it might be a blowout.

Disappointingly it isn't, though the Mariners win 4–1.

Go Mariners! Elliot and I clink beer bottles.

As the postgame analysis drones on, my phone buzzes and Miss Steele's number flashes on the screen.

It's her.

"Anastasia?" I don't hide my surprise or my pleasure. The background is noisy and it sounds like she's at a party or in a bar. Elliot glances at me, so I get up off the sofa and out of his earshot.

"Why did you send me the books?" She's slurring her words, and a wave of apprehension ripples down my spine.

"Anastasia, are you okay? You sound strange."

"I'm not the strange one, you are." Her tone is accusatory.

"Anastasia, have you been drinking?"

Hell. Who is she with? The photographer? Where's her friend Kate?

"What's it to you?" She sounds surly and belligerent, and I know she's drunk, but I also need to know that she's okay.

"I'm . . . curious. Where are you?"

"In a bar."

"Which bar?" *Tell me.* Anxiety blooms in my gut. She's a young woman, drunk, somewhere in Portland. She's not safe.

"A bar in Portland."

"How are you getting home?" I pinch the bridge of my nose in the vain hope that the action will distract me from my fraying temper.

"I'll find a way."

What the hell? Will she drive? I ask her again which bar she's in and she ignores my question.

"Why did you send me the books, Christian?"

"Anastasia, where are you? Tell me now."

How will she get home?

"You're so . . . domineering." She giggles. In any other situation I would find this charming. But right now—I want to show her how domineering I can be. She's driving me crazy.

"Ana, so help me, where the fuck are you?"

She giggles again. *Shit, she's laughing at me!*

Again!

"I'm in Portland . . . 's a long way from Seattle."

"Where in Portland?"

"Good night, Christian." The line goes dead.

"Ana!"

She hung up on me! I stare at the phone in disbelief. No one has ever hung up on me. *What the fuck!*

"What's the problem?" Elliot calls over from the sofa.

"I've just been drunk-dialed." I peer at him and his mouth drops open in surprise.

"You?"

"Yep." I press the callback button, trying to contain my temper, and my anxiety.

"Hi," she says, all breathy and timid, and she's in quieter surroundings.

"I'm coming to get you." My voice is arctic as I wrestle with my anger and snap my phone shut.

"I've got to go get this girl and take her home. Do you want to come?"

Elliot is staring at me as if I've grown three heads.

"You? With a chick? This I have to see." Elliot grabs his sneakers and starts putting them on.

"I just have to make a call." I wander into his bedroom while I decide if I should call Barney or Welch. Barney is the most senior engineer in the telecommunications division of my company. He's a tech genius. But what I want is not strictly legal.

Best to keep this away from my company.

I speed-dial Welch and within seconds his rasping voice answers.

"Mr. Grey?"

"I'd really like to know where Anastasia Steele is right now."

"I see." He pauses for a moment. "Leave it to me, Mr. Grey."

I know this is outside the law, but she could be getting herself into trouble.

"Thank you."

"I'll get back to you in a couple of minutes."

Elliot is rubbing his hands with glee, with a stupid smirk on his face when I return to the living room.

Oh, for fuck's sake.

"I wouldn't miss this for the world," he says, gloating.

"I'm just going to get the car keys. I'll meet you in the garage in five," I growl, ignoring his smug face.

THE BAR IS CROWDED, full of students determined to have a good time. There's some indie crap thumping over the sound system and the dance floor is crowded with heaving bodies.

It makes me feel old.

She's here somewhere.

Elliot has followed me in through the front door. "Do you see her?" he shouts over the noise. Scanning the room, I spot Katherine Kavanagh. She's with a group of friends, all of them men, sitting in a booth. There's no sign of Ana, but the table is littered with shot glasses and tumblers of beer.

Well, let's see if Miss Kavanagh is as loyal to her friend as Ana is to her.

She looks at me in surprise when we arrive at her table.

"Katherine," I say by way of greeting, and she interrupts me before I can ask her Ana's whereabouts.

"Christian, what a surprise to see you here," she shouts above the noise. The three guys at the table regard Elliot and me with hostile wariness.

"I was in the neighborhood."

"And who's this?" She smiles rather too brightly at Elliot, interrupting me again. What an exasperating woman.

"This is my brother Elliot. Elliot, Katherine Kavanagh. Where's Ana?"

Her smile broadens at Elliot, and I'm surprised by his answering grin.

"I think she went outside for some fresh air," Kavanagh responds, but she doesn't look at me. She has eyes only for Mr. Love 'Em and Leave 'Em. Well, it's her funeral.

"Outside? Where?" I shout.

"Oh. That way." She points to double doors at the far end of the bar.

Pushing through the throng, I make my way to the door, leaving the three disgruntled men and Kavanagh and Elliot engaged in a grin-off.

Through the double doors there is a line for the ladies' washroom, and beyond that a door that's open to the outside. It's at the back of the bar. Ironically, it leads to the parking lot where Elliot and I have just been.

Walking outside, I find myself in a gathering space adjacent to the parking lot—a hangout flanked by raised flowerbeds, where a few people are smoking, drinking, chatting. Making out. I spot her.

Hell! She's with the photographer, I think, though it's difficult to tell in the dim light. She's in his arms, but she seems to be twisting away from him. He mutters something to her, which I don't hear, and kisses her, along her jaw.

"José, no," she says, and then it's clear. She's trying to push him off.

She doesn't want this.

For a moment I want to rip his head off. With my hands fisted at my side I march up to them. "I think the lady said no." My voice carries, cold and sinister, in the relative quiet, while I struggle to contain my anger.

He releases Ana and she squints at me with a dazed, drunken expression.

"Grey," he says, his voice terse, and it takes every ounce of my self-control not to smash the disappointment off his face.

Ana heaves, then buckles over and vomits on the ground.

Oh, shit!

"Ugh—*Dios mío*, Ana!" José leaps out of the way in disgust.

Fucking idiot.

Ignoring him, I grab her hair and hold it out of the way as she continues to throw up everything she's had this evening. It's with some annoyance that I note she doesn't appear to have eaten. With my arm around her shoulders I lead her away from the curious onlookers toward one of the flowerbeds. "If you're going to throw up again, do it here. I'll hold you." It's darker here. She can puke in peace. She vomits again and again, her hands on the brick. It's pitiful. Once her stomach is empty, she continues to retch, long dry heaves.

Boy, she's got it bad.

Finally her body relaxes and I think she's finished. Releasing her, I give her my handkerchief, which by some miracle I have in the inside pocket of my jacket.

Thank you, Mrs. Jones.

Wiping her mouth, she turns and rests against the bricks, avoiding eye contact because she's ashamed and embarrassed. And

yet I'm so pleased to see her. Gone is my fury at the photographer.
I'm delighted to be standing in the parking lot of a student bar in
Portland with Miss Anastasia Steele.

She puts her head in her hands, cringes, then peeks up at me,
still mortified. Turning to the door, she glares over my shoulder. I
assume it's at her "friend."

"I'll, um, see you inside," José says, but I don't turn to stare him
down, and to my delight, she ignores him, too, returning her eyes
to mine.

"I'm sorry," she says finally, while her fingers twist the soft linen.
Okay, let's have some fun.

"What are you sorry for, Anastasia?"

"The phone call, mainly. Being sick. Oh, the list is endless,"
she mumbles.

"We've all been here, perhaps not quite as dramatically as you."
Why is it such fun to tease this young woman? "It's about knowing your limits, Anastasia. I mean, I'm all for pushing limits, but
really this is beyond the pale. Do you make a habit of this kind of
behavior?"

Perhaps she has a problem with alcohol. The thought is worrying, and I consider whether I should call my mother for a referral
to a detox clinic.

Ana frowns for a moment, as if angry, that little *v* forming
between her brows, and I suppress the urge to kiss it. But when she
speaks she sounds contrite.

"No," she says. "I've never been drunk before and right now I
have no desire to ever be again." She looks up at me, her eyes unfocused, and she sways a little. She might pass out, so without giving
it a thought I scoop her up into my arms.

She's surprisingly light. Too light. The thought irks me. No
wonder she's drunk.

"Come on, I'll take you home."

"I need to tell Kate," she says, as her head rests on my shoulder.

"My brother can tell her."

"What?"

"My brother Elliot is talking to Miss Kavanagh."

"Oh?"

"He was with me when you called."

"In Seattle?"

"No, I'm staying at The Heathman."

And my wild-goose chase has paid off.

"How did you find me?"

"I tracked your cell phone, Anastasia." I head toward the car. I want to drive her home. "Do you have a jacket or a purse?"

"Er . . . yes, I came with both. Christian, please, I need to tell Kate. She'll worry."

I stop and bite my tongue. Kavanagh wasn't worried about her being out here with the overamorous photographer. *Rodriguez.* That's his name. What kind of *friend* is she? The lights from the bar illuminate her anxious face.

As much as it pains me, I put her down and agree to take her inside. Holding hands, we walk back into the bar, stopping at Kate's table. One of the young men is still sitting there, looking annoyed and abandoned.

"Where's Kate?" Ana shouts above the noise.

"Dancing," the guy says, his dark eyes staring at the dance floor. Ana collects her jacket and purse and, reaching out, she unexpectedly clutches my arm.

I freeze.

Shit.

My heart rate catapults into overdrive as the darkness surfaces, stretching and tightening its claws around my throat.

"She's on the dance floor," she shouts, her words tickling my ear, distracting me from my fear. And suddenly the darkness disappears and the pounding in my heart ceases.

What?

I roll my eyes to hide my confusion and take her to the bar, order a large glass of water, and pass it to her.

"Drink."

Eyeing me over the glass, she takes a tentative sip.

"All of it," I command. I'm hoping this will be enough damage control to avoid one hell of a hangover tomorrow.

What might have happened to her if I hadn't intervened? My mood sinks.

And I think of what just happened to me.

Her touch. My reaction.

My mood plummets further.

Ana sways a little as she's drinking, so I steady her with a hand on her shoulder. I like the connection—me touching her. She's oil on my troubled, deep, dark waters.

Hmm . . . flowery, Grey.

She finishes her drink, and retrieving the glass, I place it on the bar.

Okay. She wants to talk to her so-called friend. I survey the crowded dance floor, uneasy at the thought of all those bodies pressing in on me as we fight our way through.

Steeling myself, I grab her hand and lead her toward the dance floor. She hesitates, but if she wants to talk to her friend, there's only one way; she's going to have to dance with me. Once Elliot gets his groove on, there's no stopping him; so much for his quiet night in.

With a tug, she's in my arms.

This I can handle. When I know she's going to touch me, it's okay. I can deal, especially since I'm wearing my jacket. I weave us through the crowd to where Elliot and Kate are making a spectacle of themselves.

Still dancing, Elliot leans toward me in mid-strut when we're beside him and sizes us up with a look of incredulity.

"I'm taking Ana home. Tell Kate," I shout in his ear.

He nods and pulls Kavanagh into his arms.

Right. Let me take Miss Drunk Bookworm home, but for some reason she seems reluctant to go. She's watching Kavanagh with concern. When we're off the dance floor she looks back at Kate, then at me, swaying and a little dazed.

"Fuck—" By some miracle I catch her as she passes out in the middle of the bar. I'm tempted to haul her over my shoulder, but we'd be too conspicuous, so I pick her up once more, cradling her against my chest, and take her outside to the car.

"Christ," I mutter as I fish the key out of my jeans and hold her at the same time. Amazingly, I manage to get her into the front seat and strap her in.

"Ana." I give her a little shake, because she's worryingly quiet. "Ana!"

She mumbles something incoherent and I know she's still conscious. I know I should take her home, but it's a long drive to Vancouver, and I don't know if she'll be sick again. I don't relish the idea of my Audi reeking of vomit. The smell emanating from her clothes is already noticeable.

I head to The Heathman, telling myself that I'm doing this for her sake.

Yeah, tell yourself that, Grey.

SHE SLEEPS IN MY arms as we travel up in the elevator from the garage. I need to get her out of her jeans and her shoes. The stale stench of vomit pervades the space. I'd really like to give her a bath, but that would be stepping beyond the bounds of propriety.

And this isn't?

In my suite, I drop her purse on the sofa, then carry her into the bedroom and lay her down on the bed. She mumbles once more but doesn't wake.

Briskly I remove her shoes and socks and put them in the plastic laundry bag provided by the hotel. Then I unzip her jeans and pull them off, check the pockets before stuffing the jeans in the laundry bag. She falls back on the bed, splayed out like a starfish, all pale arms and legs, and for a moment I picture those legs wrapped around my waist as her wrists are bound to my Saint Andrew's cross. There's a fading bruise on her knee and I wonder if that's from the fall she took in my office.

She's been marked since then . . . like me.

I sit her up and she opens her eyes.

"Hello, Ana," I whisper, as I remove her jacket slowly and without her cooperation.

"Grey. Lips," she mutters.

"Yes, sweetheart." I ease her down onto the bed. She closes her eyes again and rolls onto her side, but this time huddles into a ball, looking small and vulnerable. I pull the covers over her and plant a kiss in her hair. Now that her filthy clothes have gone, a trace of her scent has reappeared. Apples, fall, fresh, delicious . . . Ana. Her lips are parted, eyelashes fanning out over pale cheeks, and her skin looks flawless. One more touch is all I allow myself as I stroke her cheek with the back of my index finger.

"Sleep well," I murmur, and then head into the living room to complete the laundry list. When it's done, I place the offending bag outside my suite so the contents will be collected and laundered.

Before I check my e-mails I text Welch, asking him to see if José Rodriguez has any police records. I'm curious. I want to know if he preys on drunk young women. Then I address the issue of clothes for Miss Steele: I send a quick e-mail to Taylor.

From: Christian Grey
RE: Miss Anastasia Steele
Date: May 20, 2011 23:46
To: J B Taylor

Good morning,
Can you please find the following items for Miss Steele and have them delivered to my usual room before 10:00.

Jeans: Blue Denim Size 4
Blouse: Blue. Pretty. Size 4
Converse: Black Size 7
Socks: Size 7
Lingerie: Underwear—Size Small. Bra—Estimate 34C.

Thank you.

Christian Grey
CEO, Grey Enterprises Holdings, Inc.

Once it's disappeared from my outbox, I text Elliot.

> Ana is with me.
> If you're still with Kate, tell her.

He texts by return.

> Will do.
> Hope you get laid.
> You soooo need it. ;)

His response makes me snort.
I so do, Elliot. I so do.
I open my work e-mail and begin to read.

SATURDAY, MAY 21, 2011

Nearly two hours later, I come to bed. It's just after 1:45. She's fast asleep and hasn't moved from where I left her. I strip, pull on my PJ pants and a T-shirt, and climb in beside her. She's comatose; it's unlikely she's going to thrash around and touch me. I hesitate for a moment as the darkness swells within me, but it doesn't surface and I know it's because I'm watching the hypnotic rise and fall of her chest and I'm breathing in sync with her. In. Out. In. Out. In. Out. For seconds, minutes, hours, I don't know, I watch her. And while she sleeps I survey every beautiful inch of her lovely face. Her dark lashes fluttering while she sleeps, her lips slightly parted so I glimpse her even white teeth. She mutters something unintelligible and her tongue darts out and licks her lips. It's arousing, very arousing. Finally I fall into a deep and dreamless slumber.

IT'S QUIET WHEN I open my eyes, and I'm momentarily disoriented. Oh yes. I'm at The Heathman. The clock at my bedside says 7:43.

When was the last time I slept this late?

Ana.

Slowly I turn my head, and she's fast asleep, facing me. Her beautiful face soft in repose.

I have never slept with a woman. I've fucked many, but to wake up beside an alluring young woman is a new and stimulating experience. My cock agrees.

This will not do.

Reluctantly, I climb out of bed and change into my running

gear. I need to burn off this . . . excess energy. As I change into my sweats I can't remember the last time I've slept so well.

In the living room, I fire up my laptop, check my e-mail, and respond to two from Ros and one from Andrea. It takes me a little longer than usual, as I'm distracted knowing that Ana is asleep in the next room. I wonder how she'll feel when she wakes.

Hungover. *Ah.*

In the minibar I find a bottle of orange juice and empty it into a glass. She's still asleep when I enter, her hair a riot of mahogany spread across her pillow, and the covers have slipped below her waist. Her T-shirt has ridden up, exposing her belly and her navel. The sight stirs my body once more.

Stop standing here ogling the girl, for fuck's sake, Grey.

I have to get out of here before I do something I'll regret. Placing the glass on the bedside table, I duck into the bathroom, find two Advil in my travel kit, and deposit them beside the glass of orange juice.

With one last lingering look at Anastasia Steele—the first woman I've ever slept with—I head out for my run.

WHEN I RETURN FROM my exercise, there's a bag in the living room from a store I don't recognize. I take a peek and see it contains clothes for Ana. From what I can see, Taylor has done well— and all before 9:00.

The man is a marvel.

Her purse is on the sofa where I dropped it last night, and the door to the bedroom is closed, so I assume she's not left and that she's still asleep.

It's a relief. Poring over the room-service menu, I decide to order some food. She'll be hungry when she wakes, but I have no idea what she'll eat, so in a rare moment of indulgence I order a selection from the breakfast menu. I'm informed it will take half an hour.

Time to wake the delectable Miss Steele; she's slept enough.

Grabbing my workout towel and the shopping bag, I knock on

the door and enter. To my delight, she's sitting up in bed. The tablets are gone and so is the juice.

Good girl.

She pales as I saunter into the room.

Keep it casual, Grey. You don't want to be charged with kidnapping.

She closes her eyes, and I assume it's because she's embarrassed.

"Good morning, Anastasia. How are you feeling?"

"Better than I deserve," she mutters, as I place the bag on the chair. When she turns her gaze to me her eyes are impossibly big and blue, and though her hair is a tangled mess . . . she looks stunning.

"How did I get here?" she asks, as though she's afraid of the answer.

Reassure her, Grey.

I sit down on the edge of the bed and stick to the facts. "After you passed out, I didn't want to risk the leather upholstery in my car, taking you all the way to your apartment. So I brought you here."

"Did you put me to bed?"

"Yes."

"Did I throw up again?"

"No." Thank God.

"Did you undress me?"

"Yes." *Who else would have undressed you?*

She blushes, and at last she has some color in her cheeks. Perfect teeth bite down on her lip. I suppress a groan.

"We didn't—?" she whispers, staring at her hands.

Christ, what kind of animal does she think I am?

"Anastasia, you were comatose. Necrophilia is not my thing." My tone is dry. "I like my women sentient and receptive." She sags with relief, which makes me wonder if this has happened to her before, that she's passed out and woken up in a stranger's bed and found out he's fucked her without her consent. Maybe that's the photographer's modus operandi. The thought is disturbing. But I recall her confession last night—that she'd never been drunk before. Thank God she hasn't made a habit of this.

"I'm so sorry," she says, her voice full of shame.

Hell. Maybe I should go easy on her.

"It was a very diverting evening. Not one that I'll forget in a while." I hope that sounds conciliatory, but her brow creases.

"You didn't have to track me down with whatever James Bond gadgetry you're developing for the highest bidder."

Whoa! Now she's pissed. Why?

"First, the technology to track cell phones is available over the Internet."

Well, the Deep Net . . .

"Second, my company does not invest or manufacture any kind of surveillance devices."

My temper is fraying, but I'm on a roll. "And third, if I hadn't come to get you, you'd probably be waking up in the photographer's bed, and from what I can remember, you weren't overly enthused about him pressing his suit."

She blinks a couple of times, then starts giggling.

She's laughing at me again.

"Which medieval chronicle did you escape from? You sound like a courtly knight."

She's beguiling. She's calling me out . . . again, and her irreverence is refreshing, really refreshing. However, I'm under no illusion that I'm a knight in shining armor. Boy, has she got the wrong idea. And though it may not be to my advantage, I'm compelled to warn her that there's nothing chivalrous or courtly about me. "Anastasia, I don't think so. Dark knight, maybe." If only she knew—and why are we discussing me? I change the subject. "Did you eat last night?"

She shakes her head.

I knew it!

"You need to eat. That's why you were so ill. Honestly, it's drinking rule number one."

"Are you going to continue to scold me?"

"Is that what I'm doing?"

"I think so."

"You're lucky I'm just scolding you."

"What do you mean?"

"Well, if you were mine, you wouldn't be able to sit down for a week after the stunt you pulled yesterday. You didn't eat, you got drunk, you put yourself at risk." The fear in my gut surprises me; such irresponsible, risk-taking behavior. "I hate to think what could have happened to you."

She scowls. "I would have been fine. I was with Kate."

Some help she was!

"And the photographer?" I retort.

"José just got out of line," she says, dismissing my concern and tossing her tangled hair over her shoulder.

"Well, the next time he gets out of line, maybe someone should teach him some manners."

"You're quite the disciplinarian," she snaps.

"Oh, Anastasia, you have no idea."

An image of her shackled to my bench, peeled gingerroot inserted in her ass so she can't clench her buttocks, comes to mind, followed by judicious use of a belt or strap. *Yeah . . . That would teach her not to be so irresponsible.* The thought is hugely appealing.

She's staring at me wide-eyed and dazed, and it makes me uncomfortable. *Can she read my mind? Or is she just looking at a pretty face.*

"I'm going to have a shower. Unless you'd like to shower first?" I tell her, but she continues to gape. Even with her mouth open she's quite lovely. She's hard to resist, and I grant myself permission to touch her, tracing the line of her cheek with my thumb. Her breath catches in her throat as I stroke her soft bottom lip.

"Breathe, Anastasia," I murmur, before I stand and inform her that breakfast will be here in fifteen minutes. She says nothing, her smart mouth silent for once.

In the bathroom I take a deep breath, strip, and climb into the shower. I'm half tempted to jerk off, but the familiar fear of discovery and disclosure, from an earlier time in my life, stops me.

Elena would not be pleased.

Old habits.

As the water cascades over my head I reflect on my latest interaction with the challenging Miss Steele. She's still here, in my bed, so she cannot find me completely repulsive. I noticed the way her breath caught in her throat, and how her gaze followed me around the room.

Yeah. There's hope.

But would she make a good submissive?

It's obvious she knows nothing of the lifestyle. She couldn't even say "fuck" or "sex" or whatever bookish college students use as a euphemism for fucking these days. She's quite the innocent. She's probably been subjected to a few fumbling encounters with boys like the photographer.

The thought of her fumbling with anyone irks me.

I could just ask her if she's interested.

No. I'd have to show her what she'd be taking on if she agreed to a relationship with me.

Let's see how we both fare over breakfast.

Rinsing off the soap, I stand beneath the hot stream and gather my wits for round two with Anastasia Steele. I switch off the water and, stepping out of the shower, grab a towel. A quick check in the steamed-up mirror and I decide to skip shaving today. Breakfast will be here shortly, and I'm hungry. Quickly I brush my teeth.

When I open the bathroom door she's out of bed and searching for her jeans. She looks up like the archetypal startled fawn, all long legs and big eyes.

"If you're looking for your jeans, I've sent them to the laundry." She really has great legs. She shouldn't hide them in pants. Her eyes narrow, and I think she's going to argue with me, so I tell her why. "They were spattered with your vomit."

"Oh," she says.

Yes. "Oh." Now, *what do you have to say to that, Miss Steele?*

"I sent Taylor out for another pair and some shoes. They're in the bag on the chair." I nod at the shopping bag.

She raises her eyebrows—in surprise, I think. "Um. I'll have a shower," she mutters, and then as an afterthought she adds, "Thanks."

Grabbing the bag, she dodges around me, darts into the bathroom, and locks the door.

Hmm . . . she couldn't get into the bathroom quick enough.

Away from me.

Perhaps I'm being too optimistic.

Disheartened, I briskly dry off and get dressed. In the living room I check my e-mail, but there's nothing urgent. I'm interrupted by a knock on the door. Two young women have arrived from room service.

"Where would you like breakfast, sir?"

"Set it up on the dining table."

Walking back into the bedroom, I catch their furtive looks, but I ignore them and suppress the guilt I feel over how much food I've ordered. We'll never eat it all.

"Breakfast is here," I call, and rap on the bathroom door.

"O-okay." Ana's voice sounds a little muted.

Back in the living room, our breakfast is on the table. One of the women, who has dark, dark eyes, hands me the check to sign, and from my wallet I pull a couple of twenties for them.

"Thank you, ladies."

"Just call room service when you want the table cleared, sir," Miss Dark Eyes says with a coquettish look, as if she's offering more.

My chilly smile warns her off.

Sitting down at the table with the newspaper, I pour myself a coffee and make a start on my omelet. My phone buzzes—a text from Elliot.

> **Kate wants to know if Ana is still alive.**

I chuckle, somewhat mollified that Ana's so-called friend is thinking about her. It's obvious that Elliot hasn't given his dick a rest after all his protestations yesterday. I text back.

> Alive and kicking ;)

Ana appears a few moments later: hair wet, in the pretty blue blouse that matches her eyes. Taylor has done well; she looks lovely. Scanning the room, she spots her purse.

"Crap, Kate!" she blurts.

"She knows you're here and still alive. I texted Elliot."

She gives me an uncertain smile as she walks toward the table.

"Sit," I say, pointing to the place that's been set for her. She frowns at the amount of food on the table, which only accentuates my guilt.

"I didn't know what you liked, so I ordered a selection from the breakfast menu," I mutter by way of an apology.

"That's very profligate of you," she says.

"Yes, it is." My guilt blooms. But as she opts for the pancakes, scrambled eggs, and bacon with maple syrup, and tucks in, I forgive myself. It's good to see her eat.

"Tea?" I ask.

"Yes, please," she says between mouthfuls. She's obviously famished. I pass her the small teapot of water. She gives me a sweet smile when she notices the Twinings English Breakfast tea.

I have to catch my breath at her expression. And it makes me uneasy.

It gives me hope.

"Your hair's very damp," I observe.

"I couldn't find the hair dryer," she says, embarrassed.

She'll get sick.

"Thank you for the clothes," she adds.

"It's a pleasure, Anastasia. That color suits you."

She stares down at her fingers.

"You know, you really should learn to take a compliment."

Perhaps she doesn't get many . . . but why? She's gorgeous in an understated way.

"I should give you some money for these clothes."

What?

I glare at her, and she continues quickly, "You've already given me the books, which, of course, I can't accept. But these, please let me pay you back."

Sweetheart.

"Anastasia, trust me, I can afford it."

"That's not the point. Why should you buy these for me?"

"Because I can." *I'm a very rich man, Ana.*

"Just because you can doesn't mean that you should." Her voice is soft, but suddenly I'm wondering if she's looked through me and seen my darkest desires. "Why did you send me the books, Christian?"

Because I wanted to see you again, and here you are . . .

"Well, when you were nearly run over by the cyclist—and I was holding you and you were looking up at me—all 'kiss me, kiss me, Christian'—" I stop, recalling that moment, her body pressed against mine. *Shit.* Quickly I shrug off the memory. "I felt I owed you an apology and a warning. Anastasia, I'm not a hearts-and-flowers kind of man. I don't do romance. My tastes are very singular. You should steer clear of me. There's something about you, though, and I'm finding it impossible to stay away. But I think you've figured that out already."

"Then don't," she whispers.

What?

"You don't know what you're saying."

"Enlighten me, then."

Her words travel straight to my cock.

Fuck.

"You're not celibate?" she asks.

"No, Anastasia, I'm not celibate." And if you'd let me tie you up I'd prove it to you right now.

Her eyes widen and her cheeks pink.

Oh, Ana.

I have to show her. It's the only way I'll know. "What are your plans for the next few days?" I ask.

"I'm working today, from midday. What time is it?" she exclaims in panic.

"It's just after ten; you've plenty of time. What about tomorrow?"

"Kate and I are going to start packing. We're moving to Seattle next weekend, and I'm working at Clayton's all this week."

"You have a place in Seattle already?"

"Yes."

"Where?"

"I can't remember the address. It's in the Pike Market District."

"Not far from me." *Good!* "So what are you going to do for work in Seattle?"

"I've applied for some internships. I'm waiting to hear."

"Have you applied to my company, as I suggested?"

"Um . . . no."

"And what's wrong with my company?"

"Your company or your *company*?" She arches an eyebrow.

"Are you smirking at me, Miss Steele?" I can't hide my amusement.

Oh, she'd be a joy to train . . . challenging, maddening woman.

She examines her plate, chewing at her lip.

"I'd like to bite that lip," I whisper, because it's true.

Her face flies to mine and she shuffles in her seat. She tilts her chin toward me, her eyes full of confidence. "Why don't you?" she says quietly.

Oh. Don't tempt me, baby. I can't. Not yet.

"Because I'm not going to touch you, Anastasia—not until I have your written consent to do so."

"What does that mean?" she asks.

"Exactly what I say. I need to show you, Anastasia." So you know what you're getting yourself into. "What time do you finish work this evening?"

"About eight."

"Well, we could go to Seattle this evening or next Saturday for dinner at my place, and I'll acquaint you with the facts then. The choice is yours."

"Why can't you tell me now?"

"Because I'm enjoying my breakfast and your company. Once you're enlightened, you probably won't want to see me again."

She frowns as she processes what I've said. "Tonight," she says.

Whoa. That didn't take long.

"Like Eve, you're so quick to eat from the tree of knowledge," I taunt her.

"Are you smirking at me, Mr. Grey?" she asks.

I look at her through narrowed eyes.

Okay, baby, you asked for this.

I pick up my phone and press Taylor on speed dial. He answers almost immediately.

"Mr. Grey."

"Taylor. I'm going to need *Charlie Tango.*"

She watches me closely as I make arrangements to bring my EC135 to Portland.

I'll show her what I have in mind . . . and the rest will be up to her. She may want to come home once she knows. I'll need Stephan, my pilot, to be on standby so he can bring her back to Portland if she decides to have nothing more to do with me. I hope that's not the case.

And it dawns on me that I'm thrilled that I can take her to Seattle in *Charlie Tango.*

It'll be a first.

"Standby pilot from 22:30," I confirm with Taylor and hang up.

"Do people always do what you tell them?" she asks, and the disapproval in her voice is obvious. Is she scolding me now? Her challenge is annoying.

"Usually, if they want to keep their jobs." *Don't question how I treat my staff.*

"And if they don't work for you?" she adds.

"Oh, I can be very persuasive, Anastasia. You should finish your breakfast. And then I'll drop you off at home. I'll pick you up at Clayton's at eight when you finish. We'll fly up to Seattle."

"Fly?"

"Yes. I have a helicopter."

Her mouth drops open, forming a small *o.* It's a pleasing moment.

"We'll go by helicopter to Seattle?" she whispers.

"Yes."

"Why?"

"Because I can." I grin. Sometimes it's just fucking great to be me. "Finish your breakfast."

She seems stunned.

"Eat!" My voice is more forceful. "Anastasia, I have an issue with wasted food. Eat."

"I can't eat all this." She studies all the food on the table and I feel guilty once more. Yes, there is too much food here.

"Eat what's on your plate. If you'd eaten properly yesterday, you wouldn't be here, and I wouldn't be declaring my hand so soon."

Hell. This could be a huge mistake.

She gives me a sideways look as she chases her food around on the plate with a fork, and her mouth twitches.

"What's so funny?"

She shakes her head and pops the last piece of pancake into her mouth, and I try not to laugh. As ever, she surprises me. She's awkward, unexpected, and disarming. She really makes me want to laugh, and what's more, it's at myself.

"Good girl," I mutter. "I'll take you home when you've dried your hair. I don't want you getting ill."

You'll need all your strength for tonight, for what I have to show you.

Suddenly, she gets up from the table and I have to stop myself from telling her that she doesn't have permission.

She's not your submissive . . . yet, Grey.

On the way back to the bedroom, she pauses by the sofa.

"Where did you sleep last night?" she asks.

"In my bed." *With you.*

"Oh."

"Yes, it was quite a novelty for me, too."

"Not having . . . sex."

She said the s-word . . . and the telltale pink cheeks appear.

"No."

How can I tell her this, without it sounding weird?

Just tell her, Grey.

"Sleeping with someone." Nonchalantly, I turn my attention

back to the sports section and the write-up on last night's game, then watch as she disappears into the bedroom.

No, that didn't sound weird at all.

Well, I have another date with Miss Steele. No, not a date. She needs to know about me. I let out a long breath and drink what's left of my orange juice. This is shaping up to be a very interesting day. I'm pleased when I hear the buzz of the hair dryer and surprised that she's doing what she's been told.

While I'm waiting for her, I phone the valet to bring my car up from the garage and check her address once more on Google Maps. Next, I text Andrea to send me an NDA via e-mail; if Ana wants enlightenment, she'll need to keep her mouth shut. My phone buzzes. It's Ros.

As I'm on the phone, Ana emerges from the bedroom and picks up her purse. Ros is talking about Darfur, but my attention is on Miss Steele. She rummages around in her purse and she's pleased when she finds a hair tie.

Her hair is beautiful. Lush. Long. Thick. Idly, I wonder what it would be like to braid. She ties it back and puts on her jacket, then sits down on the sofa, waiting for me to finish my call.

"Okay, let's do it. Keep me abreast of progress." I conclude my conversation with Ros. She's been working miracles and it looks like our food shipment to Darfur is happening.

"Ready to go?" I ask Ana. She nods. I grab my jacket and car keys and follow her out the door. She peeks at me through long lashes as we walk toward the elevator, and her lips curl into a shy smile. My lips twitch in response.

What the hell is she doing to me?

The elevator arrives, and I allow her to step in first. I press the first-floor button and the doors close. In the confines of the elevator, I'm completely aware of her. A trace of her sweet fragrance invades my senses . . . Her breathing alters, hitching a little, and she peeks up at me with a bright come-hither look.

Shit.

She bites her lip.

She's doing this on purpose. And for a split second I'm lost in her sensual, mesmerizing stare. She doesn't back down.

I'm hard.

Instantly.

I want her.

Here.

Now.

In the elevator.

"Oh, fuck the paperwork." The words come from nowhere and on instinct I grab her and push her against the wall. Clasping both her hands, I pin them above her head so she can't touch me, and once she's secure, I twist my other hand in her hair while my lips seek and find hers.

She moans into my mouth, the call of a siren, and finally I can sample her: mint and tea and an orchard of mellow fruitfulness. She tastes every bit as good as she looks. Reminding me of a time of plenty. *Good Lord.* I'm yearning for her. I grasp her chin, deepening the kiss, and her tongue tentatively touches mine . . . exploring. Considering. Feeling. Kissing me back.

Oh, God in heaven.

"You. Are. So. Sweet," I murmur against her lips, completely intoxicated, punch-drunk with her scent and taste.

The elevator stops and the doors begin to open.

Get a fucking grip, Grey.

I push myself off her and stand beyond her reach.

She's breathing hard.

As am I.

When was the last time I lost control?

Three men in business suits give us knowing looks as they join us.

And I stare at the poster that's above the buttons in the elevator advertising a sensual weekend at The Heathman. I glance at Ana and exhale.

She grins.

And my lips twitch once more.

What the fuck has she done to me?

The elevator stops at the second floor and the guys get out, leaving me alone with Miss Steele.

"You've brushed your teeth," I observe with wry amusement.

"I used your toothbrush," she says, eyes shining.

Of course she has . . . and for some reason, I find this pleasing, too pleasing. I stifle my smile. "Oh, Anastasia Steele, what am I going to do with you?" I take her hand as the elevator doors open on the ground floor, and I mutter under my breath, "What is it about elevators?" She gives me a knowing look as we stroll across the polished marble of the lobby.

The car is waiting in one of the bays in front of the hotel; the valet is pacing impatiently. I give him an obscene tip and open the passenger door for Ana, who is quiet and introspective.

But she hasn't run.

Even though I jumped her in the elevator.

I should say something about what happened in there—but what?

Sorry?

How was that for you?

What the hell are you doing to me?

I start the car and decide that the less said, the better. The soothing sound of Delibes's "Flower Duet" fills the car and I begin to relax.

"What are we listening to?" Ana inquires, as I turn onto Southwest Jefferson Street. I tell her and ask her if she likes it.

"Christian, it's wonderful."

To hear my name on her lips is a strange delight. She's said it about half a dozen times now, and each time it's different. Today, it's with wonder—at the music. It's great that she likes this piece: it's one of my favorites. I find myself beaming; she's obviously excused me for the elevator outburst.

"Can I hear that again?"

"Of course." I tap the touch screen to replay the music.

"You like classical music?" she asks, as we cross the Fremont Bridge, and we fall into an easy conversation about my taste in music. While we're talking I get a call on the hands-free.

"Grey," I answer.

"Mr. Grey, it's Welch here. I have the information you require."

Oh yes, details about the photographer.

"Good. E-mail it to me. Anything to add?"

"No, sir."

I press the button and the music is back. We both listen, now lost in the raw sound of the Kings of Leon. But it doesn't last long—our listening pleasure is disturbed once more by the hands-free.

What the hell?

"Grey," I snap.

"The NDA has been e-mailed to you, Mr. Grey."

"Good. That's all, Andrea."

"Good day, sir."

I sneak a look at Ana, to see if she's picked up on that conversation, but she's studying the Portland scenery. I suspect she's being polite. It's difficult to keep my eyes on the road. I want to stare at her. For all her maladroitness, she has a beautiful neckline, one that I'd like to kiss from the bottom of her ear right down to her shoulder.

Hell. I shuffle in my seat. I hope she agrees to sign the NDA and to take what I have to offer.

When we join I-5 I get another call.

It's Elliot.

"Hi, Christian, d'you get laid?"

Oh . . . smooth, dude, smooth.

"Hello, Elliot—I'm on speakerphone, and I'm not alone in the car."

"Who's with you?"

"Anastasia Steele."

"Hi, Ana!"

"Hello, Elliot," she says, animated.

"Heard a lot about you," Elliot says.

Shit. What has he heard?

"Don't believe a word Kate says," she responds good-naturedly. Elliot laughs.

"I'm dropping Anastasia off now. Shall I pick you up?" I interject.

There's no doubt Elliot will want to make a quick getaway.

"Sure."

"See you shortly." I hang up.

"Why do you insist on calling me Anastasia?" she asks.

"Because it's your name."

"I prefer Ana."

"Do you, now?"

"Ana" is too everyday and ordinary for her. And too familiar. Those three letters have the power to wound . . .

And in that moment I know that her rejection, when it comes, will be hard to take. It's happened before, but I've never felt this . . . invested. I don't even know this girl, but I want to know her, all of her. Maybe it's because I've never chased a woman.

Grey, get control of yourself and follow the rules, otherwise this will all go to shit.

"Anastasia," I say, ignoring her disapproving look. "What happened in the elevator—it won't happen again—well, not unless it's premeditated."

That keeps her quiet as I park outside her apartment. Before she can answer me I climb out of the car, walk around and open her door.

As she steps onto the sidewalk, she gives me a fleeting glance. "I liked what happened in the elevator," she says.

You did? Her confession halts me in my tracks. I'm pleasantly surprised again by little Miss Steele. As she walks up the steps to the front door, I have to scramble to keep up with her.

Elliot and Kate look up when we enter. They're sitting at a dining table in a sparsely furnished room, befitting a couple of students. There are a few packing boxes beside a bookshelf. Elliot looks relaxed and not in a hurry to leave, which surprises me.

Kavanagh jumps up and gives me a critical once-over as she hugs Ana.

What did she think I was going to do to the girl?

I know what I'd like to do to her . . .

As Kavanagh holds her at arm's length I'm reassured; maybe she does care for Ana, too.

"Good morning, Christian," she says, her tone cool and condescending.

"Miss Kavanagh." And what I want to say is something sarcastic about how she's finally showing some interest in her friend, but I hold my tongue.

"Christian, her name is Kate," Elliot says with mild irritation.

"Kate," I mutter, to be polite. Elliot hugs Ana, holding her for a moment too long.

"Hi, Ana," he says, all fucking smiles.

"Hi, Elliot." She beams.

Okay, this is becoming unbearable. "Elliot, we'd better go." *And take your hands off her.*

"Sure," he says, releasing Ana, but grabbing Kavanagh and making an unseemly show of kissing her.

Oh, for fuck's sake.

Ana's uncomfortable watching them. I don't blame her. But when she turns to me it's with a speculative look through narrowed eyes.

What is she thinking?

"Laters, baby," Elliot mutters, slobbering over Kavanagh.

Dude, show some dignity, for heaven's sake.

Ana's reproachful eyes are on me, and for a moment I don't know if it's because of Elliot and Kate's lascivious display or—

Hell! This is what she wants. To be courted and wooed.

I don't do romance, sweetheart.

A lock of her hair has broken free, and without thinking, I tuck it behind her ear. She leans her face into my fingers, the tender gesture surprising me. My thumb strays to her soft bottom lip, which I'd like to kiss again. But I can't. Not until I have her consent.

"Laters, baby," I whisper, and her face softens with a smile. "I'll pick you up at eight." Reluctantly, I turn away and open the front door, Elliot behind me.

"Man, I need some sleep," Elliot says, as soon as we're in the car. "That woman is voracious."

"Really . . ." My voice drips with sarcasm. The last thing I want is a blow-by-blow account of his assignation.

"How about you, hotshot? Did she pop your cherry?"

I give him a sideways "fuck off" glare.

Elliot laughs. "Man, you are one uptight son of a bitch." He pulls his Sounders cap over his face and nestles down in his seat for a nap.

I turn up the volume of the music.

Sleep through that, Lelliot!

Yeah. I envy my brother: his ease with women, his ability to sleep . . . and the fact that he's not the son of a bitch.

JOSÉ LUIS RODRIGUEZ'S BACKGROUND check reveals a ticket for possession of marijuana. There is nothing in his police records for sexual harassment. Maybe last night would have been a first if I hadn't intervened. And the little prick smokes weed? I hope he doesn't smoke around Ana—and I hope she doesn't smoke, period.

Opening Andrea's e-mail, I send the NDA to the printer in my study at home in Escala. Ana will need to sign it before I show her my playroom. And in a moment of weakness, or hubris, or perhaps unprecedented optimism—I don't know which—I fill in her name and address on my standard Dom/sub contract and send that to print, too.

There's a knock at the door.

"Hey, hotshot. Let's go hiking," Elliot says through the door.

Ah . . . the child has woken from his nap.

THE SCENT OF PINE, fresh damp earth, and late spring is a balm to my senses. The smell reminds me of those heady days of my childhood, running through a forest with Elliot and my sister Mia under the watchful eyes of our adoptive parents. The quiet, the space, the freedom . . . the scrunch of dry pine needles underfoot.

Here in the great outdoors I could forget.

Here was a refuge from my nightmares.

Elliot chatters away, needing only the occasional grunt from me to keep talking. As we make our way along the pebbled shore of the Willamette my mind strays to Anastasia. For the first time in a long time, I have a sweet sense of anticipation. I'm excited.

Will she say yes to my proposal?

I picture her sleeping beside me, soft and small . . . and my cock twitches with expectation. I could have woken her and fucked her then—what a novelty that would have been.

I'll fuck her in time.

I'll fuck her bound and with her smart mouth gagged.

CLAYTON'S IS QUIET. The last customer left five minutes ago. And I'm waiting—again—drumming my fingers on my thighs. Patience is not my forte. Even the long hike with Elliot today has not dampened my restlessness. He's having dinner with Kate this evening at The Heathman. Two dates on consecutive nights is not his usual style.

Suddenly the fluorescent lights inside the store flicker off, the front door opens, and Ana steps out into a mild Portland evening. My heart begins to hammer. This is it: either the beginning of a new relationship or the beginning of the end. She waves good-bye to a young man who's followed her out. It's not the same man I met the last time I was here—it's someone new. He watches her walk toward the car, his eyes on her ass. Taylor distracts me by making a move to climb out of the car, but I stop him. This is my call. When I'm out of the car holding the door open for her, the new guy is locking up the store and no longer ogling Miss Steele.

Her lips curve into a shy smile as she approaches, her hair in a jaunty ponytail swinging in the evening breeze.

"Good evening, Miss Steele."

"Mr. Grey," she says. She's dressed in black jeans . . . *Jeans again.* She greets Taylor as she climbs into the backseat of the car.

Once I'm beside her I clasp her hand, while Taylor pulls out onto the empty road and heads to the Portland helipad. "How was work?" I ask, enjoying the feel of her hand in mine.

"Very long," she says, her voice husky.

"Yes, it's been a long day for me, too."

It's been hell waiting for the last couple of hours!

"What did you do?" she asks.

"I went hiking with Elliot." Her hand is warm and soft. She glances down at our joined fingers and I brush her knuckles with my thumb over and over. Her breath catches and her eyes meet mine. In them I see her longing and desire . . . and her sense of anticipation. I just hope she accepts my proposition.

Mercifully, the drive to the helipad is short. When we're out of the car I take her hand again. She looks a little perplexed.

Ah. She's wondering where the helicopter might be.

"Ready?" I ask. She nods, and I lead her into the building toward the elevator. She gives me a quick knowing look.

She's remembering the kiss from this morning, but then . . . so am I.

"It's only three floors," I mutter.

As we stand inside I make a mental note to fuck her in an elevator one day. That's if she agrees to my deal.

On the roof *Charlie Tango*, newly arrived from Boeing Field, is prepped and ready to fly, though there's no sign of Stephan, who's brought her down here. But Joe, who runs the helipad in Portland, is in the small office. He salutes when I see him. He's older than my grandpa, and what he doesn't know about flying is not worth knowing; he flew Sikorskys in Korea for casualty evacuation, and boy, does he have some hair-raising stories.

"Here's your flight plan, Mr. Grey," Joe says, his gravelly voice betraying his age. "All external checks are done. She's ready and waiting, sir. You're good to go."

"Thank you, Joe."

A quick glance at Ana tells me that she's excited . . . and so am I. This is a first.

"Let's go." With her hand in mine once more, I lead Ana over the helipad to *Charlie Tango*. The safest Eurocopter in her class and a delight to fly. She's my pride and joy. I hold the door open for Ana; she scrambles inside and I climb in behind her.

"Over there," I order, pointing to the front passenger seat. "Sit. Don't touch anything." I'm amazed when she does as she's told.

Once in her seat, she examines the array of instruments with a mixture of awe and enthusiasm. Crouching down beside her, I strap her into the seat harness, trying not to imagine her naked as I do it. I take a little longer than is necessary because this might be my last chance to be this close to her, my last chance to inhale her sweet, evocative scent. Once she knows about my predilections she may flee . . . on the other hand, she may embrace the lifestyle. The possibilities this conjures in my mind are almost overwhelming. She's watching me intently, she's so close . . . so lovely. I tighten the last strap. She's not going anywhere. Not for an hour at least.

Suppressing my excitement, I whisper, "You're secure. No escaping." She inhales sharply. "Breathe, Anastasia," I add, and caress her cheek. Holding her chin, I lean down and kiss her quickly. "I like this harness," I mutter. I want to tell her I have others, in leather, in which I'd like to see her trussed and suspended from the ceiling. But I behave, sit down, and buckle up.

"Put your cans on." I point to the headset in front of Ana. "I'm just going through all the preflight checks." All instruments look good. I press the throttle to 1500 rpm, transponder to stand-by, and position beacon on. Everything is set and ready to go.

"Do you know what you're doing?" she asks with wonder. I inform her that I've been a fully qualified pilot for four years. Her smile is infectious.

"You're safe with me," I reassure her, and add, "Well, while we're flying." I give her a wink, she beams, and I'm dazzled.

"Are you ready?" I ask—and I can't quite believe how excited I am to have her here beside me.

She nods.

I talk to the tower—they're awake—and increase the throttle to 2000 rpm. Once they've given us clearance I do my final checks. Oil temperature is at 104. *Good.* I increase the manifold pressure to 14, the engine to 2500 rpm, and pull back on the throttle. And like the elegant bird she is . . . *Charlie Tango* rises into the air.

Anastasia gasps as the ground disappears below us, but she

holds her tongue, entranced by the waning lights of Portland. Soon we are shrouded in darkness; the only light emanates from the instruments before us. Ana's face is illuminated by the red and green glow as she stares into the night.

"Eerie, isn't it?"

Though I don't find it so. To me this is a comfort. Nothing can harm me here.

I'm safe and hidden in the dark.

"How do you know you're going the right way?" Ana asks.

"Here." I point to the panel. I don't want to bore her talking about instrument flight rules, but the fact is it's *all* the equipment in front of me that guides us to our destination: the attitude indicator, the altimeter, the VSI, and of course the GPS. I tell her about *Charlie Tango*, and how she's equipped for night flight.

Ana looks at me, amazed.

"There's a helipad on top of the building I live in. That's where we're heading."

I look back at the panel, checking all the data. This is what I love: the control, my safety and well-being reliant on my mastery of the technology in front of me. "When you fly at night, you fly blind. You have to trust the instrumentation," I tell her.

"How long will the flight be?" she asks, a little breathless.

"Less than an hour—the wind is in our favor." I glance at her again. "You okay, Anastasia?"

"Yes," she says, her voice oddly abrupt.

Is she nervous? Or maybe she's regretting her decision to be here with me. The thought is unsettling. She hasn't given me a chance. I'm distracted by air-traffic control for a moment. Then, as we clear cloud cover, I see Seattle in the distance, a beacon blazing in the dark.

"Look, over there." I direct Ana's attention to the bright lights.

"Do you always impress women this way? 'Come and fly in my helicopter'?"

"I've never brought a girl up here, Anastasia. It's another first for me. Are you impressed?"

"I'm awed, Christian," she whispers.

"Awed?" My smile is spontaneous. And I remember Grace, my mother, stroking my hair as I read out loud from *The Once and Future King*.

"*Christian, that was wonderful. I'm awed, darling boy.*"

I was seven and had only recently started speaking.

"You're just so . . . competent," Ana continues.

"Why, thank you, Miss Steele." My face warms with pleasure at her unexpected praise. I hope she doesn't notice.

"You obviously enjoy this," she says a little later.

"What?"

"Flying."

"It requires control and concentration." Two qualities I most enjoy. "How could I not love it? Though my favorite is soaring."

"Soaring?"

"Yes. Gliding, to the layperson. Gliders and helicopters—I fly them both."

Perhaps I should take her soaring?

Getting ahead of yourself, Grey.

And since when do you take anyone soaring?

Since when do I bring anyone in *Charlie Tango*?

ATC refocuses me on the flight path, halting my rogue thoughts as we approach the outskirts of Seattle. We're close. And I'm closer to knowing whether this is a pipe dream or not. Ana is staring out the window, entranced.

I can't keep my eyes off her.

Please say yes.

"Looks good, doesn't it?" I ask, so that she'll turn and I can see her face. She does, with a huge cock-tightening grin. "We'll be there in a few minutes," I add.

Suddenly the atmosphere in the cabin shifts and I have a more heightened awareness of her. Breathing deeply, I inhale her scent and sense the anticipation. Ana's. Mine.

As we descend I take *Charlie Tango* through the downtown area toward Escala, my home, and my heart rate increases. Ana starts fidgeting. She's nervous, too. I hope she doesn't flee.

As the helipad comes into view, I take another deep breath.
This is it.

We land smoothly and I power down, watching the rotor blades
slow and come to a stop. All I can hear is the hiss of white noise
over our headphones as we sit in silence. I remove my cans, then
remove Ana's, too. "We're here," I say quietly. Her face is pale in
the glow of the landing lights, her eyes luminous.

Sweet Lord, she's beautiful.

I unbuckle my harness and reach over to undo hers.

She peers up at me. Trusting. Young. Sweet. Her delicious
scent is almost my undoing.

Can I do this with her?

She's an adult.

She can make her own decisions.

And I want her to look at me this way once she knows me . . .
knows what I'm capable of. "You don't have to do anything you don't
want to do. You know that, don't you?" She needs to understand
this. I want her submission, but more than that I want her consent.

"I'd never do anything I didn't want to do, Christian." She
sounds sincere and I want to believe her. With those pacifying
words ringing in my head, I climb out of my seat and open the
door, then jump down onto the helipad. I take her hand as she
exits the aircraft. The wind whips her hair around her face, and
she looks anxious. I don't know if it's because she's here with me,
alone, or if it's because we're thirty stories high. I know it's a giddy
feeling being up here.

"Come." Wrapping my arm around her to shield her from the
wind, I guide her to the elevator.

We are both quiet as we make the short journey to the penthouse. She's wearing a pale green shirt beneath her black jacket. It
suits her. I make a mental note to include blues and greens in the
clothes I'll provide if she agrees to my terms. She should be better
dressed. Her eyes meet mine in the elevator's mirrors as the doors
open to my apartment.

She follows me through the foyer, across the corridor, and into the living room. "Can I take your jacket?" I ask. Ana shakes her head and clutches the lapels to emphasize that she wants to keep her jacket on.

Okay.

"Would you like a drink?" I try a different approach and decide that I need a drink to steady my nerves.

Why am I so nervous?

Because I want her . . .

"I'm going to have a glass of white wine. Would you like to join me?"

"Yes, please," she says.

In the kitchen I slip off my jacket and open the wine fridge. A sauvignon blanc would be a good icebreaker. Pulling out a service-able Pouilly-Fumé, I watch Ana peer through the balcony doors at the view. When she turns and walks back toward the kitchen I ask if she'd be happy with the wine I've selected.

"I know nothing about wine, Christian. I'm sure it will be fine." She sounds subdued.

Shit. This isn't going well. Is she overwhelmed? Is that it?

I pour two glasses and walk to where she stands in the middle of my living room, looking every bit the sacrificial lamb. Gone is the disarming woman. She looks lost.

Like me . . .

"Here." I hand her the glass, and she immediately takes a sip, closing her eyes in obvious appreciation of the wine. When she lowers the glass her lips are moist.

Good choice, Grey.

"You're very quiet, and you're not even blushing. In fact, I think this is the palest I've ever seen you, Anastasia. Are you hungry?"

She shakes her head and takes another sip. Maybe she's in need of some liquid courage, too. "It's a very big place you have here," she says, her voice timid.

"Big?"

"Big."

"It's big." There's no arguing with that; it is more than ten thousand square feet.

"Do you play?" She looks at the piano.

"Yes."

"Well?"

"Yes."

"Of course you do. Is there anything you can't do well?"

"Yes . . . a few things."

Cook.

Tell jokes.

Make free and easy conversation with a woman I'm attracted to.

Be touched . . .

"Do you want to sit?" I gesture toward the sofa. A brisk nod tells me that she does. Taking her hand, I lead her there, and she sits down, giving me an impish look.

"What's so amusing?" I ask, as I take a seat beside her.

"Why did you give me *Tess of the d'Urbervilles*, specifically?"

Oh. Where is this going? "Well, you said you liked Thomas Hardy."

"Is that the only reason?"

I don't want to tell her that she has *my* first edition, and that it was a better choice than *Jude the Obscure*. "It seemed appropriate. I could hold you to some impossibly high ideal like Angel Clare or debase you completely like Alec d'Urberville." My answer is truthful enough and has a certain irony to it. What I'm about to propose I suspect will be very far from her expectations.

"If there are only two choices, I'll take the debasement," she whispers.

Damn. Isn't that what you want, Grey?

"Anastasia, stop biting your lip, please. It's very distracting. You don't know what you're saying."

"That's why I'm here," she says, her teeth leaving little indentations on a bottom lip moist with wine.

And there she is: disarming once more, surprising me at every turn. My cock concurs.

We are cutting to the chase on this deal, but before we explore the details, I need her to sign the NDA. I excuse myself and head into my study. The contract and NDA are ready on the printer.

Leaving the contract on my desk—I don't know if we'll ever get to it—I staple the NDA together and take it back to Ana.

"This is a nondisclosure agreement." I place it on the coffee table in front of her. She looks confused and surprised. "My lawyer insists on it," I add. "If you're going for option two, debasement, you'll need to sign this."

"And if I don't want to sign anything?"

"Then it's Angel Clare high ideals, well, for most of the book anyway." And I won't be able to touch you. I'll send you home with Stephan, and I will try my very best to forget you. My anxiety mushrooms; this deal could all go to shit.

"What does this agreement mean?"

"It means you cannot disclose anything about us. Anything, to anyone."

She searches my face and I don't know if she's confused or displeased.

This could go either way.

"Okay. I'll sign," she says.

Well, that was easy. I hand her my Mont Blanc and she places the pen at the signature line.

"Aren't you even going to read it?" I ask, suddenly annoyed.

"No."

"Anastasia, you should always read anything you sign." *How could she be so foolish?* Have her parents taught her nothing?

"Christian, what you fail to understand is that I wouldn't talk about us to anyone anyway. Even Kate. So it's immaterial whether I sign an agreement or not. If it means so much to you, or your lawyer, whom *you* obviously talk to, then fine. I'll sign."

She has an answer for everything. It's refreshing. "Fair point well made, Miss Steele," I note dryly.

With a quick, disapproving glance, she signs.

And before I can begin my pitch, she asks, "Does this mean you're going to make love to me tonight, Christian?"

What?

Me?

Make love?

Oh, Grey, let's disabuse her of this straightaway. "No, Anastasia, it doesn't. First, I don't make love. I fuck, hard."

She gasps. That's made her think.

"Second, there's a lot more paperwork to do. And third, you don't yet know what you're in for. You could still run from here screaming! Come, I want to show you my playroom."

She's nonplussed, the little *v* forming between her brows. "You want to play on your Xbox?"

I laugh out loud.

Oh, baby.

"No, Anastasia, no Xbox, no PlayStation. Come." Standing, I offer her my hand, which she takes willingly. I lead her to the hallway and upstairs, where I stop outside the door to my playroom, my heart hammering in my chest.

This is it. Pay or play. Have I ever been this nervous? Realizing my desires depend on the turn of this key, I unlock the door, and in that moment I need to reassure her. "You can leave anytime. The helicopter is on standby to take you whenever you want to go; you can stay the night and go home in the morning. It's fine, whatever you decide."

"Just open the damn door, Christian," she says with a mulish expression and her arms crossed.

This is the crossroads. I don't want her to run. But I've never felt this exposed. Even in Elena's hands . . . and I know it's because she knows nothing about the lifestyle.

I open the door and follow her into my playroom.

My safe place.

The only place where I'm truly myself.

Ana stands in the middle of the room, studying all the paraphernalia that is so much a part of my life: the floggers, the canes, the bed, the bench . . . She's silent, drinking it in, and all I hear is the deafening pounding of my heart as the blood rushes past my eardrums.

Now you know.

This is me.

She turns and gives me a piercing stare as I wait for her to say something, but she prolongs my agony and walks farther into the room, forcing me to follow her.

Her fingers trail over a suede flogger, one of my favorites. I tell her what it's called, but she doesn't respond. She walks over to the bed, her hands exploring, her fingers running over one of the carved pillars.

"Say something," I ask. Her silence is unbearable. I need to know if she's going to run.

"Do you do this to people or do they do it to you?"

Finally!

"People?" I want to snort. "I do this to women who want me to." She's willing to have a dialogue. There's hope.

She frowns. "If you have willing volunteers, why am I here?"

"Because I want to do this with you, very much." Visions of her tied up in various positions around the room overwhelm my imagination; on the cross, on the bed, over the bench . . .

"Oh," she says, and wanders to the bench. My eyes are drawn to her inquisitive fingers stroking the leather. Her touch is curious, slow, and sensual—is she even aware?

"You're a sadist?" she says, startling me.

Fuck. She sees me.

"I'm a Dominant," I say quickly, hoping to move the conversation on.

"What does that mean?" she inquires, shocked, I think.

"It means I want you to willingly surrender yourself to me, in all things."

"Why would I do that?"

"To please me," I whisper. *This is what I need from you.* "In very simple terms, I want you to want to please me."

"How do I do that?" she breathes.

"I have rules, and I want you to comply with them. They are for your benefit and for my pleasure. If you follow these rules to my satisfaction, I shall reward you. If you don't, I shall punish you, and you will learn."

And I can't wait to train you. In every way.

She stares at the canes behind the bench. "And where does all this fit in?" She waves at her surroundings.

"It's all part of the incentive package. Both reward and punishment."

"So you'll get your kicks by exerting your will over me."

Spot on, Miss Steele.

"It's about gaining your trust and your respect, so you'll let me exert my will over you." *I need your permission, baby.* "I will gain a great deal of pleasure, joy even, in your submission. The more you submit, the greater my joy—it's a very simple equation."

"Okay, and what do I get out of this?"

"Me." I shrug. *That's it, baby. Just me. All of me. And you'll find pleasure, too . . .*

Her eyes widen fractionally as she stares at me, saying nothing. It's exasperating. "You're not giving anything away, Anastasia. Let's go back downstairs where I can concentrate better. It's very distracting having you in here."

I hold out my hand to her and for the first time she looks from my hand to my face, undecided.

Shit.

I've frightened her. "I'm not going to hurt you, Anastasia."

Tentatively she puts her hand in mine. I'm elated. She hasn't run.

Relieved, I decide to show her the submissive's bedroom.

"If you do this, let me show you." I lead her down the corridor. "This will be your room. You can decorate it how you like, have whatever you like in here."

"My room? You're expecting me to move in?" she squeaks in disbelief.

Okay. Maybe I should have left this until later.

"Not full-time," I reassure her. "Just, say, Friday evening through Sunday. We have to talk about all that. Negotiate. If you want to do this."

"I'll sleep here?"

"Yes."

"Not with you."

"No. I told you, I don't sleep with anyone, except you when you're stupefied with drink."

"Where do you sleep?"

"My room is downstairs. Come, you must be hungry."

"Weirdly, I seem to have lost my appetite," she declares, with her familiar stubborn expression.

"You must eat, Anastasia."

Her eating habits will be one of the first issues I'll work on if she agrees to be mine . . . that, and her fidgeting.

Stop getting ahead of yourself, Grey!

"I'm fully aware that this is a dark path I'm leading you down, Anastasia, which is why I really want you to think about this."

She follows me downstairs into the living room once more. "You must have some questions. You've signed your NDA; you can ask me anything you want and I'll answer."

If this is going to work, she's going to have to communicate. In the kitchen I open the fridge and find a large plate of cheese and some grapes. Gail wasn't expecting me to have company, and this is not enough . . . I wonder if I should order some takeout. Or perhaps take her out?

Like a date.

Another date.

I don't want to raise expectations like that.

I don't do dates.

Only with her . . .

The thought is irritating. There's a fresh baguette in the bread basket. Bread and cheese will have to do. Besides, she says she's not hungry.

"Sit." I point to one of the barstools and Ana sits down and gives me a level gaze.

"You mentioned paperwork," she says.

"Yes."

"What paperwork?"

"Well, apart from the NDA, a contract saying what we will and

won't do. I need to know your limits, and you need to know mine.
This is consensual, Anastasia."

"And if I don't want to do this?"

Shit.

"That's fine," I lie.

"But we won't have any sort of relationship?"

"No."

"Why?"

"This is the only sort of relationship I'm interested in."

"Why?"

"It's the way I am."

"How did you become this way?"

"Why is anyone the way they are? That's kind of hard to answer.
Why do some people like cheese and other people hate it? Do you
like cheese? Mrs. Jones—my housekeeper—has left this for a late
supper." I place the plate in front of her.

"What are your rules that I have to follow?"

"I have them written down. We'll go through them once we've
eaten."

"I'm really not hungry," she whispers.

"You will eat."

The look she gives me is defiant.

"Would you like another glass of wine?" I ask, as a peace offering.

"Yes, please."

I pour wine into her glass and sit down beside her. "Help yourself to food, Anastasia."

She takes a few grapes.

That's it? That's all you're eating?

"Have you been like this for a while?" she asks.

"Yes."

"Is it easy to find women who want to do this?"

Oh, if you only knew. "You'd be amazed." My tone is wry.

"Then why me? I really don't understand." She's utterly
bemused.

Baby, you're beautiful. Why wouldn't I want to do this with you?

"Anastasia, I've told you. There's something about you. I can't leave you alone. I'm like a moth to a flame. I want you very badly, especially now, when you're biting your lip again."

"I think you have that cliché the wrong way around," she says softly, and it's a disturbing confession.

"Eat!" I order, to change the subject.

"No. I haven't signed anything yet, so I think I'll hang on to my free will for a bit longer, if that's okay with you."

Oh . . . her smart mouth.

"As you wish, Miss Steele." And I hide my smirk.

"How many women?" she asks, and she pops a grape into that mouth.

"Fifteen." I have to look away.

"For long periods of time?"

"Some of them, yes."

"Have you ever hurt anyone?"

"Yes."

"Badly?"

"No." Dawn was fine, if a little shaken by the experience. And if I'm honest, so was I.

"Will you hurt me?"

"What do you mean?"

"Physically, will you hurt me?"

Only what you can take.

"I will punish you when you require it, and it will be painful."

For example, when you get drunk and put yourself at risk.

"Have you ever been beaten?" she asks.

"Yes."

Many, many times. Elena was devilishly handy with a cane. It's the only touch I could tolerate.

Her eyes widen and she puts the uneaten grapes on her plate and takes another sip of wine. Her lack of appetite is irritating and is affecting mine. Perhaps I should just bite the bullet and show her the rules.

"Let's discuss this in my study. I want to show you something."

She follows me and sits in the leather chair in front of my desk as I lean against it, arms folded.

This is what she wants to know. It's a blessing that she's curious—she hasn't run yet. From the contract laid out on my desk I take one of the pages and hand it to her. "These are the rules. They may be subject to change. They form part of the contract, which you can also have. Read these rules and let's discuss."

Her eyes scan the page. "Hard limits?" she asks.

"Yes. What you won't do, what I won't do, we need to specify in our agreement."

"I'm not sure about accepting money for clothes. It feels wrong."

"I want to lavish money on you. Let me buy you some clothes. I may need you to accompany me to functions."

Grey, what are you saying? This would be a first. "And I want you dressed well. I'm sure your salary, when you do get a job, won't cover the kind of clothes I'd like you to wear."

"I don't have to wear them when I'm not with you?"

"No."

"Okay. I don't want to exercise four times a week."

"Anastasia, I need you supple, strong, and with stamina. Trust me, you need to exercise."

"But surely not four times a week. How about three?"

"I want you to do four."

"I thought this was a negotiation?"

Again, she's disarming, calling me out on my shit. "Okay, Miss Steele, another point well made. How about an hour on three days and one day half an hour?"

"Three days, three hours. I get the impression you're going to keep me exercised when I'm here."

Oh, I hope so.

"Yes, I am. Okay, agreed. Are you sure you don't want to intern at my company? You're a good negotiator."

"No, I don't think that's a good idea."

Of course she's right. And it's my number-one rule: never fuck the staff.

"So, limits. These are mine." I hand her the list.

This is it, shit-or-bust time. I know my limits by heart, and mentally tick off the list as I watch her read through. Her face grows paler and paler as she nears the end.

Fuck, I hope this isn't frightening her off.

I want her. I want her submission . . . badly. She swallows, glancing nervously up at me. *How can I persuade her to give this a try?* I should reassure her, show her that I'm capable of caring.

"Is there anything you'd like to add?"

Deep down I hope she won't add anything. I want carte blanche with her. She stares at me, still at a loss for words. It's irritating. I'm not used to waiting for answers. "Is there anything you won't do?" I prompt.

"I don't know."

Not the response I was expecting.

"What do you mean you don't know?"

She shifts in her seat, looking uncomfortable, her teeth toying with her bottom lip. *Again.* "I've never done anything like this."

Hell, of course she hasn't.

Patience, Grey. For fuck's sake. You've thrown a great deal of information at her. I continue my gentle approach. It's novel.

"Well, when you've had sex, was there anything that you didn't like doing?" And I'm reminded of the photographer fumbling all over her yesterday.

She flushes and my interest is piqued. What has she done that she didn't like? Is she adventurous in bed? She seems so—innocent. Normally I don't find that attractive.

"You can tell me, Anastasia. We have to be honest with each other or this isn't going to work." I really have to encourage her to loosen up—she won't even talk about sex. She's squirming again and staring at her fingers.

Come on, Ana.

"Tell me," I order. *Sweet Lord, she's frustrating.*

"Well, I've not had sex before, so I don't know," she whispers.

The earth stops spinning.

I don't fucking believe it.

How?

Why?

Fuck!

"Never?" I'm incredulous.

She shakes her head, eyes wide.

"You're a virgin?" I don't believe it.

She nods, embarrassed. I close my eyes. I can't look at her.

How the hell did I get this so wrong?

Anger lances through me. *What can I do with a virgin?* I glare at her as fury surges through my body.

"Why the fuck didn't you tell me?" I growl, and start pacing my study. *What do I want with a virgin?* She shrugs apologetically, at a loss for words.

"I don't understand why you didn't tell me." The exasperation is clear in my voice.

"The subject never came up," she says. "I'm not in the habit of revealing my sexual status to everyone I meet. I mean, we hardly know each other."

As ever, it's a fair point. I can't believe I've given her the bus tour of my playroom—thank heavens for the NDA.

"Well, you know a lot more about me now," I snarl. "I knew you were inexperienced, but a *virgin*! Hell, Ana, I just showed you . . ."

Not only the playroom: my rules, hard limits. She knows nothing. How could I do this? "May God forgive me," I mutter under my breath. I'm at a loss.

A startling thought occurs to me—our one kiss in the elevator, where I could have fucked her there and then—was that her first kiss?

"Have you ever been kissed, apart from by me?" Please say yes.

"Of course I have." She looks offended. Yeah, she's been kissed, but not often. And for some reason the thought is . . . pleasing.

"And a nice young man hasn't swept you off your feet? I just don't understand. You're twenty-one, nearly twenty-two. You're beautiful." Why hasn't some guy taken her to bed?

Shit, maybe she's religious. No, Welch would have uncovered that. She gazes down at her fingers, and I think she's smiling. She thinks this is funny? I could kick myself. "And you're seriously discussing what I want to do, when you have no experience."

Words fail me. How can this be?

"How have you avoided sex? Tell me, please." Because I don't get it. She's in college—and from what I remember of college all the kids were fucking like rabbits.

All of them. Except me.

The thought is a dark one, but I push it aside for the moment.

Ana shrugs, her small shoulders lifting slightly. "No one's really, you know . . ." She trails off.

No one has what? Seen how attractive you are? No one's lived up to your expectations—and I do?

Me?

She really knows nothing. How could she ever be a submissive if she has no idea about sex? This is not going to fly . . . and all the groundwork I've done has been for nothing. I can't close this deal.

"Why are you so angry with me?" she whispers.

Of course she would think that. *Make this right, Grey.*

"I'm not angry with you, I'm angry at myself. I just assumed—"
Why the hell would I be angry with you? What a mess this is. I run my hands through my hair, trying to rein in my temper.

"Do you want to go?" I ask, concerned.

"No, unless you want me to go," she says softly, her voice tinged with regret.

"Of course not. I like having you here." The statement surprises me as I say it. I *do* like having her here. Being with her. She's so . . . different. And I want to fuck her, and spank her, and watch her alabaster skin pink beneath my hands. That's out of the question now—isn't it? Perhaps not the fucking . . . perhaps I could. The thought is a revelation. I could take her to bed. Break her in. It would be a novel experience for both of us. Would she want to? She asked me earlier if I was going to make love to her. I could try, without tying her up.

But she might touch me.

Fuck. I glance down at my watch and note the time. It's late. When I look back at her the sight of her toying with her bottom lip arouses me.

I still want her, in spite of her innocence. Could I take her to bed? Would she want to, knowing what she knows about me now? *Hell*, I have no idea. Do I just ask her? But she's turning me on, biting her lip again. I point it out and she apologizes.

"Don't apologize. It's just that I want to bite it, too, hard."

Her breath hitches.

Oh. Maybe she's interested. *Yes. Let's do this.* My decision is made.

"Come," I offer, holding out my hand.

"What?"

"We're going to rectify the situation right now."

"What do you mean? What situation?"

"Your situation. Ana, I'm going to make love to you, now."

"Oh."

"That's if you want to. I mean, I don't want to push my luck."

"I thought you didn't make love. I thought you fucked hard," she says, her voice husky and so damned seductive, her eyes wide, pupils dilating. She's flushed with desire—she wants this, too.

And a wholly unexpected thrill unfurls inside me. "I can make an exception, or maybe combine the two, we'll see. I really want to make love to you. Please, come to bed with me. I want our arrangement to work, but you really need to have some idea what you're getting yourself into. We can start your training tonight—with the basics. This doesn't mean I've come over all hearts and flowers—it's a means to an end, but one that I want, and hopefully you do, too." The words rush out in a torrent.

Grey! Get ahold of yourself.

Her cheeks pink.

Come on, Ana, yes or no. I'm dying here.

"But I haven't done all the things you require from your list of rules." Her voice is timid. Is she afraid? I hope not. I don't want her to be afraid.

"Forget about the rules. Forget about all those details for tonight. I want you. I've wanted you since you fell into my office, and I know you want me. You wouldn't be sitting here calmly discussing punishment and hard limits if you didn't. Please, Ana, spend the night with me."

I offer her my hand again, and this time she takes it, and I pull her into my arms, holding her flush against my body. She gasps with surprise and I feel her against me. The darkness is quiet, perhaps subdued by my libido. I want her. She's so alluring. This girl confounds me, every step of the way. I've revealed my dark secret, yet she's still here; she hasn't run.

My fingers tug at her hair, pulling her face up to mine, and I gaze into captivating eyes.

"You are one brave young woman," I breathe. "I am in awe of you." I lean down and gently kiss her, then tease her lower lip with my teeth. "I want to bite this lip." I tug harder and she whimpers. My cock hardens in response.

"Please, Ana, let me make love to you," I whisper against her mouth.

"Yes," she responds—and my body lights up like the Fourth of July.

Get a grip, Grey. We have no arrangement in place, no limits set, she's not mine to do with as I please—and yet I'm excited. Aroused. It's an unfamiliar but exhilarating feeling, desire for this woman coursing through me. I'm at the tipping edge of a giant roller coaster.

Vanilla sex?

Can I do this?

Without another word I lead her out of my study, through the living room, and down the corridor to my bedroom. She follows, her hand tightly holding mine.

Shit. Contraception. I'm sure she's not on the pill . . . Fortunately, I have condoms for backup. At least I don't have to worry about every dick she's slept with. I release her by the bed, walk over to my chest of drawers, and remove my watch, shoes, and socks.

"I assume you're not on the pill."

She shakes her head.

"I didn't think so." From the drawer I take out a packet of condoms, letting her know I'm prepared. She studies me, her eyes impossibly large in her beautiful face, and I have a moment's hesitation. This is supposed to be a big deal for her, isn't it? I remember my first time with Elena, how embarrassing it was . . . but what a heaven-sent relief. Deep down I know I should send her home. But the simple truth is, I don't want her to go, and I want her. What's more, I can see my desire reflected in her expression, in her darkening eyes.

"Do you want the blinds drawn?" I ask.

"I don't mind," she says. "I thought you didn't let anyone sleep in your bed."

"Who says we're going to sleep?"

"Oh." Her lips form a perfect small o. My cock hardens further. Yes, I'd like to fuck that mouth, that o. I stalk toward her like she's my prey. *Oh, baby, I want to bury myself in you.* Her breathing is shallow and quick. Her cheeks are rosy . . . she's wary, but excited. She's at my mercy, and knowing that makes me feel powerful. She has no idea what I'm going to do to her. "Let's get this jacket off, shall we?" Reaching up, I gently push her jacket off her shoulders, fold it, and place it on my chair.

"Do you have any idea how much I want you, Ana Steele?"

Her lips part as she inhales, and I reach up to touch her cheek. Her skin is petal-soft beneath my fingertips as they glide down to her chin. She's entranced—lost—under my spell. She's already mine. It's intoxicating.

"Do you have any idea what I'm going to do to you?" I murmur, and hold her chin between my thumb and forefinger. Leaning down, I kiss her firmly, molding her lips to mine. Returning my kiss, she's soft and sweet and willing, and I have an overwhelming need to see her, all of her. I make quick work of her buttons, slowly peeling off her blouse and letting it fall to the floor. I stand back to look at her. She's wearing the pale blue bra that Taylor bought.

She's stunning.

"Oh, Ana. You have the most beautiful skin, pale and flawless. I want to kiss every single inch of it." There's not a mark on her.

The thought is unsettling. I want to see her marked . . . pink . . . with tiny, thin welts from a crop maybe.

She colors a delicious rose—embarrassed, no doubt. If I do nothing else, I will teach her not to be shy of her body. Reaching up, I pull her hair tie, freeing her hair. It tumbles lush and chestnut around her face, down to her breasts.

"Mmm, I like brunettes." She's lovely, exceptional, a jewel.

Holding her head, I run my fingers through her hair and pull her to me, kissing her. She moans against me and parts her lips, allowing me access to her warm, wet mouth. The sweet appreciative noise echoes through me—to the end of my cock. Her tongue shyly meets mine, tentatively probing my mouth, and for some reason, her fumbling inexperience is . . . hot.

She tastes luscious. Wine, grapes, and innocence—a potent, heady mix of flavors. I fold my arms tightly around her, relieved that she grips only my upper arms. With one hand in her hair, holding her in place, I run my other hand down her spine to her ass and push her against me, against my erection. She moans again. I continue to kiss her, coaxing her unschooled tongue to explore my mouth as I explore hers. My body tenses when she moves her hands up my arms—and for a moment I worry where she'll touch me next. She caresses my cheek, then strokes my hair. It's a little unnerving. But when she twists her fingers in my hair, pulling gently . . .

Damn, that feels good.

I groan in response but can't let her continue. Before she can touch me again, I push her against the bed and drop to my knees. I want her out of these jeans—I want to strip her, arouse her some more, and . . . keep her hands off me. Grasping her hips, I run my tongue just north of the waistband up to her navel. She tenses and inhales sharply. Fuck, does she smell and taste good, an orchard in springtime, and I want my fill. Her hands fist in my hair once more; this I don't mind—in fact, I like it. I nip her hipbone and her grip tightens in my hair. Her eyes are closed, her mouth slack, and she's panting. As I reach up and undo the button on her jeans, she opens her eyes and we study each other. Slowly I ease down the zipper and move my hands around her ass. Slipping my hands inside the waistband, my palms against the soft cheeks of her behind, I slide her jeans off.

I can't stop myself. I want to shock her . . . test her boundaries right now. Not taking my eyes off hers, I deliberately lick my lips, then lean forward and run my nose up the center of her panties, inhaling her arousal. Closing my eyes, I savor her.

Lord, she's enticing.

"You smell so good." My voice is husky with want and my jeans are becoming extremely uncomfortable. I need to take them off. Gently, I push her onto the bed and, grasping her right foot, I make quick work of removing her sneaker and sock. To tease her I run my thumbnail along her instep and she writhes gratifyingly on the bed, her mouth open, watching me, fascinated. Leaning down, I trace my tongue along her instep, and my teeth graze the little line that my thumbnail has left in its wake. She lies back on the bed, eyes closed, groaning. She's so responsive, it's delightful.

"Oh, Ana, what I could do to you," I whisper, as images of her writhing beneath me in my playroom flash through my mind: shackled to my four-poster bed, bent over the table—suspended from the cross. I could tease and torture her until she begged for release . . . the images make my jeans even tighter.

Hell.

Quickly I remove her other shoe and sock, and pull off her jeans. She's almost naked on my bed, her hair framing her face perfectly, her long, pale legs stretched out in invitation before me. I have to make allowances for her inexperience. But she's panting. Wanting. Her eyes fixed on me.

I've never fucked anyone in my bed before. *Another first with Miss Steele.*

"You're very beautiful, Anastasia Steele. I can't wait to be inside you." My voice is gentle; I want to tease her some more, find out what she does know. "Show me how you pleasure yourself," I ask, gazing intently down at her.

She frowns.

"Don't be coy, Ana, show me." Part of me wants to spank the shyness out of her.

She shakes her head. "I don't know what you mean."

Is she playing games?

"How do you make yourself come? I want to see."

She remains mute. Clearly I've shocked her again. "I don't," she mutters finally, her voice breathless. I gaze at her in disbelief. Even I used to masturbate, before Elena sunk her claws into me.

She's probably never had an orgasm—though I find this hard to believe. *Whoa.* I'm responsible for her first fuck and her first orgasm. I'd better make this good.

"Well, we'll have to see what we can do about that." *I'm going to make you come like a freight train, baby.*

Hell—she's probably never seen a naked man, either. Not taking my eyes off hers, I undo the top button on my jeans and ease them onto the floor, though I can't risk taking my shirt off, because she might touch me.

But if she did . . . it wouldn't be so bad . . . would it? Being touched?

I banish the thought before the darkness surfaces, and grasping her ankles, I spread her legs. Her eyes widen and her hands clench my sheets.

Yes. Keep your hands there, baby.

I crawl slowly up the bed, between her legs. She squirms beneath me.

"Keep still," I tell her, and lean down to kiss the delicate skin of her inner thigh. I trail kisses up her thighs, over her panties, across her belly, nipping and sucking as I go. She writhes beneath me.

"We're going to have to work on keeping you still, baby."

If you'll let me.

I'll teach her to just absorb the pleasure and not move, intensifying every touch, every kiss, every nip. The thought alone is enough to make me want to bury myself in her, but before I do, I want to know how responsive she is. So far she hasn't held back.

She's allowing me free rein over her body. She's not hesitant at all. She wants this . . . she really wants this. I dip my tongue into her navel and continue my leisurely journey north, savoring her. I shift, lying beside her, one leg still between hers. My hand ghosts up her body, over her hip, up her waist, on to her breast. Gently I cup her breast, trying to gauge her reaction. She doesn't stiffen. She doesn't stop me . . . she trusts me. Can I extend her trust to letting me have complete dominion over her body . . . over her? The thought is exhilarating.

"You fit my hand perfectly, Anastasia." Dipping my finger into her bra cup, I jerk it down, freeing her breast. The nipple is small, rose pink, and it's already hard. I drag the cup down so that the fabric and underwire rest under her breast, forcing it upward. I repeat the process with the other cup and watch, fascinated, as her nipples grow under my steady gaze. *Whoa* . . . I haven't even touched her yet.

"Very nice," I whisper in awed appreciation, and blow gently on the nearest nipple, watching in delight as it hardens and extends. Anastasia closes her eyes and arches her back.

Keep still, baby, just absorb the pleasure, it will feel so much more intense.

Blowing on one nipple, I roll the other gently between my thumb and forefinger. She grasps the sheets tightly as I lean down and suck—hard. Her body bows again and she cries out.

"Let's see if we can make you come like this," I whisper, and I don't stop. She starts to whimper.

Oh, yes, baby . . . feel this. Her nipples extend farther and she starts grinding her hips, around and around. *Keep still, baby. I will teach you to keep still.*

"Oh, please," she begs. Her legs stiffen. It's working. She's close. I continue my lascivious assault. Concentrating on each nipple, watching her response, sensing her pleasure, is driving me to distraction. Lord, I want her.

"Let go, baby," I murmur, and pull her nipple with my teeth. She cries out as she climaxes.

Yes! I move quickly to kiss her, capturing her cries in my mouth. She's breathless and panting, lost in her pleasure . . . *Mine.* I own her first orgasm, and I'm ridiculously pleased by the thought.

"You're very responsive. You're going to have to learn to control that, and it's going to be so much fun teaching you how." I can't wait . . . but right now, I want her. All of her. I kiss her once more and let my hand travel down her body, down to her vulva. I hold her, feeling her heat. Slipping my index finger through the lace of her panties, I slowly circle around her . . . *fuck, she's soaking.*

"You're so deliciously wet. God, I want you." I thrust my finger inside her, and she cries out. She's hot and tight and wet, and I want her. I thrust into her again, taking her cries into my mouth. I press my palm to her clitoris . . . pushing down . . . pushing around. She cries out and writhes beneath me. *Fuck,* I want her—now. She's ready. Sitting up, I drag her panties off, then my boxers, and reach for a condom. I kneel up between her legs, pushing them farther apart. Anastasia watches me with—what? Trepidation? She's probably never seen an erect penis before.

"Don't worry. You expand, too," I mutter. Stretching out over her, I put my hands on either side of her head, taking my weight on my elbows. God, I want her . . . but I check she's still keen. "You really want to do this?" I ask.

For fuck's sake, please don't say no.

"Please," she begs.

"Pull your knees up," I instruct her. This'll be easier. Have I ever been so aroused? I can barely contain myself. I don't get it . . . it must be her.

Why?

Grey, focus!

I position myself so I can take her at my whim. Her eyes are open wide, imploring me. She really wants this . . . as much as I do. Should I be gentle and prolong the agony, or do I go for it?

I go for it. I need to possess her.

"I'm going to fuck you now, Miss Steele. Hard."

One thrust and I'm inside her.

F. U. C. K.

She's so fucking tight. She cries out.

Shit! I've hurt her. I want to move, to lose myself in her, and it takes all my restraint to stop. "You're so tight. You okay?" I ask, my voice a hoarse, anxious whisper, and she nods, eyes wider. She's like heaven on earth, so tight around me. And even though her hands are on my forearms, I don't care. The darkness is slumbering, perhaps because I've wanted her for so long. I've never felt this desire, this . . . *hunger* before. It's a new feeling, new and shiny. I want so much from her: her trust, her obedience, her submission. I want her to be mine, but right now . . . I'm hers.

"I'm going to move, baby." My voice is strained as I ease back slowly. It's such an extraordinary, exquisite feeling: her body cradling my cock. I push into her again and claim her, knowing no one has before. She whimpers.

I stop. "More?"

"Yes," she breathes, after a moment.

This time I thrust into her more deeply.

"Again?" I plead, as sweat beads on my body.

"Yes."

Her trust in me—it's suddenly overwhelming, and I start to move, really move. I want her to come. I will not stop until she comes. I want to own this woman, body and soul. I want her clenching around me.

Fuck—she starts meeting every thrust, matching my rhythm. *See how well we fit together, Ana?* I grasp her head, holding her in place while I claim her body and kiss her hard, claiming her mouth. She stiffens beneath me . . . *fuck yes.* Her orgasm is close.

"Come for me, Ana," I demand, and she cries out as she's consumed, tipping her head back, her mouth open, her eyes closed . . . and just the sight of her ecstasy is enough. I explode in her, losing all sense and reason, as I call out her name and come violently inside her.

When I open my eyes I'm panting, trying to catch my breath, and we're forehead to forehead and she's staring up at me.

Fuck. I'm undone.

I plant a swift kiss on her forehead and pull out of her and lie down beside her.

She winces as I withdraw, but other than that she looks okay.

"Did I hurt you?" I ask, and I tuck her hair behind her ear, because I don't want to stop touching her.

Ana beams with incredulity. "You are asking me if you hurt me?"

And for a moment I don't know why she's grinning.

Oh. My playroom.

"The irony is not lost on me," I mutter. Even now she confounds me. "Seriously, are you okay?"

She stretches out beside me, testing her body and teasing me with an amused but sated expression.

"You haven't answered me," I growl. I need to know if she found that enjoyable. All the evidence points to a "yes"—but I need to hear it from her. While I'm waiting for her reply I remove the condom. Lord, I hate these things. I discard it discreetly on the floor.

She peers up at me. "I'd like to do that again," she says with a shy giggle.

What?

Again?

Already?

"Would you now, Miss Steele?" I kiss the corner of her mouth. "Demanding little thing, aren't you? Turn on your front."

That way I know you won't touch me.

She gives me a brief sweet smile, then rolls onto her stomach. My cock stirs with approval. I unhook her bra and run my hand down her back to her pert behind. "You really have the most beautiful skin," I say, as I brush her hair off her face and push her legs apart. Gently I plant soft kisses on her shoulder.

"Why are you wearing your shirt?" she asks.

She's so damn inquisitive. While she's on her front I know she can't touch me, so I lean back and pull my shirt over my head and let it drop to the floor. Fully naked, I lie on top of her. Her skin is warm, and melts against mine.

Hmm . . . I could get used to this.

"So you want me to fuck you again?" I whisper in her ear, kissing her. She squirms deliciously against me.

Oh, this will never do. Keep still, baby.

I skim my hand down her body to the back of her knee, then hitch it up high, parting her legs wide so that she's spread beneath me. Her breath catches and I hope it's with anticipation. She stills beneath me.

Finally!

I palm her ass as I ease my weight onto her. "I'm going to take you from behind, Anastasia." With my other hand I grab her hair at the nape and tug gently, holding her in place. She cannot move. Her hands are helpless and splayed against the sheets, out of harm's way.

"You are mine," I whisper. "Only mine. Don't forget it."

With my free hand I move from her ass to her clitoris and begin circling slowly.

Her muscles flex beneath me as she tries to move, but my weight keeps her in place. I run my teeth along her jawline. Her sweet fragrance lingers over the scent of our coupling. "You smell divine," I whisper, as I nuzzle behind her ear.

She starts to circle her hips against my moving hand.

"Keep still," I warn.

Or I might stop . . .

Slowly I insert my thumb inside her and circle it around and around, taking particular care to stroke the front wall of her vagina.

She groans and tenses beneath me, trying to move again.

"You like this?" I tease, and my teeth trace her outer ear. I don't stop my fingers from tormenting her clitoris, but I begin to ease my thumb in and out of her. She stiffens, but can't move.

She groans loudly, her eyes scrunched up tight.

"You're so wet, so quickly. So responsive. Oh, Anastasia, I like that. I like that a lot."

Right. Let's see how far you'll go.

I withdraw my thumb from her vagina. "Open your mouth," I order, and when she does I thrust my thumb between her lips. "See how you taste. Suck me, baby."

She sucks my thumb . . . hard.

Fuck.

And for a moment I imagine it's my cock in her mouth.

"I want to fuck your mouth, Anastasia, and I will soon." I'm breathless.

She closes her teeth around me, biting me hard.

Ow! Fuck.

I grip her hair tightly and she loosens her mouth. "Naughty, sweet girl." My mind flits through a number of punishments worthy of such a bold move that, if she were my submissive, I could inflict on her. My cock expands to bursting at the thought. I release her and sit back on my knees.

"Stay still, don't move." I grab another condom from my bedside table, rip open the foil, and roll the latex over my erection.

Watching her, I see that she's still, except for the rise and fall of her back as she pants in anticipation.

She's gorgeous.

Leaning over her again, I grasp her hair and hold her so she can't move her head.

"We're going to go real slow this time, Anastasia."

She gasps, and gently I ease into her until I can go no farther.

Fuck. She feels good.

As I ease out I circle my hips and slowly slip into her again. She whimpers and her limbs tense beneath me as she tries to move.

Oh no, baby.

I want you still.

I want you to feel this.

Take all the pleasure.

"You feel so good," I tell her, and repeat the move again, circling my hips as I go. Slowly. In. Out. In. Out. Her insides start to tremble.

"Oh no, baby, not yet."

No way am I letting you come.

Not when I'm enjoying this so much.

"Oh, please," she cries.

"I want you sore, baby." I pull out and sink into her again.

"Every time you move tomorrow, I want you to be reminded that I've been here. Only me. You are mine."

"Please, Christian," she begs.

"What do you want, Anastasia? Tell me." I continue the slow torture. "Tell me."

"You, please." She's desperate.

She wants me.

Good girl.

I increase the pace and her insides begin to quiver, responding immediately.

Between each thrust I utter one word. "You. Are. So. Sweet. I. Want. You. So. Much. You. Are. Mine." Her limbs tremble with the strain of keeping still. She's on the edge. "Come for me, baby," I growl.

And on command she shudders around me as her orgasm rips through her and she screams my name into the mattress.

My name on her lips is my undoing, and I climax and collapse on top of her.

"Fuck. Ana," I whisper, drained yet elated. I pull out of her almost immediately and roll onto my back. She curls up at my side, and as I pull off the condom, she closes her eyes and falls asleep.

I wake with a start and a pervading sense of guilt, as if I've committed a terrible sin.

Is it because I've fucked Anastasia Steele? Virgin?

She's snuggled up fast asleep beside me. I check the radio alarm: it's after three in the morning. Ana sleeps the sound sleep of an innocent. Well, not so innocent now. My body stirs as I watch her.

I could wake her.

Fuck her again.

There are definitely some advantages to having her in my bed.

Grey. Stop this nonsense.

Fucking her was merely a means to an end and a pleasant diversion.

Yes. Very pleasant.

More like incredible.

It was just sex, for fuck's sake.

I close my eyes in what will probably be a futile attempt to sleep. But the room is too full of Ana: her scent, the sound of her soft breathing, and the memory of my first vanilla fuck. Visions of her head thrown back in passion, of her crying out a barely recognizable version of my name, and her unbridled enthusiasm for sexual congress overwhelm me.

Miss Steele is a carnal creature.

She will be a joy to train.

My cock twitches in agreement.

Shit.

I can't sleep, though tonight it's not nightmares that keep me awake, it's little Miss Steele. Climbing out of bed, I collect the used condoms from the floor, knot them, and dispose of them in the wastepaper basket. From the chest of drawers I pull out a pair of PJ pants and drag them on. With a lingering look at the enticing woman in my bed, I venture into the kitchen. I'm thirsty.

Once I've had a glass of water, I do what I always do when I can't sleep—I check my e-mail in my study. Taylor has returned and is asking if he can stand *Charlie Tango* down. Stephan must be asleep upstairs. I e-mail him back with a "yes," though at this time of night it's a given.

Back in the living room I sit down at my piano. This is my solace, where I can lose myself for hours. I've been able to play well since I was nine, but it wasn't until I had my own piano, in my own place, that it really became a passion. When I want to forget everything, this is what I do. And right now I don't want to think about having propositioned a virgin, fucked her, or revealed my lifestyle to someone with no experience. With my hands on the keys, I begin to play and lose myself in the solitude of Bach.

A movement distracts me from the music, and when I look up Ana's standing by the piano. Wrapped in a comforter, her hair wild and curling down her back, eyes luminous, she looks stunning.

"Sorry," she says. "I didn't mean to disturb you."

Why is she apologizing? "Surely, I should be saying that to you." I play the last notes and stand. "You should be in bed," I chide.

"That was a beautiful piece. Bach?"

"Transcription by Bach, but it's originally an oboe concerto by Alessandro Marcello."

"It was exquisite, but very sad, such a melancholy melody."

Melancholy? It wouldn't be the first time someone has used that word to describe me.

"May I speak freely? Sir." Leila is kneeling beside me while I work.

"You may."

"Sir, you are most melancholy today."

"Am I?"

"Yes, Sir. Is there something that you would like me to do . . . ?"

I shake off the memory. Ana should be in bed. I tell her so again.

"I woke and you weren't there."

"I find it difficult to sleep, and I'm not used to sleeping with anyone." I've told her this—and why am I justifying myself? I wrap my arm around her naked shoulders, enjoying the feel of her skin, and guide her back to the bedroom.

"How long have you been playing? You play beautifully."

"Since I was six." I'm abrupt.

"Oh," she says. I think she's taken the hint—I don't want to talk about my childhood.

"How are you feeling?" I ask as I switch on the bedside light.

"I'm good."

There's blood on my sheets. Her blood. Evidence of her now-absent virginity. Her eyes dart from the stains to me and she looks away, embarrassed.

"Well, that's going to give Mrs. Jones something to think about." She looks mortified.

It's just your body, sweetheart. I grasp her chin and tip her head back so I can see her expression. I'm about to give her a short lecture on how not to be ashamed of her body, when she reaches out to touch my chest.

Fuck.

I step out of her reach as the darkness surfaces.

No. Don't touch me.

"Get into bed," I order, rather more sharply than I'd intended, but I hope she doesn't detect my fear. Her eyes widen with confusion and maybe hurt.

Damn.

"I'll come and lie down with you," I add, as a peace offering, and from the chest of drawers I pull out a T-shirt and quickly slip it on, for protection.

She's still standing, staring at me. "Bed," I command more forcefully. She scrambles into my bed and lies down and I climb in behind her, folding her in my arms. I bury my face in her hair and inhale her sweet scent: autumn and apple trees. Facing away, she can't touch me, and while I lie there I resolve to spoon with her until she's asleep. Then I'll get up and do some work.

"Sleep, sweet Anastasia." I kiss her hair and close my eyes. Her scent fills my nostrils, reminding me of a happy time and leaving me replete . . . content, even . . .

Mommy is happy today. She is singing.
Singing about what love has to do with it.
And cooking. And singing.
My tummy gurgles. She is cooking bacon and waffles.
They smell good. My tummy likes bacon and waffles.
They smell so good.

Opening my eyes, light is flooding through the windows and there's a mouthwatering aroma coming from the kitchen. Bacon. Momentarily I'm confused. Is Gail back from her sister's?

Then I remember.

Ana.

A look at the clock tells me it's late. I bounce out of bed and follow my nose to the kitchen.

There's Ana. She's wearing my shirt, her hair in braids, dancing around to some music. Only I can't hear it. She's wearing earbuds. Unobserved, I take a seat at the kitchen counter and watch the show. She's whisking eggs, making breakfast, her braids bouncing as she jiggles from foot to foot, and I realize she's not wearing underwear.

Good girl.

She has to be one of the most uncoordinated females I've ever seen. It's amusing, charming, and strangely arousing at the same time; I think of all the ways I can improve her coordination. When she turns and spots me, she freezes.

"Good morning, Miss Steele. You're very . . . energetic this morning." She looks even younger in her braids.

"I-I slept well," she stammers.

"I can't imagine why," I quip, admitting to myself that I did, too. It's after nine. When did I last sleep past 6:30?

Yesterday.

After I'd slept with her.

"Are you hungry?" she asks.

"Very." And I'm not sure if it's for breakfast or for her.

"Pancakes, bacon, and eggs?" she says.

"Sounds great."

"I don't know where you keep your placemats," she says, seeming at a loss, and I think she's embarrassed, because I caught her dancing. Taking pity on her, I offer to set places for breakfast and add, "Would you like me to put some music on so you can continue your . . . er . . . dancing?"

Her cheeks pink and she looks down at the floor.

Damn. I've upset her. "Please, don't stop on my account. It's very entertaining."

With a pout she turns her back on me and continues to whisk the eggs with gusto. I wonder if she has any idea how disrespectful this is to someone like me . . . but of course she doesn't, and for some unfathomable reason it makes me smile. Sidling up to her, I gently tug one of her braids. "I love these. They won't protect you."

Not from me. Not now that I've had you.

"How would you like your eggs?" Her tone is unexpectedly haughty. And I want to laugh out loud, but I resist.

"Thoroughly whisked and beaten," I reply, trying and failing to sound deadpan. She attempts to hide her amusement, too, and continues her task.

Her smile is bewitching.

Hastily, I set up the placemats, wondering when I last did this for someone else.

Never.

Normally over the weekend my submissive would take care of all domestic tasks.

Not today, Grey, because she's not your submissive . . . yet.

I pour us both orange juice and put the coffee on. She doesn't drink coffee, only tea. "Would you like some tea?"

"Yes, please. If you have some."

In the cupboard I find the Twinings teabags I'd asked Gail to buy.

Well, well, who would have thought I'd ever get to use them?

She frowns when she sees them. "Bit of a foregone conclusion, wasn't I?"

"Are you? I'm not sure we've concluded anything yet, Miss Steele," I answer with a stern look.

And don't talk about yourself like that.

I add her self-deprecation to the list of behaviors that will need modifying.

She avoids my gaze, busy with serving up breakfast. Two plates are placed on the placemats, then she fetches the maple syrup out of the fridge.

When she looks up at me I'm waiting for her to sit down. "Miss Steele." I indicate where she should sit.

"Mr. Grey," she replies, with contrived formality, and winces as she sits.

"Just how sore are you?" I'm surprised by an uneasy sense of guilt. I want to fuck her again, preferably after breakfast, but if she's too sore that will be out of the question. Perhaps I could use her mouth this time.

The color in her face rises. "Well, to be truthful, I have nothing to compare this to," she says tartly. "Did you wish to offer your commiserations?" Her sarcastic tone takes me by surprise. If she were mine, it would earn her a spanking at least, maybe over the kitchen counter.

"No. I wondered if we should continue your basic training."

"Oh." She startles.

Yes, Ana, we can have sex during the day, too. And I'd like to fill that smart mouth of yours.

I take a bite of my breakfast and close my eyes in appreciation. It tastes mighty fine. When I swallow she's still staring at me. "Eat, Anastasia," I order. "This is delicious, incidentally."

She can cook, and well.

Ana takes one bite of her food, then pushes her breakfast

around on her plate. I ask her to stop biting her lip. "It's very dis-tracting, and I happen to know you're not wearing anything under my shirt."

She fidgets with her teabag and the teapot, ignoring my irri-tation. "What sort of basic training did you have in mind?" she asks.

She's ever-curious—let's see how far she'll go.

"Well, as you're sore, I thought we could stick to oral skills."

She splutters into her teacup.

Hell. I don't want to choke the girl. Gently, I pat her on the back and hand her a glass of orange juice. "That's if you want to stay." I shouldn't push my luck.

"I'd like to stay for today. If that's okay. I have to work tomor-row."

"What time do you have to be at work tomorrow?"

"Nine."

"I'll get you to work by nine tomorrow."

What? I want her to stay?

It's a surprise to me.

Yes, I want her to stay.

"I'll need to go home tonight—I need clean clothes."

"We can get you some here."

She flips her hair and gnaws nervously at her lip . . . again.

"What is it?" I ask.

"I need to be home this evening."

Boy, she's stubborn. I don't want her to go, but at this stage, with no agreement, I can't insist that she stay. "Okay, this evening. Now eat your breakfast."

She examines her food.

"Eat, Anastasia. You didn't eat last night."

"I'm really not hungry," she says.

Well, this is frustrating. "I would really like you to finish your breakfast." My voice is low.

"What is it with you and food?" she snaps.

Oh, baby, you really don't want to know. "I told you, I have issues with wasted food. Eat." I glare at her. *Don't push me on this, Ana.* She gives me a mulish look and starts to eat.

As I watch her place a forkful of eggs in her mouth, I relax. She's quite challenging in her own way. And it's unique. I've never dealt with this. *Yes.* That's it. She's a novelty. That's the fascination . . . isn't it?

When she finishes her food I take her plate.

"You cooked, I'll clear."

"That's very democratic," she says, arching an eyebrow.

"Yes. Not my usual style. After I've done this, we'll take a bath."

And I can test her oral skills. I take a swift breath to control my instant arousal at the thought.

Hell.

Her phone rings and she wanders to the end of the room, deep in conversation. I pause by the sink and watch her. As she stands against the glass wall, the morning light silhouettes her body in my white shirt. My mouth dries. She's slim, with long legs, perfect breasts, and a perfect ass.

Still on her call, she turns toward me and I pretend my attention is elsewhere. For some reason I don't want her to catch me ogling.

Who is it on the phone?

I hear Kavanagh's name mentioned and I tense. *What is she saying?* Our eyes lock.

What are you saying, Ana?

She turns away and a moment later hangs up, then walks back toward me, her hips swaying in a soft, seductive rhythm beneath my shirt. *Should I tell her what I can see?*

"The NDA, does it cover everything?" she asks, halting me in my tracks as I shut the pantry cupboard.

"Why?" *Where's she going with this? What has she said to Kavanagh?*

She takes a deep breath. "Well, I have a few questions, you know, about sex. And I'd like to ask Kate."

"You can ask me."

"Christian, with all due respect—" She stops.

She's embarrassed?

"It's just about mechanics. I won't mention the Red Room of Pain," she says in a rush.

"Red Room of Pain?"

What the hell?

"It's mostly about pleasure, Anastasia. Believe me. Besides, your roommate is making the beast with two backs with my brother. I'd really rather you didn't."

I don't want Elliot to know anything about my sex life. He'd never let me live it down.

"Does your family know about your . . . um, predilection?"

"No. It's none of their business."

She's burning to ask something.

"What do you want to know?" I ask, standing in front of her, scrutinizing her face.

What is it, Ana?

"Nothing specific at the moment," she whispers.

"Well, we can start with: how was last night for you?" My breathing shallows as I wait for her answer. Our whole deal could hang on her response.

"Good," she says, and gives me a soft, sexy smile.

It's what I want to hear.

"For me, too. I've never had vanilla sex before. There's a lot to be said for it. But then, maybe it's because it's with you."

Her surprise and pleasure at my words are obvious. I brush her plump lower lip with my thumb. I'm itching to touch her . . . again. "Come, let's have a bath." I kiss her and take her into my bathroom.

"Stay there," I order, turning the faucet, then adding scented oil to the steaming water. The tub fills quickly as she watches me. Normally, I would expect any woman I was about to bathe with to have her eyes cast down in modesty.

But not Ana.

She doesn't drop her gaze, and her eyes glow with anticipation and curiosity. But she has her arms wrapped around herself; she's shy.

It's arousing.

And to think she's never bathed with a man.

I can claim another first.

When the bath is full I peel off my T-shirt and hold out my hand. "Miss Steele."

She accepts my invitation and steps into the bath.

"Turn around, face me," I instruct. "I know that lip is delicious, I can attest to that, but will you stop biting it? Your chewing it makes me want to fuck you, and you're sore, okay?"

She inhales sharply, releasing her lip.

"Yeah. Get the picture?"

Still standing, she gives me an emphatic nod.

"Good." She's still wearing my shirt and I take the iPod from the breast pocket and place it by the sink. "Water and iPods—not a clever combination." I grab the hem and pull it off her. Immediately she hangs her head when I step back to admire her.

"Hey." My voice is gentle and encourages her to peek up at me. "Anastasia, you're a very beautiful woman, the whole package. Don't hang your head like you're ashamed. You have nothing to be ashamed of, and it's a real joy to stand here and look at you." Holding her chin, I tip her head back.

Don't hide from me, baby.

"You can sit down now."

She sits down with indecent haste and winces as her sore body hits the water.

Okay . . .

She screws her eyes shut as she lies back, but when she opens them, she looks more relaxed. "Why don't you join me?" she asks with a coy smile.

"I think I will. Move forward." Stripping, I climb in behind her, pull her to my chest, and place my legs around hers, my feet over her ankles, and then I pull her legs apart.

She wriggles against me, but I ignore her motion and bury my nose in her hair. "You smell so good, Anastasia," I whisper.

She settles and I grab the body wash from the shelf beside us. Squeezing some into my hand, I work the soap into a lather and start massaging her neck and shoulders. She moans as her head lolls to one side under my tender ministration.

"You like that?" I ask.

"Hmm," she hums in contentment.

I wash her arms and her underarms, then reach my first goal: her breasts.

Lord, the feel of her.

She has perfect breasts. I knead and tease them. She groans and flexes her hips and her breathing accelerates. She's aroused. My body responds in kind, growing beneath her.

My hands skim over her torso and her belly toward my second goal. Before I reach her pubic hair I stop and grab a washcloth. Squirting some soap onto the cloth, I begin the slow process of washing between her legs. Gentle, slow but sure, rubbing, washing, cleaning, stimulating. She starts to pant and her hips move in synchronization with my hand. Her head resting against my shoulder, her eyes closed, her mouth open in a silent moan as she surrenders to my relentless fingers.

"Feel it, baby." I run my teeth along her earlobe. "Feel it for me."

"Oh, please," she whines, and she tries to straighten her legs, but I have them pinioned under mine.

Enough.

Now that she's all worked up into a lather I'm ready to proceed.

"I think you're clean enough now," I announce, and take my hands off of her.

"Why are you stopping?" she protests, her eyes fluttering open, revealing frustration and disappointment.

"Because I have other plans for you, Anastasia."

She's panting and, if I'm not mistaken, pouting.

Good.

"Turn around. I need washing, too."

She does, her face rosy, her eyes bright, pupils large.

Lifting my hips, I grab my cock. "I want you to become well acquainted, on first-name terms, if you will, with my favorite and most cherished part of my body. I'm very attached to this."

Her mouth drops open as she looks from my penis to my face . . . and back again. I can't help my wicked grin. Her face is a picture of maidenly outrage.

But as she stares, her expression changes. First thoughtful, then assessing, and when her eyes meet mine, the challenge in them is clear.

Oh, bring it on, Miss Steele.

Her smile is one of delight as she reaches for the body wash. Taking her sweet time, she drizzles some of the soap into her palm and, without taking her eyes off mine, rubs her hands together. Her lips part and she bites her bottom lip, running her tongue across the little indentations left by her teeth.

Ana Steele, seductress!

My cock responds in appreciation, hardening further. Reaching forward, she grabs me, her hand fisting around me. My breath hisses out through clenched teeth and I close my eyes, savoring the moment.

Here, I don't mind being touched.

No, I don't mind at all . . . Placing my hand over hers, I show her what to do. "Like this." My voice is hoarse as I guide her. She tightens her hold around me and her hand moves up and down beneath mine.

Oh yes.

"That's right, baby."

I release her and let her continue, closing my eyes and surrendering to the rhythm she's set.

Oh, God.

What is it about her inexperience that is so arousing? Is it that I'm enjoying all her firsts?

Suddenly she draws me into her mouth, sucking hard, her tongue torturing me.

Fuck.

"Whoa . . . Ana."

She sucks harder; her eyes are alight with feminine cunning. This is her revenge, her tit for tat. She looks stunning.

"Christ," I growl, and close my eyes so I don't come immediately.

She continues her sweet torture, and as her confidence grows I flex my hips, pushing myself farther into her mouth.

How far can I go, baby?

Watching her is stimulating, so stimulating. I grab her hair and start to work her mouth as she supports herself with her hands on my thighs.

"Oh. Baby. That. Feels. Good."

She confines her teeth behind her lips and pulls me into her mouth once more.

"Ah!" I groan, and wonder how deep she'll allow me. Her mouth torments me, her shielded teeth squeezing hard. And I want more. "Jesus. How far can you go?"

Her eyes meet mine and she frowns. Then, with a look of determination, she slides down on me until I hit the back of her throat.

Fuck.

"Anastasia, I'm going to come in your mouth," I warn her, breathless. "If you don't want me to, stop now." I thrust into her again and again, watching my cock disappear and reappear from her mouth. It's beyond erotic. I'm so close. Suddenly she bares her teeth, gently squeezing me, and I'm undone, ejaculating into the back of her throat, crying out my pleasure.

Fuck.

My breathing is labored. She's completely disarmed me . . . again!

When I open my eyes she's glowing with pride.

As she should be. That was one hell of a blow job.

"Don't you have a gag reflex?" I marvel at her as I catch my breath. "Christ, Ana . . . that was . . . good, really good. Unexpected, though. You know, you never cease to amaze me." Praise for a job well done.

Wait, that was so good, perhaps she has some experience after all. "Have you done that before?" I ask, and I'm not sure I want to know.

"No," she says with obvious pride.

"Good." I hope my relief is not too obvious. "Yet another first,

Miss Steele. Well, you get an A in oral skills. Come, let's go to bed,
I owe you an orgasm."

I climb out of the bath a little dazed and wrap a towel around
my waist. Grabbing another, I hold it up and help her out of the
bath, swathing her in it so she's trapped. I hold her against me, kissing her, really kissing her. Exploring her mouth with my tongue.

I taste my ejaculate in her mouth. Grasping her head, I deepen
the kiss.

I want her.

All of her.

Her body and soul.

I want her to be mine.

Staring down into bemused eyes, I implore her. "Say yes."

"To what?" she whispers.

"Yes to our arrangement. To being mine. Please, Ana." And it's
the closest I've come to begging in a long time. I kiss her again,
pouring my fervor into my kiss. When I take her hand, she looks
dazed.

Dazzle her further, Grey.

In my bedroom, I release her. "Trust me?" I ask.

She nods.

"Good girl."

Good. Beautiful. Girl.

I head into my closet to select one of my ties. When I'm back
in front of her, I take her towel and drop it on the floor. "Hold your
hands together in front of you."

She licks her lips in what I think is a moment of uncertainty,
then holds out her hands. Swiftly I bind her wrists together with
the tie. I test the knot. *Yes.* It's secure.

Time for more training, Miss Steele.

Her lips part as she inhales . . . she's excited.

Gently I tug both her braids. "You look so young with these."
But they're not going to stop me. I drop my towel. "Oh, Anastasia, what shall I do to you?" I grasp her upper arms and push her
gently back on the bed, keeping hold of her so that she doesn't

fall. Once she's prostrate, I lie down beside her, grab her fists, and raise them above her head. "Keep your hands up here, don't move them. Understand?"

She swallows.

"Answer me."

"I won't move my hands," she says, her voice husky.

"Good girl." I can't help my smile. She lies beside me, wrists bound, helpless. *Mine.*

Not quite to do with as I wish—yet—but getting there.

Leaning down, I kiss her lightly and let her know that I'll kiss her all over.

She sighs as my lips move from the base of her ear down to the hollow at the bottom of her neck. I'm rewarded with her appreciative moan. Abruptly she lowers her arms so that they circle my neck.

No. No. No. This will not do, Miss Steele.

Glaring down at her, I place them firmly back above her head. "Don't move your hands, or we just have to start all over again."

"I want to touch you," she whispers.

"I know." *But you can't.* "Keep your hands above your head."

Her lips are parted and her chest is heaving with each rapid breath. She's turned on.

Good.

Cupping her chin, I start kissing my way down her body. My hand travels over her breasts, my lips in hot pursuit. With one hand on her belly, holding her in place, I pay homage to each of her nipples, sucking and nipping gently, delighting in their hardening response.

She mewls and her hips start to move.

"Keep still," I warn against her skin. I plant kisses across her belly, where my tongue explores the taste and depth of her navel.

"Ah," she moans and squirms.

I will have to teach her to keep still . . .

My teeth graze her skin. "Hmm. You are so sweet, Miss Steele." I gently nip between her navel and pubic hair, then sit up between her legs. Grabbing both her ankles, I spread her legs wide. Like this, naked, vulnerable, she is a glorious sight to behold. Holding her left foot, I bend her knee and raise her toes to my lips, watching her face as I do. I kiss each toe, then bite the soft pad on each.

Her eyes are wide and her mouth is open, moving alternately from a small to a capital O. When I bite the pad on her little toe a little harder, her pelvis flexes and she whimpers. I run my tongue over her instep to her ankle. She scrunches her eyes closed, her head twisting from side to side, as I continue to torment her.

"Oh, please," she begs when I suck and bite her little toe.

"All good things, Miss Steele," I tease.

When I get to her knee, I don't stop but continue, licking, sucking, and biting up the inside of her thigh, spreading her legs wide as I do.

She trembles, in shock, anticipating my tongue at the apex of her thighs.

Oh no . . . not yet, Miss Steele.

I return my attentions to her left leg, kissing and nipping from her knee up the inside of her thigh.

She tenses when I finally lie between her legs. But she keeps her arms raised.

Good girl.

Gently, I run my nose up and down her vulva.

She writhes beneath me.

I stop. She has to learn to keep still.

She raises her head to look at me.

"Do you know how intoxicating you smell, Miss Steele?" Holding her stare with my own, I push my nose into her pubic hair and breathe deeply. Her head flops back in the bed and she groans.

I blow gently up and down over her pubic hair. "I like this," I mutter. It's been a long time since I've seen pubic hair up close and personal like this. I tug it gently. "Perhaps we'll keep this."

Though it's no good for wax play . . .

"Oh, please," she pleads.

"Hmm, I like it when you beg me, Anastasia."

She moans.

"Tit for tat is not my usual style, Miss Steele," I whisper

against her flesh. "But you've pleased me today, and you should be rewarded." And I hold down her thighs, opening her up to my tongue, and slowly start circling her clitoris.

She cries out, her body rising off the bed.

But I don't stop. My tongue is ruthless. Her legs stiffen, her toes pointed.

Ah, she's close, and slowly I slip my middle finger inside her.

She's wet.

Wet and waiting.

"Oh, baby. I love that you're so wet for me." I start to move my finger clockwise, stretching her. My tongue continues to torment her clitoris, over and over. She stiffens beneath me and finally cries out as her orgasm crashes through her.

Yes!

I kneel up and grab a condom. Once it's on, slowly I ease myself into her.

Fuck, she feels good.

"How's this?" I check.

"Fine. Good." Her voice is hoarse.

Oh . . . I start to move, reveling in the feel of her around me, beneath me. Again and again, faster and faster, losing myself in this woman. I want her to come again.

I want her sated.

I want her happy.

Finally, she stiffens once more and whimpers.

"Come for me, baby," I utter through clenched teeth, and she detonates around me.

"Thank fuck," I cry, and let go, finding my own sweet release. Briefly I collapse on her, glorying in her softness. She moves her hands so they are around my neck, but because she's tied she can't touch me.

Taking a deep breath, I rest my weight on my arms and stare down at her in wonder.

"See how good we are together? If you give yourself to me, it will be so much better. Trust me, Anastasia, I can take you places you don't even know exist." Our foreheads touch and I close my eyes.

Please say yes.

We hear voices outside the door.

What the hell?

It's Taylor and Grace.

"Shit! It's my mother."

Ana cringes as I pull out of her.

Leaping out of bed, I throw the condom in the wastepaper basket.

What the hell is my mother doing here?

Taylor has diverted her, thank heaven. Well, she's about to get a surprise.

Ana is still prostrate on the bed. "Come on, we need to get dressed—that's if you want to meet my mother." I smile at Ana as I pull on my jeans. She looks adorable.

"Christian—I can't move," she protests, but she's grinning, too.

Leaning down, I undo the tie and kiss her forehead.

My mother is going to be thrilled.

"Another first," I whisper, unable to shift my grin.

"I have no clean clothes in here."

I slip on a white T-shirt, and when I turn around she's sitting up, hugging her knees. "Perhaps I should stay here."

"Oh no you don't," I warn. "You can wear something of mine."

I like her wearing my clothes.

Her face falls.

"Anastasia, you could be wearing a sack and you'd look lovely. Please don't worry. I'd like you to meet my mother. Get dressed. I'll just go and calm her down. I'll expect you in that room in five minutes, otherwise I'll come and drag you out of here myself in whatever you're wearing. My T-shirts are in this drawer. My shirts are in the closet. Help yourself."

Her eyes widen.

Yes. I'm serious, baby.

Cautioning her with a pointed look, I open the door and exit to find my mother.

Grace is standing in the corridor opposite the foyer door, and Taylor is talking to her. Her face lights up when she sees me. "Darling, I had no idea you might have company," she exclaims, and she looks a little embarrassed.

"Hello, Mother." I kiss her proffered cheek. "I'll deal with her from here," I say to Taylor.

"Yes, Mr. Grey." He nods, looking exasperated, and heads back into his office.

"Thank you, Taylor," Grace calls after him, then turns her full attention to me. "Deal with me?" she says in rebuke. "I was shopping downtown and I thought I might pop in for coffee." She stops. "If I'd known you weren't alone . . ." She shrugs in an awkward, girlish way.

She has often stopped by for coffee and there *was* a woman here . . . she just never knew.

"She'll join us in a moment," I admit, putting her out of her misery. "Do you want to sit down?" I wave in the direction of the sofa.

"She?"

"Yes, Mother. She." My tone is dry as I try not to laugh. And for once she's silent as she wanders through the living room.

"I see you've had breakfast," she observes, eyeing the unwashed pans.

"Would you like some coffee?"

"No. Thank you, darling." She sits down. "I'll meet your . . . friend and then I'll go. I don't want to interrupt you. I had a feeling that you'd be slaving away in your study. You work too hard, darling. I thought I might drag you away." She looks almost apologetic when I join her on the sofa.

"Don't worry." I'm thoroughly amused by her reaction. "Why aren't you at church this morning?"

"Carrick had to work, so we thought we'd go to evening Mass. I suppose it's too much to hope that you'll come with us."

I raise an eyebrow in cynical contempt. "Mother, you know that's not for me."

God and I turned our backs on each other a long time ago.

She sighs, but then Ana appears—dressed in her own clothes,

standing shyly in the doorway. The tension between mother and son is averted, and I stand in relief. "Here she is."

Grace turns and gets to her feet.

"Mother, this is Anastasia Steele. Anastasia, this is Grace Trevelyan-Grey."

They shake hands.

"What a pleasure to meet you," Grace says with a little too much enthusiasm for my liking.

"Dr. Trevelyan-Grey," Ana says politely.

"Call me Grace," she says, all at once amiable and informal.

What? Already?

Grace continues, "I'm usually Dr. Trevelyan, and Mrs. Grey is my mother-in-law." She winks at Ana and sits down. I motion to Ana and pat the cushion beside me, and she comes and takes a seat.

"So how did you two meet?" Grace asks.

"Anastasia interviewed me for the student paper at WSU because I'm conferring the degrees there this week."

"So you're graduating this week?" Grace beams at Ana.

"Yes."

Ana's cell phone starts ringing and she excuses herself to answer it.

"And I'll be giving the commencement address," I say to Grace, but my attention is on Ana.

Who is it?

"Look, José, now's not a good time," I hear her say.

That fucking photographer. What does he want?

"I left a message for Elliot, then found out he was in Portland. I haven't seen him since last week," Grace is saying.

Ana hangs up.

Grace continues as Ana approaches us again, ". . . and Elliot called to say you were around—I haven't seen you for two weeks, darling."

"Did he now?" I remark.

What does the photographer want?

"I thought we might have lunch together, but I can see you

have other plans, and I don't want to interrupt your day." Grace stands, and for once I'm grateful that she's intuitive and can read a situation. She offers me her cheek again. I kiss her good-bye.

"I have to drive Anastasia back to Portland."

"Of course, darling." Grace turns her bright—and if I'm not mistaken, grateful—smile on Ana.

It's irritating.

"Anastasia, it's been such a pleasure." Grace beams and takes Ana's hand. "I do hope we meet again."

"Mrs. Grey?" Taylor appears on the threshold of the room.

"Thank you, Taylor," Grace responds, and he escorts her from the room and through the double doors to the foyer.

Well, that was interesting.

My mother's always thought I was gay. But as she's always respected my boundaries, she's never asked me.

Well, now she knows.

Ana is worrying her bottom lip, radiating anxiety . . . as she should be.

"So the photographer called?" I sound gruff.

"Yes."

"What did he want?"

"Just to apologize, you know—for Friday."

"I see." Maybe he wants another shot at her. The thought is displeasing.

Taylor clears his throat. "Mr. Grey, there's an issue with the Darfur shipment."

Shit. This is what I get for not checking my e-mail this morning. I've been too preoccupied with Ana.

"*Charlie Tango* back at Boeing Field?" I ask Taylor.

"Yes, sir."

Taylor acknowledges Ana with a nod. "Miss Steele."

She gives him a broad smile and he leaves.

"Does he live here? Taylor?" Ana asks.

"Yes."

Heading into the kitchen, I pick up my phone and quickly

check my e-mail. There's a flagged message from Ros and a couple of texts. I call her immediately.

"Ros, what's the issue?"

"Christian, hi. The report back from Darfur is not good. They can't guarantee the safety of the shipments or road crew, and the State Department isn't willing to sanction the relief without the NGO's backing."

Fuck this.

"I'm not having either crew put at risk." Ros knows this.

"We could try and pull in mercenaries," she says.

"No, cancel—"

"But the cost," she protests.

"We'll air-drop instead."

"I knew that's what you'd say, Christian. I have a plan in the works. It will be costly. In the meantime, the containers can go to Rotterdam out of Philly and we can take it from there. That's it."

"Good." I hang up. More support from the State Department would be helpful. I resolve to call Blandino to discuss this further.

My attention reverts to Miss Steele, who's standing in my living room, regarding me warily. I need to get us back on track.

Yes. The contract. That's the next step in our negotiation.

In my study, I gather the papers that are on my desk and stuff them into a manila envelope.

Ana's not moved from where I left her in the living room. Perhaps she's been thinking about the photographer . . . my mood takes a nosedive.

"This is the contract." I hold up the envelope. "Read it, and we'll discuss it next weekend. May I suggest you do some research, so you know what's involved?" She looks from the manila envelope to me, her face pale. "That's if you agree, and I really hope you do," I add.

"Research?"

"You'll be amazed what you can find on the Internet."

She frowns.

"What is it?" I ask.

"I don't have a computer. I usually use the computers at school. I'll see if I can use Kate's laptop."

No computer? How can a student not have a computer? Is she that broke? I hand her the envelope. "I'm sure I can, um—lend you one. Get your things, we'll drive back to Portland and grab some lunch on the way. I need to dress."

"I'll just make a call," she says, her voice soft and hesitant.

"The photographer?" I snap. She looks guilty.

What the hell? "I don't like to share, Miss Steele. Remember that." I storm out of the room before I say anything else.

Is she hung up on him?

Was she just using me to break her in?

Fuck.

Maybe it's the money. That's a depressing thought . . . though she doesn't strike me as a gold digger. She was quite vehement about me not buying her any clothing. I remove my jeans and put on a pair of boxer briefs. My Brioni tie is on the floor. I stoop to pick it up.

She took to being tied up well . . . *There's hope, Grey. Hope.*

I stuff the tie and two others into a messenger bag along with socks, underwear, and condoms.

What am I doing?

Deep down I know I'm going to stay at The Heathman all next week . . . to be near her. I gather a couple of suits and shirts that Taylor can bring down later in the week. I'll need one for the graduation ceremony.

I slip on some clean jeans and grab a leather jacket, and my phone buzzes. It's a text from Elliot.

> I'm driving back today in your car.
> Hope that doesn't screw up your plans.

I text back.

> No. I'm coming back to Portland now.
> Let Taylor know when you arrive.

I buzz Taylor through the internal phone system.

"Mr. Grey?"

"Elliot is bringing the SUV back sometime this afternoon. Bring it down to Portland tomorrow. I'm going to stay at The Heathman until the graduation ceremony. I've left some clothes that I'd like you to bring down as well."

"Yes, sir."

"And call Audi. I may need the A3 sooner than I thought."

"It's ready, Mr. Grey."

"Oh. Good. Thanks."

So that's the car taken care of; now it's the computer. I call Barney, assuming he'll be in his office, and knowing he'll have a state-of-the-art laptop lying around.

"Mr. Grey?" he answers.

"What are you doing in the office, Barney? It's Sunday."

"I'm working on the tablet design. The solar-cell issue is bugging me."

"You need a home life."

Barney has the grace to laugh. "What can I do for you, Mr. Grey?"

"Do you have any new laptops?"

"I have two right here from Apple."

"Great. I need one."

"Sure thing."

"Can you set it up with an e-mail account for Anastasia Steele? She'll be the owner."

"How are you spelling 'Steal'?"

"S.T.E.E.L.E."

"Cool."

"Great. Andrea will be in touch today to arrange delivery."

"Sure thing, sir."

"Thanks, Barney—and go home."

"Yes, sir."

I text Andrea with instructions to send the laptop to Ana's home address, then return to the living room. Ana is sitting on the sofa, fidgeting with her fingers. She gives me a cautious look and rises.

"Ready?" I ask.

She nods.

Taylor appears from his office. "Tomorrow, then," I tell him.

"Yes, sir. Which car are you taking, sir?"

"The R8."

"Safe trip, Mr. Grey. Miss Steele," Taylor says, as he opens the foyer doors for us. Ana fidgets beside me as we wait for the elevator, her teeth on her plump lower lip.

It reminds me of her teeth on my cock.

"What is it, Anastasia?" I ask, as I reach out and pluck her chin. "Stop biting your lip, or I will fuck you in the elevator, and I don't care who gets in with us," I growl.

She's shocked, I think—though why would she be after all we've done . . . My mood softens.

"Christian, I have a problem," she says.

"Oh?"

In the elevator I press the button for the garage.

"W-Well," she stutters, uncertain. Then she squares her shoulders. "I need to talk to Kate. I've so many questions about sex, and you're too involved. If you want me to do all these things, how do I know—?" She stops, as if weighing her words. "I just don't have any terms of reference."

Not this again. We've been over this. I don't want her talking to anyone. She's signed an NDA. But she's asked, again. So it must be important to her. "Talk to her if you must. Make sure she doesn't mention anything to Elliot."

"She wouldn't do that, and I wouldn't tell you anything she tells me about Elliot—if she were to tell me anything," she insists.

I remind her that I'm not interested in Elliot's sex life but agree that she can talk about what we've done so far. Her roommate would have my balls if she knew my real intentions.

"Okay," Ana says, and gives me a bright smile.

"The sooner I have your submission the better, and we can stop all this."

"Stop all what?"

"You, defying me." I kiss her quickly and her lips on mine immediately make me feel better.

"Nice car," she says, as we approach the R8 in the underground garage.

"I know." I flash her a quick grin, and I'm rewarded with another smile—before she rolls her eyes. I open the door for her, wondering if I should comment about the eye rolling.

"So what sort of car is this?" she asks, when I'm behind the wheel.

"It's an Audi R8 Spyder. It's a lovely day; we can take the top down. There's a baseball cap in there. In fact there should be two."

I start the ignition and retract the roof, and the Boss fills the car. "Gotta love Bruce." I grin at Ana and steer the R8 out of her safe place in the garage.

Weaving in and out of the traffic on I-5, we head toward Portland. Ana is quiet, listening to the music and staring out the window. It's difficult to see her expression, behind oversized Wayfarers and under my Mariners cap. The wind whistles over us as we speed past Boeing Field.

So far, this weekend has been unexpected. But what did I expect? I thought we'd have dinner, discuss the contract, and then what . . . ? Perhaps fucking her was inevitable.

I glance across at her.

Yes . . . And I want to fuck her again.

I wish I knew what she was thinking. She gives little away, but I've learned some things about Ana. In spite of her inexperience, she's willing to learn. Who would have thought that under that shy exterior she has the soul of a siren? An image of her lips around my dick comes to mind and I suppress a moan.

Yeah . . . she's more than willing.

The thought is arousing.

I hope I can see her before next weekend.

Even now I'm itching to touch her again. Reaching across, I put my hand on her knee.

"Hungry?"

"Not particularly," she responds, subdued.

This is getting old.

"You must eat, Anastasia. I know a great place near Olympia. We'll stop there."

CUISINE SAUVAGE IS SMALL, and crowded with couples and families enjoying Sunday brunch. With Ana's hand in mine, we follow the hostess to our table. The last time I came here was with Elena. I wonder what she'd make of Anastasia.

"I've not been here for a while. We don't get a choice—they cook whatever they've caught or gathered," I say, grimacing, feigning my horror. Ana laughs.

Why do I feel ten feet tall when I make her laugh?

"Two glasses of the pinot grigio," I order from the waitress, who's making eyes at me from beneath blond bangs. It's annoying. Ana scowls.

"What?" I ask, wondering if the waitress is annoying her, too.

"I wanted a Diet Coke."

Why didn't you say so? I frown. "The pinot grigio here is a decent wine. It will go well with the meal, whatever we get."

"Whatever we get?" she asks, her eyes round with alarm.

"Yes." And I give her my megawatt smile to make amends for not letting her order her own drink. I'm just not used to asking . . . "My mother liked you," I add, hoping this will please her and remembering Grace's reaction to Ana.

"Really?" she says, looking flattered.

"Oh yes. She's always thought I was gay."

"Why?"

"Because she's never seen me with a girl."

"Oh, not even one of the fifteen?"

"You remembered. No, none of the fifteen."

"Oh."

Yes . . . only you, baby. The thought is unsettling.

"You know, Anastasia, it's been a weekend of firsts for me, too."

"It has?"

"I've never slept with anyone, never had sex in my bed, never flown a girl in *Charlie Tango*, never introduced a woman to my mother. What are you doing to me?"

Yeah. What the hell are you doing to me? This isn't me.

The waitress brings us our chilled wine, and Ana immediately takes a quick sip, her bright eyes on me. "I've really enjoyed this weekend," she says, with bashful delight in her voice. I have, too, and I realize I haven't enjoyed a weekend for a while . . . since Susannah and I parted ways. I tell her so.

"What's vanilla sex?" she asks.

I laugh at her unexpected question and complete change of topic.

"Just straightforward sex, Anastasia. No toys, no add-ons." I shrug. "You know—well, actually you don't, but that's what it means."

"Oh," she says, and she looks a little crestfallen.

What now?

The waitress diverts us, putting down two soup bowls full of greenery. "Nettle soup," she announces, and struts back into the kitchen. We glance at each other, then back at the soup. A quick taste informs us both that it's delicious. Ana giggles at my exaggerated expression of relief.

"That's a lovely sound," I say softly.

"Why have you never had vanilla sex before? Have you always done, what you've done?" She's as inquisitive as ever.

"Sort of." And then I wonder if I should expand on this. More than anything, I want her to be forthcoming with me; I want her to trust me. I'm never this candid, but I think I can trust her so I choose my words carefully.

"One of my mother's friends seduced me when I was fifteen."

"Oh." Ana's spoon pauses midway from the bowl to her mouth.

"She had very particular tastes. I was her submissive for six years."

"Oh," she breathes.

"So I do know what it involves, Anastasia." *More than you know.* "I didn't really have a run-of-the-mill introduction to sex." I couldn't be touched. I still can't.

I wait for her reaction but she continues with her soup, mulling over this tidbit of information. "So you never dated anyone in college?" she asks, when she's finished her last spoonful.

"No."

The waitress interrupts us to clear our empty bowls. Ana waits for her to leave. "Why?"

"Do you really want to know?"

"Yes."

"I didn't want to. She was all I wanted, needed. And besides, she'd have beaten the shit out of me."

She blinks a couple of times as she absorbs this news. "So if she was a friend of your mother's, how old was she?"

"Old enough to know better."

"Do you still see her?" She sounds shocked.

"Yes."

"Do you still . . . er—" She blushes crimson, her mouth turned down.

"No," I say quickly. I don't want her to have the wrong idea about my relationship with Elena. "She's a very good friend," I reassure her.

"Oh. Does your mother know?"

"Of course not."

My mother would kill me—and Elena, too.

The waitress returns with the main entrée: venison. Ana takes a long sip of her wine. "But it can't have been full-time?" She's ignoring her food.

"Well, it was, though I didn't see her all the time. It was . . . difficult. After all, I was still at school and then at college. Eat up, Anastasia."

"I'm really not hungry, Christian," she says.

I narrow my eyes. "Eat." I keep my voice low, as I try to check my temper.

"Give me a moment," she says, her tone as quiet as mine.

What's her problem? Elena?

"Okay," I agree, wondering if I've told her too much, and I take a bite of my venison.

Finally, she picks up her cutlery and starts eating.

Good.

"Is this what our, um . . . relationship will be like?" she asks. "You ordering me around?" She scrutinizes the plate of food in front of her.

"Yes."

"I see." She tosses her ponytail over her shoulder.

"And what's more, you'll want me to."

"It's a big step," she says.

"It is." I close my eyes. I want to do this with her, now more than ever. What can I say to convince her to give our arrangement a try?

"Anastasia, you have to go with your gut. Do the research, read the contract. I'm happy to discuss any aspect. I'll be in Portland until Friday if you want to talk about it before then. Call me—maybe we can have dinner—say, Wednesday? I really want to make this work. In fact, I've never wanted anything as much as I want this."

Whoa. Big speech, Grey. Did you just ask her on a date?

"What happened to the fifteen?" she asks.

"Various things, but it boils down to incompatibility."

"And you think that I might be compatible with you?"

"Yes."

I hope so . . .

"So you're not seeing any of them anymore?"

"No, Anastasia, I'm not. I am monogamous in my relationships."

"I see."

"Do the research, Anastasia."

She puts her knife and fork down, signaling that she's finished her meal.

"That's it? That's all you're going to eat?"

She nods, placing her hands in her lap, and her mouth sets in that mulish way she has . . . and I know it will be a fight to persuade her to clean her plate. No wonder she's so slim. Her eating issues will be something to work on, if she agrees to be mine. As I continue to eat, her eyes dart to me every few seconds and a slow flush stains her cheeks.

Oh, what's this?

"I'd give anything to know what you're thinking right at this moment." She's clearly thinking about sex. "I can guess," I tease.

"I'm glad you can't read my mind."

"Your mind, no, Anastasia, but your body—*that* I've gotten to know quite well since yesterday." I give her a wolfish grin and ask for the check.

When we leave, her hand is firmly in mine. She's quiet—deep in thought, it seems—and remains so all the way to Vancouver. I've given her a great deal to think about.

But she's also given me a great deal to think about.

Will she want to do this with me?

Damn, I hope so.

It's still light when we arrive at her home, but the sun is sinking to the horizon and shining pink and pearl light on Mount St. Helens. Ana and Kate live in a scenic spot with an amazing view.

"Do you want to come in?" she asks, after I've switched off the engine.

"No. I have work to do." I know that if I accept her invitation I'll be crossing a line I'm not prepared to cross. I'm not boyfriend material—and I don't want to give her any false expectations of the kind of relationship she'll have with me.

Her face falls and, deflated, she looks away.

She doesn't want me to go.

It's humbling. Reaching across, I grasp her hand and kiss her knuckles, hoping to take the sting out of my rejection.

"Thank you for this weekend, Anastasia. It's been . . . the best." She turns shining eyes to me. "Wednesday?" I continue. "I'll pick you up from work, from wherever?"

"Wednesday," she says, and the hope in her voice is disconcerting.

Shit. It's not a date.

I kiss her hand again and climb out of the car to open her door. I have to get out of here before I do something I'll regret.

When she gets out of the car, she brightens, at odds with how she looked a moment ago. She marches up to her front door but before reaching the steps she turns suddenly. "Oh, by the way, I'm wearing your underwear," she says in triumph, and she yanks the waistband up so I can see the words "Polo" and "Ralph" peeking over her jeans.

She's stolen my underwear!

I'm stunned. And in that instant I want nothing more than to see her in my boxer briefs . . . and only them.

She tosses back her hair and swaggers into her apartment, leaving me standing on the curb, staring like a fool.

Shaking my head, I climb back into the car, and as I start the engine I cannot help my shit-eating grin.

I hope she says yes.

I FINISH MY WORK and take a sip of the fine Sancerre, delivered from room service by the woman with dark, dark eyes. Trawling through my e-mails and answering where required has been a welcome distraction from thoughts of Anastasia. And now I'm pleasantly tired. Is it the five hours of work? Or all the sexual activity last night and this morning? Memories of the delectable Miss Steele invade my mind: in *Charlie Tango*, in my bed, in my bath, dancing around my kitchen. And to think it all started here on Friday . . . and now she's considering my proposal.

Has she read the contract? Is she doing her homework?

I check my phone once again for a text or a missed call but, of course, there's nothing.

Will she agree?

I hope so . . .

Andrea has sent me Ana's new e-mail address and assured me the laptop will be delivered tomorrow morning. With that in mind, I type out an e-mail.

From: Christian Grey
Subject: Your New Computer
Date: May 22 2011 23:15
To: Anastasia Steele

Dear Miss Steele,
I trust you slept well. I hope that you put this laptop to good
use, as discussed.

I look forward to dinner Wednesday.

Happy to answer any questions before then, via e-mail,
should you so desire.

Christian Grey
CEO, Grey Enterprises Holdings, Inc.

The e-mail doesn't bounce, so the address is live. I wonder
how Ana will react in the morning when she reads it. I hope she
likes the laptop. Guess I'll know tomorrow. Picking up my latest
read, I settle onto the sofa. It's a book by two renowned economists
who examine why the poor think and behave the way they do. An
image of a young woman brushing out her long, dark hair comes
to mind; her hair shines in the light from the cracked, yellowed
window, and the air is filled with dancing dust motes. She's singing
softly, like a child.

I shudder.

Don't go there, Grey.

I open the book and start to read.

MONDAY, MAY 23, 2011

I t's after one in the morning when I go to bed. Staring at the ceiling, I'm tired, relaxed, but also excited, anticipating what the week will bring. I hope to have a new project: Miss Anastasia Steele.

MY FEET POUND THE sidewalk on Main Street as I run toward the river. It's 6:35 in the morning and the sun's rays are shimmering through the high-rise buildings. The sidewalk trees are newly green with spring leaves; the air is clean, the traffic quiet. I've slept well. "O Fortuna" from Orff's *Carmina Burana* is blaring in my ears. Today the streets are paved with possibility.

Will she respond to my e-mail?

It's too early, far too early for any response, but feeling lighter than I have for weeks, I run past the statue of the elk and toward the Willamette.

BY 7:45 I'M IN front of my laptop, having showered and ordered breakfast. I e-mail Andrea to let her know I'll be working from Portland for the week and to ask her to reschedule any meetings so that they can take place by phone or videoconference. I e-mail Gail to let her know I won't be home until Thursday evening at the earliest. Then I work through my inbox and find among other things a proposal for a joint venture with a shipyard in Taiwan. I forward it to Ros to add to the agenda of items we need to discuss.

Then I turn to my other outstanding matter: Elena. She's texted me a couple of times over the weekend and I've not replied.

From: Christian Grey
Subject: The Weekend
Date: May 23 2011 08:15
To: Elena Lincoln

Good morning, Elena.
Sorry not to get back to you. I've been busy all weekend,
and I'll be in Portland all this week. I don't know about next
weekend, either, but if I'm free, I'll let you know.
Latest results for the beauty business look promising.
Good going, Ma'am . . .

Best
C

Christian Grey
CEO, Grey Enterprises Holdings, Inc.

I press send, wondering again what Elena would make of
Ana . . . and vice versa. There's a ping from my laptop as a new
e-mail arrives.

It's from Ana.

From: Anastasia Steele
Subject: Your New Computer (on loan)
Date: May 23 2011 08:20
To: Christian Grey

I slept very well, thank you—for some strange reason—*Sir*.
I understood that this computer was on loan, ergo not mine.

Ana

"Sir" with a capital *S*; the girl has been reading, and possibly researching. And she's still talking to me. I grin stupidly at the e-mail. This is good news. Though she is also telling me that she doesn't want the computer.

Well, that's frustrating.

I shake my head, amused.

From: Christian Grey
Subject: Your New Computer (on loan)
Date: May 23 2011 08:22
To: Anastasia Steele

The computer is on loan. Indefinitely, Miss Steele.
I note from your tone that you have read the documentation
I gave you.

Do you have any questions so far?

Christian Grey
CEO, Grey Enterprises Holdings, Inc.

I hit send. How long will it be before she responds? I resume reading my e-mail as a distraction while I wait for her reply. There's an executive summary from Fred, the head of my telecom division, about the development of our solar-powered tablet—one of my pet projects. It's ambitious but few of my business ventures matter more than this one and I'm excited about it. Bringing affordable first world technology to the third world is something I'm determined to do.

There's a ping from my computer.

Another e-mail from Miss Steele.

From: Anastasia Steele
Subject: Inquiring Minds
Date: May 23 2011 08:25
To: Christian Grey

I have many questions, but not suitable for e-mail, and some of us have to work for a living.

I do not want or need a computer indefinitely.

Until later, good day. *Sir.*

Ana

The tone of her e-mail makes me smile, but it seems she's off to work, so this might be the last one for a while. Her reluctance to accept the damned computer is annoying. But I suppose it shows she's not acquisitive. She's no gold digger—rare among the women I've known . . . yet Leila was the same.

"Sir, I am not deserving of this beautiful dress."
"You are. Take it. And I'll not hear another word on this.
Understand?"
"Yes, Master."
"Good. And the style will suit you."

Ah, Leila. She was a good submissive, but she became too attached and I was the wrong man. Fortunately, that wasn't for long. She's married now and happy. I turn my attention back to Ana's e-mail and reread.
"Some of us have to work for a living."
The sassy wench is implying I don't do any work.
Well to hell with that!
I spy Fred's rather dry summary report open on my desktop and decide to set the record straight with Ana.

From: Christian Grey
Subject: Your New Computer (again on loan)
Date: May 23 2011 08:26
To: Anastasia Steele

Laters, baby.
P.S.: I work for a living, too.

Christian Grey
CEO, Grey Enterprises Holdings, Inc.

I find it impossible to concentrate on my work, waiting for the telltale ping to announce a new e-mail from Ana. When it comes, I look up immediately—but it's from Elena. And I'm surprised by my disappointment.

From: Elena Lincoln
Subject: The Weekend
Date: May 23 2011 08:33
To: Christian Grey

Christian, you work too hard. What's in Portland? Work?
Ex

ELENA LINCOLN
ESCLAVA
For The Beauty That Is You™

Do I tell her? If I do, she'll call immediately with questions, and I'm not ready to divulge my weekend experiences yet. I type her a quick e-mail saying it's work, and get back to my reading.

Andrea calls me at nine and we run through my schedule. As

I'm in Portland, I ask her to set up a meeting with the president and the AVP of economic development at WSU, to discuss the soil science project we've set up and their need for additional funding in the next fiscal year. She agrees to cancel all my social engagements this week, and then connects me through to my first videoconference of the day.

AT 3:00 I'M PORING over some tablet design schematics that Barney has sent me when I'm disturbed by a knock at my door. The interruption is annoying but for a moment I hope that it's Miss Steele. It's Taylor.

"Hello." I hope my voice doesn't reveal my disappointment.

"I have your clothes, Mr. Grey," he says politely.

"Come in. Can you hang them in the closet? I'm expecting my next conference call."

"Certainly, sir." He hurries into the bedroom, carrying a couple of suit bags and a duffel.

When he returns I'm still waiting for my call.

"Taylor, I don't think I'm going to need you for the next couple of days. Why don't you take the time to see your daughter?"

"That's very good of you, sir, but her mother and I—" He stops, embarrassed.

"Ah. Like that, is it?" I ask.

He nods. "Yes, sir. It will take some negotiating."

"Okay. Would Wednesday be better?"

"I'll ask. Thank you, sir."

"Anything I can do to help?"

"You do enough, sir."

He doesn't want to talk about this. "Okay. I think I'm going to need a printer—can you arrange it?"

"Yes, sir." He nods. As he leaves, closing the door softly behind him, I frown. I hope his ex-wife isn't giving him grief. I pay for his daughter's schooling as another incentive for him to stay in my employment; he's a good man, and I don't want to lose him. The phone rings—it's my conference call with Ros and Senator Blandino.

MY LAST CALL WRAPS up at 5:20. Stretching in my chair, I think about how productive I've been today. It's amazing how much more I get done when I'm not in the office. Only a couple of reports to read and I'm finished for the day. As I look out the window at the early-evening sky, my mind strays to a certain potential submissive.

I wonder how her day at Clayton's has been, pricing cable ties and measuring out lengths of rope. I hope one day I'll get to use them on her. The thought conjures images of her tethered in my playroom. I dwell on this for a moment . . . then quickly send her an e-mail. All this waiting, working, and e-mailing is making me restless. I know how I'd like to release this pent-up energy, but I have to settle for a run.

From: Christian Grey
Subject: Working for a Living
Date: May 23 2011 17:24
To: Anastasia Steele

Dear Miss Steele,
I do hope you had a good day at work.

Christian Grey
CEO, Grey Enterprises Holdings, Inc.

I change back into my running gear. Taylor has brought me two more pairs of sweatpants. I'm sure that's Gail's doing. As I head toward the door I check my e-mail. She's replied.

From: Anastasia Steele
Subject: Working for a Living
Date: May 23 2011 17:48
To: Christian Grey

Sir . . . I had a very good day at work.
Thank you.

Ana

But she hasn't done her homework. I e-mail her back.

From: Christian Grey
Subject: Do the Work!
Date: May 23 2011 17:50
To: Anastasia Steele

Miss Steele,
Delighted you had a good day.

While you are e-mailing, you are not researching.

Christian Grey
CEO, Grey Enterprises Holdings, Inc.

And rather than leave the room, I wait for her reply. She doesn't keep me waiting long.

From: Anastasia Steele
Subject: Nuisance
Date: May 23 2011 17:53
To: Christian Grey

Mr. Grey, stop e-mailing me, and I can start my assignment.
I'd like another A.

Ana

I laugh out loud. *Yes.* That A was something else. Closing my eyes, I see and feel her mouth around my cock once more.
Fuck.
Bringing my errant body to heel, I press send on my reply, and wait.

From: Christian Grey
Subject: Impatient
Date: May 23 2011 17:55
To: Anastasia Steele

Miss Steele,
Stop e-mailing *me*—and do your assignment.

I'd like to award another A.

The first one was so well deserved. ;)

Christian Grey
CEO, Grey Enterprises Holdings, Inc.

Her response is not as immediate, and feeling a little crest-fallen, I turn away and decide to go on my run. But as I open the door the ping from my inbox pulls me back.

From: Anastasia Steele
Subject: Internet Research
Date: May 23 2011 17:59
To: Christian Grey

Mr. Grey,
What would you suggest I put into a search engine?

Ana

Shit! Why didn't I think about this? I could have given her some books. Numerous websites spring to mind—but I don't want to frighten her off.

Perhaps she should start with the most vanilla . . .

From: Christian Grey
Subject: Internet Research
Date: May 23 2011 18:02
To: Anastasia Steele

Miss Steele,
Always start with Wikipedia.

No more e-mails unless you have questions.

Understood?

Christian Grey
CEO, Grey Enterprises Holdings, Inc.

I get up from my desk, thinking she won't respond, but as usual she surprises me and does. I can't resist.

From: Anastasia Steele
Subject: Bossy!
Date: May 23 2011 18:04
To: Christian Grey

Yes . . . *Sir.*
You are so bossy.

Ana

Damned right, baby.

From: Christian Grey
Subject: In Control
Date: May 23 2011 18:06
To: Anastasia Steele

Anastasia, you have no idea.
Well, maybe an inkling now.

Do the work.

Christian Grey
CEO, Grey Enterprises Holdings, Inc.

Show some restraint, Grey. Before she can distract me again, I'm out the door. With the Foo Fighters blaring in my ears I run to the river; I've seen the Willamette at dawn, now I want to see it at dusk. It's a fine evening: couples are walking by the riverside, some sitting on the grass, and a few tourists are cycling up and down the concourse. I avoid them, the music blasting in my ears.

Miss Steele has questions. She is still in the game—this is not a "no." Our e-mail exchange has given me hope. As I run under the Hawthorne Bridge I reflect on how at ease she is with the written word, more so than when she's speaking. Maybe this is her preferred medium of expression. Well, she has been studying English literature. I'm hoping that by the time I get back there'll be another e-mail, maybe with questions, maybe with some more of her sassy banter.

Yeah. That's something to look forward to.

As I sprint down Main Street I dare to hope that she'll accept my proposition. The thought is exciting, invigorating even, and I pick up my pace, sprinting back to The Heathman.

IT'S 8:15 WHEN I sit back in my dining chair. I've eaten the wild Oregon salmon for dinner, courtesy of Miss Dark, Dark Eyes again, and I still have half a glass of Sancerre to finish. My laptop is open and powered up, should any important e-mails arrive. I pick up the report that I've printed out, on the brownfield sites in Detroit. "It would have to be Detroit," I grumble out loud, and start to read.

A few minutes later, I hear a ping.

It's an e-mail with "Shocked of WSUV" written in the subject line. The heading makes me sit up.

From: Anastasia Steele
Subject: Shocked of WSUV
Date: May 23 2011 20:33
To: Christian Grey

Okay, I've seen enough.
It was nice knowing you.

Ana

Shit!

I read it again.

Fuck.

It's a "no." I stare at the screen in disbelief.

That's it?

No discussion?

Nothing.

Just "It was nice knowing you"?

What. The. Fuck.

I sit back in my chair, dumbfounded.

Nice?

Nice.

NICE.

She thought it was more than nice when her head was thrown back as she came.

Don't be so hasty, Grey.

Maybe it's a joke?

Some joke!

I pull my laptop toward me to write a reply.

From: Christian Grey
Subject: NICE?
Date: May 23 2011
To: Anastasia Steele

But as I stare at the screen, my fingers hovering over the keys, I can't think of what to say.

How could she dismiss me so easily?

Her first fuck.

Get it together, Grey. What are your options? Maybe I should pay her a visit, just to make sure it's a "no." Maybe I can persuade her otherwise. I certainly don't know what to say to this e-mail. Perhaps she's looked at some particularly hardcore sites. Why didn't I give her a few books? I don't believe this. She needs to look me in the eye and say no.

Yep. I rub my chin as I formulate a plan, and moments later I'm in my closet, retrieving my tie.

That tie.

This deal isn't dead yet. From my messenger bag I take some condoms and slide them into the back pocket of my pants, then grab my jacket and a bottle of white wine from the minibar. Damn, it's a chardonnay—but it will have to do. Snatching my room key, I close the door and head toward the elevator to collect my car from the valet.

AS I PULL UP in the R8 outside the apartment she shares with Kavanagh, I wonder if this is a wise move. I've never visited any of my previous submissives at their homes—they always came to me. I'm pushing all the boundaries that I've set for myself. Opening the door of the car and climbing out, I'm uneasy; it's reckless and too presumptuous of me to come here. Then again, I've already been here twice, though for only a few minutes. If she does agree, I'll have to manage her expectations. This won't happen again.

Getting ahead of yourself, Grey.

You're here because you think it's a "no."

Kavanagh answers when I knock at the door. She's surprised to see me. "Hi, Christian. Ana didn't say you were coming over." She stands aside to let me enter. "She's in her room. I'll call her."

"No. I'd like to surprise her." I give her my most earnest and endearing look and in response she blinks a couple of times. *Whoa. That was easy. Who would have thought?* How gratifying. "Where's her room?"

"Through there, the first door." She points to a door off the empty living room.

"Thanks."

Leaving my jacket and the chilled wine on one of the packing crates, I open the door to find a small hallway with a couple of rooms off it. I assume one is a bathroom, so I knock on the other door. After a beat, I open it and there's Ana, sitting at a small desk, reading what looks like the contract. She has her earbuds in as she idly drums her fingers to an unheard beat. Standing there for a moment, I watch her. Her face is scrunched in concentration; her hair is braided and she's wearing sweats. Perhaps she's been for a run this evening . . . perhaps she's suffering from excess energy, too. The thought is pleasing. Her room is small, neat, and girlish: all whites, creams, and baby blues, and bathed in the soft glow of her bedside lamp. It's also a little empty, but I spy a closed packing crate with *Ana's room* scrawled on the top. At least she has a double bed—with a white wrought-iron bedstead. *Yes.* That has possibilities.

Ana suddenly jumps, startled by my presence.

Yes. I'm here because of your e-mail.

She pulls out her earbuds and the sound of tinny music fills the silence between us.

"Good evening, Anastasia."

She stares at me dumbfounded, her eyes widening.

"I felt that your e-mail warranted a reply in person." I try to keep my voice neutral. Her mouth opens and closes, but she remains mute.

Miss Steele is speechless. This I like. "May I sit?"

She nods, continuing to stare in disbelief as I perch on her bed.

"I wondered what your bedroom would look like," I offer as an icebreaker, though chitchat is not my area of expertise. She scans her room as if seeing it for the first time. "It's very serene and peaceful in here," I add, though I feel anything but serene or peaceful right now. I want to know why she's said no to my proposal with no discussion whatsoever.

"How . . . ?" she whispers, but she stops, her disbelief still evident in her quiet tone.

"I'm still at The Heathman." She knows this.

"Would you like a drink?" she squeaks.

"No thank you, Anastasia." *Good.* She's found her manners. But I want to get on with the business at hand: her alarming e-mail. "So, it was *nice* knowing me?" I emphasize the word that offends me most in that sentence.

Nice? Really?

She examines her hands in her lap, her fingers nervously tapping against her thighs. "I thought you'd reply by e-mail," she says, her voice as small as her room.

"Are you biting your lower lip deliberately?" I inquire, my voice sterner than I'd intended.

"I wasn't aware I was biting my lip," she whispers, her face pale.

We gaze at each other.

And the air almost crackles between us.

Fuck.

Can't you feel this, Ana? This tension. This attraction. My breathing shallows as I watch her pupils dilate. Slowly, deliberately, I reach for her hair and gently tug on the elastic, freeing one of her braids. She watches me, captivated, her eyes never leaving mine. I loosen her second braid.

"So you decided on some exercise?" My fingers trace the soft shell of her ear. With great care, I tug and squeeze the plump skin of her earlobe. She's not wearing earrings, though she does have pierced ears. I wonder what a diamond would look like twinkling there. I ask her why she's been exercising, keeping my voice low. Her breathing quickens.

"I needed time to think," she says.

"Think about what, Anastasia?"

"You."

"And you decided that it was nice knowing me? Do you mean knowing me in the biblical sense?"

Her cheeks pink. "I didn't think you were familiar with the Bible."

"I went to Sunday school, Anastasia. It taught me a great deal." *Catechism. Guilt. And that God abandoned me long ago.*

"I don't remember reading about nipple clamps in the Bible. Perhaps you were taught from a modern translation," she goads me, her eyes shining and provocative.

Oh, that smart mouth.

"Well, I thought I should come and remind you how *nice* it was knowing me." The challenge is there in my voice, and now between us. Her mouth drops open in surprise, but I glide my fingers to her chin and coax it closed. "What do you say to that, Miss Steele?" I whisper, as we stare at each other.

Suddenly she launches herself at me.

Shit.

Somehow I grab her arms before she can touch me, and twist so that she lands on the bed, beneath me, and I have her arms stretched out above her head. Turning her face to mine, I kiss her, hard, my tongue exploring and reclaiming her. Her body rises in response as she kisses me back with equal ardor.

Oh, Ana. What you do to me.

Once she's squirming for more, I stop and gaze down at her. It's time for plan B.

"Trust me?" I ask, when her eyelids flutter open.

She nods enthusiastically. From the back pocket of my pants I extract the tie so she can see it, then sit astride her and, taking both of her offered wrists, bind her to one of the iron spindles of her bedstead.

She wriggles beneath me, testing her bindings, but the tie holds fast. She's not escaping. "That's better." I smile with relief because I have her where I want her. Now to undress her.

Grabbing her right foot, I start to undo her sneakers.

"No," she grumbles with embarrassment, trying to withdraw her foot, and I know it's because she's been running and she doesn't want me to remove her shoes. Does she think perspiration would put me off?

Sweetheart!

"If you struggle, I'll tie your feet, too. If you make a noise, Anastasia, I will gag you. Keep quiet. Katherine is probably outside listening right now."

She stops. And I know that my instincts are right. She's worried about her feet. When will she understand that none of that stuff bothers me?

Quickly I remove her shoes, socks, and sweatpants. Then shift her so she's stretched out and lying on her sheets, and not that dainty, homemade quilt. We're going to make a mess.

Stop biting that fucking lip.

I brush my finger over her mouth as a carnal warning. She purses her lips in the semblance of a kiss, prompting my smile. She's a beautiful, sensual creature.

Now that she's where I want her, I take my shoes and socks off, undo the top button of my pants, and remove my shirt. She doesn't take her eyes off me.

"I think you've seen too much." I want to keep her guessing, and not knowing what's coming next. It will be a carnal treat. I've not blindfolded her before, so this will count toward her training. *That's if she says yes . . .*

Sitting astride her once more, I grab the hem of her T-shirt and roll it up her body. But rather than taking it off, I leave it rolled over her eyes: an effective blindfold.

She looks fantastic, laid out and bound. "Mmm, this just gets better and better. I'm going to get a drink," I whisper, and kiss her. She gasps as I climb off the bed. Outside her room, I leave her door slightly ajar and enter the living room to retrieve the bottle of wine.

Kavanagh looks up from where she's sitting on the sofa, reading, and her eyebrows rise in surprise. *Don't tell me you've never seen a shirtless man, Kavanagh, because I won't believe you.* "Kate, where would I find glasses, ice, and a corkscrew?" I ask, ignoring her scandalized expression.

"Um. In the kitchen. I'll get them for you. Where's Ana?"

Ah, some concern for her friend. Good.

"She's a little tied up at the moment, but she wants a drink." I grab the bottle of chardonnay.

"Oh, I see," Kavanagh says, and I follow her into the kitchen, where she points to some glasses on the counter. All the glasses are out, I assume to be packed for their move. She hands me a corkscrew and from the fridge she removes a tray of ice and breaks out the ice cubes.

"We still have to pack in here. You know Elliot is helping us move." Her tone is critical.

"Is he?" I sound uninterested as I open the wine. "Just put the ice in the glasses." With my chin I indicate two glasses. "It's a chardonnay. It'll be more drinkable with the ice."

"I figured you for a red-wine kind of guy," she says, when I pour the wine. "Are you going to come and help Ana with the move?" Her eyes flash. She's challenging me.

Shut her down now, Grey.

"No. I can't." My voice is clipped, because she's pissing me off, trying to make me feel guilty. Her lips thin, and I turn around to leave the kitchen, but not before I catch the disapproval in her face.

Fuck off, Kavanagh.

No way am I going to help. Ana and I don't have that kind of relationship. Besides, I can't spare the time.

I return to Ana's room and shut the door behind me, blotting out Kavanagh and her disdain. Immediately I'm appeased by the sight of the enchanting Ana Steele, breathless and waiting, on her bed. Setting the wine down on her bedside table, I take the foil packet out of my pants and place it beside the wine, then drop my pants and underwear on the floor, freeing my erection.

I take a sip of wine—surprisingly, it's not bad—and gaze down at Ana. She hasn't said a word. Her face is turned toward me, her lips parted with anticipation. Taking the glass, I sit astride her once more. "Are you thirsty, Anastasia?"

"Yes," she whispers.

Taking a sip of wine, I lean down and kiss her, pouring the wine into her mouth. She laps it up, and deep in her throat I hear a faint hum of appreciation.

"More?" I ask.

She nods, smiling, and I oblige.

"Let's not go too far; we know your capacity for alcohol is limited, Anastasia," I tease, and her mouth splits in the widest of grins. Leaning down, I let her have another drink from my mouth, and she wriggles beneath me.

"Is this *nice?*" I ask, as I lay down beside her.

She stills, all seriousness now, but her lips part as she inhales sharply.

I take another swig of wine, this time with two ice cubes. When I kiss her, I push a small shard of ice between her lips, then lay a trail of icy kisses down her sweet-smelling skin from her throat to her navel. There, I place the other shard, and a little wine.

She sucks in a breath.

"Now you have to keep still. If you move, Anastasia, you'll get wine all over the bed." My voice is low, and I kiss her again just above her navel. Her hips shift. "Oh no. If you spill the wine, I will punish you, Miss Steele."

She moans in response and pulls at the tie.

All good things, Ana . . .

I release each of her breasts from her bra so they're supported by the underwire cups; her breasts are pert and vulnerable, just how I like them. Slowly I tease them both with my lips.

"How *nice* is this?" I whisper, and blow gently on one nipple. Her mouth slackens in a silent "Ah." Taking another piece of ice in my mouth, I slowly trace down her sternum to her nipple, circling a couple of times with the ice. She moans beneath me. Transferring the ice to my fingers, I continue to torture each nipple with cool lips and the remaining ice cube that's melting in my fingers.

Whining and panting beneath me, she's tensing but managing to stay still. "If you spill the wine, I won't let you come," I warn.

"Oh. Please. Christian. Sir. Please," she begs.

Oh, to hear her use those words.

There's hope.

This is not a "no."

I skim my fingers over her body toward her panties, teasing her soft skin. Suddenly her pelvis flexes, spilling the wine and the now-melted ice from her navel. I move quickly to lap it up, kissing and sucking it off her body.

"Oh dear, Anastasia, you moved. What am I going to do to

you?" I slip my fingers into her panties and brush her clitoris as I do.

"Ah!" she whines.

"Oh, baby," I whisper with reverence. She's wet. Very wet.

See. See how nice *this is?*

I push my index and middle finger inside her and she trembles.

"Ready for me so soon," I murmur, and push my fingers slowly in and out of her, eliciting a long sweet moan. Her pelvis starts lifting to meet my fingers.

Oh, she wants this.

"You are a greedy girl." My voice is still low and she matches the pace I'm setting as I begin to circle her clitoris with my thumb, teasing and tormenting her.

She cries out, her body bucking beneath me. I want to see her expression, and reaching up with my other hand, I slip her T-shirt off her head. She opens her eyes, blinking in the soft light.

"I want to touch you," she says, her voice husky and full of need.

"I know," I breathe against her lips, and kiss her, all the while keeping up the relentless rhythm with my fingers and thumb. She tastes of wine and need and Ana. And she kisses me back with a hunger I've not felt in her before. I cradle the top of her head, keeping her in place, and continue to kiss and finger-fuck her. As her legs stiffen, I drop the pace of my hand.

Oh, no, baby. You're not coming yet.

I do this three more times while kissing her warm, sweet mouth. The fifth time I still my fingers inside her, and I hum soft and slow in her ear, "This is your punishment, so close and yet so far. Is this *nice?*"

"Please," she whimpers.

God, I love to hear her beg.

"How shall I fuck you, Anastasia?"

My fingers start again and her legs begin to quiver, and I gentle my hand once more.

"Please," she breathes again, the word so low I barely hear her.

"What do you want, Anastasia?"

"You . . . now," she pleads.

"Shall I fuck you this way, or this way, or this way? There's an endless choice," I murmur. Withdrawing my hand, I snatch the condom from the bedside table and kneel up between her legs. Keeping my eyes on hers, I pull her panties off and discard them on the floor. Her eyes are dark, full of promise and longing. They widen as I slowly put the condom on.

"How *nice* is this?" I ask, as I wrap my fist around my erection.

"I meant it as a joke," she whimpers.

Joke?

Thank. The. Lord.

All is not lost.

"A joke?" I query, as my fist slides up and down my cock.

"Yes. Please, Christian," she begs.

"Are you laughing now?"

"No." Her voice is barely audible, but the little shake of her head tells me all I need to know.

Watching her needing me . . . I could explode in my hand just looking at her. Grabbing her, I flip her over, keeping her fine, fine ass in the air. It's too tempting. I slap her cheek, hard, then plunge inside her.

Oh, fuck. She's so ready.

She tightens around me and cries out as she comes.

Fuck. That's too quick.

Holding her hips in place, I fuck her, hard, riding through her orgasm. Gritting my teeth, I grind into her, again and again, as she begins to build once more.

Come on, Ana. Again, I will her, pounding on.

She moans and whimpers beneath me, a sheen of sweat appearing on her back.

Her legs begin to quiver.

She's close.

"Come on, Anastasia, again," I growl, and by some miracle her orgasm spirals through her body and into mine. *Thank fuck.* Wordlessly I come, pouring myself into her.

Sweet Lord. I collapse on top of her. That was exhausting.

"How *nice* was that?" I hiss against her ear as I draw air into my lungs.

As she lies flat on the bed, panting, I pull out of her and remove the wretched condom. I get off the bed and quickly get dressed. When I'm done, I reach down and unfasten my tie, freeing her. Turning over, she stretches her hands and fingers and readjusts her bra. Once I cover her with the comforter I lie down beside her, propped up on my elbow.

"That was really nice," she says with a mischievous smile.

"There's that word again." I smirk at her.

"You don't like that word?"

"No. It doesn't do it for me at all."

"Oh—I don't know . . . it seems to have a very beneficial effect on you."

"I'm a beneficial effect now, am I? Could you wound my ego any further, Miss Steele?"

"I don't think there's anything wrong with your ego." Her frown is fleeting.

"You think?"

Dr. Flynn would have plenty to say about that.

"Why don't you like to be touched?" she asks, her voice sweet and soft.

"I just don't." I kiss her forehead to distract her from this line of questioning. "So, that e-mail was your idea of a joke?"

She gives me a coy look and an apologetic shrug.

"I see. So you are still considering my proposition?"

"Your indecent proposal . . . yes, I am."

Well, thank fuck for that.

Our deal is still in play. My relief is palpable; I can almost taste it.

"I have issues, though," she adds.

"I'd be disappointed if you didn't."

"I was going to e-mail them to you, but you kind of interrupted me."

"Coitus interruptus."

"See? I knew you had a sense of humor somewhere in there." The light in her eyes dances with mirth.

"Only certain things are funny, Anastasia. I thought you were saying no—no discussion at all."

"I don't know yet. I haven't made up my mind. Will you collar me?"

Her question surprises me. "You have been doing your research. I don't know, Anastasia. I've never collared anyone."

"Were you collared?" she asks.

"Yes."

"By Mrs. Robinson?"

"Mrs. Robinson?" I laugh out loud. Anne Bancroft in *The Graduate*. "I'll tell her you said that; she'll love it."

"You still talk to her regularly?" Her voice is high-pitched with shock and indignation.

"Yes." Why's that such a big deal?

"I see." Now her voice is clipped. She's mad? Why? I don't understand. "So you have someone you can discuss your alternative lifestyle with, but I'm not allowed." Her tone is petulant, but once again she's calling me out on my shit.

"I don't think I've ever thought about it like that. Mrs. Robinson is part of that lifestyle. I told you, she's a good friend now. If you'd like, I can introduce you to one of my former subs. You could talk to her."

"Is this *your* idea of a joke?" she demands.

"No, Anastasia." I'm surprised by her vehemence and shake my head to reinforce my denial. It's perfectly normal for a submissive to check with exes that their new Dominant knows what he's doing.

"No—I'll do this on my own, thank you very much," she insists, and reaches for her comforter and quilt, pulling them up to her chin.

What? She's upset?

"Anastasia, I . . . I didn't mean to offend you."

"I'm not offended. I'm appalled."

"Appalled?"

"I don't want to talk to one of your ex-girlfriends, slave, sub, whatever you call them."

Oh.

"Anastasia Steele, are you jealous?" I sound bewildered . . . because I am. She flushes beet red, and I know I've found the root of her problem. How the hell can she be jealous?

Sweetheart, I had a life before you.

A very active life.

"Are you staying?" she snaps.

What? Of course not. "I have a breakfast meeting tomorrow at The Heathman. Besides, I told you, I don't sleep with girlfriends, slaves, subs, or anyone. Friday and Saturday were exceptions. It won't happen again."

She presses her lips together with her stubborn expression. "Well, I'm tired now," she says.

Fuck.

"Are you kicking me out?"

This is not how this is supposed to go.

"Yes."

What the hell?

Disarmed again, by Miss Steele. "Well, that's another first," I mutter.

Kicked out. I can't believe it.

"So nothing you want to discuss now? About the contract?" I ask, as an excuse to prolong my stay.

"No," she grunts. Her petulance is irritating, and were she truly mine, it would not be tolerated.

"God, I'd like to give you a good hiding. You'd feel a lot better, and so would I," I tell her.

"You can't say things like that. I haven't signed anything yet." Her eyes flash with defiance.

Oh, baby, I can say it. I just can't do it. Not until you let me. "A man can dream, Anastasia. Wednesday?" I still want this. Why, though, I don't know; she's so difficult. I give her a brief kiss.

"Wednesday," she agrees, and I'm relieved once again. "I'll see you out," she adds, her tone softer. "If you give me a minute." She pushes me off the bed and pulls on her T-shirt. "Please pass me my sweatpants," she orders, pointing to them.

Wow. Miss Steele can be a bossy little thing.

"Yes, ma'am," I quip, knowing that she won't get the reference. But she narrows her eyes. She knows I'm making fun of her, but she says nothing as she slips her pants on.

Feeling a little bemused at the prospect of being tossed out onto the street, I follow her through the living room to the front door.

When was the last time this happened?

Never.

She opens the door, but she's staring down at her hands.

What is going on here?

"You okay?" I ask, and brush her lower lip with my thumb. Perhaps she doesn't want me to go—or perhaps she can't wait for me to leave?

"Yes," she says, her tone soft and subdued. I'm not sure I believe her.

"Wednesday," I remind her. I'll see her then. Bending down, I kiss her, and she closes her eyes. And I don't want to go. Not with her uncertainty on my mind. I hold her head and deepen the kiss and she responds, surrendering her mouth to me.

Oh, baby, don't give up on me. Give it a try.

She grasps my arms, kissing me back, and I don't want to stop. She's intoxicating and the darkness is quiet, calmed by the young woman in front of me. Reluctantly, I pull back and lean my forehead against hers.

She's breathless, like me. "Anastasia, what are you doing to me?"

"I could say the same to you," she whispers.

I know I have to leave. She has me in a tailspin, and I don't know why. I kiss her forehead and walk down the path toward the R8. She stands watching me from the doorway. She hasn't gone in. I smile, pleased that she's still watching as I climb into the car.

When I look back, she's gone.

Shit. What just happened? No wave good-bye?

I start the car and begin the drive back to Portland, analyzing what's taken place between us.

She e-mailed me.

I went to her.

We fucked.

She threw me out before I was ready to leave.

For the first time—well, maybe not the first time—I feel a little used, for sex. It's a disturbing feeling that reminds me of my time with Elena.

Hell! Miss Steele is topping from the bottom, and she doesn't even know it. And fool that I am, I'm letting her.

I have to turn this around. This soft-sell approach is messing with my head.

But I want her. I need her to sign.

Is it just the chase? Is that what's turning me on? Or is it her?

Fuck, I don't know. But I hope to find out more on Wednesday. And on a positive note, that was one hell of a *nice* way to spend an evening. I smirk in the rearview mirror and pull into the garage at the hotel.

When I'm back in my room I sit down at my laptop.

Focus on what you want, where you want to be. Isn't that what Flynn is always harassing me about, his solution-based shit?

From: Christian Grey
Subject: This Evening
Date: May 23 2011 23:16
To: Anastasia Steele

Miss Steele,
I look forward to receiving your notes on the contract.

Until then, sleep well, baby.

Christian Grey
CEO, Grey Enterprises Holdings, Inc.

And I want to add, *Thank you for another diverting evening* . . . but that seems a little over the top. Pushing my laptop aside because Ana will probably be asleep, I pick up the Detroit report and continue reading.

TUESDAY, MAY 24, 2011

The thought of siting the electronics plant in Detroit is depressing. I loathe Detroit; it holds nothing but bad memories for me. Memories I do my damnedest to forget. They surface, mainly at night, to remind me of what I am and where I came from.

But Michigan is offering excellent tax incentives. It's hard to ignore what they are proposing in this report. I toss it on the dining table and take a sip of my Sancerre. *Shit.* It's warm. It's late. I should sleep. As I stand and stretch, there's a ping on my computer. An e-mail. It might be from Ros, so I have a quick look.

It's from Ana. Why is she still awake?

From: Anastasia Steele
Subject: Issues
Date: May 24 2011 00:02
To: Christian Grey

Dear Mr. Grey,
Here is my list of issues. I look forward to discussing them
more fully at dinner on Wednesday.

The numbers refer to clauses:

She's referring to the clauses? Miss Steele has been thorough. I pull a copy up on screen for my reference.

CONTRACT

Made this day _____ of 2011 ("The Commencement Date")

BETWEEN

MR. CHRISTIAN GREY of 301 Escala, Seattle, WA 98889

("The Dominant")

MISS ANASTASIA STEELE of 1114 SW Green Street,

Apartment 7, Haven Heights, Vancouver, WA 98888

("The Submissive")

THE PARTIES AGREE AS FOLLOWS

1   The following are the terms of a binding contract between the Dominant and the Submissive.

FUNDAMENTAL TERMS

2   The fundamental purpose of this contract is to allow the Submissive to explore her sensuality and her limits safely, with due respect and regard for her needs, her limits, and her well-being.

3   The Dominant and the Submissive agree and acknowledge that all that occurs under the terms of this contract will be consensual, confidential, and subject to the agreed limits and safety procedures set out in this contract. Additional limits and safety procedures may be agreed in writing.

4   The Dominant and the Submissive each warrant that they suffer from no sexual, serious, infectious, or life-threatening illnesses, including but not limited to HIV, herpes, and hepatitis. If during the Term (as defined below) or any extended term of this contract either party should be diagnosed with or become aware of any such illness, he or she undertakes to inform the other immediately and in any event prior to any form of physical contact between the parties.

5   Adherence to the above warranties, agreements, and undertakings (and any additional limits and safety procedures agreed under clause 3 above) are fundamental to this contract. Any breach shall render it void with immediate effect and each party agrees to be fully responsible to the other for the consequence of any breach.

6   Everything in this contract must be read and interpreted in the

light of the fundamental purpose and the fundamental terms set out in clauses 2–5 above.

ROLES

7   The Dominant shall take responsibility for the well-being and the proper training, guidance, and discipline of the Submissive. He shall decide the nature of such training, guidance, and discipline and the time and place of its administration, subject to the agreed terms, limitations, and safety procedures set out in this contract or agreed additionally under clause 3 above.

8   If at any time the Dominant should fail to keep to the agreed terms, limitations, and safety procedures set out in this contract or agreed additionally under clause 3 above, the Submissive is entitled to terminate this contract forthwith and to leave the service of the Dominant without notice.

9   Subject to that proviso and to clauses 2–5 above, the Submissive is to serve and obey the Dominant in all things. Subject to the agreed terms, limitations, and safety procedures set out in this contract or agreed additionally under clause 3 above, she shall without query or hesitation offer the Dominant such pleasure as he may require and she shall accept without query or hesitation his training, guidance, and discipline in whatever form it may take.

COMMENCEMENT AND TERM

10   The Dominant and Submissive enter into this contract on the Commencement Date fully aware of its nature and undertake to abide by its conditions without exception.

11   This contract shall be effective for a period of three calendar months from the Commencement Date ("the Term"). On the expiry of the Term the parties shall discuss whether this contract and the arrangements they have made under this contract are satisfactory and whether the needs of each party have been met. Either party may propose the extension of this contract subject to adjustments to its terms or to the arrangements they have made under it. In the absence of agreement to such extension this contract shall terminate and both parties shall be free to resume their lives separately.

AVAILABILITY

12   The Submissive will make herself available to the Dominant from Friday evenings through to Sunday afternoons each week during the Term at times to be specified by the Dominant ("the Allotted Times"). Further allocated time can be mutually agreed to on an ad hoc basis.

13   The Dominant reserves the right to dismiss the Submissive from his service at any time and for any reason. The Submissive may request her release at any time, such request to be granted at the discretion of the Dominant subject only to the Submissive's rights under clauses 2–5 and 8 above.

LOCATION

14   The Submissive will make herself available during the Allotted Times and agreed additional times at locations to be determined by the Dominant. The Dominant will ensure that all travel costs incurred by the Submissive for that purpose are met by the Dominant.

SERVICE PROVISIONS

15   The following service provisions have been discussed and agreed and will be adhered to by both parties during the Term. Both parties accept that certain matters may arise that are not covered by the terms of this contract or the service provisions, or that certain matters may be renegotiated. In such circumstances, further clauses may be proposed by way of amendment. Any further clauses or amendments must be agreed, documented, and signed by both parties and shall be subject to the fundamental terms set out under clauses 2–5 above.

DOMINANT

15.1   The Dominant shall make the Submissive's health and safety a priority at all times. The Dominant shall not at any time require, request, allow, or demand the Submissive to participate at the hands of the Dominant in the activities detailed in Appendix 2 or in any act that either party deems to be unsafe. The Dominant will not undertake or permit to be undertaken any action which could cause serious injury or any risk to the Submissive's life. The remaining subclauses of this clause 15 are to be read subject to this proviso and to the fundamental matters agreed in clauses 2–5 above.

15.2   The Dominant accepts the Submissive as his, to own, control, dominate, and discipline during the Term. The Dominant may use the Submissive's body at any time during the Allotted Times or any agreed additional times in any manner he deems fit, sexually or otherwise.

15.3   The Dominant shall provide the Submissive with all necessary training and guidance in how to properly serve the Dominant.

15.4   The Dominant shall maintain a stable and safe environment in which the Submissive may perform her duties in service of the Dominant.

15.5   The Dominant may discipline the Submissive as necessary to ensure the Submissive fully appreciates her role of subservience to the Dominant and to discourage unacceptable conduct. The Dominant may flog, spank, whip, or corporally punish the Submissive as he sees fit, for purposes of discipline, for his own personal enjoyment, or for any other reason, which he is not obliged to provide.

15.6   In training and in the administration of discipline the Dominant shall ensure that no permanent marks are made upon the Submissive's body nor any injuries incurred that may require medical attention.

15.7   In training and in the administration of discipline the Dominant shall ensure that the discipline and the instruments used for the purposes of discipline are safe, shall not be used in such a way as to cause serious harm, and shall not in any way exceed the limits defined and detailed in this contract.

15.8   In case of illness or injury the Dominant shall care for the Submissive, seeing to her health and safety, encouraging and, when necessary, ordering medical attention when it is judged necessary by the Dominant.

15.9   The Dominant shall maintain his own good health and seek medical attention when necessary in order to maintain a risk-free environment.

15.10   The Dominant shall not loan his Submissive to another Dominant.

15.11   The Dominant may restrain, handcuff, or bind the Submissive at any time during the Allotted Times or any agreed additional times for any reason and for extended periods of time, giving due regard to the health and safety of the Submissive.

15.12   The Dominant will ensure that all equipment used for the purposes of training and discipline shall be maintained in a clean, hygienic, and safe state at all times.

SUBMISSIVE

15.13   The Submissive accepts the Dominant as her master, with the understanding that she is now the property of the Dominant, to be dealt with as the Dominant pleases during the Term generally but specifically during the Allotted Times and any additional agreed allotted times.

15.14   The Submissive shall obey the rules ("the Rules") set out in Appendix 1 to this agreement.

15.15   The Submissive shall serve the Dominant in any way the Dominant sees fit and shall endeavor to please the Dominant at all times to the best of her ability.

15.16   The Submissive shall take all measures necessary to maintain her good health and shall request or seek medical attention whenever it is needed, keeping the Dominant informed at all times of any health issues that may arise.

15.17   The Submissive will ensure that she procures oral contraception and ensure that she takes it as and when prescribed to prevent any pregnancy.

15.18   The Submissive shall accept without question any and all disciplinary actions deemed necessary by the Dominant and remember her status and role in regard to the Dominant at all times.

15.19   The Submissive shall not touch or pleasure herself sexually without permission from the Dominant.

15.20   The Submissive shall submit to any sexual activity demanded by the Dominant and shall do so without hesitation or argument.

15.21   The Submissive shall accept whippings, floggings, spankings, canings, paddlings, or any other discipline the Dominant should decide to administer, without hesitation, inquiry, or complaint.

15.22   The Submissive shall not look directly into the eyes of the Dominant except when specifically instructed to do so. The Submissive shall keep her eyes cast down and maintain a quiet and respectful bearing in the presence of the Dominant.

15.23   The Submissive shall always conduct herself in a respectful manner to the Dominant and shall address him only as Sir, Mr. Grey, or such other title as the Dominant may direct.

15.24   The Submissive will not touch the Dominant without his express permission to do so.

ACTIVITIES

16   The Submissive shall not participate in activities or any sexual acts that either party deems to be unsafe or any activities detailed in Appendix 2.

17   The Dominant and the Submissive have discussed the activities set out in Appendix 3 and recorded in writing on Appendix 3 their agreement in respect of them.

SAFE WORDS

18   The Dominant and the Submissive recognize that the Dominant may make demands of the Submissive that cannot be met without incurring physical, mental, emotional, spiritual, or other harm at the time the demands are made to the Submissive. In such circumstances related to this, the Submissive may make use of a safe word ("the Safe Word[s]"). Two Safe Words will be invoked depending on the severity of the demands.

19   The Safe Word "Yellow" will be used to bring to the attention of the Dominant that the Submissive is close to her limit of endurance.

20   The Safe Word "Red" will be used to bring to the attention of the Dominant that the Submissive cannot tolerate any further demands. When this word is said, the Dominant's action will cease completely with immediate effect.

CONCLUSION

21   We the undersigned have read and understood fully the provisions of this contract. We freely accept the terms of this contract and have acknowledged this by our signatures below.

_____

The Dominant: Christian Grey
Date

_____

The Submissive: Anastasia Steele
Date

APPENDIX 1
RULES
Obedience:

The Submissive will obey any instructions given by the Dominant immediately without hesitation or reservation and in an expeditious manner. The Submissive will agree to any sexual activity deemed fit and pleasurable by the Dominant excepting those activities that are outlined in hard limits (Appendix 2). She will do so eagerly and without hesitation.

Sleep:

The Submissive will ensure she achieves a minimum of eight hours' sleep a night when she is not with the Dominant.

Food:

The Submissive will eat regularly to maintain her health and well-being from a prescribed list of foods (Appendix 4). The Submissive will not snack between meals, with the exception of fruit.

Clothes:

During the Term the Submissive will wear clothing only approved by the Dominant. The Dominant will provide a clothing budget for the Submissive, which the Submissive shall utilize. The Dominant shall accompany the Submissive to purchase clothing on an ad hoc basis. If the Dominant so requires, the Submissive shall, during the Term, wear adornments the Dominant shall require, in the presence of the Dominant and at any other time the Dominant deems fit.

Exercise:

The Dominant shall provide the Submissive with a personal trainer four times a week in hour-long sessions at times to be mutually agreed between the personal trainer and the Submissive. The personal trainer will report to the Dominant on the Submissive's progress.

Personal Hygiene/Beauty:

The Submissive will keep herself clean and shaved and/or waxed at all times. The Submissive will visit a beauty salon of the Dominant's choosing at times to be decided by the Dominant and undergo whatever treatments the Dominant sees fit. All costs will be met by the Dominant.

Personal Safety:

The Submissive will not drink to excess, smoke, take recreational drugs, or put herself in any unnecessary danger.

Personal Qualities:

The Submissive will not enter into any sexual relations with anyone other than the Dominant. The Submissive will conduct herself in a respectful and modest manner at all times. She must recognize that her behavior is a direct reflection on the Dominant. She shall be held accountable for any misdeeds, wrongdoings, and misbehavior committed when not in the presence of the Dominant.

Failure to comply with any of the above will result in immediate punishment, the nature of which shall be determined by the Dominant.

APPENDIX 2

Hard Limits

No acts involving fire play.

No acts involving urination or defecation and the products thereof.

No acts involving needles, knives, cutting, piercing, or blood.

No acts involving gynecological medical instruments.

No acts involving children or animals.

No acts that will leave any permanent marks on the skin.

No acts involving breath control.

No activity that involves the direct contact of electric current (whether alternating or direct), fire, or flames to the body.

APPENDIX 3

Soft Limits

To be discussed and agreed between both parties:

Does the Submissive consent to:

- Masturbation
- Cunnilingus
- Fellatio
- Swallowing Semen
- Vaginal intercourse
- Vaginal fisting
- Anal intercourse
- Anal fisting

Does the Submissive consent to the use of:

- Vibrators
- Butt plugs
- Dildos
- Other vaginal/anal toys

Does the Submissive consent to:

- Bondage with rope
- Bondage with leather cuffs
- Bondage with handcuffs/
  shackles/manacles
- Bondage with tape
- Bondage with other

Does the Submissive consent to be restrained with:

- Hands bound in front
- Ankles bound
- Elbows bound
- Hands bound behind back
- Knees bound
- Wrists bound to ankles
- Binding to fixed items,
  furniture, etc.
- Binding with spreader bar
- Suspension

Does the Submissive consent to be blindfolded?

Does the Submissive consent to be gagged?

How much pain is the Submissive willing to experience?

Where 1 is likes intensely and 5 is dislikes intensely:
1—2—3—4—5

Does the Submissive consent to accept the following forms of
pain/punishment/discipline:

- Spanking
- Whipping
- Biting
- Genital clamps
- Hot wax

- Paddling
- Caning
- Nipple clamps
- Ice
- Other types/methods of
  pain

So, her points.

2: Not sure why this is solely for MY benefit—i.e., to explore
MY sensuality and limits. I'm sure I wouldn't need a ten-page
contract to do that! Surely this is for YOUR benefit.

Fair point well made, Miss Steele!

4: As you are aware, you are my only sexual partner. I don't
take drugs, and I've not had any blood transfusions. I'm
probably safe. What about you?

*Another fair point! And it dawns on me that this is the first time
I haven't had to consider the sexual history of a partner. Well, that's
one advantage of screwing a virgin.*

8: I can terminate at any time if I don't think you're sticking to
the agreed limits. Okay—I like this.

*I hope it won't come to that, but it wouldn't be the first time if
it did.*

9: Obey you in all things? Accept without hesitation your
discipline? We need to talk about this.

11: One-month trial period. Not three.

Only a month? That's not long enough. How far can we go in a month?

12: I cannot commit every weekend. I do have a life, or will have. Perhaps three out of four?

And she'll have the opportunity to socialize with other men? She'll realize what she's missing. I'm not sure about this.

15.2: Using my body as you see fit sexually or otherwise— please define "or otherwise."

15.5: This whole discipline clause. I'm not sure I want to be whipped, flogged, or corporally punished. I am sure this would be in breach of clauses 2–5. And also "for any other reason." That's just mean—and you told me you weren't a sadist.

Shit! Read on, Grey.

15.10: Like loaning me out to someone else would ever be an option. But I'm glad it's here in black and white.

15.14: The Rules. More on those later.

15.19: Touching myself without your permission. What's the problem with this? You know I don't do it anyway.

15.21: Discipline—please see clause 15.5 above.

15.22: I can't look into your eyes? Why?

15.24: Why can't I touch you?

Rules:

Sleep—I'll agree to six hours.

Food—I am not eating food from a prescribed list. The food list goes or I do—deal breaker.

Well, this is going to be an issue!

Clothes—as long as I only have to wear your clothes when
I'm with you . . . okay.

Exercise—We agreed on three hours, this still says four.

Soft Limits:

Can we go through all of these? No fisting of any kind. What is
suspension? Genital clamps—you have got to be kidding me.

Can you please let me know the arrangements for
Wednesday? I am working until five p.m. that day.

Good night.

Ana

Her response is a relief. Miss Steele has put some thought into
this, more so than anyone else I've dealt with over this contract.
She's really engaged. She seems to be taking it seriously and we'll
have much to discuss on Wednesday. The uncertainty that I felt
when leaving her apartment this evening recedes. There's hope for
our relationship, but first—she needs to sleep.

From: Christian Grey
Subject: Issues
Date: May 24 2011 00:07
To: Anastasia Steele

Miss Steele,
That's a long list. Why are you still up?

Christian Grey
CEO, Grey Enterprises Holdings, Inc.

A few minutes later her answer is in my inbox.

From: Anastasia Steele
Subject: Burning the Midnight Oil
Date: May 24 2011 00:10
To: Christian Grey

Sir,
If you recall, I was going through this list when I was
distracted and bedded by a passing control freak.

Good night.

Ana

Her e-mail makes me laugh out loud but it irritates me in equal
measure. She's much more sassy in print and she has a great sense
of humor, but the woman needs sleep.

From: Christian Grey
Subject: Stop Burning the Midnight Oil
Date: May 24 2011 00:12
To: Anastasia Steele

GO TO BED, ANASTASIA.

Christian Grey
CEO & Control Freak, Grey Enterprises Holdings, Inc.

A few minutes pass and once I'm convinced she's gone to bed,
persuaded by my capital letters, I head into my bedroom. I take my
laptop just in case she replies again.

Once in bed, I grab my book and read. After half an hour I give up. I can't concentrate; my mind keeps straying to Ana, how she was this evening, and her e-mail.

I need to remind her of what I expect from our relationship. I don't want her getting the wrong idea. I've strayed too far from my goal.

"Are you going to come and help Ana with the move?" Kavanagh's words remind me that unrealistic expectations have been set.

Perhaps I could help them move?

No. Stop now, Grey.

Opening my laptop, I read through her "Issues" e-mail again. I need to manage her expectations and try to find the right words to express how I feel.

Finally, I'm inspired.

From: Christian Grey
Subject: Your Issues
Date: May 24 2011 01:27
To: Anastasia Steele

Dear Miss Steele,
Following my more thorough examination of your issues, may I bring to your attention the definition of submissive.

submissive [*suh*b-mis-iv]—adjective

1. inclined or ready to submit; unresistingly or humbly obedient: *submissive servants.*

2. marked by or indicating submission: *a submissive reply.*

Origin: 1580–90; submiss + -ive

Synonyms: 1. tractable, compliant, pliant, amenable.
2. passive, resigned, patient, docile, tame, subdued.
Antonyms: 1. rebellious, disobedient.

Please bear this in mind for our meeting on Wednesday.

Christian Grey
CEO, Grey Enterprises Holdings, Inc.

That's it. I hope she'll find it amusing, but it gets my point across.

With that thought, I switch off my bedside light and fall asleep and dream.

> His name is Lelliot. He's bigger than me. He laughs. And smiles. And shouts. And talks all the time. He talks all the time to Mommy and Daddy. He is my brother. *Why don't you talk?* Lelliot says again and again and again. *Are you stupid?* Lelliot says again and again and again. I jump on him and smack his face again and again and again. He cries. He cries a lot. I don't cry. I never cry. Mommy is angry with me. I have to sit on the bottom stair. I have to sit for the longest time. But Lelliot never asks me why I don't talk ever again. If I make my hand into a fist he runs away. Lelliot is scared of me. He knows I'm a monster.

WHEN I RETURN FROM my run the next morning, I check my e-mail before having a shower. Nothing from Miss Steele, but then it's only 7:30. Maybe it's a little early.

Grey, snap out of this. Get a grip.

I glare at the gray-eyed prick who stares back at me from the mirror as I shave. *No more. Forget about her for today.*

I have a job to do and a breakfast meeting to attend.

"FREDDIE WAS SAYING BARNEY may have a prototype of the tablet for you in a couple of days," Ros tells me during our video-conference.

"I was studying the schematics yesterday. They were impressive, but I'm not sure we're there yet. If we get this right there's no telling where the technology could go, and what it could do in developing countries."

"Don't forget the home market," she interjects.

"As if."

"Christian, just how long are you going to be in Portland?" Ros sounds exasperated. "What's going on down there?" Eyeing the webcam, she then peers hard at her screen, looking for clues in my expression.

"A merger." I try to hide my smile.

"Does Marco know?"

I snort. Marco Inglis is the head of my mergers and acquisitions division. "No. It's not that kind of merger."

"Oh." Ros is silenced momentarily and, from her look, surprised.

Yeah. It's private.

"Well, I hope you're successful," she says, smirking.

"Me, too," I acknowledge with a smirk of my own. "Now, can we talk about Woods?"

Over the past year, we've acquired three tech companies. Two are booming, surpassing all targets, and one is struggling despite Marco's initial optimism. Lucas Woods heads it up; he's turned out to be an idiot—all show, no substance. The money has gone to his head and he's lost focus and squandered the lead his company once had in fiber optics. My gut says asset-strip the company, fire Woods, and merge their technology division into GEH.

But Ros thinks Lucas needs more time—and that we need time to plan if we're going to liquidate and rebrand his company. If we do, it will involve expensive redundancies.

"I think Woods has had enough time to turn this around. He just won't accept reality," I say emphatically. "We need him gone, and I'd like Marco to estimate the costs of liquidating."

"Marco wants to join us for this part of the call. I'll get him to log in."

AT 12:30 IN THE afternoon Taylor drives me out to WSU in Vancouver for lunch with the president, the head of the environmental sciences department, and the vice president of economic development. As we approach the long driveway I can't help looking out at all the students to see if I can spy Miss Steele. Alas, I don't see her; she's probably holed up in the library reading a classic. The thought of her curled up somewhere with a book is comforting. There has been no reply to my last e-mail, but then she's been working. Perhaps there'll be something after lunch.

As we pull up outside the administration building my phone buzzes. It's Grace. She never calls during the week.

"Mom?"

"Hello, darling. How are you?"

"Fine. I'm about to go into a meeting."

"Your PA said you were in Portland." Her voice is full of hope.

Damn. She thinks I'm with Ana.

"Yeah, on business."

"How's Anastasia?" *There it is!*

"Fine as far as I know, Grace. What do you want?"

Oh, Good Lord. My mother is someone else whose expectations I have to manage.

"Mia's coming home a week early, on Saturday. I'm on call that day and your father is away at a legal conference presenting a panel on philanthropy and aid," she says.

"You want me to meet her?"

"Will you?"

"Sure. Ask her to send me her flight details."

"Thank you, darling. Say hi to Anastasia for me."

"I have to go. Good-bye, Mom." I hang up before she can ask any more awkward questions. Taylor opens the car door.

"I should be out of here by three."

"Yes, Mr. Grey."

"Will you be able to see your daughter tomorrow, Taylor?"

"Yes, sir." His expression is warm and full of paternal pride.

"Great."

"I'll be here at three," he confirms.

I head into the university's administration building . . . This is going to be a long lunch.

I HAVE MANAGED TO keep Anastasia Steele out of every waking thought today. Almost. During lunch there were times when I found myself imagining us in my playroom . . . What did she call it? *The Red Room of Pain.* I shake my head, smiling, and check my e-mail. That woman has a way with words, but so far there are no words from her today.

I change from my suit to my sweats to get ready for the hotel gym. As I'm about to leave my room, I hear a ping. It's her.

From: Anastasia Steele
Subject: My Issues . . . What about Your Issues?
Date: May 24 2011 18:29
To: Christian Grey

Sir,
Please note the date of origin: 1580–90. I would respectfully remind Sir that the year is 2011. We have come a long way since then.

May I offer a definition for *you* to consider for our meeting:

compromise [kom-pr*uh*-mahyz]—*noun*

1. a settlement of differences by mutual concessions; an agreement reached by adjustment of conflicting or opposing claims, principles, etc., by reciprocal modification of demands. 2. the result of such a settlement. 3. something intermediate between different things: *The split-level is a compromise between a ranch house and a multistoried house.* 4. an endangering, esp. of reputation; exposure to danger, suspicion, etc.: *a compromise of one's integrity.*

Ana

What a surprise, a provocative e-mail from Miss Steele, but our meeting is still happening. *Well, that's a relief.*

From: Christian Grey
Subject: What about My Issues?
Date: May 24 2011 18:32
To: Anastasia Steele

Good point, well made, as ever, Miss Steele. I will collect you from your apartment at 7:00 tomorrow.

Christian Grey
CEO, Grey Enterprises Holdings, Inc.

My phone buzzes. It's Elliot.

"Hey, hotshot. Kate's asked me to hassle you about the move."

"The move?"

"Kate and Ana, help moving, you dipshit."

I give him an exaggerated sigh. He really is a crude asshole. "I can't help. I'm meeting Mia at the airport."

"What? Can't Mom do that, or Dad?"

"No. Mom called me this morning."

"Then I guess that settles it. You never told me how you got on with Ana? Did you f—"

"Good-bye, Elliot." I hang up. It's none of his business and there's an e-mail waiting for me.

From: Anastasia Steele
Subject: 2011—Women Can Drive
Date: May 24 2011 18:40
To: Christian Grey

Sir,
I have a car. I can drive.

I would prefer to meet you somewhere.

Where shall I meet you?

At your hotel at 7:00?

Ana

How irritating. I write back immediately.

From: Christian Grey
Subject: Stubborn Young Women
Date: May 24 2011 18:43
To: Anastasia Steele

Dear Miss Steele,
I refer to my e-mail dated May 24, 2011, sent at 1:27, and the
definition contained therein.

Do you ever think you'll be able to do what you're told?

Christian Grey
CEO, Grey Enterprises Holdings, Inc.

Her response is slow, which does nothing for my mood.

From: Anastasia Steele
Subject: Intractable Men
Date: May 24 2011 18:49
To: Christian Grey

Mr. Grey,
I would like to drive.

Please.

Ana

Intractable? Me? Fuck. If our meeting goes as planned, her contrary behavior will be a thing of the past. With that in mind, I agree.

From: Christian Grey
Subject: Exasperated Men
Date: May 24 2011 18:52
To: Anastasia Steele

Fine.
My hotel at 7:00.

I'll meet you in the Marble Bar.

Christian Grey
CEO, Grey Enterprises Holdings, Inc.

From: Anastasia Steele
Subject: Not So Intractable Men
Date: May 24 2011 18:55
To: Christian Grey

Thank you.

Ana x

And I'm rewarded with a kiss. Ignoring how that makes me feel, I let her know that she's welcome. My mood has lifted as I head to the hotel gym.

She sent me a kiss . . .

I order a glass of Sancerre and stand at the bar. I've been waiting for this moment all day and look repeatedly at my watch. This feels like a first date, and in a way it is. I've never taken a prospect out to dinner. I've sat through interminable meetings today, bought a business, and fired three people. Nothing I've done today, including running—twice—and a quick circuit in the gym, has dispelled the anxiety I've wrestled with all day. That power is in the hands of Anastasia Steele. I want her submission.

I hope she's not going to be late. I glance toward the entrance of the bar . . . and my mouth dries. She's standing on the threshold, and for a second I don't realize it's her. She looks exquisite: her hair falls in soft waves to her breast on one side, and on the other it's pinned back so it's easier to see her delicate jawline and the gentle curve of her slender neck. She's wearing high heels and a tight dark purple dress that accentuates her lithe, alluring figure.

Wow.

I step forward to meet her. "You look stunning," I whisper, and kiss her cheek. Closing my eyes, I savor her scent; she smells heavenly. "A dress, Miss Steele. I approve." Diamonds in her ears would complete the ensemble; I must buy her a pair.

Taking her hand, I lead her to a booth. "What would you like to drink?"

I'm rewarded with a knowing smile as she sits down. "I'll have what you're having, please."

Ah, she's learning. "Another glass of the Sancerre," I tell the waiter, and I slide into the booth, opposite her. "They have an excellent wine cellar here," I add, and take a moment to look at her. She's wearing a little makeup. Not too much. And I remember when she first fell into my office how ordinary I thought she looked. She is anything but ordinary. With a little makeup and the right clothes, she's a goddess.

She shifts in her seat and her eyelashes flutter.

"Are you nervous?" I ask.

"Yes."

This is it, Grey.

Leaning forward, in a candid whisper, I tell her that I'm nervous, too. She looks at me as if I've grown three heads.

Yeah, I'm human, too, baby . . . just.

The waiter places Ana's wine and two small plates of mixed nuts and olives between us.

Ana squares her shoulders, an indication that she means business, like she did when she first interviewed me. "So, how are we going to do this? Run through my points one by one?" she asks.

"Impatient as ever, Miss Steele."

"Well, I could ask you what you thought of the weather today," she retorts.

Oh, that smart mouth.

Let her stew for a moment, Grey.

Keeping my eyes on hers, I pop an olive into my mouth and lick my index finger. Her eyes grow wider and darker.

"I thought the weather was particularly unexceptional today." I try for nonchalance.

"Are you smirking at me, Mr. Grey?"

"I am, Miss Steele."

She purses her lips to stifle her smile. "You know this contract is legally unenforceable."

"I am fully aware of that, Miss Steele."

"Were you going to tell me that at any point?"

What? I didn't think I'd have to . . . and you've worked it out for yourself. "You'd think I'd coerce you into something you don't want to do, and then pretend that I have a legal hold over you?"

"Well, yes."

Whoa. "You don't think very highly of me, do you?"

"You haven't answered my question."

"Anastasia, it doesn't matter if it's legal or not. It represents an arrangement that I would like to make with you—what I would like from you and what you can expect from me. If you don't like it, then don't sign. If you do sign and then decide you don't like it, there are enough get-out clauses so you can walk away. Even if it were legally binding, do you think I'd drag you through the courts if you did decide to run?"

What does she take me for?

She considers me with her unfathomable blue eyes.

What I need her to understand is that this contract isn't about the law, it's about trust.

I want you to trust me, Ana.

As she takes a sip of her wine I rush on, endeavoring to explain. "Relationships like this are built on honesty and trust. If you don't trust me—trust me to know how I'm affecting you, how far I can go with you, how far I can take you—if you can't be honest with me, then we really can't do this."

She rubs her chin as she considers what I've said.

"So it's quite simple, Anastasia. Do you trust me or not?"

And if she thinks so little of me, then we shouldn't do this at all.

My gut is knotting with tension.

"Did you have similar discussions with, um . . . the fifteen?"

"No." *Why is she going off on this tangent?*

"Why not?" she asks.

"Because they were all established submissives. They knew what they wanted out of a relationship with me and generally what I expected. With them, it was just a question of fine-tuning the soft limits, details like that."

"Is there a store you go to? Submissives 'R' Us?" She arches an eyebrow and I laugh out loud. And like a magician's rabbit the tension in my body disappears. "Not exactly." My tone is wry.

"Then how?" She's ever-curious, but I don't want to talk about Elena again. Last time I mentioned her Ana turned frosty. "Is that what you want to discuss? Or shall we get down to the nitty-gritty? Your issues, as you say."

She frowns.

"Are you hungry?" I ask.

She looks suspiciously at the olives. "No."

"Have you eaten today?"

She hesitates.

Shit.

"No," she says. I try not to let her admission anger me.

"You have to eat, Anastasia. We can eat down here or in my suite. Which would you prefer?"

She'll never go for this.

"I think we should stay in public, on neutral ground."

As predicted—sensible, Miss Steele.

"Do you think that would stop me?" My voice is husky.

She swallows. "I hope so."

Put the girl out of her misery, Grey.

"Come, I have a private dining room booked. No public." Rising, I hold out my hand to her.

Will she take it?

She looks from my face to my hand.

"Bring your wine," I order. And she picks up her glass and places her hand in mine.

As we leave the bar, I notice admiring glances from other guests, and in the case of one handsome, athletic guy, overt appreciation of my date. It's not something I've dealt with before . . . and I don't think I like it.

Upstairs on the mezzanine, the liveried young host dispatched by the maître d' leads us to the room I've booked. He only has eyes for Miss Steele, and I give him a withering look that sends him in retreat from the opulent dining room. An older waiter seats Ana and drapes a napkin on her lap.

"I've ordered already. I hope you don't mind."

"No, that's fine," she says with a gracious nod.

"It's good to know that you can be amenable." I smirk. "Now, where were we?"

"The nitty-gritty," she says, focused on the task at hand, but then she takes a large gulp of wine and her cheeks color. She must be looking for courage. I'll have to watch how much she's drinking, because she's driving.

She could always spend the night here . . . then I could peel her out of that enticing dress.

Regaining my focus, I return to business—Ana's issues. From the inside pocket of my jacket I retrieve her e-mail. She squares her shoulders once more and gives me an expectant look, and I have to hide my amusement. "Clause two. Agreed. This is for the benefit of us both. I shall redraft."

She takes another sip.

"My sexual health? Well, all of my previous partners have had blood tests, and I have regular tests every six months for all the health risks you mention. All my recent tests are clear. I have never taken drugs. In fact, I'm vehemently antidrug. I have a strict no-tolerance policy with regards to drugs for all my employees, and I insist on random drug testing."

In fact, one of the people I fired today failed his drug test.

She's shocked, but I plow on. "I've never had any blood transfusions. Does that answer your question?"

She nods.

"Your next point I mentioned earlier. You can walk away anytime, Anastasia. I won't stop you. If you go, however—that's it. Just so you know."

No. Second. Chances. Ever.

"Okay," she replies, though she doesn't sound certain.

We both fall silent as the waiter enters with our appetizers. For a moment I wonder if I should have held this meeting at my office, then dismiss the thought as ridiculous. Only fools mix business with pleasure. I've kept my work and private life separate; it's one of my golden rules, and the only exception to that is my relationship with Elena . . . but then she helped me start my business.

"I hope you like oysters," I remark to Ana as the waiter leaves.

"I've never had one."

"Really? Well. All you do is tip and swallow. I think you can manage that." I stare pointedly at her mouth, remembering how well she can swallow. On cue she blushes and I squeeze lemon juice on the shellfish and tip it into my mouth. "Hmm, delicious. Tastes of the sea." I grin as she watches me, fascinated. "Go on," I encourage her, knowing that she's not one to back down from a challenge.

"So, I don't chew it?"

"No, Anastasia, you don't." And I try not to think about her teeth toying with my favorite part of my anatomy.

She presses them into her bottom lip, leaving little indentation marks.

Damn. The sight stirs my body and I shift in my chair. She reaches for an oyster, squeezes the lemon, holds back her head, and opens wide. As she tips the oyster into her mouth my body hardens.

"Well?" I ask, and I sound a little hoarse.

"I'll have another," she says with wry humor.

"Good girl."

She asks me if I've chosen oysters deliberately, knowing their reputed aphrodisiac qualities. I surprise her when I tell her they were simply at the top of the menu. "I don't need an aphrodisiac near you."

Yeah, I could fuck you right now.

Behave, Grey. Get this negotiation back on track.

"So where were we?" I return to her e-mail and concentrate on her outstanding issues. Clause nine. "Obey me in all things. Yes, I want you to do that." This is important to me. I need to know she's safe and will do *anything* for me. "I need you to do that. Think of it as role-play, Anastasia."

"But I'm worried you'll hurt me."

"Hurt you how?"

"Physically."

"Do you really think I would do that? Go beyond any limit you can't take?"

"You've said you've hurt someone before."

"Yes, I have. It was a long time ago."

"How did you hurt her?"

"I suspended her from my playroom ceiling. In fact, that's one of your questions. Suspension—that's what the karabiners are for in the playroom. Rope play. One of the ropes was tied too tightly."

Appalled, she holds up her hand in a plea for me to stop.

Too much information.

"I don't need to know any more. So you won't suspend me, then?" she asks.

"Not if you really don't want to. You can make that a hard limit."

"Okay." She exhales, relieved.

Move on, Grey. "So, obeying, do you think you can manage that?"

She stares at me with those eyes that see through to my dark soul, and I don't know what she's going to say.

Shit. This could be the end.

"I could try," she says, her voice low.

It's my turn to exhale. *I'm still in the game.* "Good."

"Now term." Clause eleven. "One month instead of three is no time at all, especially if you want a weekend away from me each month." We'll get nowhere in that time. She needs training and I can't stay away from her for any length of time. I tell her as much. Maybe we can compromise, as she suggested. "How about one day over one weekend per month you get to yourself—but I get a mid-week night that week?"

I watch her weighing the possibility. "Okay," she says eventually, her expression serious.

Good.

"And please, let's try it for three months. If it's not for you, then you can walk away anytime."

"Three months," she says. Is she agreeing? I'll take it as a "yes."

Right. Here goes.

"The ownership thing, that's just terminology and goes back to the principle of obeying. It's to get you into the right frame of mind, to understand where I'm coming from. And I want you to know that as soon as you cross my threshold as my submissive, I will do what I like to you. You have to accept that, and willingly. That's why you have to trust me. I will fuck you, anytime, any way I want—anywhere I want. I will discipline you, because you will screw up. I will train you to please me.

"But I know you've not done this before. Initially, we'll take it slowly, and I will help you. We'll build up to various scenarios. I want you to trust me, but I know I have to earn your trust, and I will. The 'or otherwise'—again, it's to help you get into the mindset; it means anything goes."

Some speech, Grey.

She sits back—overwhelmed, I think.

"Still with me?" I ask, gently. The waiter sneaks into the room, and with a nod I give him permission to clear our table.

"Would you like some more wine?" I ask her.

"I have to drive."

Good answer.

"Some water, then?"

She nods.

"Still or sparkling?"

"Sparkling, please."

The waiter leaves with our plates.

"You're very quiet," I whisper. She's barely said a word.

"You're very verbose," she shoots straight back at me.

Fair point, Miss Steele.

Now for the next item on her list of issues: clause fifteen. I take a deep breath. "Discipline. There's a very fine line between pleasure and pain, Anastasia. They are two sides of the same coin, one not existing without the other. I can show you how pleasurable pain can be. You don't believe me now, but this is what I mean about trust. There will be pain, but nothing that you can't handle." I cannot emphasize this enough. "Again, it comes down to trust. Do you trust me, Ana?"

"Yes, I do," she says immediately. Her response knocks me sideways: it's completely unexpected.

Again.

Have I gained her trust already?

"Well, then, the rest of this stuff is just details." I feel ten feet tall.

"Important details."

She's right. *Concentrate, Grey.*

"Okay, let's talk through those."

The waiter reenters with our entrées.

"I hope you like fish," I say, as he places our food before us. The black cod looks delicious. Ana takes a bite.

Finally, she's eating!

"The rules," I continue. "Let's talk about them. The food is a deal breaker?"

"Yes."

"Can I modify to say that you will eat at least three meals a day?"

"No."

Suppressing an irritated sigh, I persist. "I need to know that you're not hungry."

She frowns. "You'll have to trust me."

"Oh, touché, Miss Steele," I mutter to myself. These are battles I'm not going to win. "I concede the food and the sleep."

She gives me a small, relieved smile. "Why can't I look at you?" she asks.

"That's a Dom/sub thing. You'll get used to it."

She frowns once more, but looks pained this time. "Why can't I touch you?" she asks.

"Because you can't."

Shut her down, Grey.

"Is it because of Mrs. Robinson?"

What? "Why would you think that? You think she traumatized me?"

She nods.

"No, Anastasia. She's not the reason. Besides, Mrs. Robinson wouldn't take any of that shit from me."

"So nothing to do with her," she asks, looking confused.

"No."

I can't bear to be touched. And, baby, you really don't want to know why.

"And I don't want you touching yourself, either," I add.

"Out of curiosity, why?"

"Because I want all your pleasure."

In fact, I want it now. I could fuck her here to see if she can be quiet. Real quiet, knowing we're within earshot of the hotel staff and guests. After all, that's why I've booked this room.

She opens her mouth as if to say something, but closes it again and takes another bite of food from her largely untouched plate. "I've given you a great deal to think about, haven't I?" I say, folding up her e-mail and tucking it into my inside pocket.

"Yes."

"Do you want to go through the soft limits now, too?"

"Not over dinner."

"Squeamish?"

"Something like that."

"You've not eaten very much."

"I've had enough."

This is getting old. "Three oysters, four bites of cod, and one asparagus stalk, no potatoes, no nuts, no olives, and you've not eaten all day. You said I could trust you."

Her eyes widen.

Yeah. I've been keeping count, Ana.

"Christian, please, it's not every day I sit through conversations like this."

"I need you fit and healthy, Anastasia." My tone is adamant.

"I know."

"And right now, I want to peel you out of that dress."

"I don't think that's a good idea," she whispers. "We haven't had dessert."

"You want dessert?" When you haven't eaten your main course?

"Yes."

"You could be dessert."

"I'm not sure I'm sweet enough."

"Anastasia, you're deliciously sweet. I know."

"Christian. You use sex as a weapon. It really isn't fair." She looks down at her lap, and her voice is low and a little melancholy. She looks up again, pinning me with an intense stare, her powder-blue eyes unnerving . . . and arousing.

"You're right. I do," I admit. "In life you use what you know. Doesn't change how much I want you. Here. Now." *And we could fuck here, right now.* I know you're interested, Ana. I hear how your breathing has changed. "I'd like to try something." I really want to know how quiet she can be, and if she can do this with the fear of discovery.

Her brow creases once more; she's confused.

"If you were my sub, you wouldn't have to think about this. It would be easy. All those decisions—all the wearying thought processes behind them. The 'Is this the right thing to do? Should this happen here? Can it happen now?' You wouldn't have to worry about any of that detail. That's what I'd do as your Dom. And right now, I know you want me, Anastasia."

She tosses her hair over her shoulder, and her frown intensifies as she licks her lips.

Oh yes. She wants me.

"I can tell because your body gives you away. You're pressing your thighs together, you're flushed, and your breathing has changed."

"How do you know about my thighs?" she asks, her voice high-pitched, shocked, I think.

"I felt the tablecloth move, and it's a calculated guess based on years of experience. I'm right, aren't I?"

She's quiet for a moment and looks away. "I haven't finished my cod," she says, evasive but still blushing.

"You'd prefer cold cod to me?"

Her eyes meet mine, and they're wide, pupils dark and large. "I thought you liked me to clear my plate."

"Right now, Miss Steele, I couldn't give a fuck about your food."

"Christian. You just don't fight fair."

"I know. I never have."

We stare at each other in a battle of wills, both aware of the sexual tension stretching between us across the table.

Please, would you just do as you're told? I implore her with a look. But her eyes glint with sensual disobedience and a smile lifts her lips. Still holding my stare, she picks up an asparagus spear and deliberately bites her lip.

What is she doing?

Very slowly, she places the tip of the spear in her mouth and sucks it.

Fuck.

She's trifling with me—a dangerous tactic that will have me fucking her over this table.

Oh, bring it on, Miss Steele.

I watch, mesmerized, hardening by the second.

"Anastasia. What are you doing?" I warn.

"Eating my asparagus," she says with a coy smile.

"I think you're toying with me, Miss Steele."

"I'm just finishing my food, Mr. Grey." Her lips curl wider, slowly, carnal, and the heat between us rises several degrees. She really has no idea how sexy she is . . . I'm about to pounce when the waiter knocks and enters.

Damn it.

I let him clear the plates, then turn my attention back to Miss Steele. But her frown is back, and she's fidgeting with her fingers.

Hell.

"Would you like some dessert?" I ask.

"No thank you. I think I should go," she says, still staring at her hands.

"Go?" *She's leaving?*

The waiter exits quickly with our plates.

"Yes," Ana says, her voice firm with resolve. She gets to her feet to leave. And automatically I stand, too. "We both have the graduation ceremony tomorrow," she says.

This is not going according to plan at all.

"I don't want you to go," I state, because it's the truth.

"Please, I have to," she insists.

"Why?"

"Because you've given me so much to consider, and I need some distance." Her eyes are pleading with me to let her go.

But we've gotten so far in our negotiation. We've made compromises. We can make this work. *I have to make this work.*

"I could make you stay," I tell her, knowing that I could seduce her right now, in this room.

"Yes, you could easily, but I don't want you to."

This is all going south—I've overplayed my hand. This isn't how I thought the night would end. I rake my hands through my hair in frustration.

"You know, when you fell into my office to interview me, you were all 'Yes, sir,' 'No, sir.' I thought you were a natural-born submissive. But quite frankly, Anastasia, I'm not sure you have a submissive bone in your delectable body." I walk the few steps that separate us and look down into eyes that shine with determination.

"You may be right," she says.

No. No. I don't want to be right.

"I want the chance to explore the possibility that you do." I caress her face and her lower lip with my thumb. "I don't know any other way, Anastasia. This is who I am."

"I know," she says.

Lowering my head so my lips hover over hers, I wait until she raises her mouth to mine and closes her eyes. I want to give her a brief, chaste kiss, but as our lips touch, she leans in to me, her hands suddenly fisting in my hair, her mouth opening to me, her tongue insistent. I press my hand to the base of her spine, holding her against me, and deepen the kiss, mirroring her fervor.

Christ, I want her.

"I can't persuade you to stay?" I whisper against the corner of her mouth, as my body responds, hardening with desire.

"No."

"Spend the night with me."

"And not touch you? No."

Damn. The darkness uncoils in my guts, but I ignore it.

"You impossible girl," I mutter, and pull back, examining her face and her tense, brooding expression.

"Why do I think you're telling me good-bye?"

"Because I'm leaving now."

"That's not what I mean, and you know it."

"Christian, I have to think about this. I don't know if I can have the kind of relationship you want."

I close my eyes and rest my forehead against hers.

What did you expect, Grey? She's not cut out for this.

I take a deep breath and kiss her forehead, then bury my nose in her hair, inhaling her sweet, autumnal scent and committing it to memory.

That's it. Enough.

Stepping back, I release her. "As you wish, Miss Steele. I'll escort you to the lobby." I hold out my hand for what could be the last time, and I'm surprised how painful this thought is. She places her hand in mine, and in silence we head down to reception.

"Do you have your valet ticket?" I ask as we reach the lobby. I sound calm and collected, but inside I'm in knots.

From her purse she retrieves the ticket, which I hand to the doorman.

"Thank you for dinner," she says.

"It's a pleasure as always, Miss Steele."

This cannot be the end. I have to show her—demonstrate what this all means, what we can do together. Show her what we can do in the playroom. Then she'll know. This might be the only way to save this deal. Quickly I turn to her. "You're moving this weekend to Seattle. If you make the right decision, can I see you on Sunday?" I ask.

"We'll see. Maybe," she says.

That's not a "no."

I notice the goose bumps on her arms. "It's cooler now, don't you have a jacket?" I ask.

"No."

This woman needs looking after. I take off my jacket. "Here. I don't want you catching cold." I slip it over her shoulders and she hugs it around herself, closes her eyes, and inhales deeply.

Is she drawn to my scent? Like I am to hers?

Perhaps all is not lost?

The valet pulls up in an ancient VW Beetle.

What the hell is that?

"That's what you drive?" This must be older than Grandpa Theodore. *Jesus!* The valet hands over the keys and I tip him generously. He deserves danger pay.

"Is this roadworthy?" I glare at Ana. How can she be safe in this rust bucket?

"Yes."

"Will it make it to Seattle?"

"Yes. She will."

"Safely?"

"Yes." She tries to reassure me. "Okay, she's old. But she's mine, and she's roadworthy. My stepdad bought it for me."

When I suggest that we could do better than this she realizes what I'm offering and her expression changes immediately.

She's mad.

"You are *not* buying me a car," she says emphatically.

"We'll see," I mutter, trying to keep calm. I hold open the driver's door, and as she climbs in I wonder if I should ask Taylor to take her home. *Damn.* I remember that he's off this evening.

Once I've shut the door, she rolls down the window . . . painfully slowly.

For Christ's sake!

"Drive safely," I growl.

"Good-bye, Christian," she says, and her voice falters, as if she's trying not to cry.

Shit. My whole mood shifts from irritation and concern for her well-being to helplessness as her car roars off up the street.

I don't know if I'll see her again.

I stand like a fool on the sidewalk until her rear lights disappear into the night.

Fuck. Why did that go so wrong?

I stalk back into the hotel, make for the bar, and order a bottle of the Sancerre. Taking it with me, I head up to my room. My laptop lies open on my desk, and before I uncork the wine, I sit down and start typing an e-mail.

From: Christian Grey
Subject: Tonight
Date: May 25 2011 22:01
To: Anastasia Steele

I don't understand why you ran this evening. I sincerely hope I answered all your questions to your satisfaction. I know I have given you a great deal to contemplate, and I fervently hope that you will give my proposal your serious consideration. I really want to make this work. We will take it slow.
Trust me.

Christian Grey
CEO, Grey Enterprises Holdings, Inc.

I glance at my watch. It will take her at least twenty minutes to get home, probably longer in that deathtrap. I e-mail Taylor.

From: Christian Grey
Subject: Audi A3
Date: May 25 2011 22:04
To: J B Taylor

I need that Audi delivered here tomorrow.
Thanks.

Christian Grey
CEO, Grey Enterprises Holdings, Inc.

Opening the Sancerre, I pour myself a glass, and picking up my book, I sit and read, trying hard to concentrate. My eyes keep straying to my laptop screen. When will she reply?

As the minutes tick by, my anxiety balloons; why hasn't she returned my e-mail?

At 11:00, I text her.

> Are you home safe?

But I get nothing in response. Perhaps she's gone straight to bed. Before midnight I send another e-mail.

From: Christian Grey
Subject: Tonight
Date: May 25 2011 23:58
To: Anastasia Steele

I hope you made it home in that car of yours.
Let me know if you're okay.

Christian Grey
CEO, Grey Enterprises Holdings, Inc.

I'll see her tomorrow at the graduation ceremony and I'll find out then if she's turning me down. With that depressing thought I strip and climb into bed and stare at the ceiling.

You've really fucked up this deal, Grey.

Mommy is gone. Sometimes she goes outside.
And it is only me. Me and my cars and my blankie.
When she comes home she sleeps on the couch. The couch
is brown and sticky. She is tired. Sometimes I cover her with
my blankie.
Or she comes home with something to eat. I like those days.
We have bread and butter. And sometimes we have macrami
and cheese. That is my favorite.
Today Mommy is gone. I play with my cars. They go fast on
the floor. My mommy is gone. She will come back. She will.
When is Mommy coming home?
It is dark now, and my mommy is gone. I can reach the light
when I stand on the stool.
On. Off. On. Off. On. Off.
Light. Dark. Light. Dark. Light.
I'm hungry. I eat the cheese. There is cheese in the fridge.
Cheese with blue fur.
When is Mommy coming home?
Sometimes she comes home with him. I hate him. I hide
when he comes. My favorite place is in my mommy's closet.
It smells of Mommy. It smells of Mommy when she's happy.
When is Mommy coming home?
My bed is cold. And I am hungry. I have my blankie and my
cars but not my mommy. When is Mommy coming home?

I wake with a start.
Fuck. Fuck. Fuck.

I hate my dreams. They're riddled with harrowing memories, distorted reminders of a time I want to forget. My heart is pounding and I'm drenched with sweat. But the worst consequence of these nightmares is dealing with the overwhelming anxiety when I wake.

My nightmares have recently become more frequent, and more vivid. I have no idea why. Damned Flynn—he's not back until sometime next week. I run both of my hands through my hair and check the time. It's 5:38, and the dawn light is seeping through the curtains. It's nearly time to get up.

Go for a run, Grey.

THERE IS STILL NO text or e-mail from Ana. As my feet pound the sidewalk, my anxiety grows.

Leave it, Grey.

Just fucking leave it!

I know I'll see her at the graduation ceremony.

But I can't leave it.

Before my shower, I send her another text.

> Call me.

I just need to know she's safe.

AFTER BREAKFAST THERE'S STILL no word from Ana. To get her out of my head I work for a couple of hours on my commencement speech. At the graduation ceremony later this morning I'll be honoring the extraordinary work of the environmental sciences department and the progress they've made in partnership with GEH in arable technology for developing countries.

"All part of your feed-the-world plan?" Ana's shrewd words echo in my head, and they nudge at last night's nightmare.

I shrug it off as I rewrite. Sam, my VP for publicity, has sent a draft that is way too pretentious for me. It takes me an hour to rework his media-speak bullshit into something more human.

Nine thirty and still no word from Ana. Her radio silence is worrying—and frankly rude. I call, but her phone goes straight to a generic voice mail message.

I hang up.

Show some dignity, Grey.

There's a ping in my inbox, and my heartbeat spikes—but it's from Mia. In spite of my bad mood, I smile. I've missed that kid.

From: Mia G. Chef Extraordinaire
Subject: Flights
Date: May 26 2011 18:32 GMT-1
To: Christian Grey

Hey, Christian,

I can't wait to get out of here!

Rescue me. Please.

My flight number on Saturday is AF3622. It arrives at 12:22

p.m. and Dad is making me fly coach! *pouting!

I will have lots of luggage. Love. Love. Love Paris fashion.

Mom says you have a girlfriend.

Is this true?

What's she like?

I NEED TO KNOW!!!!!

See you Saturday. Missed you so much.

À bientôt mon frère.

Mxxxxxxxxx

Oh hell! My mother's big mouth. Ana is not my girlfriend! And come Saturday I'll have to fend off my sister's equally big mouth and her inherent optimism and her prying questions. She can be exhausting. Making a mental note of the flight number and time, I send Mia a quick e-mail to let her know I'll be there.

At 9:45 I get ready for the ceremony. Gray suit, white shirt, and of course *that* tie. It will be my subtle message to Ana that I haven't given up, and a reminder of good times.

Yeah, real good times . . . images of her bound and wanting come to mind. *Damn it. Why hasn't she called?* I press redial.

Shit.

Still no fucking answer!

At 10:00 precisely, there's a knock on my door. It's Taylor.

"Good morning," I say, as he comes in.

"Mr. Grey."

"How was yesterday?"

"Good, sir." Taylor's demeanor shifts, and his expression warms. He must be thinking of his daughter.

"Sophie?"

"She's a doll, sir. And doing very well at school."

"That's great to hear."

"The A3 will be in Portland later this afternoon."

"Excellent. Let's go."

And though I'm loath to admit it, I'm anxious to see Miss Steele.

THE CHANCELLOR'S SECRETARY USHERS me into a small room adjacent to the WSU auditorium. She blushes, almost as much as a certain young woman I know intimately. There, in the greenroom, academics, administrative staff, and a few students are having pre-graduation coffee. Among them, to my surprise, is Katherine Kavanagh.

"Hi, Christian," she says, strutting toward me with the confidence of the well-heeled. She's in her graduation gown and appears cheerful enough; surely she's seen Ana.

"Hi, Katherine. How are you?"

"You seem baffled to see me here," she says, ignoring my greeting and sounding a little affronted. "I'm valedictorian. Didn't Elliot tell you?"

"No, he didn't." *We're not in each other's pockets, for Christ's sake.* "Congratulations," I add as a courtesy.

"Thank you." Her tone is clipped.

"Is Ana here?"

"Soon. She's coming with her dad."

"You saw her this morning?"

"Yes. Why?"

"I wanted to know if she made it home in that deathtrap she calls a car."

"Wanda. She calls it Wanda. And yes, she did." She gazes at me with a quizzical expression.

"I'm glad to hear it."

At that point the chancellor joins us, and with a polite smile to Kavanagh, escorts me over to meet the other academics.

I'm relieved that Ana is in one piece, but pissed that she hasn't replied to any of my messages.

It's not a good sign.

But I don't have long to dwell on this discouraging state of affairs—one of the faculty members announces it's time to begin and herds us out into the corridor.

In a moment of weakness I try Ana's phone once more. It goes straight to voice mail, and I'm interrupted by Kavanagh. "I'm looking forward to your commencement address," she says as we walk down the hallway.

When we reach the auditorium I notice it's larger than I expected, and packed. The audience, as one, rises and applauds as we file onto the stage. The clapping intensifies, then slowly subsides to an expectant buzz as everyone takes their seats.

Once the chancellor begins his welcome address I'm able to scan the room. The front rows are filled with students, in identical black-and-red WSU robes. *Where is she?* Methodically I inspect each row.

There you are.

I find her huddled in the second row. She's alive. I feel foolish for expending so much anxiety and energy on her whereabouts last night and this morning. Her brilliant blue eyes are wide as they lock with mine, and she shifts in her seat, a slow flush coloring her cheeks.

Yes. I've found you. And you haven't replied to my messages.

She's avoiding me and I'm pissed. Really pissed. Closing my eyes, I imagine dripping hot wax onto her breasts and her squirming beneath me. This has a radical effect on my body.

Shit.

Get it together, Grey.

Dismissing her from my mind, I marshal my lascivious thoughts and concentrate on the speeches.

Kavanagh gives an inspiring address about embracing opportunities—*yes, carpe diem, Kate*—and gets a rousing reception when she's finished. She's obviously smart and popular and confident. Not the shy and retiring wallflower that is the lovely Miss Steele. It really amazes me that these two are friends.

I hear my name announced; the chancellor has introduced me. I rise and approach the lectern. *Showtime, Grey.*

"I'm profoundly grateful and touched by the great compliment accorded to me by the authorities of WSU today. It offers me a rare opportunity to talk about the impressive work of the environmental sciences department here at the university. Our aim is to develop viable and ecologically sustainable methods of farming for third world countries; our ultimate goal is to help eradicate hunger and poverty across the globe. Over a billion people, mainly in sub-Saharan Africa, South Asia, and Latin America, live in abject poverty. Agricultural dysfunction is rife within these parts of the world, and the result is ecological and social destruction. I have known what it's like to be profoundly hungry. This is a very personal journey for me.

"As partners, WSU and GEH have made tremendous progress in soil fertility and arable technology. We are pioneering low-input systems in developing countries, and our test sites have increased crop yields up to thirty percent per hectare. WSU has been instrumental in this fantastic achievement. And GEH is proud of those students who join us through internships to work at our test sites in Africa. The work they do there benefits the local communities and the students themselves. Together we can fight hunger and the abject poverty that blights these regions.

"But in this age of technological evolution, as the first world races ahead, widening the gap between the haves and the have-nots, it's vital to remember that we must not squander the world's finite resources. These resources are for all humanity, and we need to harness them, find ways of renewing them, and develop new solutions to feed our overpopulated planet.

"As I've said, the work that GEH and WSU are doing together will provide solutions, and it's our job to get the message out there. It's through GEH's telecommunications division that we intend to supply information and education to the developing world. I'm proud to say that we're making impressive progress in solar technology, battery life, and wireless distribution that will bring the Internet to the remotest parts of the world—and our goal is to make it free to users at the point of delivery. Access to education and information, which we take for granted here, is the crucial component for ending poverty in these developing regions.

"We're lucky. We're all privileged here. Some more than others, and I include myself in that category. We have a moral obligation to offer those less fortunate a decent life that's healthy, secure, and well nourished, with access to more of the resources that we all enjoy here.

"I'll leave you with a quote that has always resonated with me. And I'm paraphrasing a Native American saying: 'Only when the last leaf has fallen, the last tree has died, and the last fish been caught will we realize that we cannot eat money.' "

As I sit down to rousing applause, I resist looking at Ana and examine the WSU banner hanging at the back of the auditorium. If she wants to ignore me, fine. Two can play at that game.

The vice chancellor rises to commence handing out the degrees. And so begins the agonizing wait until we reach the S's and I can see her again.

After an eternity I hear her name called: "Anastasia Steele." A ripple of applause, and she's walking toward me looking pensive and worried.

Shit.

What is she thinking?

Hold it together, Grey.

"Congratulations, Miss Steele," I say as I give Ana her degree. We shake hands, but I don't let hers go. "Do you have a problem with your laptop?"

She looks perplexed. "No."

"Then you *are* ignoring my e-mails?" I release her.

"I only saw the mergers and acquisitions one."

What the hell does that mean?

Her frown deepens, but I have to let her go—there's a line forming behind her.

"Later." I let her know that we're not finished with this conversation as she moves on.

I'm in purgatory by the time we've reached the end of the line. I've been ogled, and had eyelashes batted at me, silly giggling girls squeezing my hand, and five notes with phone numbers pressed into my palm. I'm relieved as I exit the stage along with the faculty, to the strains of some dreary processional music and applause.

In the corridor I grab Kavanagh's arm. "I need to speak to Ana. Can you find her? Now."

Kavanagh is taken aback, but before she can say anything I add, in as polite a tone as I can manage, "Please."

Her lips thin with disapproval, but she waits with me as the academics file past and then she returns to the auditorium. The chancellor stops to congratulate me on my speech.

"It was an honor to be asked," I respond, shaking his hand once again. Out of the corner of my eye I spy Kate in the corridor—with Ana at her side. Excusing myself, I stride toward Ana.

"Thank you," I say to Kate, who gives Ana a worried glance. Ignoring her, I take Ana's elbow and lead her through the first door I find. It's a men's locker room, and from the fresh smell I can tell it's empty. Locking the door, I turn to face Miss Steele. "Why haven't you e-mailed me? Or texted me back?" I demand.

She blinks a couple of times, consternation writ large on her face. "I haven't looked at my computer today, or my phone." She seems genuinely bewildered by my outburst. "That was a great speech," she adds.

"Thank you," I mutter, derailed. How can she not have checked her phone or e-mail?

"Explains your food issues to me," she says, her tone gentle—and if I'm not mistaken, pitying, too.

"Anastasia, I don't want to go there at the moment."

I don't need your pity.

I close my eyes. All this time I thought she didn't want to talk to me. "I've been worried about you."

"Worried, why?"

"Because you went home in that deathtrap you call a car."

And I thought I'd blown the deal between us.

Ana bristles. "What? It's not a deathtrap. It's fine. José regularly services it for me."

"José, the photographer?" This just gets better and fucking better.

"Yes, the Beetle used to belong to his mother."

"Yes, and probably her mother and her mother before her. It's not safe." I'm almost shouting.

"I've been driving it for over three years. I'm sorry you were worried. Why didn't you call?"

I called her cell phone. Does she not use her damned cell phone? Is she talking about the house phone? Running my hand through my hair in exasperation, I take a deep breath. This is not addressing the fucking elephant in the room.

"Anastasia, I need an answer from you. This waiting around is driving me crazy."

Her face falls.

Shit.

"Christian, I . . . look, I've left my stepdad on his own."

"Tomorrow. I want an answer by tomorrow."

"Okay. Tomorrow, I'll tell you then," she says with an anxious look.

Well, it's still not a "no." And once more, I'm surprised by my relief.

What the hell is it about this woman? She stares up at me with sincere blue eyes, her face etched in concern, and I resist the urge to touch her. "Are you staying for drinks?" I ask.

"I don't know what Ray wants to do." She looks uncertain.

"Your stepfather? I'd like to meet him."

Her uncertainty magnifies. "I'm not sure that's a good idea," she says darkly, as I unlock the door.

What? Why? Is this because she now knows I was dirt-poor as a kid? Or because she knows how I like to fuck? That I'm a freak?

"Are you ashamed of me?"

"No!" she exclaims, and she rolls her eyes in frustration. "Introduce you to my dad as what?" She raises her hands in exasperation. " 'This is the man who deflowered me and wants us to start a BDSM relationship'? You're not wearing running shoes."

Running shoes?

Her dad is going to come after me? And just like that she has injected a little humor between us. My mouth twitches in response and she returns my smile, her face lighting up like a summer dawn.

"Just so you know, I can run quite fast," I respond playfully. "Just tell him I'm your friend, Anastasia." I open the door and follow her out but stop when I reach the chancellor and his colleagues. As one they turn and stare at Miss Steele, but she's disappearing into the auditorium. They turn back to me.

Miss Steele and I are none of your business, people.

I give the chancellor a brief, polite nod and he asks if I'll come and meet more of his colleagues and enjoy some canapés.

"Sure," I reply.

It takes me thirty minutes to escape from the faculty gathering, and as I make my way out of the crowded reception Kavanagh falls into step beside me. We head to the lawn where the graduates and their families are enjoying a post-graduation drink in a large tented pavilion.

"So have you asked Ana to dinner on Sunday?" she asks.

Sunday? Has Ana mentioned that we're seeing each other on Sunday?

"At your parents' house," Kavanagh explains.

My parents?

I spot Ana.

What the fuck?

A tall blond guy who looks as if he's walked off a beach in California has his hands all over her.

Who the hell is that? Is this why she didn't want me to come for a drink?

Ana looks up, catches my expression, and pales as her roommate stands beside that guy. "Hello, Ray," Kavanagh says, and she kisses a middle-aged man in an ill-fitting suit standing beside Ana.

This must be Raymond Steele.

"Have you met Ana's boyfriend?" Kavanagh asks him. "Christian Grey."

Boyfriend!

"Mr. Steele, it's a pleasure to meet you."

"Mr. Grey," he says, quietly surprised. We shake hands; his grip is firm, and his fingers and palm are rough to the touch. This man works with his hands. Then I remember—he's a carpenter. His dark brown eyes give nothing away.

"And this is my brother, Ethan Kavanagh," says Kate, introducing the beach bum who has his arm wrapped around Ana.

Ah. The Kavanagh offspring, together.

I mutter his name as we shake hands, noting that they are soft, unlike Ray Steele's.

Now stop pawing my girl, you fucker.

"Ana, baby," I whisper, holding out my hand, and like the good woman she is, she steps into my embrace. She's discarded her graduation robe and wears a pale gray halter-neck dress, exposing her flawless shoulders and back.

Two dresses in two days. She's spoiling me.

"Ethan, Mom and Dad wanted a word." Kavanagh hauls her brother away, leaving me with Ana and her father.

"So how long have you kids known each other?" Mr. Steele asks.

As I reach across to grasp Ana's shoulder I gently trace my

thumb across her naked back and she trembles in response. I tell
him we've known each other for a couple of weeks. "We met when
Anastasia came to interview me for the student newspaper."

"Didn't know you worked on the student newspaper, Ana," Mr.
Steele says.

"Kate was ill," she says.

Ray Steele eyes his daughter and frowns. "Fine speech you
gave, Mr. Grey," he says.

"Thank you, sir. I understand that you're a keen fisherman."

"Indeed I am. Annie tell you that?"

"She did."

"You fish?" There's a spark of curiosity in his brown eyes.

"Not as much as I'd like to. My dad used to take my brother
and me when we were kids. For him it was all about the steelheads.
Guess I caught the bug from him." Ana listens for a moment, then
excuses herself and moves off through the crowd to join the Kavanagh clan.

Damn, she looks sensational in that dress.

"Oh? Where d'you fish?" Ray Steele's question pulls me back
into the conversation. I know it's a test.

"All over the Pacific Northwest."

"You grew up in Washington?"

"Yes, sir. My dad started us on the Wynoochee River."

A smile tugs at Steele's mouth. "Know it well."

"But his favorite is the Skagit. The U.S. side. He'd get us out of
bed at some ungodly hour of the morning and we'd drive up there.
He's caught some mighty fine fish in that river."

"That's some sweet water. Caught me some rod breakers in the
Skagit. On the Canadian side, mind."

"It's one of the best stretches for wild steelheads. Give you a
much better chase than those that are clipped," I say, my eyes on
Ana.

"Couldn't agree more."

"My brother's caught a couple of wild monsters. Me, I'm still
waiting for the big one."

"One day, huh?"

"I hope so."

Ana is deep in a passionate discussion with Kavanagh. *What are those two women talking about?*

"You still get out much to fish?" I refocus on Mr. Steele.

"Sure do. Annie's friend José, his father, and I sneak out as often as we can."

The fucking photographer! Again?

"He's the guy that looks after the Beetle?"

"Yeah, that's him."

"Great car, the Beetle. I'm a fan of German-made cars."

"Yeah? Annie loves that old car, but I guess it's getting past its sell-by date."

"Funny you should mention that. I was thinking of loaning her one of my company cars. Do you think she'd go for it?"

"I guess. That would be up to Annie, mind."

"Great. I take it Ana's not into fishing."

"No. That girl takes after her mother. She couldn't stomach seeing the fish suffer. Or the worms, for that matter. She's a gentle soul." He gives me a pointed look. *Oh.* A warning from Raymond Steele. I turn it into a joke.

"No wonder she wasn't keen on the cod we ate the other day."

Steele chuckles. "She's fine with eating them."

Ana has finished talking to the Kavanaghs and is heading our way. "Hi," she says, beaming at us.

"Annie, where are the restrooms?" Steele asks.

She directs him to go outside the pavilion and to the left.

"See you in a moment. You kids enjoy yourselves," he says.

She watches him go, then peers nervously up at me. But before she or I can say anything we're interrupted by a photographer. She snaps a quick still of us together before hurrying away.

"So you've charmed my father as well?" Ana says, her voice sweet and teasing.

"As well?" *Have I charmed you, Miss Steele?*

With my fingers I trace the rosy flush that appears on her cheek.

"Oh, I wish I knew what you were thinking, Anastasia." When my fingers reach her chin I tilt her head back so I can scrutinize her expression. She stills and stares back at me, her pupils darkening.

"Right now," she whispers, "I'm thinking, nice tie."

I was expecting some kind of declaration; her response makes me laugh. "It's recently become my favorite."

She smiles.

"You look lovely, Anastasia. This halter-neck dress suits you, and I get to stroke your back, feel your beautiful skin."

Her lips part and her breath hitches, and I can feel the pull of the attraction between us.

"You know it's going to be good, don't you, baby?" My voice is low, betraying my longing.

She closes her eyes, swallows, and takes a deep breath. When she opens them again, she's radiating anxiety. "But I want more," she says.

"More?"

Fuck. What is this?

She nods.

"More?" I whisper again. Her lip is pliant beneath my thumb. "You want hearts and flowers." *Fuck.* It will never work with her. How can it? I don't do romance. My hopes and dreams begin to crumble between us.

Her eyes are wide, innocent, and beseeching.

Damn. She's so beguiling. "Anastasia. It's not something I know."

"Me, neither."

Of course; she's never had a relationship before. "You don't know much."

"You know all the wrong things," she breathes.

"Wrong? Not to me. Try it," I plead.

Please. Try it my way.

Her gaze is intense as she searches my face, looking for clues. And for a moment I'm lost in blue eyes that see everything.

"Okay," she whispers.

"What?" Every hair on my body stands to attention.

"Okay. I'll try."

"You're agreeing?" I don't believe it.

"Subject to the soft limits, yes. I'll try."

Sweet. Lord. I pull her into my arms and wrap her in my embrace, burying my face in her hair, inhaling her seductive scent. And I don't care that we're in a crowded space. It's just her and me. "Jesus, Ana, you're so unexpected. You take my breath away."

A moment later I'm aware that Raymond Steele has returned and is examining his watch to cover his embarrassment. Reluctantly, I release her. I'm on top of the world.

Deal done, Grey!

"Annie, should we get some lunch?" Steele asks.

"Okay," she says with a shy smile directed at me.

"Would you like to join us, Christian?" For a moment I'm tempted, but Ana's anxious glance in my direction says, *Please, no.* She wants alone time with her dad. I get it.

"Thank you, Mr. Steele, but I have plans. It's been great to meet you, sir."

Try and control your stupid grin, Grey.

"Likewise," Steele replies—sincerely, I think. "Look after my baby girl."

"Oh, I fully intend to," I respond, shaking his hand.

In ways that you can't possibly imagine, Mr. Steele.

I take Ana's hand and bring her knuckles to my lips. "Later, Miss Steele," I murmur. *You've made me a happy, happy man.*

Steele gives me a brief nod, and taking his daughter's elbow, leads her out of the reception. I stand dazed but brimming with hope.

She's agreed.

"Christian Grey?" My joy is interrupted by Eamon Kavanagh, Katherine's father.

"Eamon, how are you?" We shake hands.

TAYLOR COLLECTS ME AT 3:30. "Good afternoon, sir," he says, opening my car door.

En route he informs me that the Audi A3 has been delivered to The Heathman. Now I just have to give it to Ana. No doubt this will involve a discussion, and deep down I know it will be more than just a discussion. Then again, she's agreed to be my submissive, so maybe she'll accept my gift without any fuss.

Who are you kidding, Grey?

A man can dream. I hope we can meet this evening; I'll give it to her as her graduation present.

I call Andrea and tell her to put a WebEx breakfast meeting into my schedule tomorrow with Eamon Kavanagh and his associates in New York. Kavanagh is interested in upgrading his fiber-optic network. I ask Andrea to have Ros and Fred on standby for the meeting, too. She relays some messages—nothing important—and reminds me I have to attend a charity function tomorrow evening in Seattle.

Tonight will be my last night in Portland. It's almost Ana's last night here, too . . . I contemplate calling her, but there's little point since she doesn't have her cell phone. And she's enjoying time with her dad.

Staring out the car window as we drive toward The Heathman, I watch the good people of Portland go about their afternoon. At a stoplight there's a young couple arguing on the sidewalk over a spilled bag of groceries. Another couple, even younger, walks hand in hand past them, eyes locked and giggling. The girl leans up and whispers something in the ear of her tattooed beau. He laughs, leans down, and kisses her quickly, then opens the door to a coffee shop and steps aside to let her enter.

Ana wants "more." I sigh heavily and plow my fingers through my hair. They always want more. All of them. What can I do about that? The hand-in-hand couple strolling to the coffee shop—Ana and I did that. We've eaten together at two restaurants, and it was . . . fun. Perhaps I could try. After all, she's giving me so much. I loosen my tie.

Could I do more?

———————

BACK IN MY ROOM, I strip down, pull on my sweats, and head downstairs for a quick circuit in the gym. Enforced socializing has stretched the limits of my patience and I need to work off some excess energy.

And I need to think about *more*.

ONCE I'M SHOWERED AND dressed and back in front of my laptop, Ros calls via WebEx to check in and we talk for forty minutes. We cover all of the items on her agenda, including the Taiwan proposal and Darfur. The cost of the airdrop is staggering, but it's safer for all involved. I give her the go-ahead. Now we have to wait for the shipment to arrive in Rotterdam.

"I'm up to date on Kavanagh Media. I think Barney should be in on the meeting, too," Ros says.

"If you think so. Let Andrea know."

"Will do. How was the graduation ceremony?" she asks.

"Good. Unexpected."

Ana agreed to be mine.

"Unexpected good?"

"Yes."

From the screen Ros peers at me, intrigued, but I say nothing more.

"Andrea tells me you're back in Seattle tomorrow."

"Yes. I have a function to attend in the evening."

"Well, I hope your 'merger' has been successful."

"I would say affirmative at this point, Ros."

She smirks. "Glad to hear it. I have another meeting, so if there's nothing else, I'll say good-bye for now."

"Good-bye." I log out of WebEx and into e-mail, turning my attention to this evening.

From: Christian Grey
Subject: Soft Limits
Date: May 26 2011 17:22
To: Anastasia Steele

What can I say that I haven't already?
Happy to talk these through anytime.

You looked beautiful today.

Christian Grey
CEO, Grey Enterprises Holdings, Inc.

And to think this morning I was convinced it was all over between us.

Jesus, Grey. You need to get a grip. Flynn would have a field day.

Of course, part of the reason was she didn't have her phone. Perhaps she needs a more reliable form of communication.

From: Christian Grey
Subject: BlackBerry
Date: May 26 2011 17:36
To: J B Taylor
Cc: Andrea Ashton

Taylor
Please source a new BlackBerry for Anastasia Steele with
her e-mail preinstalled. Andrea can get the account details
from Barney and get them to you.
Please deliver it tomorrow either to her home or to Clayton's.

Christian Grey
CEO, Grey Enterprises Holdings, Inc.

Once that's sent, I pick up the latest *Forbes* and start to read.

By 6:30 there's no response from Ana, so I assume she's still entertaining the quiet and unassuming Ray Steele. Given that they aren't related, they're remarkably similar.

I order the seafood risotto from room service and while I wait I read more of my book.

GRACE CALLS WHILE I'M reading.

"Christian, darling."

"Hello, Mother."

"Did Mia get in touch?"

"Yes. I have her flight details. I'll pick her up."

"Great. Now, I hope you'll stay for dinner on Saturday."

"Sure."

"And then on Sunday Elliot is bringing his friend Kate to dinner. Would you like to come? You could bring Anastasia."

That's what Kavanagh was talking about today.

I play for time. "I'll have to see if she's free."

"Let me know. It will be lovely to have all the family together again."

I roll my eyes. "If you say so, Mother."

"I do, darling. See you Saturday."

She hangs up.

Take Ana to meet my parents? How the hell do I get out of that?

As I contemplate this predicament, an e-mail arrives.

From: Anastasia Steele
Subject: Soft Limits
Date: May 26 2011 19:23
To: Christian Grey

I can come over this evening to discuss if you'd like.

Ana

No, no baby. Not in that car. And my plans fall into place.

From: Christian Grey
Subject: Soft Limits
Date: May 26 2011 19:27
To: Anastasia Steele

I'll come to you. I meant it when I said I wasn't happy about
you driving that car.
I'll be with you shortly.

Christian Grey
CEO, Grey Enterprises Holdings, Inc.

I print out another copy of the "Soft Limits" from the contract
and her "Issues" e-mail because I've left my first copy in my jacket,
which she still has in her possession. Then I call Taylor in his room.

"I'm going to deliver the car to Anastasia. Can you pick me up
from her place—say, nine thirty?"

"Certainly, sir."

Before I leave I stuff two condoms into the back pocket of my
jeans.

I might get lucky.

THE A3 IS FUN to drive, though it's got less torque than I'm used
to. I pull up outside a liquor store on the outskirts of Portland to
buy some celebratory champagne. I forgo the Cristal and the Dom
Pérignon for a Bollinger, mostly because it's the 1999 vintage,
and chilled, but also because it's pink . . . symbolic, I think with a
smirk, as I hand my AmEx to the cashier.

Ana is still wearing the stunning gray dress when she opens the
door. I look forward to peeling it off her later.

"Hi," she says, her eyes large and luminous in her pale face.

"Hi."

"Come in." She seems shy and awkward. *Why? What's happened?*

"If I may." I hold up the bottle of champagne. "I thought we'd celebrate your graduation. Nothing beats a good Bollinger."

"Interesting choice of words." Her voice is sardonic.

"Oh, I like your ready wit, Anastasia." There she is . . . my girl.

"We only have teacups. We've packed all the glasses."

"Teacups? Sounds good to me."

I watch her wander into the kitchen. She's nervous and skittish. Perhaps because she's had a big day, or because she's agreed to my terms, or because she's here alone—I know Kavanagh is with her own family this evening; her father told me. I hope the champagne will help Ana relax . . . and talk.

The room is empty, except for packing crates, the sofa, and the table. There's a brown parcel on the table with a handwritten note attached.

> *"I agree to the conditions, Angel; because you know*
> *best what my punishment ought to be; only—only—*
> *don't make it more than I can bear!"*

"Do you want saucers as well?" she calls.

"Teacups will be fine, Anastasia," I respond, distracted. She's wrapped up the books—the first editions I sent her. She's giving them back to me. She doesn't want them. This is why she's nervous.

How the hell will she react to the car?

Looking up, I see her standing there, watching me. And carefully she places the cups on the table.

"That's for you." Her voice is small and strained.

"Hmm, I figured as much," I mutter. "Very apt quote." I trace her handwriting with my finger. The letters are small and neat, and I wonder what a graphologist would make of them. "I thought I was d'Urberville, not Angel. You decided on the debasement." Of course it's the perfect quote. My smile is ironic. "Trust you to find something that resonates so appropriately."

"It's also a plea," she whispers.

"A plea? For me to go easy on you?"

She nods.

To me these books were an investment, but for her I thought they'd mean something.

"I bought these for you." It's a small white lie—as I've replaced them. "I'll go easier on you if you accept them." I keep my voice calm and quiet, masking my disappointment.

"Christian, I can't accept them, they're just too much."

Here we go, another battle of wills.

Plus ça change, plus c'est la même chose.

"You see, this is what I was talking about, you defying me. I want you to have them, and that's the end of the discussion. It's very simple. You don't have to think about this. As a submissive you would just be grateful for them. You just accept what I buy you because it pleases me for you to do so."

"I wasn't a submissive when you bought them for me," she says quietly.

As ever, she has an answer for everything.

"No . . . but you've agreed, Anastasia."

Is she reneging on our deal? God, this girl has me on a roller coaster.

"So they are mine to do with as I wish?"

"Yes." *I thought you loved Hardy?*

"In that case, I'd like to give them to a charity—one working in Darfur, since that seems to be close to your heart. They can auction them."

"If that's what you want to do." I'm not going to stop you.

You can burn them, for all I care . . .

Her pale face colors. "I'll think about it," she mutters.

"Don't think, Anastasia. Not about this." Keep them, please. They're for you, because your passion is books. You've told me more than once. Enjoy them.

Placing the champagne on the table, I stand in front of her and cup her chin, tipping back her head so my eyes are on hers. "I will buy you lots of things, Anastasia. Get used to it. I can afford it. I'm a very wealthy man." I kiss her quickly. "Please," I add, and release her.

"It makes me feel cheap," she says.

"It shouldn't. You're overthinking it. Don't place some vague moral judgment on yourself based on what others might think. Don't waste your energy. It's only because you have reservations about our arrangement; that's perfectly natural. You don't know what you're getting yourself into."

Anxiety is etched all over her lovely face.

"Hey, stop this. There is nothing about you that is cheap, Anastasia. I won't have you thinking that. I just sent you some old books that I thought might mean something to you, that's all."

She blinks a couple of times and stares at the package, obviously conflicted.

Keep them, Ana—they're for you.

"Have some champagne," I whisper, and she rewards me with a small smile.

"That's better." I open the champagne and fill the dainty teacups she's placed in front of me.

"It's pink." She's surprised, and I haven't the heart to tell her why I chose pink.

"Bollinger La Grande Année Rosé 1999—an excellent vintage."

"In teacups." She grins. It's infectious.

"In teacups. Congratulations on your degree, Anastasia."

We touch cups, and I drink. It tastes good, as I knew it would.

"Thank you." She raises the cup to her lips and takes a quick sip. "Shall we go through the soft limits?"

"Always so eager." Taking her hand, I lead her to the sofa—one of the only remaining pieces of furniture in the living room—and we sit, surrounded by boxes.

"Your stepfather's a very taciturn man."

"You managed to get him eating out of your hand."

I chuckle. "Only because I know how to fish."

"How did you know he liked fishing?"

"You told me. When we went for coffee."

"Oh, did I?" She takes another sip and closes her eyes, savoring the taste. Opening them again, she asks, "Did you try the wine at the reception?"

"Yes. It was foul." I grimace.

"I thought of you when I tasted it. How did you get to be so knowledgeable about wine?"

"I'm not knowledgeable, Anastasia, I just know what I like." And I like you. "Some more?" I nod toward the bottle on the table.

"Please."

I fetch the champagne and refill her cup. She regards me suspiciously. She knows I'm plying her with alcohol.

"This place looks pretty bare. Are you ready for the move?" I ask, to distract her.

"More or less."

"Are you working tomorrow?"

"Yes, my last day at Clayton's."

"I'd help you move, but I promised to meet my sister at the airport. Mia arrives from Paris early on Saturday. I'm heading back to Seattle tomorrow, but I hear Elliot is giving you two a hand."

"Yes, Kate is very excited about that."

I'm surprised Elliot is still interested in Ana's friend; it's not his usual MO. "Yes, Kate and Elliot, who would have thought?" Their liaison makes matters complicated. My mother's voice rings in my head: *You could bring Anastasia.*

"So what are you doing about work in Seattle?" I ask.

"I have a couple of interviews for intern places."

"You were going to tell me this when?"

"Um . . . I'm telling you now," she says.

"Where?" I ask, hiding my frustration.

"A couple of publishing houses."

"Is that what you want to do, something in publishing?"

She nods, but she's still not forthcoming.

"Well?" I prompt.

"Well, what?"

"Don't be obtuse, Anastasia. Which publishing houses?" I mentally run through all the publishing houses I know of in Seattle. There are four . . . I think.

"Just small ones," she says evasively.

"Why don't you want me to know?"

"Undue influence," she says.

What does that mean? I frown.

"Oh, now *you're* being obtuse," she says, her eyes twinkling with mirth.

"Obtuse?" I laugh. "Me? God, you're challenging. Drink up, let's talk about these limits."

Her eyelashes flutter and she takes a shaky breath, then drains her cup. She's really nervous about this. I offer her more liquid courage.

"Please," she responds.

Bottle in hand, I pause. "Have you eaten anything?"

"Yes. I had a three-course meal with Ray," she says, exasperated, and rolls her eyes.

Oh, Ana. At last I can do something about this disrespectful habit.

Leaning forward, I take hold of her chin and glare at her. "Next time you roll your eyes at me, I will take you across my knee."

"Oh." She looks a little shocked, but a little intrigued, too.

"Oh. So it begins, Anastasia." With a wolfish grin I fill her teacup, and she takes a long sip.

"Got your attention now, haven't I?"

She nods.

"Answer me."

"Yes, you've got my attention," she says with a contrite smile.

"Good." I fish out her e-mail, and Appendix 3 of my contract, from my jacket. "So, sexual acts. We've done most of this." She shuffles closer to me and we read down the list.

APPENDIX 3
Soft Limits
To be discussed and agreed between both parties:
Does the Submissive consent to:

- Masturbation
- Cunnilingus
- Fellatio
- Swallowing Semen

- Vaginal intercourse
- Vaginal fisting
- Anal intercourse
- Anal fisting

"No fisting, you say. Anything else you object to?" I ask.

She swallows. "Anal intercourse doesn't exactly float my boat."

"I'll agree to the fisting, but I'd really like to claim your ass, Anastasia."

She inhales sharply, gazing at me.

"But we'll wait for that. Besides, it's not something we can dive into." I can't help my smirk. "Your ass will need training."

"Training?" Her eyes widen.

"Oh yes. It'll need careful preparation. Anal intercourse can be very pleasurable, trust me. But if we try it and you don't like it, we don't have to do it again." I delight in her shocked expression.

"Have you done that?" she asks.

"Yes."

"With a man?"

"No. I've never had sex with a man. Not my scene."

"Mrs. Robinson?"

"Yes." And her large rubber strap-on.

Ana frowns and I move on quickly, before she can ask me any more questions about that.

"And . . . swallowing semen. Well, you get an A in that." I expect a smile from her, but she's studying me intently, as if seeing me in a new light. I think she's still reeling over Mrs. Robinson and anal intercourse. *Oh, baby,* Elena had my submission. She could do with me as she pleased. And I enjoyed it.

"So, swallowing semen okay?" I ask, trying to bring her back to the now. She nods and finishes her champagne.

"More?" I ask.

Steady, Grey, you just want her tipsy, not drunk.

"More," she whispers.

I refill her cup and get back to the list. "Sex toys?"

Does the Submissive consent to the use of:

- Vibrators
- Butt plugs

- Dildos
- Other vaginal/anal toys

"Butt plug? Does it do what it says on the box?" She grimaces.

"Yes. And I refer to anal intercourse above. Training."

"Oh. What's in 'other'?"

"Beads, eggs, that sort of stuff."

"Eggs?" Her hands shoot to her mouth in shock.

"Not real eggs." I laugh.

"I'm glad you find me funny." The hurt in her voice is sobering.

"I apologize. I'm sorry."

For fuck's sake, Grey. Go easy on her.

"Any problem with toys?"

"No," she snaps.

Shit. She's sulking.

"Anastasia, I am sorry. Believe me. I don't mean to laugh. I've never had this conversation in so much detail. You're just so inexperienced. I'm sorry."

She pouts and takes another sip of champagne.

"Right—bondage," I say, and we return to the list.

Does the Submissive consent to:

- Bondage with rope
- Bondage with leather cuffs
- Bondage with handcuffs/
   shackles/manacles

- Bondage with tape
- Bondage with other

"Well?" I ask, gently this time.
"Fine," she whispers and continues reading.

Does the Submissive consent to be restrained with:

- Hands bound in front
- Ankles bound
- Elbows bound
- Hands bound behind back
- Knees bound

- Wrists bound to ankles
- Binding to fixed items,
   furniture, etc.
- Binding with spreader bar
- Suspension

Does the Submissive consent to be blindfolded?
Does the Submissive consent to be gagged?

"We've talked about suspension. And it's fine if you want to set that up as a hard limit. It takes a great deal of time, and I only have you for short periods anyway. Anything else?"

"Don't laugh at me, but what's a spreader bar?"

"I promise not to laugh. I've apologized twice." *For Christ's sake.* "Don't make me do it again." My voice is sharper than I intended, and she leans away from me.

Shit.

Ignore her reaction, Grey. Get on with it. "A spreader is a bar with cuffs for ankles and/or wrists. They're fun."

"Okay. Well, gagging me. I'd be worried I wouldn't be able to breathe."

"*I'd* be worried if you couldn't breathe. I don't want to suffocate you." Breath play is not my scene at all.

"And how will I use safe words if I'm gagged?" she inquires.

"First of all, I hope you never have to use them. But if you're gagged, we'll use hand signals."

"I'm nervous about the gagging."

"Okay. I'll take note."

She studies me for a moment as if she's solved the riddle of the sphinx. "Do you like tying your submissives up so they can't touch you?" she asks.

"That's one of the reasons."

"Is that why you've tied my hands?"

"Yes."

"You don't like talking about that," she says.

"No, I don't."

I'm not going there with you, Ana. Give it up.

"Would you like another drink?" I ask. "It's making you brave, and I need to know how you feel about pain." I refill her cup and she takes a sip, wide-eyed and anxious. "So, what's your general attitude to receiving pain?"

She remains mute.

I suppress a sigh. "You're biting your lip." Fortunately, she stops, but now she's pensive and staring down at her hands.

"Were you physically punished as a child?" I prompt her gently.

"No."

"So you have no sphere of reference at all?"

"No."

"It's not as bad as you think. Your imagination is your worst enemy in this." *Trust me on this, Ana. Please.*

"Do you have to do it?"

"Yes."

"Why?"

You really don't want to know.

"Goes with the territory, Anastasia. It's what I do. I can see you're nervous. Let's go through methods."

We read through the list:

• Spanking	• Paddling
• Whipping	• Caning
• Biting	• Nipple clamps
• Genital clamps	• Ice
• Hot wax	• Other types/methods of pain

"Well, you said no to genital clamps. That's fine. It's caning that hurts the most."

Ana pales.

"We can work up to that," I state quickly.

"Or not do it at all," she counters.

"This is part of the deal, baby, but we'll work up to all of this. Anastasia, I won't push you too far."

"This punishment thing, it worries me the most."

"Well, I'm glad you've told me. We'll keep caning off the list for now. And as you get more comfortable with everything else, we'll increase intensity. We'll take it slow."

She looks uncertain, so I lean forward and kiss her. "There, that wasn't so bad, was it?"

She shrugs, still doubtful.

"Look, I want to talk about one more thing, then I'm taking you to bed."

"Bed?" she exclaims and color flushes her cheeks.

"Come on, Anastasia, talking through all this, I want to fuck you into next week, right now. It must be having some effect on you, too."

She squirms beside me and takes a husky breath, her thighs pressing together.

"See? Besides, there's something I want to try."

"Something painful?"

"No—stop seeing pain everywhere. It's mainly pleasure. Have I hurt you yet?"

"No."

"Well, then. Look, earlier today you were talking about wanting more." I stop.

Fuck. I'm on a precipice.

Okay, Grey, are you sure about this?

I have to try. I don't want to lose her before we start.

Jump.

I take her hand. "Outside of the time you're my sub, perhaps we could try. I don't know if it will work. I don't know about separating everything. It may not work. But I'm willing to try. Maybe one night a week. I don't know."

Her mouth drops open.

"I have one condition."

"What?" she asks, her breath hitching.

"You graciously accept my graduation present to you."

"Oh," she says, her eyes widening with uncertainty.

"Come." I pull her to her feet, slip off my leather jacket, and drape it over her shoulders. Taking a deep breath, I open the front door and reveal the Audi A3 parked at the curb. "It's for you. Happy graduation." I wrap my arms around her and kiss her hair.

When I release her she stares dumbfounded at the car.

Okay . . . this could go either way.

Taking her hand, I lead her down the steps and she follows as if in a trance.

"Anastasia, that Beetle of yours is old and, frankly, dangerous. I would never forgive myself if something happened to you when it's so easy for me to make it right."

She gapes at the car, speechless.

Shit.

"I mentioned it to your stepfather. He was all for it."

Perhaps I'm overstating this.

Her mouth is still open in dismay when she turns to glare at me.

"You mentioned this to Ray? How *could* you?" She's annoyed, really annoyed.

"It's a gift, Anastasia. Can't you just say thank you?"

"But you know it's too much."

"Not to me it isn't, not for my peace of mind."

Come on, Ana. You want more. This is the price.

Her shoulders sag, and she turns to me, resigned, I think. Not quite the reaction I was hoping for. The rosy glow from the champagne has disappeared and her face is pale once more. "I'm happy for you to loan this to me, like the laptop."

I shake my head. Why is she so difficult? I've never had this reaction to a car from any of my submissives. They're usually delighted.

"Okay. On loan. Indefinitely," I agree through gritted teeth.

"No, not indefinitely, but for now. Thank you," she says quietly, and leaning up, she kisses me on the cheek. "Thank you for the car, Sir."

That word. From her sweet, sweet mouth. I grab her and press her body to mine, her hair pooling in my fingers. "You are one challenging woman, Ana Steele." I kiss her forcefully, coaxing her lips apart with my tongue, and a moment later she's responding, matching my ardor, her tongue caressing mine. My body reacts—I want her. Here. Now. In the open. "It's taking all my self-control not to fuck you on the hood of this car right now, just to show you that you are mine, and if I want to buy you a fucking car, I'll buy you a fucking car. Now let's get you inside and naked," I growl. Then I kiss her once more, demanding and possessive. Taking her hand, I stride back into the apartment, slamming the front door behind us and heading straight for her bedroom. There I release her and switch on her bedside light.

"Please don't be angry with me," she whispers.

Her words douse the fire of my anger.

"I'm sorry about the car and the books—" She halts and licks her lips. "You scare me when you're angry."

Shit. No one has ever said that to me before. I close my eyes. The last thing I want to do is frighten her.

Calm down, Grey.

She's here. She's safe. She's willing. Don't blow it, just because she doesn't understand how to behave.

Opening my eyes, I find Ana watching me, not in fear, but with anticipation.

"Turn around," I demand, my voice soft. "I want to get you out of that dress."

She obeys immediately.

Good girl.

I remove my jacket from her shoulders and discard it on the floor, then lift her hair off her neck. The feel of her soft skin beneath my index finger is soothing. Now that she's doing what she's told, I relax. With the tip of my finger I follow the line of her spine down her back to the start of the zipper bound in gray chiffon. "I like this dress. I like to see your flawless skin."

Hooking my finger into the back of her dress, I pull her close so she's flush against me. I bury my face in her hair and breathe in her scent.

"You smell so good, Anastasia. So sweet."

Like fall.

Her fragrance is comforting, reminding me of a time of plenty and happiness. Still inhaling her delicious scent, I skim my nose from her ear down her neck to her shoulder, kissing her as I go. Slowly I unzip her dress and kiss, and lick, and suck my way across her skin to her other shoulder.

She shivers beneath my touch.

Oh, baby. "You are going to have to learn to keep still," I whisper between kisses, and unfasten her halter neck. The dress falls to her feet.

"No bra, Miss Steele. I like that."

Reaching forward, I cup her breasts and feel her nipples pebble against my palm.

"Lift your arms and put them around my head," I order, my lips brushing her neck. She does as she's told and her breasts lift farther into my palms. She twists her fingers into my hair, the way I like, and she tugs.

Ah . . . That feels so good.

Her head lolls to the side, and I take advantage, kissing her where her pulse hammers beneath her skin.

"Mmm . . ." I murmur in appreciation, my fingers teasing and tugging at her nipples.

She groans, arching her back, pushing her perfect tits even farther into my hands. "Shall I make you come this way?"

Her body bows a little more.

"You like this, don't you, Miss Steele?"

"Mmm . . ."

"Tell me," I insist, continuing my sensual assault on her nipples.

"Yes," she breathes.

"Yes, what?"

"Yes . . . Sir."

"Good girl."

Gently I pinch and twist with my fingers and her body bucks convulsively against me while she moans, her hands tugging harder at my hair.

"I don't think you're ready to come yet." And I still my hands, just holding her breasts, while my teeth tug at her earlobe. "Besides, you have displeased me. So perhaps I won't let you come after all."

I knead her breasts and my fingers return my attention to her nipples, twisting and tugging. She groans and grinds her ass against my erection. Shifting my hands to her hips, I hold her steady and glance down at her panties.

Cotton. White. Easy.

I hook my fingers into them and stretch them as far as they'll go, then push my thumbs through the seam at the back. They tear apart in my hands and I throw them at Ana's feet.

She gasps.

I trace my fingers around her ass and insert one into her vagina. She's wet. Very wet.

"Oh yes. My sweet girl is ready."

I spin her around and slip my finger into my mouth.

Mmm. Salty. "You taste so fine, Miss Steele."

Her lips part and her eyes darken with want. I think she's a little shocked.

"Undress me." I keep my eyes on hers. She tilts her head, processing my command, but hesitates. "You can do it," I encourage her. She lifts her hands and all of a sudden I think she's going to touch me, and I'm not ready. *Shit.*

Instinctively I grab her hands.

"Oh no. Not the T-shirt."

I want her on top. We've not done this yet, and she may lose her balance, so I'll need the T-shirt for protection. "You may need to touch me for what I have planned." I release one of her hands, but the other I place over my erection, which is fighting for space in my jeans.

"This is the effect you have on me, Miss Steele."

She inhales, gazing at her hand. Then her fingers tighten around my cock and she glances up at me with appreciation.

I grin. "I want to be inside you. Take my jeans off. You're in charge."

Her mouth drops open.

"What are you going to do with me?" My voice is husky.

Her face transforms, bright with delight, and before I can react she pushes me. I laugh as I fall onto the bed, mainly at her bravado, but also because she touched me and I didn't panic. She removes my shoes, then my socks, but she's all fingers and thumbs, reminding me of the interview and her attempts to set up the recorder.

I watch her. Amused. Aroused. Wondering what she'll do next. It's going to be one hell of a task for her to remove my jeans while I'm lying down. Stepping out of her pumps, she crawls up the bed, sits astride the top of my thighs, and slips her fingers beneath the waistband of my jeans.

I close my eyes and flex my hips, enjoying shameless Ana.

"You'll have to learn to keep still," she castigates me, and tugs at my pubic hair.

Ah! *So bold, ma'am.*

"Yes, Miss Steele," I tease through clenched teeth. "In my pocket, condom."

Her eyes flash with obvious delight and her fingers rifle through my pocket, diving deep, brushing my erection.

Ah . . .

She produces both foil packets and tosses them onto the bed beside me. Her fumbling fingers reach for the button on my waistband, and after two attempts she undoes it.

Her naïveté is captivating. It's obvious that she's never done this before. Another first . . . and it's fucking arousing.

"So eager, Miss Steele," I tease.

She yanks down my zipper and, pulling at my waistband, gives me a look of frustration.

I try hard not to laugh.

Yeah, baby, how are you going to get these off me now?

Shuffling down my legs, she tugs at my jeans, concentrating hard, looking adorable. And I decide to help her out. "I can't keep still if you're going to bite that lip," I say while arching my hips, lifting them off the bed.

Rising up on her knees, she pulls down my jeans and boxers and I kick them off, onto the floor. She sits across me, eyeing my cock and licking her lips.

Whoa.

She looks hot, her dark hair falling in soft waves around her breasts.

"Now what are you going to do?" I whisper. Her eyes flick to my face and she reaches up and grasps me firmly, squeezing hard, her thumb brushing over the tip.

Jesus.

She leans down.

And I'm in her mouth.

Fuck.

She sucks hard. And my body flexes beneath her. "Jeez, Ana, steady," I hiss through my teeth. But she shows no mercy as she fellates me again and again. *Fuck.* Her enthusiasm is disarming. Her tongue is up and down, I'm in and out of her mouth to the back of her throat, her lips tight around me. It's an overwhelming erotic vision. I could come just watching her.

"Stop, Ana, stop. I don't want to come."

She sits up, her mouth moist and her eyes two dark pools directed down at me.

"Your innocence and enthusiasm are very disarming." *But right now I want to fuck you so I can see you.* "You, on top, that's what we need to do. Here, put this on." I place a condom in her hand. She examines it with consternation, then rips the packet open with her teeth.

She's keen.

She removes the condom and looks to me for direction.

"Pinch the top and then roll it down. You don't want any air in the end of that sucker."

She nods and does exactly that, absorbed in her task, concentrating hard, her tongue peeking between her lips.

"Christ, you're killing me here," I exclaim through clenched teeth.

When she's done she sits back and admires her handiwork, or me—I'm not quite sure, but I don't care. "Now. I want to be buried inside you." I sit up suddenly so we're face-to-face, surprising her. "Like this," I whisper, and, wrapping my arm around her, I lift her. With my other hand I position my cock and lower her slowly onto me.

My breath escapes from my body as her eyes close and pleasure thrums noisily in her throat.

"That's right, baby, feel me, all of me."

She. Feels. So. Good.

I hold her, letting her get used to the feel of me. Like this. Inside her. "It's deep this way." My voice is hoarse, as I flex and tilt my pelvis, pushing deeper into her.

Her head lolls as she moans. "Again," she breathes. And she opens her eyes and they blaze into mine. Wanton. Willing. I love that she loves this. I do as I'm asked and she moans again, throwing back her head, her hair tumbling in a riot over her shoulders. Slowly I recline onto the bed to watch the show.

"You move, Anastasia, up and down, how you want. Take my hands." I hold them out and she grabs them, steadying herself on top of me. Slowly she eases herself up, then sinks back down onto me.

My breath is coming in short, sharp pants as I restrain myself. She lifts herself again and this time I raise my hips to meet her as she comes down.

Oh yes.

Closing my eyes, I savor every delicious inch of her. Together we find our rhythm as she rides me. Over and over and over. She looks fantastic: her breasts bouncing, her hair swinging, her mouth slack as she absorbs each stab of pleasure.

Her eyes meet mine, full of carnal need and wonder. God, she's beautiful.

She cries out as her body takes over. She's almost there, so I tighten my grip on her hands, and she ignites around me. I grab her hips, holding her as she shouts incoherently through her orgasm. Then I tighten my hold on her hips and silently lose myself as I explode inside her.

She flops down onto my chest, and I lie, panting, beneath her.

My God, she's a good fuck.

We lie together for a moment, her weight a comfort. She stirs and nuzzles me through my shirt, then splays her hand on top of my chest.

The darkness slithers, quick and strong, into my chest, into my throat, threatening to suffocate and choke me.

No. Don't touch me.

I grab her hand and bring her knuckles to my lips, and roll over on top of her so she's no longer able to touch me.

"Don't," I plead, and kiss her lips as I dampen down my fear.

"Why don't you like to be touched?"

"Because I'm fifty shades of fucked up, Anastasia." After years and years of therapy, it's the one thing I know to be true.

Her eyes widen, inquisitive; she's thirsty for more information. But she doesn't need to know this shit. "I had a very tough introduction to life. I don't want to burden you with the details. Just don't." I gently brush my nose against hers and, withdrawing from her, I sit up and remove the condom and drop it by the bed. "I think that's all the very basics covered. How was that?"

For a moment she seems distracted, then she tilts her head to one side and smiles. "If you imagine for one minute that I think you ceded control to me, well, you haven't taken into account my GPA. But thank you for the illusion."

"Miss Steele, you are not just a pretty face. You've had six orgasms so far and all of them belong to me." Why does that mere fact make me glad?

Her eyes stray to the ceiling, and a fleeting guilty expression crosses her face.

What's this? "Do you have something to tell me?" I ask.

She hesitates. "I had a dream this morning."

"Oh?"

"I came in my sleep." She flings her arm over her face, hiding from me, embarrassed. I'm stunned by her confession but aroused and delighted, too.

Sensual creature.

She peeks over her arm. Does she expect me to be angry?

"In your sleep?" I clarify.

"Woke me up," she whispers.

"I'm sure it did." I'm fascinated. "What were you dreaming about?"

"You," she says in a small voice.

Me!

"What was I doing?"

She hides beneath her arm again.

"Anastasia, what was I doing? I won't ask you again." Why is she so embarrassed? Her dreaming about me is . . . endearing.

"You had a riding crop," she mumbles. I move her arm so I can see her face.

"Really?"

"Yes." Her face is bright red. The research must be affecting her, in a good way. I smile down at her.

"There's hope for you yet. I have several riding crops."

"Brown plaited leather?" Her voice is tinged with quiet optimism.

I laugh. "No, but I'm sure I could get one."

I give her a swift kiss and stand to dress. Ana does the same, pulling on sweatpants and a camisole. Collecting the condom off the floor, I knot it quickly. Now that she's agreed to be mine, she needs contraception. Fully dressed, she sits cross-legged on the bed watching me as I grab my pants. "When is your period due?" I ask. "I hate wearing these things." I hold up the knotted condom and pull on my jeans.

She's taken aback.

"Well?" I prod.

"Next week," she answers, her cheeks pink.

"You need to sort out some contraception."

I sit on the bed to slip on my socks and shoes. She says nothing.

"Do you have a doctor?" I ask. She shakes her head. "I can have mine come and see you at your apartment—Sunday morning, before you come and see me. Or he can see you at my place. Which would you prefer?"

I'm sure Dr. Baxter will make a house call for me, although I haven't seen him for a while.

"Your place," she says.

"Okay. I'll let you know the time."

"Are you leaving?"

She seems surprised that I'm going. "Yes."

"How are you getting back?" she asks.

"Taylor will pick me up."

"I can drive you. I have a lovely new car."

That's better. She's accepted the car as she should, but after all that champagne she shouldn't be driving. "I think you've had too much to drink."

"Did you get me tipsy on purpose?"

"Yes."

"Why?"

"Because you overthink everything, and you're reticent, like your stepdad. A drop of wine in you and you start talking, and I need you to communicate honestly with me. Otherwise you clam up, and I have no idea what you're thinking. In vino veritas, Anastasia."

"And you think you're always honest with me?"

"I endeavor to be. This will only work if we're honest with each other."

"I'd like you to stay and use this." She grabs the other condom and waves it at me.

Manage her expectations, Grey.

"I have crossed so many lines here tonight. I have to go. I'll see you on Sunday." I stand up. "I'll have the revised contract ready for you, and then we can really start to play."

"Play?" she squeaks.

"I'd like to do a scene with you. But I won't until you've signed, so I know you're ready."

"Oh. So I could stretch this out if I don't sign?"

Shit. I hadn't thought of that.

Her chin tilts up in defiance.

Ah . . . topping from the bottom, again. She always finds a way.

"Well, I suppose you could, but I may crack under the strain."

"Crack? How?" she queries, her eyes alive with curiosity.

"Could get really ugly," I tease, narrowing my eyes.

"Ugly, how?" Her grin matches mine.

"Oh, you know, explosions, car chases, kidnapping, incarceration."

"You'd kidnap me?"

"Oh yes."

"Hold me against my will?"

"Oh yes." *Now, that's an interesting idea.* "And then we're talking TPE twenty-four-seven."

"You've lost me," she says, perplexed and a little breathless.

"Total Power Exchange—around the clock." My mind whirls as I think of the possibilities. She's curious. "So you have no choice," I add, with a playful tone.

"Clearly." Her tone is sarcastic and she rolls her eyes to the heavens, perhaps looking for divine inspiration to understand my sense of humor.

Oh, sweet joy.

"Anastasia Steele, did you just roll your eyes at me?"

"No!"

"I think you did. What did I say I'd do to you if you rolled your eyes at me again?" My words hang between us and I sit down again on the bed. "Come here."

For a moment she stares at me, blanching. "I haven't signed," she whispers.

"I told you what I'd do. I'm a man of my word. I'm going to spank you, and then I'm going to fuck you very quick and very hard. Looks like we'll need that condom after all."

Will she? Won't she? This is it. Proof of whether she can do this or not. I watch her, impassive, waiting for her to decide. If she says no, it means she's paying lip service to the idea of being my submissive.

And that will be it.

Make the right choice, Ana.

Her expression is grave, her eyes wide, and I think she's weighing up her decision.

"I'm waiting," I murmur. "I'm not a patient man."

Taking a deep breath, she unfurls her legs and crawls toward me, and I hide my relief.

"Good girl. Now stand up."

She does as she's told, and I offer her my hand. She lays the condom on my palm, and I grasp her hand and abruptly pull her over my left knee, so that her head, shoulders, and chest are resting on the bed. I drape my right leg over her legs, holding her in place. I've wanted to do this since she asked me if I was gay. "Put your hands up on either side of your head," I order and she complies immediately. "Why am I doing this, Anastasia?"

"Because I rolled my eyes at you," she says in a hoarse whisper.

"Do you think that's polite?"

"No."

"Will you do it again?"

"No."

"I will spank you each time you do it, do you understand?"

I'm going to savor this moment. It's another first.

With great care—relishing the deed—I tug down her sweat-pants. Her beautiful behind is naked and ready for me. As I place my hand on her backside, she tenses every muscle in her body . . . waiting. Her skin is soft to the touch and I sweep my palm across both cheeks, fondling each. She has a fine, fine ass. And I'm going to make it pink . . . like the champagne.

Lifting my palm, I smack her, hard, just above the junction of her thighs.

She gasps and tries to rise, but I hold her down with my other hand at the small of her back, and I soothe the area I've just hit with a slow, gentle caress.

She stays still.

Panting.

Anticipating.

Yes. I'm going to do that again.

I smack her once, twice, three times.

She grimaces at the pain, her eyes screwed shut. But she doesn't ask me to stop even though she's squirming beneath me.

"Keep still, or I'll spank you for longer," I warn.

I rub her sweet flesh and start again, taking turns: left cheek, right cheek, middle.

She cries out. But she doesn't move her arms, and she still doesn't ask me to stop.

"I'm just getting warmed up." My voice is husky. I smack her again, and trace the pink handprint I've left on her skin. Her ass is pinking up nicely. It looks glorious.

I smack her once more.

And she cries out again.

"No one to hear you, baby, just me."

I spank her over and over—the same pattern, left cheek, right cheek, middle—and she yelps each time. When I reach eighteen I stop. I'm breathless, my palm is stinging, and my cock is rigid.

"Enough," I rasp, trying to catch my breath. "Well done, Anastasia. Now I'm going to fuck you."

I stroke her pink behind gently, round and round, moving down. She's wet.

And my body gets harder.

I insert two fingers into her vagina.

"Feel this. See how much your body likes this. You're soaking, just for me." I slide my fingers in and out, and she groans, her body curling around them with each push and her breathing accelerating.

I withdraw them.

I want her. Now.

"Next time, I will get you to count. Now, where's that condom?" Grabbing it from beside her head, I ease her gently off my lap and onto the bed, facedown. Unzipping my fly, I don't bother to remove my jeans, and I make short work of the foil packet, rolling the condom on quickly and efficiently. I lift her hips until she's kneeling and her ass in all its rosy glory is poised in the air as I stand behind her.

"I'm going to take you now. You can come," I growl, caressing her behind and grabbing my cock. With one swift thrust I'm inside her.

She moans as I move. In. Out. In. Out. I pound into her, watching my cock disappear beneath her pink backside.

Her mouth is open wide and she grunts and groans with each thrust, her cries getting higher and higher.

Come on, Ana.

She clenches around me and cries out as she comes, hard.

"Oh, Ana!" I follow her over the edge as I climax into her and lose all time and perspective.

I collapse at her side, pull her on top of me, and, wrapping my arms around her, I whisper into her hair, "Oh, baby, welcome to my world."

Her weight anchors me, and she makes no attempt to touch my chest. Her eyes are closed and her breathing is returning to normal. I stroke her hair. It's soft, a rich mahogany, shining in the glow of her bedside light. She smells of Ana and apples and sex. It's heady. "Well done, baby."

She's not in tears. She did as she was asked. She's faced every challenge I've thrown at her; she really is quite remarkable. I finger the thin strap of her cheap cotton camisole. "Is this what you sleep in?"

"Yes." She sounds drowsy.

"You should be in silks and satins, you beautiful girl. I'll take you shopping."

"I like my sweats," she argues.

Of course she does.

I kiss her hair. "We'll see."

Closing my eyes, I relax in our quiet moment, a strange contentment warming me, filling me up inside.

This feels right. *Too right.*

"I have to go," I murmur, and kiss her forehead. "Are you okay?"

"I'm okay," she says, sounding a little subdued.

Gently I roll out from underneath her and get up. "Where's your bathroom?" I ask, taking off the used condom and zipping up my jeans.

"Down the hall to the left."

In the bathroom I discard the condoms in a trash bin and spy a bottle of baby oil on the shelf.

That's what I need.

She's dressed when I return, evading my gaze. *Why so shy suddenly?*

"I found some baby oil. Let me rub it into your behind."

"No. I'll be fine," she says, examining her fingers, still avoiding eye contact.

"Anastasia," I warn her.

Please just do as you're told.

I sit down behind her and tug down her sweatpants. Squirting some baby oil on my hand, I rub it tenderly into her sore ass.

She puts her hands on her hips in an obstinate stance, but stays silent.

"I like my hands on you," I admit out loud to myself. "There." I pull her sweatpants up. "I'm leaving now."

"I'll see you out," she says quietly, standing aside. I take her hand and reluctantly let go when we reach the front door. Part of me doesn't want to leave.

"Don't you have to call Taylor?" she asks, her eyes fixed on the zipper of my leather jacket.

"Taylor's been here since nine. Look at me."

Large blue eyes peek up at me through long, dark lashes.

"You didn't cry." My voice is low.

And you let me spank you. You're amazing.

I grab her and kiss her, pouring my gratitude into the kiss and holding her close. "Sunday," I whisper, fevered, against her lips. I release her abruptly before I'm tempted to ask her if I can stay, and I head out to where Taylor is waiting in the SUV. Once I'm in the car I look back, but she's gone. She's probably tired . . . like me.

Pleasantly tired.

That has to have been the most pleasurable "soft limits" conversation I've ever had.

Damn, that woman is unexpected. Closing my eyes, I see her riding me, her head tipped back in ecstasy. Ana does not do things halfheartedly. She commits. And to think she had sex for the first time only a week ago.

With me. And no one else.

I grin as I stare out the car window, but all I see is my ghostly face reflected in the glass. So I close my eyes and allow myself to daydream.

Training her will be fun.

TAYLOR WAKES ME FROM my doze. "We're here, Mr. Grey."

"Thank you," I mumble. "I have a meeting in the morning."

"At the hotel?"

"Yes. Videoconference. I won't need to be driven anywhere. But I'd like to leave before lunch."

"What time would you like me to pack?"

"Ten thirty."

"Very good, sir. The BlackBerry you asked for will be delivered to Miss Steele tomorrow."

"Good. That reminds me. Can you collect her old Beetle tomorrow and dispose of it? I don't want her driving it."

"Of course. I have a friend who restores vintage cars. He might be interested. I'll deal with it. Will there be anything else?"

"No thank you. Good night."

"Good night."

I leave Taylor to park the SUV and make my way up to my suite.

Opening a bottle of sparkling water from the fridge, I sit down at the desk and switch on my laptop.

No urgent e-mails.

But my real purpose is to say good night to Ana.

From: Christian Grey
Subject: You
Date: May 26 2011 23:14
To: Anastasia Steele

Dear Miss Steele,
You are quite simply exquisite. The most beautiful, intelligent, witty, and brave woman I have ever met. Take some Advil— this is not a request. And don't drive your Beetle again. I will know.

Christian Grey
CEO, Grey Enterprises Holdings, Inc.

She'll probably be asleep, but I keep my laptop open just in case and check e-mail. A few minutes later her response arrives.

From: Anastasia Steele
Subject: Flattery
Date: May 26 2011 23:20
To: Christian Grey

Dear Mr. Grey,
Flattery will get you nowhere, but since you've been *everywhere,* the point is moot.

I will need to drive my Beetle to a garage so I can sell it—so will not graciously accept any of your nonsense over that. Red wine is always more preferable to Advil.

Ana

P.S.: Caning is a HARD limit for me.

Her opening line makes me laugh out loud. *Oh, baby, I have not been everywhere I want to go with you.* Red wine on top of champagne? Not a clever mix, and caning is off the list. I wonder what else she'll object to as I compose my reply.

From: Christian Grey
Subject: Frustrating Women Who Can't Take Compliments
Date: May 26 2011 23:26
To: Anastasia Steele

Dear Miss Steele,
I am not flattering you. You should go to bed.

I accept your addition to the hard limits.

Don't drink too much.

Taylor will dispose of your car and get a good price for it, too.

Christian Grey
CEO, Grey Enterprises Holdings, Inc.

I hope she's in bed now.

From: Anastasia Steele
Subject: Taylor—Is He the Right Man for the Job?
Date: May 26 2011 23:40
To: Christian Grey

Dear Sir,
I am intrigued that you are happy to risk letting your right-hand man drive my car but not some woman you fuck occasionally. How can I be sure that Taylor is the man to get me the best deal for said car? I have, in the past, probably before I met you, been known to drive a hard bargain.

Ana

What the hell? Some woman I fuck occasionally?
I have to take a deep breath. Her response irks me . . . no, infuriates me. How *dare* she talk about herself like that? As my submissive she'll be so much more than that. I'll be devoted to her. Does she not realize this?

And she has driven a hard bargain with me. *Good God!* Look at all the concessions I've made with regard to the contract.

I count to ten, and to calm down, I visualize myself aboard *The Grace*, my catamaran, sailing on the Sound.

Flynn would be proud.
I respond.

From: Christian Grey
Subject: Careful!
Date: May 26 2011 23:44
To: Anastasia Steele

Dear Miss Steele,
I am assuming it is the RED WINE talking, and that you've
had a very long day.

Though I am tempted to drive back over there to ensure that
you don't sit down for a week, rather than an evening.

Taylor is ex-army and capable of driving anything from a
motorcycle to a Sherman tank. Your car does not present a
hazard to him.

Now please do not refer to yourself as "some woman I fuck
occasionally" because, quite frankly, it makes me MAD, and
you really wouldn't like me when I'm angry.

Christian Grey
CEO, Grey Enterprises Holdings, Inc.

I exhale slowly, steadying my heart rate. Who else on earth has
the ability to get under my skin like this?

She doesn't write back immediately. Perhaps she's intimidated
by my response. I pick up my book, but soon find that I've read the
same paragraph three times while awaiting her reply. I look up for
the umpteenth time.

From: Anastasia Steele
Subject: Careful Yourself
Date: May 26 2011 23:57
To: Christian Grey

Dear Mr. Grey,
I'm not sure I like you anyway, especially at the moment.

Miss Steele

I stare at her reply, and all my anger withers and dies, to be replaced by a surge of anxiety.
Shit.
Is she saying that's it?

From: Christian Grey
Subject: Careful Yourself
Date: May 27 2011 00:03
To: Anastasia Steele

Why don't you like me?

Christian Grey
CEO, Grey Enterprises Holdings, Inc.

I get up and open another bottle of sparkling water.
And wait.

From: Anastasia Steele
Subject: Careful Yourself
Date: May 27 2011 00:09
To: Christian Grey

Because you never stay with me.

Six words.
Six little words that make my scalp tingle.
I told her that I didn't sleep with anyone.
But today was a big day.

She graduated from college.

She said yes.

We went through all those soft limits that she knew nothing about. We fucked. I spanked her. We fucked again.

Shit.

And before I can stop myself, I grab the garage ticket for my car, pick up a jacket, and I'm out the door.

THE ROADS ARE EMPTY and I'm at her place twenty-three minutes later.

I knock quietly, and Kavanagh opens the door.

"What the fuck do you think you're doing here?" she shouts, her eyes blazing with anger.

Whoa. Not the reception I was expecting.

"I've come to see Ana."

"Well, you can't!" Kavanagh stands with arms folded and legs braced in the doorway, like a gargoyle.

I try reasoning with her. "But I need to see her. She sent me an e-mail." *Get out of my way!*

"What the fuck have you done to her now?"

"That's what I need to find out." I grit my teeth.

"Ever since she met you she cries all the time."

"What?" I can't deal with her shit anymore, and I barge past her.

"You can't come in here!" Kavanagh follows me, shrieking like a harpy, as I storm through the apartment to Ana's bedroom.

I open Ana's door and switch on the main light. She's huddled in her bed, wrapped in her comforter. Her eyes are red and puffy, and squinting in the overhead light. Her nose is swollen and blotchy.

I've seen women in this state many times, especially after I've punished them. But I'm surprised by the unease that grips my gut.

"Jesus, Ana." I flick the main light off so she doesn't have to squint and I sit on the bed beside her.

"What are you doing here?" She's sniffling. I turn on her bedside light.

"Do you want me to throw this asshole out?" Kate barks from the doorway.

Fuck you, Kavanagh. Raising an eyebrow, I pretend to ignore her.

Ana shakes her head, but her watery eyes are on me.

"Just holler if you need me," Kate says to Ana, as if she were a child. "Grey," she snaps, so I'm obliged to look at her. "You're on my shit list, and I'm watching you." She sounds shrill, her eyes glinting with fury, but I don't give a fuck.

Fortunately she leaves, pulling the door to, but not shutting it. I check in my inside pocket, and once again Mrs. Jones has exceeded all expectations; I fish out the handkerchief and give it to Ana. "What's going on?"

"Why are you here?" Her voice is shaky.

I don't know.

You said you didn't like me.

"Part of my role is to look after your needs. You said you wanted me to stay, so here I am." *Nice save, Grey.* "And yet I find you like this." *You weren't like this when I left.* "I'm sure I'm responsible, but I have no idea why. Is it because I hit you?"

She struggles to sit up and flinches when she does.

"Did you take some Advil?" *As instructed?*

She shakes her head.

When will you do as you're told?

I go to find Kavanagh, who's on the sofa, seething.

"Ana has a headache. Do you have any Advil?"

She raises her eyebrows, surprised, I think, by my concern for her friend. Glowering, she gets up and stomps into the kitchen. After some rustling through boxes she hands me a couple of tablets and a teacup of water.

Back in the bedroom I offer them to Ana and sit on the bed. "Take these."

She does, her eyes clouded with apprehension.

"Talk to me. You told me you were okay. I'd never have left you if I thought you were like this." Distracted, she toys with a loose thread on her quilt. "I take it that when you said you were okay, you weren't."

"I thought I was fine," she admits.

"Anastasia, you can't tell me what you think I want to hear. That's not very honest. How can I trust anything you've said to me?" This will never work if she's not honest with me.

The thought is depressing.

Talk to me, Ana.

"How did you feel while I was hitting you, and after?"

"I didn't like it. I'd rather you didn't do it again."

"You weren't meant to like it."

"Why do you like it?" she asks, and her voice is stronger.

Shit. I can't tell her why.

"You really want to know?"

"Oh, trust me, I'm fascinated." Now she's being sarcastic.

"Careful," I warn her.

She pales at my expression. "Are you going to hit me again?"

"No, not tonight." *I think you've had enough.*

"So." She still wants an answer.

"I like the control it gives me, Anastasia. I want you to behave in a particular way, and if you don't, I shall punish you, and you will learn to behave the way I desire. I enjoy punishing you. I've wanted to spank you since you asked me if I was gay."

And I don't want you rolling your eyes at me, or being sarcastic.

"So you don't like the way I am." Her voice is small.

"I think you're lovely the way you are."

"So why are you trying to change me?"

"I don't want to change you." *God forbid. You're enchanting.* "I'd like you to be courteous and to follow the set of rules I've given you and not defy me. Simple." *I want you safe.*

"But you want to punish me?"

"Yes, I do."

"That's what I don't understand."

I sigh. "It's the way I'm made. I need to control you. I need you to behave in a certain way, and if you don't—" My mind drifts. *I find it arousing, Ana. You did, too. Can't you accept that?*

Bending you over my knee . . . feeling your ass beneath my palm.
"I love to watch your beautiful alabaster skin pink and warm up under my hands. It turns me on." Just thinking about it stirs my body.

"So it's not the pain you're putting me through?"

Hell.

"A bit, to see if you can take it." Actually, it's a lot, but I don't want to go there right now. If I tell her, she'll throw me out. "But that's not the whole reason. It's the fact that you are mine to do with as I see fit—ultimate control over someone else. And it turns me on. Big-time."

I must lend her a book or two on being a submissive.

"Look, I'm not explaining myself very well. I've never had to before. I've not really thought about this in any great depth. I've always been with like-minded people." I pause to check she's still with me. "And you haven't answered my question—how did you feel afterward?"

She blinks. "Confused."

"You were sexually aroused by it, Anastasia."

You have an inner freak, Ana. I know it.

Closing my eyes, I recall her wet and wanting around my fingers after I spanked her. When I open them, she's staring at me, pupils dilated, her lips parted . . . her tongue moistening her top lip. She wants it, too.

Shit. Not again, Grey. Not when she's like this.

"Don't look at me like that," I warn, my voice gruff.

Her eyebrows rise in surprise.

You know what I mean, Ana. "I don't have any condoms, and you know, you're upset. Contrary to what your roommate believes, I'm not a priapic monster. So, you felt confused?"

She remains mute.

Jesus.

"You have no problem being honest with me in print. Your e-mails always tell me exactly how you feel. Why can't you do that in conversation? Do I intimidate you that much?"

Her fingers fiddle with the quilt.

"You beguile me, Christian. Completely overwhelm me. I feel like Icarus, flying too close to the sun." Her voice is quiet, but brimming with emotion.

Her confession floors me like a swift kick to the head.

"Well, I think you've got that the wrong way round," I whisper.

"What?"

"Oh, Anastasia, you've bewitched me. Isn't it obvious?"

That's why I'm here.

She's not convinced.

Ana. Believe me. "You've still not answered my question. Write me an e-mail, please. But right now, I'd really like to sleep. Can I stay?"

"Do you want to stay?"

"You wanted me here."

"You haven't answered my question," she persists.

Impossible woman. I just drove like a maniac to get here after your fucking message. There's your answer.

I grumble that I'll respond by e-mail. I'm not talking about this. This conversation is over.

Before I can change my mind and head back to The Heathman, I stand, empty my pockets, remove my shoes and socks, and strip off my pants. Slinging my jacket over her chair, I climb into her bed.

"Lie down," I growl.

She complies, and I lean up on my elbow, looking at her. "If you are going to cry, cry in front of me. I need to know."

"Do you want me to cry?"

"Not particularly. I just want to know how you're feeling. I don't want you slipping through my fingers. Switch the light off. It's late, and we both have to work tomorrow."

She does.

"Lie on your side, facing away from me."

I don't want you to touch me.

The bed dips as she moves, and I wrap my arm around her and gently pull her against me.

"Sleep, baby," I murmur, and breathe in the scent of her hair.
Damn, she smells good.

Lelliot is running through the grass.
He's laughing. Loud.
I am running after him. My face is smiling.
I am going to catch him.
There are small trees around us.
Baby trees covered in apples.
Mommy lets me pick the apples.
Mommy lets me eat the apples.
I put the apples in my pockets. Every pocket.
I hide them in my sweater.
Apples taste good.
Apples smell good.
Mommy makes apple pie.
Apple pie and ice cream.
They make my tummy smile.
I hide the apples in my shoes. I hide them under my pillow.
There is a man. Grandpa Trev-Trev-yan.
His name is hard. Hard to say in my head.
He has another name. Thee-o-door.
Theodore is a funny name.
The baby trees are his trees.
At his house. Where he lives.
He is Mommy's daddy.
He has a loud laugh. And big shoulders.
And happy eyes.
He runs to catch Lelliot and me.
You can't catch me.
Lelliot runs. He laughs.
I run. I catch him.
And we fall down in the grass.
He is laughing.
The apples sparkle in the sun.

And they taste so good.
Yummy.
And they smell so good.
So, so good.
The apples fall.
They fall on me.
I twist and they hit my back. Stinging me.
Ow.

But the scent is still there, sweet and crisp.
Ana.

When I open my eyes I'm wrapped around her, our limbs entwined. She's regarding me with a tender smile. Her face is no longer blotchy and puffy; she looks radiant. My cock agrees, and stiffens in greeting.

"Good morning." I'm disoriented. "Jesus, even in my sleep I'm drawn to you." Stretching out, I disentangle myself from her and scan my surroundings. Of course, we're in her bedroom. Her eyes glow with eager curiosity as my cock presses against her. "Hmm, this has possibilities, but I think we should wait until Sunday." I nuzzle her just below her ear and lean up on my elbow.

She looks flushed. Warm.

"You're very hot," she scolds.

"You're not so bad yourself." I grin and flex my hips, teasing her with my favorite body part. She tries a disapproving look but fails miserably—she's highly amused. Leaning down, I kiss her.

"Sleep well?" I ask.

She nods.

"So did I."

I'm surprised. I did sleep really well. I tell her so. No nightmares. Only dreams . . .

"What's the time?" I ask.

"It's seven thirty."

"Seven thirty? Shit!" I leap out of bed and start dragging on my jeans. She watches me dress, trying to suppress her laughter.

"You are such a bad influence on me," I complain. "I have a meeting. I have to go—I have to be in Portland at eight. Are you smirking at me?"

"Yes," she admits.

"I'm late. I don't do late. Another first, Miss Steele." I tug on my jacket, reach down and take her head in both my hands. "Sunday," I whisper, and kiss her. I grab my watch, wallet, and money from her bedside table, pick up my shoes, and head for the door. "Taylor will come and sort your Beetle. I was serious. Don't drive it. I'll see you at my place on Sunday. I'll e-mail you a time."

Leaving her a little dazed, I rush out of the apartment and to my car.

I put on my shoes while I'm driving. Once they're on I open up the throttle and weave in and out of the traffic heading to Portland. I'll have to meet Eamon Kavanagh's associates in my jeans. Thankfully this meeting is via WebEx.

I burst into my room at The Heathman and switch on my laptop: 8:02. *Shit*. I haven't shaved, but I smooth my hair and straighten my jacket, and hope they don't notice I'm only wearing a T-shirt underneath.

Who gives a fuck, anyway?

I open WebEx and Andrea is online, waiting for me. "Good morning, Mr. Grey. Mr. Kavanagh is delayed, but they're ready for you in New York and here in Seattle."

"Fred and Barney?" *My Flintstones*. I smirk at the thought.

"Yes, sir. And Ros, too."

"Great. Thanks." I'm breathless. I catch Andrea's fleeting puzzled look and choose to ignore it. "Can you order me a toasted bagel with cream cheese and smoked salmon and a coffee, black. Have it sent to my suite ASAP."

"Yes, Mr. Grey." She posts the link to the conference in the window. "Here you go, sir," she says. I click the link—and I'm in.

"Good morning." There are two executives seated at a conference table in New York, both gazing expectantly at the camera. Ros, Barney, and Fred are each in separate windows.

To business. Kavanagh says he wants to upgrade his media network to high-speed fiber-optic connections. GEH can do it for them—but are they serious about buying in? It's a big investment up front, but a great payoff down the line.

While we're talking an e-mail notification with an arresting title from Ana floats onto the top right corner of my screen. As quietly as I can, I click on it.

From: Anastasia Steele
Subject: Assault and Battery: The After-Effects
Date: May 27 2011 08:05
To: Christian Grey

Dear Mr. Grey,
You wanted to know why I felt confused after you—which euphemism should we apply—spanked, punished, beat, assaulted me.

A tad overdramatic, Miss Steele. You could have said no.

Well, during the whole alarming process, I felt demeaned, debased, and abused.

If you felt that way, why didn't you stop me? You have safe words.

And much to my mortification, you're right, I was aroused, and that was unexpected.

I know. Good. You've finally acknowledged it.

As you are well aware, all things sexual are new to me—I only wish I was more experienced and therefore more prepared. I was shocked to feel aroused.

What really worried me was how I felt afterward. And that's more difficult to articulate. I was happy that you were happy. I felt relieved that it wasn't as painful as I thought it would be. And when I was lying in your arms, I felt . . . sated.

As did I, Ana, as did I . . .

But I feel very uncomfortable, guilty even, feeling that way. It doesn't sit well with me, and I'm confused as a result. Does that answer your question?

I hope the world of Mergers and Acquisitions is as stimulating as ever . . . and that you weren't too late.

Thank you for staying with me.

Ana

Kavanagh joins the conversation, apologizing for his tardiness. While the introductions are made and Fred talks about what GEH can offer, I type out my reply to Ana. I hope to those on the other side of the computer screen it looks like I'm taking notes.

From: Christian Grey
Subject: Free Your Mind
Date: May 27 2011 08:24
To: Anastasia Steele

Interesting . . . if slightly overstated title heading, Miss Steele.

To answer your points:

· I'll go with spanking—as that's what it was.

· So you felt demeaned, debased, abused, and assaulted—how very Tess Durbeyfield of you. I believe it was you who decided on the debasement, if I remember correctly. Do you really feel like this or do you think you ought to feel like this? Two very different things. If that *is* how you feel, do you think you could just try to embrace these feelings, deal with them, for me? That's what a submissive would do.

· I am grateful for your inexperience. I value it, and I'm only beginning to understand what it means. Simply put . . . it means that you are mine in every way.

· Yes, you were aroused, which in turn was very arousing, there's nothing wrong with that.

· Happy does not even begin to cover how I felt. Ecstatic joy comes close.

· Punishment spanking hurts far more than sensual spanking—so that's about as hard as it gets, unless, of course, you commit some major transgression, in which case I'll use some implement to punish you with. My hand was very sore. But I like that.

· I felt sated, too—more so than you could ever know.

· Don't waste your energy on guilt, feelings of wrong-doing, etc. We are consenting adults and what we do behind closed doors is between ourselves. You need to free your mind and listen to your body.

· The world of M&A is not nearly as stimulating as you are, Miss Steele.

Christian Grey
CEO, Grey Enterprises Holdings, Inc.

Her response is almost immediate.

From: Anastasia Steele
Subject: Consenting Adults!
Date: May 27 2011 08:26
To: Christian Grey

Aren't you in a meeting?
I'm very glad your hand was sore.
And if I listened to my body, I'd be in Alaska by now.
Ana
P.S.: I will think about embracing these feelings.

Alaska! Really, Miss Steele. I chuckle to myself and look like I'm engaged with the online conversation. There's a knock on my door, and I apologize for interrupting the conference while I let room service in with my breakfast. Miss Dark, Dark Eyes rewards me with a flirtatious smile as I sign the check.

Returning to the WebEx, I find Fred briefing Kavanagh and his associates on how successful this technology has been for another client company dealing in futures.

"Will the technology help me with the futures market?" Kavanagh asks with a sardonic smile. When I tell him that Barney's hard at work developing a crystal ball to predict prices, they all have the grace to laugh.

While Fred discusses a theoretical timeline for implementation and tech integration, I e-mail Ana.

From: Christian Grey
Subject: You Didn't Call the Cops
Date: May 27 2011 08:35
To: Anastasia Steele

Miss Steele,
I am in a meeting discussing the futures market, if you're
really interested.

For the record, you stood beside me knowing what I was going to do.

You didn't at any time ask me to stop—you didn't use either safe word.

You are an adult—you have choices.

Quite frankly, I'm looking forward to the next time my palm is ringing with pain.

You're obviously not listening to the right part of your body.

Alaska is very cold and no place to run. I would find you.

I can track your cell phone—remember?

Go to work.

Christian Grey
CEO, Grey Enterprises Holdings, Inc.

Fred is in full flow when I get Ana's response.

From: Anastasia Steele
Subject: Stalker
Date: May 27 2011 08:36
To: Christian Grey

Have you sought therapy for your stalker tendencies?

Ana

I smother my laugh. She's funny.

From: Christian Grey
Subject: Stalker? Me?
Date: May 27 2011 08:38
To: Anastasia Steele

I pay the eminent Dr. Flynn a small fortune with regard to my
stalker and other tendencies.
Go to work.

Christian Grey
CEO, Grey Enterprises Holdings, Inc.

Why hasn't she gone to work? She'll be late.

From: Anastasia Steele
Subject: Expensive Charlatans
Date: May 27 2011 08:40
To: Christian Grey

May I humbly suggest you seek a second opinion?
I am not sure that Dr. Flynn is very effective.

Miss Steele

Damn, this woman is funny . . . and intuitive; Flynn charges
me a small fortune for his advice. Surreptitiously, I type my
response.

From: Christian Grey
Subject: Second Opinions
Date: May 27 2011 08:43
To: Anastasia Steele

Not that it's any of your business, humble or otherwise, but Dr. Flynn is the second opinion.

You will have to speed, in your new car, putting yourself at unnecessary risk—I think that's against the rules.

GO TO WORK.

Christian Grey
CEO, Grey Enterprises Holdings, Inc.

Kavanagh throws me a question about future-proofing. I let him know that we've recently acquired a company that's an innovative, dynamic player in fiber optics. I don't let him know that I have doubts about the CEO, Lucas Woods. He'll be gone anyway. I'm definitely firing that idiot, no matter what Ros says.

From: Anastasia Steele
Subject: SHOUTY CAPITALS
Date: May 27 2011 08:47
To: Christian Grey

As the object of your stalker tendencies, I think it is my business, actually.

I haven't signed yet. So rules, schmules. And I don't start until 9:30.

Miss Steele

SHOUTY CAPITALS. I love it.
I respond.

From: Christian Grey
Subject: Descriptive Linguistics
Date: May 27 2011 08:49
To: Anastasia Steele

"Schmules"? Not sure where that appears in Webster's dictionary.

Christian Grey
CEO, Grey Enterprises Holdings, Inc.

"We can take this conversation offline," Ros says to Kavanagh. "Now that we have an idea of your needs and expectations, we'll prepare a detailed proposal for you and reconvene next week to discuss it."

"Great," I say, trying to look engaged.

There are nods of agreement all around, then good-byes.

"Thanks for giving us the opportunity to quote for this, Eamon," I address Kavanagh.

"It sounds like you guys know what we need," he says. "Great to see you yesterday. Good-bye."

They all hang up except Ros, who's staring at me as if I've grown two heads.

Ana's e-mail pings into my inbox.

"Hang on, Ros. I need a minute or two." I mute her.

And read.

And laugh out loud.

From: Anastasia Steele
Subject: Descriptive Linguistics
Date: May 27 2011 08:52
To: Christian Grey

It's between control freak and stalker.
And descriptive linguistics is a hard limit for me.

Will you stop bothering me now?

I'd like to go to work in my new car.

Ana

I type a quick reply.

From: Christian Grey
Subject: Challenging but Amusing Young Women
Date: May 27 2011 08:56
To: Anastasia Steele

My palm is twitching.
Drive safely, Miss Steele.

Christian Grey
CEO, Grey Enterprises Holdings, Inc.

Ros is glaring at me when I unmute her. "What the hell, Christian?"

"What?" I feign innocence.

"You know what. Don't hold a goddamn meeting when you're obviously not interested."

"Was it that obvious?"

"Yes."

"Fuck."

"Yes. Fuck. This could be a huge contract for us."

"I know. I know. I'm sorry." I grin.

"I don't know what's got into you lately." She shakes her head, but I can tell she's trying to mask her amusement with exasperation.

"It's the Portland air."

"Well, the sooner you're back here, the better."

"I'm heading back around lunchtime. In the meantime, ask Marco to investigate all the publishing houses in Seattle and see if any are ripe for a takeover."

"You want to go into publishing?" Ros splutters. "It's not a high-potential-growth sector."

She's probably right.

"Just investigate. That's all."

She sighs. "If you insist. Will you be in later this afternoon? We can have a proper catch-up."

"Depends on the traffic."

"I'll pencil in a catch-up with Andrea."

"Great. Bye for now."

I close WebEx, then phone Andrea.

"Mr. Grey."

"Call Dr. Baxter and have him come to my apartment on Sunday, around midday. If he's not available, find a good gynecologist. Get the best."

"Yes, sir," she says. "Anything else?"

"Yes. What's the name of the personal shopper I use at Neiman Marcus at the Bravern center?"

"Caroline Acton."

"Text me her number."

"Will do."

"I'll see you later this afternoon."

"Yes, sir."

I hang up.

So far it's been one interesting morning. I can't recall any exchange of e-mails being that fun, ever. I glance at the laptop, but there's nothing new. Ana must be at work.

I run my hands through my hair.

Ros noticed how distracted I was during that conversation.

Shit, Grey. Get your act together.

I wolf down my breakfast, drink some cold coffee, and head into my bedroom to shower and change. Even when I'm washing my hair I can't get that woman out of my head. Ana.

Amazing Ana.

The image of her bouncing up and down on top of me comes to mind; of her lying over my knee, ass pink; of her tethered to the bed, mouth open in ecstasy. Lord, that woman is hot. And this morning, waking up next to her, it wasn't so bad, and I slept well . . . really well.

Shouty capitals. Her e-mails make me laugh. They're entertaining. She's funny. I never knew I liked that in a woman. I'll need to think about what we'll do on Sunday in my playroom . . . something fun, something new for her.

While shaving I have an idea, and as soon as I'm dressed I get back on my laptop to browse my favorite toy store. I need a riding crop—brown plaited leather. I smirk. I'm going to make Ana's dreams come true.

Order placed, I turn to work e-mails, energized and productive, until Taylor interrupts me. "Good morning, Taylor."

"Mr. Grey." He nods, looking at me with a puzzled expression, and I realize I'm grinning because I'm thinking about her e-mails again.

Descriptive linguistics is a hard limit for me.

"I've had a good morning," I find myself explaining.

"I'm pleased to hear it, sir. I have Miss Steele's laundry from last week."

"Pack it with my things."

"Will do."

"Thank you." I watch him walk into my bedroom. Even Taylor is noticing the Anastasia Steele effect. My phone buzzes: it's a text from Elliot.

You still in Portland?

Yes. But I'm leaving soon.

I'll be there later. I'm gonna help the girls move.
Shame you can't stay.
Our first DOUBLE DATE since Ana popped your
cherry.

Fuck off. I'm picking up Mia.

I need deets bro. Kate tells me nothing.

Good. Fuck off. Again.

"Mr. Grey?" Taylor interrupts once more, my luggage in hand.
"The courier has been dispatched with the BlackBerry."

"Thanks."

He nods, and as he leaves I type up another e-mail to Miss
Steele.

From: Christian Grey
Subject: BlackBerry ON LOAN
Date: May 27 2011 11:15
To: Anastasia Steele

I need to be able to contact you at all times, and since this
is your most honest form of communication, I figured you
needed a BlackBerry.

Christian Grey
CEO, Grey Enterprises Holdings, Inc.

And maybe you'll answer this phone when I call.
At 11:30 I have another conference call, with our director of

finance, to discuss GEH's charitable giving for the next quarter. That takes the best part of an hour, and when it's over I finish a light lunch and read the rest of my *Forbes* magazine.

As I swallow the last forkful of salad, I realize I have no other reason to stay at the hotel. It's time to go, yet I'm reluctant. And deep down I have to acknowledge it's because I won't see Ana until Sunday, unless she changes her mind.

Fuck. I hope not.

Pushing that unpleasant thought aside, I start packing my papers into my messenger bag, and when I reach for my laptop to put it away, I see there's an e-mail from Ana.

From: Anastasia Steele
Subject: Consumerism Gone Mad
Date: May 27 2011 13:22
To: Christian Grey

I think you need to call Dr. Flynn right now.
Your stalker tendencies are running wild.

I am at work. I will e-mail you when I get home.

Thank you for yet another gadget.

I wasn't wrong when I said you were the ultimate consumer.

Why do you do this?

Ana

She's scolding me! I respond immediately.

From: Christian Grey
Subject: Sagacity from One So Young
Date: May 27 2011 13:24
To: Anastasia Steele

Fair point well made, as ever, Miss Steele.
Dr. Flynn is on vacation.

And I do this because I can.

Christian Grey
CEO, Grey Enterprises Holdings, Inc.

She doesn't answer straightaway, so I pack my laptop. Grabbing my bag, I head down to reception and check out. While I'm waiting for my car, Andrea calls to tell me that she's found an ob-gyn to come to Escala on Sunday.

"Her name is Dr. Greene, and she comes highly recommended by your M.D., sir."

"Good."

"She runs her practice out of Northwest."

"Okay." Where is Andrea going with this?

"There's one thing sir—she's expensive."

I dismiss her concern. "Andrea, whatever she wants is fine."

"In that case, she can be at your apartment one thirty on Sunday."

"Great. Go ahead."

"Will do, Mr. Grey."

I hang up, and I'm tempted to call my mother to check Dr. Greene's credentials, as they work in the same hospital; but that might provoke too many questions from Grace.

Once in the car I send Ana an e-mail with details about Sunday.

From: Christian Grey
Subject: Sunday
Date: May 27 2011 13:40
To: Anastasia Steele

Shall I see you at 1 p.m. Sunday?
The doctor will be at Escala to see you at 1:30.

I'm leaving for Seattle now.

I hope your move goes well, and I look forward to Sunday.

Christian Grey
CEO, Grey Enterprises Holdings, Inc.

Right. All done. I ease the R8 onto the road and roar toward I-5. As I pass the exit for Vancouver I'm inspired. I call Andrea on the hands-free and ask her to organize a housewarming present for Ana and Kate.

"What would you like to send?"

"Bollinger La Grande Année Rosé, 1999 vintage."

"Yes, sir. Anything else?"

"What do you mean, anything else?"

"Flowers? Chocolates? A balloon?"

"Balloon?"

"Yes."

"What sort of balloons?"

"Well . . . they have everything."

"Okay. Good idea—see if you can get a helicopter balloon."

"Yes, sir. And a message for the card?"

" 'Ladies, good luck in your new home. Christian Grey.' Got that?"

"I have. What's the address?"

Shit. I don't know. "I'll text it to you either later today or tomorrow. Will that work?"

"Yes, sir. I can get it delivered tomorrow."

"Thanks, Andrea."

"You're welcome." She sounds surprised.

I hang up and floor my R8.

BY 6:30 I'M HOME and my earlier ebullient mood has soured—I still haven't heard from Ana. I select a pair of cuff links from the drawers in my closet and as I knot my bow tie for the night's event I wonder if she's okay. She said she would contact me when she got home; I've called her twice, but I've heard nothing, and it's pissing me off. I try her once more and this time I leave a message.

"I think you need to learn to manage my expectations. I'm not a patient man. If you say you are going to contact me when you finish work, then you should have the decency to do so. Otherwise I worry, and it's not an emotion I'm familiar with, and I don't tolerate it very well. Call me."

If she doesn't call soon I am going to explode.

I'M SEATED AT A table with Whelan, my banker. I'm his guest at a charity function for a nonprofit that aims to raise awareness of global poverty.

"Glad you could make it," Whelan says.

"It's a good cause."

"And thank you for your generous contribution, Mr. Grey." His wife is cloying, thrusting her perfect, surgically enhanced breasts in my direction.

"Like I said, it's a good cause." I give her a patronizing smile.

Why hasn't Ana called me back?

I check my phone again.

Nothing.

I look around the table at all the middle-aged men with their second or third trophy wives. God forbid this should ever be me.

I'm bored. Seriously bored and seriously pissed.

What is she doing?

Could I have brought her here? I suspect she would have been bored stiff, too. When the conversation around the table moves to the state of the economy, I've had enough. Making my excuses, I leave the ballroom and exit the hotel. While the valet is retrieving my car, I call Ana again.

There's still no answer.

Perhaps now that I'm gone she wants nothing to do with me.

When I get home, I head straight to my study and switch on the iMac.

From: Christian Grey
Subject: Where Are You?
Date: May 27 2011 22:14
To: Anastasia Steele

"I am at work. I will e-mail you when I get home."
Are you still at work or have you packed your phone,
BlackBerry, and MacBook?

Call me, or I may be forced to call Elliot.

Christian Grey
CEO, Grey Enterprises Holdings, Inc.

I stare out of my window toward the dark waters of the Sound. Why did I volunteer to collect Mia? I could be with Ana, helping her pack all her shit, then going out for pizza with her and Kate and Elliot—or whatever ordinary people do.

For God's sake, Grey.

That's not you. *Get a grip.*

I wander around my apartment, my footsteps echoing through the living room, and it seems achingly empty since I was last here. I undo my bow tie. Perhaps it's me that's empty. I pour myself an Armagnac and stare back out at the Seattle skyline toward the Sound.

Are you thinking about me, Anastasia Steele? The winking lights of Seattle have no answer.

My phone buzzes.

Thank. Fuck. *Finally*. It's her.

"Hi." I'm relieved that she's called.

"Hi," she says.

"I was worried about you."

"I know. I'm sorry I didn't reply, but I'm fine."

Fine? I wish I was . . .

"Did you have a pleasant evening?" I ask, reining in my temper.

"Yes. We finished packing, and Kate and I had Chinese takeout with José."

Oh, this just gets better and better. The fucking photographer again. That's why she hasn't called.

"How about you?" she inquires when I don't respond, and there's a hint of desperation in her voice.

Why? What isn't she telling me?

Oh, stop overthinking this, Grey!

I sigh. "I went to a fund-raising dinner. It was deathly dull. I left as soon as I could."

"I wish you were here," she whispers.

"Do you?"

"Yes," she says fervently.

Oh. Perhaps she's missed me.

"I'll see you Sunday?" I confirm, trying to keep the hope out of my voice.

"Yes, Sunday," she says, and I think she's smiling.

"Good night."

"Good night, Sir." Her voice is husky and it takes my breath away.

"Good luck with your move tomorrow, Anastasia."

She stays on the line, her breathing soft. Why doesn't she hang up? She doesn't want to?

"You hang up," she whispers.

She doesn't want to hang up and my mood lightens immediately. I grin out at the view of Seattle.

"No, you hang up."

"I don't want to."

"Neither do I."

"Were you very angry with me?" she asks.

"Yes."

"Are you still?"

"No." *Now I know you're safe.*

"So you're not going to punish me?"

"No. I'm an in-the-moment kind of guy."

"I've noticed," she teases, and that makes me smile.

"You can hang up now, Miss Steele."

"Do you really want me to, Sir?"

"Go to bed, Anastasia."

"Yes, Sir."

She doesn't hang up, and I know she's grinning. It lifts my spirits higher. "Do you ever think you'll be able to do what you're told?" I ask.

"Maybe. We'll see after Sunday," she says, temptress that she is, and the line goes dead.

Anastasia Steele, what am I going to do with you?

Actually, I have a good idea, provided that riding crop turns up in time. And with that enticing thought I toss down the rest of the Armagnac and go to bed.

Christian!" Mia squeals with delight and runs toward me, abandoning her cartload of luggage. Throwing her arms around my neck, she hugs me tightly.

"I've missed you," she says.

"I've missed you, too." I give her a squeeze in return. She leans back and examines me with intense dark eyes.

"You look good," she gushes. "Tell me about this girl!"

"Let's get you and your luggage home first." I grab her cart, which weighs a ton, and together we head out of the airport terminal toward the parking lot.

"So how was Paris? You appear to have brought most of it home with you."

"*C'est incroyable!*" she exclaims. "Floubert, on the other hand, was a bastard. *Jesus.* He was a horrible man. A crap teacher but a good chef."

"Does that mean you're cooking this evening?"

"Oh, I was hoping Mom would cook."

Mia proceeds to talk nonstop about Paris: her tiny room, the plumbing, Sacré-Coeur, Montmartre, Parisians, coffee, red wine, cheese, fashion, shopping. But mainly about fashion and shopping. And I thought she went to Paris to learn to cook.

I've missed her chatter; it's soothing and welcome. She is the only person I know who doesn't make me feel . . . different.

This is your baby sister, Christian. Her name is Mia.

Mommy lets me hold her. She is very small. With black, black hair.

She smiles. She has no teeth. I stick out my tongue. She has a bubbly laugh.

Mommy lets me hold the baby again. Her name is Mia.

I make her laugh. I hold her and hold her. She is safe when I hold her.

Elliot is not interested in Mia. She dribbles and cries.

And he wrinkles his nose when she does a poop.

When Mia is crying Elliot ignores her. I hold her and hold her and she stops.

She falls asleep in my arms.

"Mee a," I whisper.

"What did you say?" Mommy asks, and her face is white like chalk.

"Mee a."

"Yes. Yes. Darling boy. Mia. Her name is Mia."

And Mommy starts to cry with happy, happy tears.

I TURN INTO THE driveway, pull up outside Mom and Dad's front door, unload Mia's luggage, and carry it into the hall.

"Where is everyone?" Mia is in full pout. The only person around is my parents' housekeeper—she's an exchange student, and I can't remember her name. "Welcome home," she says to Mia in her stilted English, though she's looking at me with big cow eyes.

Oh, God. It's just a pretty face, sweetheart.

Ignoring the housekeeper, I address Mia's question. "I think Mom is on call and Dad is at a conference. You did come home a week early."

"I couldn't stand Floubert another minute. I had to get out while I could. Oh, I bought you a present." She grabs one of her cases, opens it up in the hallway, and starts rummaging through it. "Ah!" She hands me a heavy square box. "Open it," she urges, beaming at me. She is an unstoppable force.

Warily I open the box, and inside I find a snow globe containing a black grand piano covered in glitter. It's the kitschiest thing I've ever seen.

"It's a music box. Here—" She takes it from me, gives it a good shake, and winds a small key on the bottom. A twinkly version of "La Marseillaise" starts to play in a cloud of colored glitter.

What am I going to do with this? I laugh, because it's so Mia. "That's great, Mia. Thank you." I give her a hug and she hugs me back.

"I knew it would make you laugh."

She's right. She knows me well.

"So tell me about this girl," she says. But we're both distracted as Grace hurries through the door, allowing me a reprieve as mother and daughter embrace. "I'm so sorry I wasn't there to meet you, darling," Grace says. "I've been on call. You look so grown up. Christian, can you take Mia's bags upstairs? Gretchen will give you a hand."

Really? I'm a porter now?

"Yes, Mom." I roll my eyes. I don't need Gretchen mooning over me.

Once that's done, I tell them that I have an appointment with my trainer. "I'll be back this evening." Quickly kissing them both, I leave before I'm pestered with more questions about Ana.

BASTILLE, MY TRAINER, WORKS me hard. Today we're kickboxing at his gym.

"You've gone soft in Portland, boy." He sneers after I'm toppled onto the mat from his roundhouse kick. Bastille is from the hard-knocks school of physical training, which suits me fine.

I scramble to my feet. I want to take him down. But he's right—he's all over my shit today, and I get nowhere.

When we finish he asks, "What gives? You're distracted, man."

"Life. You know," I answer with an air of indifference.

"Sure. You're back in Seattle this week?"

"Yeah."

"Good. We'll straighten you out."

AS I JOG BACK to the apartment I remember the housewarming present for Ana. I text Elliot.

> What's Ana and Kate's address?
>
> I want to surprise them with a present.

He texts me back an address and I forward it to Andrea. As I'm riding in the elevator up to the penthouse, Andrea texts me back.

> Champagne and balloon sent. A.

Taylor hands me a package when I arrive back at the apartment. "This came for you, Mr. Grey."

Oh yes. I recognize the anonymous wrapping: it's the riding crop.

"Thanks."

"Mrs. Jones said she'd be back tomorrow, late afternoon."

"Okay. I think that's all for today, Taylor."

"Very good, sir," he says with a polite smile, and returns to his office. Taking the crop, I stroll into my bedroom. This will be the perfect introduction to my world: by her own admission Ana has no sphere of reference with regard to corporal punishment, except the spanking I gave her that night. And that turned her on. With the crop, I'll have to take it slow and make it pleasurable.

Really pleasurable. The riding crop is perfect. I'll prove to her that the fear is in her head. Once she gets comfortable with this, we can move on.

I hope we can move on . . .

We'll take it slow. And we'll only do what she can handle. If this is going to work we're going to have to go at her pace. Not mine.

I take one more look at the crop and put it in my closet for tomorrow.

AS I FLIP OPEN my laptop to start work my phone rings. I hope it's Ana, but it's disappointingly Elena.

Was I supposed to call her?

"Hello, Christian. How are you?"

"Good, thanks."

"You're back from Portland?"

"Yes."

"Fancy dinner tonight?"

"Not tonight. Mia's just in from Paris and I've been ordered home."

"Ah. By Mama Grey. How is she?"

"Mama Grey? She's good. I think. Why? What do you know that I don't?"

"I was just asking, Christian. Don't be so touchy."

"I'll call you next week. Maybe we can do dinner then."

"Good. You've been off the radar for a while. And I've met a woman who I think might meet your needs."

So have I.

I ignore her comment. "I'll see you next week. Good-bye."

As I shower I wonder if having to chase Ana has made her more interesting . . . or is it Ana herself?

DINNER HAS BEEN FUN. My sister is back, the princess she's always been, the rest of the family merely her minions, wrapped around her little finger. With all her children home, Grace is in her element; she's cooked Mia's favorite meal—buttermilk fried chicken with mashed potatoes and gravy.

I have to say, it's one of my favorites, too.

"Tell me about Anastasia," Mia demands as we sit around the kitchen table. Elliot leans back in his chair and rests his hands behind his head.

"This I have to hear. You know she popped his cherry?"

"Elliot!" Grace scolds, and swats him with a dish towel.

"Ow!" He fends her off.

I roll my eyes at all of them. "I met a girl." I shrug. "End of story."

"You can't just say that!" Mia objects, pouting.

"Mia, I think he can. And he just did." Carrick gives her a reproving paternal stare over his glasses.

"You'll all meet her at dinner tomorrow, won't we, Christian?" Grace says with a pointed smile.

Oh, fuck.

"Kate's coming," Elliot goads.

Fucking stirrer. I glare at him.

"I can't wait to meet her. She sounds awesome!" Mia bounces up and down in her chair.

"Yeah, yeah," I mumble, wondering if there's any way I can wriggle out of dinner tomorrow.

"Elena was asking after you, darling," Grace says.

"She was?" I affect an uninterested air, developed over years of practice.

"Yes. She says she hasn't seen you in a while."

"I've been in Portland on business. Speaking of which, I should get going—I have an important call tomorrow and I need to prepare."

"But you've not had dessert. And it's apple cobbler."

Hmm . . . tempting. But if I stay they'll quiz me about Ana. "I have to go. I have work to do."

"Darling, you work too hard," Grace says, as she starts from her chair.

"Don't get up, Mom. I'm sure Elliot will help with the dishes after dinner."

"What?" Elliot scowls. I wink at him, say my good-byes, and turn to leave.

"But we'll see you tomorrow?" Grace asks, too much hope in her voice.

"We'll see."

Shit. It looks like Anastasia Steele is going to meet my family.

I don't know how I feel about this.

SUNDAY, MAY 29, 2011

With the Rolling Stones' "Shake Your Hips" blasting in my ears, I sprint down Fourth Avenue and turn right on Vine. It's 6:45 in the morning, and it's downhill all the way . . . to her apartment. I'm drawn; I just want to see where she lives.

It's between control freak and stalker.

I chuckle to myself. I'm just running. It's a free country.

The apartment block is a nondescript redbrick, with dark green painted window frames typical of the area. It's in a good location near the intersection of Vine Street and Western. I imagine Ana curled up in her bed under her comforter and her cream-and-blue quilt.

I run several blocks and turn down into the market; the vendors are setting up for business. I dodge between the fruit and vegetable trucks and the refrigerated vans delivering the catch of the day. This is the heart of the city—vibrant, even this early on a gray, cool morning. The water on the Sound is a glassy leaden color, matching the sky. But it does nothing to dampen my spirits.

Today's the day.

AFTER MY SHOWER I don jeans and a linen shirt, and from my chest of drawers I take out a hair tie. I slip it into my pocket and head into my study to e-mail Ana.

From: Christian Grey
Subject: My Life in Numbers
Date: May 29 2011 08:04
To: Anastasia Steele

If you drive you'll need this access code for the underground
garage at Escala: 146963.
Park in bay five—it's one of mine.

Code for the elevator: 1880.

Christian Grey
CEO, Grey Enterprises Holdings, Inc.

A moment or two later, there's a response.

From: Anastasia Steele
Subject: An Excellent Vintage
Date: May 29 2011 08:08
To: Christian Grey

Yes, Sir. Understood.
Thank you for the champagne and the blow-up *Charlie
Tango,* which is now tied to my bed.

Ana

An image of Ana tethered to her bed with my tie comes to
mind. I shift in my chair. I hope she's brought that bed to Seattle.

From: Christian Grey
Subject: Envy
Date: May 29 2011 08:11
To: Anastasia Steele

You're welcome.
Don't be late.

Lucky *Charlie Tango.*

Christian Grey
CEO, Grey Enterprises Holdings, Inc.

She doesn't respond, so I hunt through the refrigerator for some breakfast. Gail has left me some croissants and, for lunch, a Caesar salad with chicken, enough for two. I hope Ana will eat this; I don't mind having it two days in a row.

Taylor appears while I'm eating my breakfast.

"Good morning, Mr. Grey. Here are the Sunday papers."

"Thanks. Anastasia is coming over at one today, and a Dr. Greene at one thirty."

"Very good, sir. Anything else on the agenda today?"

"Yes. Ana and I will be going to my parents' for dinner this evening."

Taylor cocks his head, looking momentarily surprised, but he remembers himself and leaves the room. I return to my croissant and apricot jam.

Yeah. I'm taking her to meet my parents. What's the big deal?

I CAN'T SETTLE. I'M restless. It's 12:15 p.m. Time is crawling today. I give up on work and, grabbing the Sunday papers, wander back into the living room, where I switch on some music and read.

To my surprise there's a photograph of Ana and me on the local news page, taken at the graduation ceremony at WSU. She looks lovely, if a little startled.

I hear the double doors open, and there she is . . . Her hair is loose, a little wild and sexy, and she's wearing that purple dress she wore to dinner at The Heathman. She looks gorgeous.

Bravo, Miss Steele.

"Hmm, that dress." My voice is full of admiration as I saunter toward her. "Welcome back, Miss Steele," I whisper, and, holding her chin, I give her a tender kiss on the lips.

"Hi," she says, her cheeks a little rosy.

"You're on time. I like punctual. Come." Taking her hand, I lead her to the sofa. "I wanted to show you something." We both sit, and I pass her *The Seattle Times.* The photograph makes her laugh. Not quite the reaction I was expecting.

"So I'm your 'friend' now," she teases.

"So it would appear. And it's in the newspaper, so it must be true."

I'm calmer now that she's here—probably *because* she's here. She hasn't run. I tuck her soft, silky hair behind her ear; my fingers are itching to braid it.

"So, Anastasia, you have a much better idea of what I'm about since you were last here."

"Yes." Her gaze is intense . . . knowing.

"And yet you've returned."

She nods, giving me a coy smile.

I can't believe my luck.

I knew you were a freak, Ana.

"Have you eaten?"

"No."

Not at all? Okay. We'll have to fix this. I drag my hand through my hair, and in as even a tone as I can manage I ask, "Are you hungry?"

"Not for food," she teases.

Whoa. She might as well be addressing my groin.

Leaning forward, I press my lips to her ear and catch her intoxicating scent. "You are as eager as ever, Miss Steele—and just to let you in on a little secret, so am I. But Dr. Greene is due here shortly."

I lean against the sofa. "I wish you'd eat." It's a plea.

"What can you tell me about Dr. Greene?" She deftly changes the subject.

"She's the best ob-gyn in Seattle. What more can I say?"

That's what my doctor told my PA, anyway.

"I thought I was seeing *your* doctor? And don't tell me you're really a woman, because I won't believe you."

I suppress my snort. "I think it's more appropriate that you see a specialist. Don't you?"

She gives me a quizzical look, but she nods.

One more topic to tackle. "Anastasia, my mother would like you to come to dinner this evening. I believe Elliot is asking Kate, too. I don't know how you feel about that. It will be odd for me to introduce you to my family."

She takes a second to process the information, then tosses her hair over her shoulder in that way she does before a fight. But she looks hurt, not argumentative. "Are you ashamed of me?" She sounds choked.

Oh, for heaven's sake. "Of course not." *Of all the ridiculous things to say!* I glare at her, aggrieved. How could she think that about herself?

"Why is it odd?" she asks.

"Because I've never done it before." I sound irritable.

"Why are you allowed to roll your eyes, and I'm not?"

"I wasn't aware that I was." *She's calling me out. Again.*

"Neither am I, usually," she snaps.

Shit. Are we arguing?

Taylor clears his throat. "Dr. Greene is here, sir," he says.

"Show her up to Miss Steele's room."

Ana turns and looks at me and I hold out my hand to her.

"You're not going to come as well, are you?" She's horrified and amused at once.

I laugh, and my body stirs. "I'd pay very good money to watch, believe me, Anastasia, but I don't think the good doctor would approve." She places her hand in mine, and I pull her up into my arms and kiss her. Her mouth is soft and warm and inviting; my hands glide into her hair and I deepen the kiss. When I pull away, she looks dazed. I press my forehead to hers. "I'm so glad you're here. I can't wait to get you naked." *I can't believe how much I missed you.* "Come on. I want to meet Dr. Greene, too."

"You don't know her?"

"No."

I take Ana's hand and we head upstairs, to what will be her bedroom.

Dr. Greene has one of those myopic stares; it's penetrating and that makes me a tad uncomfortable. "Mr. Grey," she says, shaking my outstretched hand with a firm, no-nonsense grip.

"Thank you for coming on such short notice." I flash her my most benign smile.

"Thank you for making it worth my while, Mr. Grey. Miss Steele," she says politely to Ana, and I know she's sizing up our relationship. I'm sure that she thinks I should be twiddling a mustache like a silent-movie villain. She turns and gives me a pointed "leave now" kind of look.

Okay.

"I'll be downstairs," I acquiesce. Though I would like to watch. I'm sure the good doctor's reaction would be priceless if I made that request. I smirk at the thought and head downstairs to the living room.

Now that Ana's no longer with me, I'm restless again. As a distraction I set the counter with two placemats. It's the second time I've done this, and the first time was for Ana, too.

You're going soft, Grey.

I select a Chablis to have with lunch—one of the few chardonnays I like—and when I'm done I take a seat on the sofa and browse through the sports section of the paper. Turning up the volume via the remote for my iPod, I hope the music will help me focus on stats from last night's Mariners win against the Yankees, rather than what's happening upstairs between Ana and Dr. Greene.

Eventually their footsteps echo in the corridor, and I look up as they enter. "Are you done?" I ask, and hit the remote for the iPod, to quiet the aria.

"Yes, Mr. Grey. Look after her; she's a beautiful, bright young woman."

What has Ana told her?

"I fully intend to," I say, with a quick what-the-fuck glance at Ana.

She bats her lashes, clueless. *Good.* It's nothing she's said, then.

"I'll send you my bill," says Dr. Greene. "Good day, and good luck to you, Ana." The edges of her eyes crinkle with a warm smile as we shake hands.

Taylor escorts her toward the elevator and wisely closes the double doors to the foyer.

"How was that?" I ask, a little bemused by Dr. Greene's words.

"Fine, thank you," Ana answers. "She said that I had to abstain from all sexual activity for the next four weeks."

What the hell? I gape at her in shock.

Ana's earnest expression dissolves into one of taunting triumph. "Gotcha!"

Well played, Miss Steele.

My eyes narrow and her grin vanishes.

"Gotcha!" I can't help my smirk. Reaching around her waist, I pull her against me, my body hungering for her. "You are incorrigible, Miss Steele." I weave my hands through her hair and kiss her hard, wondering if I should fuck her over the kitchen counter as a lesson.

All in good time, Grey.

"As much as I'd like to take you here and now, you need to eat and so do I. I don't want you passing out on me later," I whisper.

"Is that all you want me for—my body?" she asks.

"That and your smart mouth." I kiss her once more, thinking of what's to come . . . My kiss deepens and desire hardens my body. I want this woman. Before I fuck her on the floor, I release her, and we're both breathless.

"What's the music?" she says, her voice hoarse.

"Villa-Lobos, an aria from *Bachianas Brasileiras*. Good, isn't it?"

"Yes," she says, gazing at the breakfast bar. I take the chicken Caesar out of the fridge, place it on the table between the place-mats, and ask her if she's okay with salad.

"Yes, fine, thank you." She smiles.

From the wine fridge I take out the Chablis, feeling her eyes on me. I didn't know I could be so domestic. "What are you think-ing?" I ask.

"I was just watching the way you move."

"And?" I ask, momentarily surprised.

"You're very graceful," she says quietly, her cheeks pink.

"Why, thank you, Miss Steele." I sit beside her, unsure how to respond to her sweet compliment. Nobody's called me graceful before. "Chablis?"

"Please."

"Help yourself to salad. Tell me—what method did you opt for?"

"Mini pill," she says.

"And will you remember to take it regularly, at the right time, every day?"

A blush steals across her surprised face. "I'm sure you'll remind me," she says with a hint of sarcasm, which I choose to ignore.

You should have had the shot.

"I'll put an alarm on my calendar. Eat."

She takes a bite, then another . . . and another. She's eating!

"So I can put chicken Caesar on the list for Mrs. Jones?" I ask.

"I thought I'd be doing the cooking."

"Yes. You will."

She finishes before I do. She must have been starving.

"Eager as ever, Miss Steele?"

"Yes," she says, giving me a demure look from beneath her lashes.

Fuck. There it is.

The attraction.

As if under her spell, I get up and tug her into my arms.

"Do you want to do this?" I whisper, inwardly begging her to say yes.

"I haven't signed anything."

"I know—but I'm breaking all the rules these days."

"Are you going to hit me?"

"Yes, but it won't be to hurt you. I don't want to punish you right now. If you'd caught me yesterday evening, well, that would have been a different story."

Her face turns to shock.

Oh, baby. "Don't let anyone try to convince you otherwise, Anastasia. One of the reasons people like me to do this is because we either like to give or receive pain. It's very simple. You don't, so I spent a great deal of time yesterday thinking about that."

I wrap my arms around her, holding her against my hardening erection.

"Did you reach any conclusions?" she whispers.

"No, and right now, I just want to tie you up and fuck you senseless. Are you ready for that?"

Her expression is darker, sensual, and full of carnal curiosity. "Yes," she says, the word as soft as a sigh.

Thank fuck.

"Good. Come." I lead her upstairs and into my playroom. My safe place. Where I can do what I wish with her. I close my eyes, briefly savoring the exhilaration.

Have I ever been this excited?

Pushing the door shut behind us, I release her hand and study her. Her lips are parted as she inhales; her breathing is quick and shallow. Her eyes are wide. Ready. Waiting.

"When you're in here, you are completely mine. To do with as I see fit. Do you understand?"

Her tongue quickly licks her upper lip, and she nods.

Good girl.

"Take your shoes off."

She swallows and proceeds to take off her high-heeled sandals. I pick them up and put them neatly by the door.

"Good. Don't hesitate when I ask you to do something. Now

I'm going to peel you out of this dress. Something I've wanted to do for a few days, if I recall."

I pause, checking that she's still with me. "I want you to be comfortable with your body, Anastasia. You have a beautiful body, and I like to look at it. It is a joy to behold. In fact, I could gaze at you all day, and I want you unembarrassed and unashamed of your nakedness. Do you understand?"

"Yes."

"Yes, what?" My tone is sharper.

"Yes, Sir."

"Do you mean that?" *I want you unashamed, Ana.*

"Yes, Sir."

"Good. Lift your arms up over your head."

Slowly she raises her arms in the air. I grab the hem and gently pull the dress up her body, revealing it inch by inch, for my eyes only. When it's off I stand back so I can have my fill of her.

Legs, thighs, belly, ass, tits, shoulders, face, mouth . . . she's perfect. Folding her dress, I place it on the toy chest. Reaching up, I tug her chin. "You're biting your lip. You know what that does to me," I scold. "Turn around."

She complies and turns to face the door. I unfasten her bra and pull the straps down her arms, skimming her skin with my fingertips as I do and feeling her tremble beneath my touch. I take off her bra and toss it on top of her dress. I stand close, not quite touching her, listening to her rapid breathing and sensing the warmth radiating off her skin. She's excited and she's not the only one. I gather her hair in both of my hands so it falls down her back. It's oh-so-silky to touch. I wind it around one hand and tug, angling her head to one side and exposing her neck to my mouth.

I run my nose from her ear to her shoulder and back again, inhaling her heavenly scent.

Fuck, she smells good.

"You smell as divine as ever, Anastasia." I place a kiss beneath her ear just above her pulse.

She moans.

"Quiet. Don't make a sound."

From my jeans pocket I grab the hair tie, and taking her hair in my hands, I braid it, slowly, enjoying the pull and twist against her beautiful, flawless back. Deftly I fasten the end with the hair tie and give it a quick tug, forcing her to step back and press her body into mine. "I like your hair braided in here," I whisper. "Turn around."

She does so, immediately.

"When I tell you to come in here, this is how you will dress. Just in your panties. Do you understand?"

"Yes."

"Yes, what?"

"Yes, Sir."

"Good girl." She's learning fast. Her arms are by her sides, her eyes trained on mine. Waiting.

"When I tell you to come in here, I expect you to kneel over there." I point to the corner of the room beside the door. "Do it now."

She blinks a couple of times, but before I have to tell her again, she turns and kneels, facing me and the room.

I give her permission to sit back on her heels and she obliges. "Place your hands and forearms flat on your thighs. Good. Now part your knees. Wider." *I want to see you, baby.* "Wider." *See your sex.* "Perfect. Look down at the floor."

Don't look at me or the room. You can sit there and let your thoughts run wild while you imagine what I'm going to do to you.

I walk over to her, and I'm pleased that she keeps her head bowed. Reaching down, I tug her braid, tilting her head so that our eyes meet. "Will you remember this position, Anastasia?"

"Yes, Sir."

"Good. Stay here, don't move."

Walking past her, I open the door and for a moment look back at her. Her head is bowed; her eyes stay fixed on the floor.

What a welcome sight. *Good girl.*

I want to run, but I contain my eagerness and walk purposefully downstairs to my bedroom.

Maintain some fucking dignity, Grey.

In my closet I strip off all my clothes and from a drawer pull out my favorite jeans. My DJs. Dom jeans.

I slip them on and fasten all the buttons except the top one. From the same drawer I retrieve the new riding crop and a gray waffle robe. As I leave I grab a few condoms and stuff them into my pocket.

Here goes.

Showtime, Grey.

When I get back she's in the same position: her head bowed, her braid hanging down her back, her hands on her knees. I close the door and hang the robe on its hook. I walk past her. "Good girl, Anastasia. You look lovely like that. Well done. Stand up."

She stands, keeping her head down.

"You may look at me."

Eager blue eyes peek up.

"I'm going to chain you now, Anastasia. Give me your right hand." I hold out mine and she places her hand in it. Without taking my eyes off hers I turn her hand palm up, and from behind my back produce the riding crop. I quickly flick the end across her palm. She startles and cups her hand, blinking at me in surprise.

"How does that feel?" I ask.

Her breathing accelerates, and she glances at me before looking back at her palm.

"Answer me."

"Okay." Her brows knit together.

"Don't frown," I warn. "Did that hurt?"

"No."

"This is not going to hurt. Do you understand?"

"Yes." Her voice is a little shaky.

"I mean it," I stress, and I show her the crop. *Brown plaited leather. See? I listen.* Her eyes meet mine, astonished. My lips twitch in amusement.

"We aim to please, Miss Steele. Come."

I lead her to the middle of the room, beneath the restraining system. "This grid is designed so the shackles move across the grid." She stares up at the intricate system, then back at me.

"We're going to start here, but I want to fuck you standing up. So we'll end up by the wall over there." I point to the Saint Andrew's cross. "Put your hands above your head."

She does, immediately. Taking the leather cuffs that hang on the grid, I fasten one to each of her wrists in turn. I'm methodical, but she's distracting. Being this close to her, sensing her excitement, her anxiety, touching her. I find it hard to concentrate. Once she's cuffed I step back and take a deep breath, relieved.

Finally I've got you where I want you, Ana Steele.

Slowly I walk around her, admiring the view. Could she look hotter? "You look mighty fine trussed up like this, Miss Steele. And your smart mouth quiet for now. I like that." I stop, facing her, curl my fingers into her panties, and oh so slowly drag them down her long legs until I'm kneeling at her feet.

Worshipping her. She's glorious.

With my eyes locked on hers, I take her panties, crush them to my nose, and inhale deeply. Her mouth pops open and her eyes widen in amused shock.

Yes. I smirk. *Perfect reaction.*

I slip the panties into the back pocket of my jeans and stand, considering my next move. Holding out the crop, I run it over her belly and gently circle her navel with the keeper . . . the leather tongue. She sucks in her breath and tremors at the touch.

This will be good, Ana. Trust me.

Slowly I begin to circle her, drawing the crop across her skin, across her belly, her flank, her back. On my second circuit I flick the tongue at the base of her behind so it makes sharp contact with her vulva.

"Ah!" she cries, and she tugs against the shackles.

"Quiet," I warn, and prowl around her once more. I flick the crop against her in the same sweet spot and she whines on contact, her eyes closed as she absorbs the sensation. With another twitch of my wrist, the crop snaps against her nipple. She throws her head back and moans. I aim again, and the crop licks her other nipple, and I watch it harden and lengthen beneath the bite of the leather keeper.

"Does that feel good?"

"Yes," she rasps, eyes closed, head back.

I smack her across her behind, harder this time.

"Yes, what?"

"Yes, Sir," she cries.

Slowly and with care, I lavish strokes, licks, and flicks over her stomach and her belly, down her body, toward my goal. With one flick, the leather tongue bites her clitoris and she shouts out in a gargled cry, "Oh, please!"

"Quiet," I command, and reprimand her with a harder flick across her backside.

I skim the leather tongue down through her pubic hair, against her vulva to her vagina. The brown leather is glistening with her arousal when I pull it back. "See how wet you are for this, Anastasia. Open your eyes and your mouth."

She's breathing hard, but she parts her lips and stares at me, her eyes dazed and lost in the carnality of the moment. And I slip the keeper into her mouth. "See how you taste. Suck. Suck hard, baby."

Her lips close around the tip and it's like they're around my dick.

Fuck.

She's so fucking hot and I can't resist her.

Easing the crop from her mouth, I wrap my arms around her. She opens her mouth for me as I kiss her, my tongue exploring her, reveling in the taste of her lust.

"Oh, baby, you taste mighty fine," I whisper. "Shall I make you come?"

"Please," she pleads.

One flick of my wrist and the crop smacks her behind. "Please, what?"

"Please, Sir," she whimpers.

Good girl. I step back. "With this?" I ask, holding up the crop so she can see it.

"Yes, Sir," she says, surprising me.

"Are you sure?" I can barely believe my luck.

"Yes, please, Sir."

Oh, Ana. You fucking goddess.

"Close your eyes."

She does as she's told. And with infinite care and not a little gratitude, I rain quick, stinging licks over her belly once more. Soon she's panting again, her arousal heightened. Moving south, I gently flick the leather tongue over her clitoris. Again. And again. And again.

She pulls at her restraints, moaning and moaning. Then she's quiet and I know she's close. Suddenly she throws her head back and mouth open and she screams her orgasm as it shudders through her entire body. Instantly I drop the crop and grab her, supporting her as her body dissolves. She sags against me.

Oh. We're not done, Ana.

With my hands under her thighs, I lift her trembling body and carry her, still shackled to the grid, toward the Saint Andrew's cross. There I release her, holding her upright, pinned between the cross and my shoulders. I tug my jeans, undoing all the buttons, and freeing my cock. Yanking a condom from my pocket, I rip the foil packet with my teeth and with one hand roll it over my erection.

Gently I pick her up again and whisper, "Lift your legs, baby, wrap them around me." Supporting her back against the wood, I help her wrap her legs around my hips, her elbows resting on my shoulders.

You are mine, baby.

With one thrust I'm inside her.

Fuck. She's exquisite.

I take a moment to savor her. Then I start to move, relishing each thrust. Feeling her, on and on, my own breathing labored as I gasp for air and lose myself in this beautiful woman. My mouth is open at her neck, tasting her. Her scent fills my nostrils, fills me. *Ana. Ana. Ana.* I don't want to stop.

Suddenly she tenses, and her body convulses around me.

Yes. Again. And I let go. Filling her. Holding her. Revering her.

Yes. Yes. Yes.

She's so beautiful. And sweet hell, was that mind-blowing.

I pull out of her, and as she collapses against me I quickly unbuckle her wrists from the grid and support her as we both sink to the floor. I cradle her between my legs, wrapping my arms around her, and she sags against me, her eyes closed, breathing hard.

"Well done, baby. Did that hurt?"

"No." Her voice is barely audible.

"Did you expect it to?" I ask, and I push stray strands of her hair off her face so I can see her better.

"Yes."

"You see? Most of your fear is in your head, Anastasia." I caress her face. "Would you do it again?" I ask.

She doesn't answer immediately, and I think she's fallen asleep.

"Yes," she whispers a moment later.

Thank you, sweet Lord.

I wrap her in my arms. "Good. So would I." *Again and again.* Tenderly I kiss the top of her head and inhale. She smells of Ana and sweat and sex. "And I haven't finished with you yet," I assert.

I'm so proud of her. She did it. She did everything I wanted.

She's everything I want.

And suddenly I'm overwhelmed by an unfamiliar emotion that rocks through me, slicing through sinew and bone, leaving unease and fear in its wake.

She turns her head and starts to nuzzle my chest.

The darkness swells, startling and familiar, replacing my unease with a sense of dread. Every muscle in my body tenses. Ana blinks up at me with clear, unflinching eyes as I struggle to control my fear.

"Don't," I whisper. *Please.*

She leans back and peers at my chest.

Get control, Grey.

"Kneel by the door," I order, uncurling around her.

Go. Don't touch me.

Shakily she gets to her feet and stumbles over to the door, where she resumes her kneeling position.

I take a deep, centering breath.

What are you doing to me, Ana Steele?

I stand and stretch, calmer now.

As she kneels by the door, she looks every bit the ideal submissive. Her eyes are glazed; she's tired. I'm sure she's coming down from the adrenaline high. Her eyelids droop.

Oh, this will never do. You want her as a submissive, Grey. Show her what that means.

From my drawer of toys I fish out one of the cable ties I bought from Clayton's, and a pair of scissors. "Boring you, am I, Miss Steele?" I ask, masking my sympathy. She startles awake and regards me guiltily. "Stand up," I order.

Slowly she gets to her feet.

"You're shattered, aren't you?"

She nods with a bashful smile.

Oh, baby, you've done so well.

"Stamina, Miss Steele. I haven't had my fill of you yet. Hold out your hands in front, as if you're praying."

A crease mars her forehead for a moment, but she presses her palms together and holds up her hands. I fasten the cable tie around her wrists. Her eyes flash to mine with recognition.

"Look familiar?" I give her a smile and run my finger around the plastic, checking that there's enough room and it's not too tight. "I have scissors here." I bring them into her view. "I can cut you out of this in a moment." She looks reassured. "Come." Taking her clasped hands, I lead her to the far corner of the four-poster bed. "I want more—much, much more," I whisper in her ear as she stares down at the bed. "But I'll make this quick. You're tired. Hold on to the post."

Halting, she grasps the wooden pillar.

"Lower," I order. She moves her hands down to the base until she's bending over. "Good. Don't let go. If you do, I'll spank you. Understand?"

"Yes, Sir," she says.

"Good." I grab her hips and lift her toward me so she's properly positioned, her beautiful behind in the air and at my disposal. "Don't let go, Anastasia," I warn her. "I'm going to fuck you hard from behind. Hold the post to support your weight. Understand?"

"Yes."

I smack her hard across her backside.

"Yes, Sir," she says immediately.

"Part your legs." I push my right foot against hers, widening her stance. "That's better. After this, I'll let you sleep."

Her back is a perfect curve, each vertebra outlined from her nape to her fine, fine ass. I trace the line with my fingers. "You have such beautiful skin, Anastasia," I say to myself. Bending over her, I follow the path my fingers have taken with tender kisses down her spine. As I do, I palm her breasts, trapping her nipples between my fingers, and tug. She writhes beneath me, and I plant a soft kiss at her waist, then suck and gently nip her skin while working her nipples.

She whimpers. I stop and stand back to admire the view, growing harder just looking at her. Reaching for a second condom from my pocket, I quickly kick my jeans off and open the foil packet. Using both hands, I wrap it around my cock.

I'd like to claim her ass. Now. But it's too soon for that.

"You have such a captivating, sexy ass. What I'd like to do to it." I stroke my hands over each cheek, fondling her, then slide two fingers inside her, stretching her.

She whimpers again.

She's ready.

"So wet. You never disappoint, Miss Steele. Hold tight. This is going to be quick, baby."

Clutching her hips, I position myself at the entrance of her vagina, then reach up, grab her braid, wind it around my wrist, and hold it tightly. With one hand on my cock and the other around her hair, I slide into her.

She. Is. So. Fucking. Sweet.

Slowly I slide out of her, then grip her hip with my free hand and tighten my hold on her hair.

Submissive.

I slam into her, forcing her forward with a cry.

"Hold on, Anastasia!" I remind her. If she doesn't she might get hurt.

Breathless, she pushes back against me, bracing her legs.

Good girl.

Then I start pounding into her, eliciting small, strangled cries from her as she clings to the post. But she doesn't back down. She pushes back.

Bravo, Ana.

And then I feel it. Slowly. Her insides curling around me. Losing control, I slam into her, and still. "Come on, Ana, give it to me," I growl, as I come, hard, her release prolonging mine as I hold her up.

Gathering her in my arms, I lower us to the floor with Ana on top of me, both of us facing the ceiling. She's utterly relaxed, exhausted no doubt; her weight a welcome comfort. I stare up at the karabiners, wondering if she'll ever let me suspend her.

Probably not.

And I don't care.

Our first time together in here, and she's been a dream. I kiss her ear. "Hold up your hands." My voice is husky. Slowly, she raises them as if they're weighted with concrete, and I slide the scissors beneath the cable tie.

"I declare this Ana open." I murmur, and snip, freeing her. She giggles, her body juddering against mine. It's a strange and not unwelcome feeling that makes me grin.

"That is such a lovely sound," I whisper as she rubs her wrists. I sit up so that she's in my lap.

I love making her laugh. She doesn't laugh enough.

"That's my fault," I admit to myself as I rub some life back into her shoulders and arms. She turns her face to me with a weary, searching look. "That you don't giggle more often," I clarify.

"I'm not a great giggler," she says, and yawns.

"Oh, but when it happens, 'tis a wonder and joy to behold."

"Very flowery, Mr. Grey," she says, teasing me.

I smile. "I'd say you're thoroughly fucked and in need of sleep."

"That wasn't flowery at all," she scoffs, scolding me.

Lifting her off my lap so I can stand up, I reach for my jeans and slip them on. "Don't want to frighten Taylor, or Mrs. Jones, for that matter."

It wouldn't be the first time.

Ana sits in a sleepy daze on the floor. I clasp her upper arms, help her to her feet, and take her to the door. From the hook on the back of the door I grab the gray robe and dress her. She's no help whatsoever; she really is exhausted.

"Bed," I announce, kissing her quickly.

An alarmed expression crosses her drowsy face.

"For sleep," I reassure her. And bending down, I gather her in my arms, cradle her against my chest, and carry her to the sub's room. There I pull back the comforter and lay her down, and in a moment of weakness climb into the bed beside her. Covering us both with the duvet, I embrace her.

I'll just hold her until she's asleep.

"Sleep now, gorgeous girl." I kiss her hair feeling utterly sated . . . and grateful. We did it. This sweet, innocent woman let me loose on her. And I think she enjoyed it. I know I did . . . more than ever before.

Mommy sits looking at me in the mirror with the big
crack.
I brush her hair. It's soft and smells of Mommy and flowers.
She takes the brush and winds her hair round and round.
So it's like a bumpy snake down her back.
There, she says.
And she turns around and smiles at me.
Today, she's happy.
I like when Mommy is happy.
I like it when she smiles at me.

She looks pretty when she smiles.
Let's bake a pie, Maggot.
Apple pie.
I like when Mommy bakes.

I wake suddenly with a sweet scent invading my mind. It's Ana.
She's fast asleep beside me. I lie back and stare at the ceiling.
When have I ever slept in this room?
Never.
The thought is unnerving, and for some unfathomable reason
it makes me uneasy.
What's going on, Grey?
I sit up carefully, not wanting to disturb her, and stare down at
her sleeping form. I know what it is—I'm unsettled because I'm in
here with her. I climb out of bed, leaving her to sleep, and head
back to the playroom. There I collect the used cable tie and condoms and stash them in my pocket, where I find Ana's panties.
With the crop, her clothes, and her shoes in hand, I leave and lock
the door. Back in her room, I hang her dress on the closet door,
place her shoes beneath the chair, and lay her bra on top. I take her
panties from my pocket—and a wicked idea comes to mind.

I head for my bathroom. I need a shower before we head to dinner with my family. I'll let Ana sleep awhile longer.

The piping-hot water cascades over me, washing away all the
anxiety and unease that I'd felt earlier. As first times go, that was
not bad, for either of us. And I'd thought that a relationship with
Ana was impossible, but now the future now seems full of possibility. I make a mental note to call Caroline Acton in the morning to
dress my girl.

After a productive hour in my study, catching up on my reading for work, I decide that Ana has had enough sleep. It's dusk
outside, and we have to leave in forty-five minutes for dinner at my
parents'. It's been easier to concentrate on my work, knowing that
she's upstairs in her bedroom.
Weird.
Well, I know she's safe up there.

From the refrigerator I take a carton of cranberry juice and a bottle of sparkling water. I mix them in a glass and head upstairs.

She's still fast asleep, curled up where I left her. I don't think she's moved at all. Her lips are parted as she breathes softly. Her hair is tousled, tendrils escaping from her braid. I sit on the edge of the bed beside her, lean down, and kiss her temple. She mumbles a protest in her sleep.

"Anastasia, wake up." My voice is gentle as I coax her awake.

"No," she grumbles, hugging her pillow.

"We have to leave in half an hour for dinner at my parents'."

Her eyes flicker open and focus on me.

"Come on, sleepyhead. Get up." I kiss her temple again. "I've brought you a drink. I'll be downstairs. Don't go back to sleep, or you'll be in trouble," I warn as she stretches her arms. I kiss her once more and with a glance at the chair, where she won't find her panties, I saunter back downstairs, unable to suppress my grin.

Playtime, Grey.

While I'm waiting for Miss Steele I press a button on the iPod remote and the music springs to life on random shuffle. Restless, I wander over to the balcony doors and stare out at the early evening sky, listening to Talking Heads' "And She Was."

Taylor enters. "Mr. Grey. Shall I bring the car around?"

"Give us five minutes."

"Yes, sir," he says, and disappears toward the service elevator.

Ana appears a few minutes later at the entrance to the living room. She looks luminous, stunning even . . . and amused. What's she going to say about her missing panties?

"Hi," she says with a cryptic smile.

"Hi. How are you feeling?"

Her smile broadens. "Good, thanks. You?" She feigns nonchalance.

"I feel mighty fine, Miss Steele." The suspense is tantalizing and I hope my anticipation is not written all over my face.

"Frank? I never figured you for a Sinatra fan," she says, cocking her head and giving me a curious look, as the rich tones of "Witch-craft" fill the room.

"Eclectic taste, Miss Steele." I step toward her until I'm stand-ing right in front of her. *Will she crack?* I'm searching for an answer in her glittering blue eyes.

Ask me for your panties, baby.

I caress her cheek with my fingertips. She leans her face into my touch—and I'm completely seduced—by her sweet gesture, by her teasing expression, and by the music. I want her in my arms.

"Dance with me," I whisper, as I remove the remote from my pocket and turn up the volume until Frank's crooning surrounds us. She gives me her hand. I circle her waist and pull her beautiful body against mine, and we start a slow, simple fox-trot. She grasps my shoulder, but I'm prepared for her touch, and together we whirl across the floor, her radiant face lighting up the room . . . and me. She falls into step with my lead, and when the song comes to an end, she's giddy and breathless.

And so am I.

"There's no nicer witch than you." I plant a chaste kiss on her lips. "Well, that's brought some color to your cheeks. Thank you for the dance. Shall we go and meet my parents?"

"You're welcome, and yes, I can't wait to meet them," she replies, looking flushed and lovely.

"Do you have everything you need?"

"Oh yes," she says with easy confidence.

"Are you sure?"

She nods, her lips carved in a smirk.

God, she has guts.

I grin. "Okay." I can't hide my delight. "If that's the way you want to play it, Miss Steele." I grab my jacket and we head to the elevator.

She never fails to surprise, impress, and disarm me. Now I will have to sit through dinner with my parents, knowing my girl is not wearing any underwear. In fact, I'm traveling down in this elevator right now, knowing she's naked beneath her skirt.

She's turned the tables on you, Grey.

_____

SHE'S QUIET AS TAYLOR drives us north on I-5. I catch a glimpse of Union Lake; the moon disappears behind a cloud, and the water darkens, like my mood. Why am I taking her to see my parents? If they meet her, they'll have certain expectations. And so will Ana. And I'm not sure if the relationship I want with Ana will live up to those expectations. And to make matters worse, I put all this in motion when I insisted she meet Grace. I'm the only one to blame. Me, and the fact that Elliot is fucking her roommate.

Who am I kidding? If I didn't want her to meet my folks, she wouldn't be here. I just wish I wasn't so anxious about it.

Yeah. That's the problem.

"Where did you learn to dance?" she asks, interrupting my chain of thoughts.

Oh, Ana. She's not going to want me to go there.

"Christian, hold me. There. Properly. Right. One step. Two. Good. Keep in time to the music. Sinatra is perfect for the fox-trot." Elena is in her element.

"Yes, Ma'am."

"Do you really want to know?" I answer.

"Yes," she replies, but her tone says otherwise.

You asked. I sigh in the darkness beside her. "Mrs. Robinson was fond of dancing."

"She must have been a good teacher." Her whisper is tinged with regret and reluctant admiration.

"She was."

"That's right. Again. One. Two. Three. Four. Baby, you've got this."

Elena and I glide across her basement.

"Again." She laughs, her head thrown back, and she looks like a woman half her age.

Ana nods and studies the landscape, no doubt concocting some theory about Elena. Or maybe she's thinking about meeting my parents. I wish I knew. Perhaps she's nervous. Like me. I've never taken a girl home.

When Ana starts fidgeting I sense something is worrying her. Is she concerned about what we did today?

"Don't," I say, my voice softer than I intend.

She turns to look at me, her expression unreadable in the dark. "Don't what?"

"Overthink things, Anastasia." Whatever you're thinking about. I reach over, take her hand, and kiss her knuckles. "I had a wonderful afternoon. Thank you."

I get a brief flash of white teeth and a timid smile.

"Why did you use a cable tie?" she asks.

Questions about this afternoon; this is good. "It's quick, it's easy, and it's something different for you to feel and experience. I know they're quite brutal, and I do like that in a restraining device." My voice is dry as I try to inject a little humor back into our conversation. "Very effective at keeping you in your place."

Her eyes dart toward Taylor in the front seat.

Sweetheart, don't worry about Taylor. He knows exactly what's going on, and he's done this for four years.

"All part of my world, Anastasia." I give her hand a reassuring squeeze before I release it. Ana returns to staring out of the window; we're surrounded by water as we cross Lake Washington on the 520 bridge, my favorite part of this journey. She draws up her feet and, curled on the seat, coils her arms around her legs.

Something is up.

When she glances at me, I ask, "Penny for your thoughts?"

She sighs.

Shit. "That bad, huh?"

"I wish I knew what you were thinking," she says.

I smirk, relieved to hear this, and glad she doesn't know what's really on my mind.

"Ditto, baby," I reply.

TAYLOR PULLS UP OUTSIDE my parents' front door. "Are you ready for this?" I ask. Ana nods and I squeeze her hand. "First for me, too," I whisper. When Taylor's out the door I give her a wicked, salacious grin. "Bet you wish you were wearing your underwear right now."

Her breath hitches and she scowls, but I climb out of the car to greet my mother and father, who are waiting on the doorstep. Ana looks cool and calm as she walks around the car to us. "Anastasia, you've met my mother, Grace. This is my dad, Carrick."

"Mr. Grey, what a pleasure to meet you." She smiles and shakes his outstretched hand.

"The pleasure is all mine, Anastasia."

"Please, call me Ana."

"Ana, how lovely to see you again." Grace hugs her. "Come in, my dear." Taking Ana's arm, she leads her inside and I follow in her pantyless wake.

"Is she here?" Mia screams from somewhere inside the house. Ana gives me a startled look.

"That would be Mia, my little sister."

We both turn in the direction of the high heels clattering through the hall. And there she is. "Anastasia! I've heard so much about you!" Mia wraps her in a big hug. Though she's taller than Ana, I remember they're almost the same age.

Mia takes her hand and drags her into the vestibule as my parents and I follow. "He's never brought a girl home before," Mia tells Ana in a shrill voice.

"Mia, calm down," Grace chides.

Yes, for fuck's sake, Mia. Stop making such a scene.

Ana catches me rolling my eyes and shoots me a withering look.

Grace greets me with a kiss on both cheeks. "Hello, darling." She's glowing, happy to have all her children home. Carrick offers his hand. "Hello, son. Long time no see." We shake hands and follow the women into the living room. "Dad, you saw me yesterday," I mutter. "Dad jokes"—my father excels at them.

Kavanagh and Elliot are cuddling on one of the sofas. But Kavanagh gets up to hug Ana when we enter.

"Christian." She gives me a polite nod.

"Kate."

And now Elliot has his big paws all over Ana.

Fuck, who knew my family was so touchy-feely all of a sudden? *Put her down.* I glare at Elliot and he grins—an I'm-just-showing-you-how-it's-done expression plastered all over his face. I slip my arm around Ana's waist and pull her to my side. All eyes are on us.

Hell. This feels like a freak show.

"Drinks?" Dad offers. "Prosecco?"

"Please," Ana and I reply together.

Mia bounces on the spot and claps her hands. "You're even saying the same things. I'll get them." She dashes out of the room.

What the hell is wrong with my family?

Ana frowns. She's probably finding them weird, too.

"Dinner's almost ready," Grace says as she follows Mia out of the room.

"Sit," I tell Ana, and I lead her over to one of the sofas. She does as she's told and I sit at her side, careful not to touch her. I need to set an example for my overly demonstrative family.

Maybe they've always been this way?

My father diverts me. "We were just talking about vacations, Ana. Elliot has decided to follow Kate and her family to Barbados for a week."

Dude! I stare at Elliot. *What the hell happened to Mr. Love 'Em and Leave 'Em?* Kavanagh must be good in the sack. She certainly looks smug enough.

"Are you taking a break now that you've finished your degree?" Carrick asks Ana.

"I'm thinking about going to Georgia for a few days," she answers.

"Georgia?" I exclaim, unable to hide my surprise.

"My mother lives there," she says, her voice wavering, "and I haven't seen her for a while."

"When were you thinking of going?" I snap.

"Tomorrow, late evening."

Tomorrow! What the fuck? And I'm only learning of this now?

Mia returns with pink prosecco for Ana and me.

"Your good health!" Dad raises his glass.

"For how long?" I persist, trying to keep my voice level.

"I don't know yet. It will depend how my interviews go tomorrow."

Interviews? Tomorrow?

"Ana deserves a break," Kavanagh interrupts, staring at me with ill-concealed antagonism. I want to tell her to mind her own fucking business, but for Ana's sake I hold my tongue.

"You have interviews?" Dad asks Ana.

"Yes, for internships at two publishers, tomorrow."

When was she going to tell me this? I'm here with her for two minutes and I'm finding out details of her life that I should know!

"I wish you the best of luck," Carrick says to her with a kind smile.

"Dinner is ready," Grace calls from across the hall.

I let the others exit the room but grab Ana's elbow before she can follow.

"When were you going to tell me you were leaving?" My temper is rapidly unraveling.

"I'm not leaving. I'm going to see my mother. And I was only thinking about it." Ana dismisses me, as if I'm a child.

"What about our arrangement?"

"We don't have an arrangement yet."

But . . .

I lead us through the living room door and into the hallway. "This conversation is not over," I warn as we enter the dining room.

Mom has gone all out—best china, best crystal—for Ana's and Kavanagh's benefit. I hold out a chair for Ana; she sits down and I take a seat beside her. Mia beams at both of us from across the table. "Where did you meet Ana?" Mia asks.

"She interviewed me for the WSU student newspaper."

"Which Kate edits," Ana interjects.

"I want to be a journalist," Kate tells Mia.

My father offers Ana some wine while Mia and Kate discuss journalism. Kavanagh has an internship at the *Seattle Times*, no doubt set up for her by her father.

From the corner of my eye I notice that Ana's studying me.

"What?" I ask.

"Please don't be mad at me," she says, so low that only I can hear.

"I'm not mad at you," I lie.

Her eyes narrow, and it's obvious she doesn't believe me.

"Yes, I am mad at you," I confess. And now I feel like I'm overreacting. I close my eyes.

Get a grip, Grey.

"Palm-twitchingly mad?" she whispers.

"What are you two whispering about?" Kavanagh interrupts.

Good God! Is she always like this? So intrusive? How the hell does Elliot put up with her? I glower at her, and she has the sense to back off.

"Just about my trip to Georgia," Ana says, with sweetness and charm.

Kate smirks. "How was José when you went to the bar with him on Friday?" she asks, with a brash look in my direction.

What. The. Fuck. Is. This?

Ana tenses beside me.

"He was fine," she says quietly.

"Palm-twitchingly mad," I whisper to her. "Especially now."

So she went to a bar with the guy who was trying to ram his tongue down her throat the last time I saw him. *And* she'd already agreed to be mine. Sneaking off to a bar with another man? And without my permission . . .

She deserves to be punished.

Around me, dinner is being served.

I've agreed not to go too hard on her . . . maybe I should use a flogger. Or maybe I should administer a straightforward spanking, harder than the last one. Here, tonight.

Yes. That has possibilities.

Ana's looking down at her fingers. Kate, Elliot, and Mia are in a conversation about French cooking, and Dad returns to the table. Where's he been?

"Call for you, darling. It's the hospital," he says to Grace.

"Please start, everyone," Mom says, passing a plate of food to Ana.

Smells good.

Ana licks her lips and the action resonates in my groin. She must be starving. *Good.* That's something.

Mom has surpassed herself: chorizo, scallops, peppers. Nice. And I realize that I, too, am hungry. That can't be helping my mood. But I brighten watching Ana eat.

Grace returns, looking worried. "Everything okay?" Dad asks, and we all look up at her.

"Another measles case." Grace sighs heavily.

"Oh no," Dad says.

"Yes, a child. The fourth case this month. If only people would get their kids vaccinated." Grace shakes her head. "I'm so glad our children never went through that. They never caught anything worse than chicken pox, thank goodness. Poor Elliot." We all look at Elliot, who stops eating, mid-chew, mouth stuffed full, bovine. He's uncomfortable being the center of attention.

Kavanagh gives Grace a questioning look.

"Christian and Mia were lucky," Grace explains. "They got it so mildly, only a spot to share between them."

Oh, give it a rest, Mom.

"So, did you catch the Mariners game, Dad?" Elliot's clearly keen to move the conversation on, as am I.

"I can't believe they beat the Yankees," Carrick says.

"Did you watch the game, hotshot?" Elliot asks me.

"No. But I read the sports column."

"The M's are going places. Nine games won out of the last eleven, gives me hope." Dad sounds excited.

"They're certainly having a better season than 2010," I add.

"Gutierrez in center field was awesome. That catch! Wow."

Elliot throws up his arms. Kavanagh fawns over him like a lovesick fool.

"How are you settling into your new apartment, dear?" Grace asks Ana.

"We've only been there one night, and I still have to unpack, but I love that it's so central—and a short walk to Pike Place, and near the water."

"Oh, so you're close to Christian, then," Grace remarks.

Mom's helper starts to clear the table. I still can't remember her name. She's Swiss, or Austrian or something, and she doesn't stop simpering and batting eyelashes at me.

"Have you been to Paris, Ana?" Mia asks.

"No, but I'd love to go."

"We honeymooned in Paris," Mom says. She and Dad exchange a look across the table, which frankly I'd prefer not to see. They obviously had a good time.

"It's a beautiful city, in spite of the Parisians. Christian, you should take Ana to Paris!" Mia exclaims.

"I think Anastasia would prefer London," I respond to my sister's ridiculous suggestion. Placing my hand on Ana's knee, I explore her thigh at a leisurely pace, her dress riding up as my fingers follow. I want to touch her; stroke her where her panties should be. As my cock rouses in anticipation I suppress a groan and shuffle in my seat.

She jerks away from me as if to cross her legs, and I close my hand around her thigh.

Don't you dare!

Ana takes a sip of wine, not taking her eyes off my mother's housekeeper, who is serving our entrées.

"So what was wrong with the Parisians? Didn't they take to your winsome ways?" Elliot teases Mia.

"Ugh, no, they didn't. And Monsieur Floubert, the ogre I was working for, he was such a domineering tyrant."

Ana chokes on her wine.

"Anastasia, are you okay?" I ask, and release her thigh.

She nods, her cheeks red, and I pat her back and gently caress her neck. Domineering tyrant? Am I? The thought amuses me. Mia shoots me a look of approval at my public display of affection.

Mom has cooked her signature dish, Beef Wellington, a recipe she picked up in London. I have to say it ranks close to yesterday's buttermilk fried chicken. In spite of her choking episode, Ana tucks into her meal and it's so good to see her eat. She's probably hungry after our energetic afternoon. I take a sip of my wine as I contemplate other ways to make her hungry.

Mia and Kavanagh are discussing the relative merits of St. Bart's vs. Barbados, where the Kavanagh family will be staying.

"Remember Elliot and the jellyfish?" Mia's eyes shine with mirth as she looks from Elliot to me.

I chuckle. "Screaming like a girl? Yeah."

"Hey, that could have been a Portuguese man-of-war! I hate jellyfish. They ruin everything." Elliot is emphatic. Mia and Kate burst into giggles, nodding in agreement.

Ana is eating heartily and listening to the banter. Everyone else has calmed down, and my family is being less weird. Why am I so tense? This happens every day all across the country, families gathering to enjoy good food and each other's company. Am I tense because I have Ana here? Am I worried they won't like her, or that she won't like them? Or is it because she's fucking off to Georgia tomorrow, and I knew nothing about that?

It's confusing.

Mia takes center stage as usual. Her tales of French life and French cooking are entertaining. "Oh, Mom, *les pâtisseries sont tout simplement fabuleuses. La tarte aux pommes de M. Floubert est incroyable,*" she says.

"*Mia, chérie, tu parles français,*" I interrupt her. "*Nous parlons anglais ici. Eh bien, à l'exception bien sûr d'Elliot. Il parle idiote, couramment.*"

Mia throws her head back with a bellowing laugh, and it's impossible not to join her.

But by the end of dinner the tension is really wearing me down. I want to be alone with my girl. I've only so much tolerance for inane chatter, even if it's with my family, and I've reached my limit.

I peer down at Ana, then reach over and tug her chin. "Don't bite your lip. I want to do that."

I also have to establish a few ground rules. We need to discuss her impromptu trip to Georgia and going out for drinks with men who are infatuated with her. I put my hand on Ana's knee again; I need to touch her. Besides, she should accept my touch, whenever I want to touch her. I gauge her reaction as my fingers travel up her thigh toward her panty-free zone, teasing her skin. Her breath catches and she squeezes her thighs together, blocking my fingers, stopping me.

That's it.

I have to excuse us from the dinner table. "Shall I give you a tour of the grounds?" I ask Ana, and I don't give her a chance to answer. Her eyes are luminous and serious as she places her hand in mine.

"Excuse me," she says to Carrick, and I lead her out of the dining room.

In the kitchen Mia and Mom are clearing up. "I'm going to show Anastasia the backyard," I announce to my mother, pretending to be cheerful.

Outside, my mood plunges south as my anger surfaces.

Panties. The photographer. Georgia.

We cross the terrace and climb the steps to the lawn. Ana pauses for a moment to admire the view.

Yeah, yeah. Seattle. Lights. Moon. Water.

I continue across the vast lawn toward my parents' boathouse.

"Stop, please," Ana pleads.

I do, and glare at her.

"My heels. I need to take my shoes off."

"Don't bother," I growl, and lift her quickly over my shoulder. She squeals in surprise.

Hell. I smack her ass, hard. "Keep your voice down!" I snap, and stride across the lawn.

"Where are we going?" she wails as she bounces on my shoulder.

"Boathouse."

"Why?"

"I need to be alone with you."

"What for?"

"Because I'm going to spank and then fuck you."

"Why?" she whines.

"You know why," I snap.

"I thought you were an in-the-moment guy?"

"Anastasia, I'm in the moment, trust me."

Throwing open the boathouse door, I step inside and switch on the light. As the fluorescents ping to life I head upstairs to the snug. There I flip another switch, and halogens illuminate the room.

I slide Ana down my body, glorying in the feel of her, and I set her on her feet. Her hair is dark and untamed, her eyes shining in the glow of the lights, and I know she's not wearing her panties. I want her. Now.

"Please don't hit me," she whispers.

I don't understand. I stare down at her blankly.

"I don't want you to spank me, not here, not now. Please don't."

But . . . I gape at her, paralyzed. *That's why we're here.* She lifts her hand, and for a moment I don't know what she's going to do. The darkness stirs and twists around my throat, threatening to choke me if she touches me. But she places her fingers on my cheek and gently skims them down to my chin. The darkness melts into oblivion and I close my eyes, feeling her gentle fingertips on me. With her other hand she ruffles my hair, running her fingers through it.

"Ah," I moan, and I don't know if it's from fear or longing. I'm breathless, standing on a precipice. When I open my eyes, she steps forward so her body is flush against mine. She fists both hands in my hair and tugs gently, raising her lips to mine. And I'm watching her do this, like a bystander, not present in my body. I'm a spectator. Our lips touch and I close my eyes as she forces her tongue into my mouth. And it's the sound of my groan that breaks the spell she's cast.

Ana.

I wrap my arms around her, kissing her back, releasing two hours of anxiety and tension into our kiss, my tongue possessing

her, reconnecting with her. My hands grip her hair and I savor her
taste, her tongue, her frame against mine as my body ignites like
gasoline.

Fuck.

When I pull away we're both dragging air into our lungs, her
hands clutching my arms. I'm confused. I wanted to spank her. But
she's said no. Like she did at the dinner table. "What are you doing
to me?" I ask.

"Kissing you."

"You said no."

"What?" She's bewildered, or maybe she's forgotten what happened.

"At the dinner table, with your legs."

"But we were at your parents' dining table."

"No one's ever said no to me before. And it's so—hot." And
different. I slide my hand around her backside and jolt her against
me, trying to regain control.

"You're mad and turned on because I said no?" Her voice is
throaty.

"I'm mad because you never mentioned Georgia to me. I'm
mad because you went drinking with that guy who tried to seduce
you when you were drunk, and who left you when you were ill with
an almost complete stranger. What kind of friend does that? And
I'm mad and aroused because you closed your legs on me."

And you're not wearing panties.

My fingers inch her dress up her legs. "I want you, and I want
you now. And if you're not going to let me spank you—which
you deserve—I'm going to fuck you on the couch, this minute,
quickly—for my pleasure, not yours."

Holding her against me, I see that she's panting as I slip my
hand through her pubic hair and slide my middle finger inside her.
I hear a low, sexy hum of appreciation in her throat. She's so ready.

"This is mine. All mine. Do you understand?" I slip my finger
in and out of her, holding her, as her lips part with shock and desire.

"Yes, yours," she whispers.

Yes. Mine. And I won't let you forget it, Ana.

I push her down onto the couch, unzip my fly, and lie down on top of her, pinning her beneath me. "Hands on your head," I growl through clenched teeth. I kneel up and spread my knees, forcing her legs wider. From the inside pocket of my jacket I take out a condom, then discard my jacket on the floor. With my eyes on hers I open the packet and roll it down my eager dick. Ana places her hands on her head, watching me, her eyes glinting with need. As I crawl over her she's squirming beneath me, her hips rising to tease and greet me.

"We don't have long. This will be quick, and it's for me, not you. Do you understand? Don't come, or I will spank you," I order, focusing on her dazed wide eyes, and with a swift, hard move I bury myself inside her. She calls out in a welcome and familiar cry of pleasure. I hold her down so she can't move, and I start to fuck her, consuming her. But greedily she tilts her pelvis, meeting me thrust for thrust, spurring me on.

Oh, Ana. Yes, baby.

She gives it back to me, matching my fervent pace, over and over.

Oh, the feel of her.

And I'm lost. In her. In this. In her scent. And I don't know if it's because I'm mad or tense or . . .

Yessss. I come quickly, losing all reason as I explode inside her. I still. Filling her. Owning her. Reminding her that she's mine.

Fuck.

That was . . .

I pull out of her and kneel up.

"Don't touch yourself." My voice is hoarse and breathless. "I want you frustrated. That's what you do to me by not talking to me, by denying me what's mine."

She nods, sprawled out beneath me, her dress bunched up around her waist so I can see she's wide and wet and wanting, and looking every bit the goddess that she is. I stand up, remove the wretched condom and knot it, then dress, picking up my jacket from the floor.

I take a deep breath. I'm calmer now. Much calmer.

Fuck, that was good.

"We'd better get back to the house."

She sits up, staring at me with dark, inscrutable eyes.

Lord, she's lovely.

"Here. You may put these on." From my jacket pocket I fish out her lacy panties and pass them to her. I think she's trying not to laugh.

Yeah, yeah. Game, set, and match to you, Miss Steele.

"*Christian!*" Mia yells from the floor below.

Shit.

"Just in time. Christ, she can be really irritating." But that's my little sister. Alarmed, I glance at Ana as she slips on her underwear. She scowls at me as she stands to straighten her dress and fixes her hair with her fingers.

"Up here, Mia," I call. "Well, Miss Steele, I feel better for that—but I still want to spank you."

"I don't believe I deserve it, Mr. Grey, especially after tolerating your unprovoked attack." She is crisp and formal.

"Unprovoked? You kissed me."

"It was attack as the best form of defense."

"Defense against what?"

"You and your twitchy palm." She's trying to suppress a smile.

Mia's high heels rattle up the stairs.

"But it was tolerable?" I ask.

Ana smirks. "Barely."

"Oh, there you are!" Mia exclaims, beaming at the two of us. Two minutes earlier and this could have been really awkward.

"I was showing Anastasia around." I hold out my hand to Ana and she takes it. I want to kiss her knuckles, but I settle for a soft squeeze.

"Kate and Elliot are about to leave. Can you believe those two? They can't keep their hands off each other." Mia wrinkles her nose in distaste. "What have you been doing in here?"

"Showing Anastasia my rowing trophies." With my free hand

I wave toward the faux-precious-metal statuettes from my sculling days at Harvard arranged on shelves at the end of the room. "Let's go say good-bye to Kate and Elliot."

Mia turns to go and I let Ana precede me, but before we get to the stairs I smack her behind.

She smothers her yelp.

"I will do it again, Anastasia, and soon," I whisper in her ear, and folding her into my arms, I kiss her hair.

We walk hand in hand across the lawn back to the house while Mia gabbles beside us. It's a beautiful evening; it's been a beautiful day. I'm glad Ana's met my family.

Why haven't I done this before?

Because I've never wanted to.

I squeeze Ana's hand, and she gives me a shy look and an oh-so-sweet smile. In my other hand I hold her shoes, and at the stone steps I bend down to fasten each of her sandals in turn.

"There," I announce when I'm done.

"Why, thank you, Mr. Grey," she says.

"The pleasure is, and was, all mine."

"I'm well aware of that, Sir," she teases.

"Oh, you two are sooo sweet!" Mia coos as we head into the kitchen. Ana gives me a sideways look.

Back in the hallway, Kavanagh and Elliot are about to leave. Ana hugs Kate, but then pulls her aside to have a heated private conversation. *What the hell is that about?* Elliot takes Kavanagh's arm and my parents wave them off as they climb into Elliot's pickup.

"We should go, too—you have interviews tomorrow." We have to drive her back to her new apartment and it's nearly 11:00.

"We never thought he'd find anyone!" Mia gushes as she hugs Ana, hard.

Oh, for fuck's sake . . .

"Take care of yourself, Ana dear," Grace says, smiling warmly at my girl. I pull Ana to my side.

"Let's not frighten her away or spoil her with too much affection."

"Christian, stop teasing," Grace chastises me in her usual manner.

"Mom." I give her a quick peck. Thank you for inviting Ana. It's been a revelation.

Ana says good-bye to my dad, and we head to the Audi, where Taylor waits, holding the rear passenger door open for her.

"Well, it seems my family likes you, too," I observe when I've joined Ana in the back. Her eyes reflect the light from my parents' porch, but I can't tell what she's thinking. Shadows shroud her face as Taylor drives smoothly out onto the road.

I catch her staring at me under the flicker of a street lamp. She's anxious. Something's wrong.

"What?" I ask.

She is quiet at first, and when she speaks there's an emptiness in her voice. "I think that you felt trapped into bringing me to meet your parents. If Elliot hadn't asked Kate, you'd never have asked me."

Damn. She doesn't understand. It was a first for me. I was nervous. Surely she knows by now that if I didn't want her here, she wouldn't be here. As we pass from light to shadow under the street lamps, she looks distant and upset.

Grey, this will not do.

"Anastasia, I'm delighted that you've met my parents. Why are you so filled with self-doubt? It never ceases to amaze me. You're such a strong, self-contained young woman, but you have such negative thoughts about yourself. If I hadn't wanted you to meet them, you wouldn't be here. Is that how you were feeling the whole time you were there?" I shake my head, reach for her hand, and give it another reassuring squeeze.

She glances nervously at Taylor.

"Don't worry about Taylor. Talk to me."

"Yes. I thought that," she says quietly. "And another thing, I only mentioned Georgia because Kate was talking about Barbados. I haven't made up my mind."

"Do you want to go and see your mother?"

"Yes."

My anxiety surfaces. Does she want out? If she goes to Georgia, her mother might persuade her to find someone more . . . suitable, someone who, like her mother, believes in romance.

I have an idea. She's met my folks; I've met Ray; perhaps I should meet her mother, the incurable romantic. Charm her.

"Can I come with you?" I ask, knowing that she'll say no.

"Um, I don't think that's a good idea," she answers, surprised by my question.

"Why not?"

"I was hoping for a break from all this . . . intensity. To try to think things through."

Shit. She does want to leave me.

"I'm too intense?"

She laughs. "That's putting it mildly!"

Damn, I love making her laugh, even if it is at my expense; and I'm relieved she's kept her sense of humor. Perhaps she doesn't want to leave me after all. "Are you laughing at me, Miss Steele?" I tease.

"I wouldn't dare, Mr. Grey."

"I think you dare, and I think you do laugh at me, frequently."

"You are quite funny."

"Funny?"

"Oh yes."

She's making fun of me. It's novel. "Funny peculiar or funny ha-ha?"

"Oh, a lot of one and some of the other."

"Which way more?"

"I'll leave you to figure that out."

I sigh. "I'm not sure if I can figure anything out around you." My tone is dry. "What do you need to think about in Georgia?"

"Us."

Fuck. "You said you'd try," I gently remind her.

"I know."

"Are you having second thoughts?"

"Possibly."

It's worse than I feared. "Why?"

She stares at me in silence. "Why, Anastasia?" I persist. She shrugs, her mouth turned down, and I hope she'll find her hand in mine reassuring. "Talk to me. I don't want to lose you. This last week—"

Has been the best in my life.

"I still want more," she breathes.

Oh no, not this again. What does she need me to say?

"I know. I'll try." I clasp her chin. "For you, Anastasia, I will try."

I've just taken you to meet my parents, for heaven's sake.

Suddenly she unbuckles her seatbelt, and before I know it she's scrambled into my lap.

What the hell?

I sit immobile as her arms slip around my head, and her lips find mine, and coax a kiss from me before the darkness has a chance to stir. My hands slide up her back until I'm cradling her head and returning her passion, exploring her sweet, sweet mouth, trying to find answers . . . Her unexpected affection is utterly disarming. And new. And confusing. I thought she wanted to leave, and now she's in my lap and turning me on, again.

I've never . . . never . . . Don't go, Ana.

"Stay with me tonight. If you go away, I won't see you all week. Please," I whisper.

"Yes," she murmurs. "And I'll try, too. I'll sign your contract."

Oh, baby.

"Sign after Georgia. Think about it. Think about it hard." I want her to do this willingly—I don't want to force this on her. Well, part of me doesn't. The rational part.

"I will," she says, and nestles against me.

This woman has me tied up in knots.

Ironic, Grey.

And I want to laugh because I'm relieved and happy, but I hold her, breathing in her redolent and comforting scent.

"You really should wear your seatbelt," I scold, but I don't want her to move. She stays wrapped in my embrace, her body slowly relaxing against mine. The darkness inside me is quiet, contained, and I'm confused by my warring emotions. What do I want out of her? What do I need out of her?

This is not how we should be progressing, but I like her in my arms; I like cradling her like this. I kiss her hair, and lean back and enjoy the ride into Seattle.

Taylor stops outside the entrance to Escala. "We're home," I whisper to Ana. I'm reluctant to release her, but I lift her onto her seat. Taylor opens her door and she joins me at the entrance to the building.

A shiver runs through her.

"Why don't you have a jacket?" I ask as I slip mine off and drape it over her shoulders.

"It's in my new car," she says, yawning.

"Tired, Miss Steele?"

"Yes, Mr. Grey. I've been prevailed upon in ways I never thought possible today."

"Well, if you're really unlucky, I may prevail upon you some more." *If I get lucky.*

She leans against the wall of the elevator as we travel up to the penthouse. Under my jacket she looks slim and small and sexy. If she wasn't wearing her underwear I could take her in here . . . I reach up and free her lip from her teeth. "One day I will fuck you in this elevator, Anastasia, but right now you're tired—so I think we should stick to a bed." I bend down and gently take her bottom lip in my teeth. Her breath catches and she returns the gesture with her teeth and my upper lip.

I feel it in my groin.

I want to take her to bed and lose myself in her. After our conversation in the car I just want to be sure she's mine. When we exit the elevator I offer her a drink, but she declines.

"Good. Let's go to bed."

She looks surprised. "You're going to settle for plain old vanilla?"

"Nothing plain or old about vanilla. It's a very intriguing flavor."

"Since when?"

"Since last Saturday. Why? Were you hoping for something more exotic?"

"Oh no. I've had enough exotic for one day."

"Sure? We cater for all tastes here—at least thirty-one flavors." I give her a lascivious look.

"I've noticed." She raises one fine eyebrow.

"Come on, Miss Steele, you have a big day tomorrow. Sooner you're in bed, sooner you'll be fucked, and sooner you can sleep."

"Mr. Grey, you are a born romantic."

"Miss Steele, you have a smart mouth. I may have to subdue it some way. Come."

Yeah. I can think of one way.

Closing the door of my bedroom, I feel lighter than I did in the car. She's still here. "Hands in the air," I order, and she does as she's told. I grip the hem of her dress and in one smooth move pull it up and over her body to reveal the beautiful woman beneath.

"Ta-da!" I'm a magician. Ana giggles and gives me a round of applause. I bow, enjoying the game, before placing her dress on my chair.

"And for your next trick?" she asks, eyes glittering.

"Oh, my dear Miss Steele. Get into my bed, and I'll show you."

"Do you think that for once I should play hard to get?" she teases, tilting her head to one side so her hair tumbles over her shoulder.

A new game. This is interesting.

"Well, the door's closed. Not sure how you're going to avoid me. I think it's a done deal."

"But I'm a good negotiator," she says, her voice soft but determined.

"So am I."

Okay, what's going on here? Is she reluctant? Too tired? What? "Don't you want to fuck?" I ask, confused.

"No," she whispers.

"Oh." Well, that's disappointing.

She swallows, then says in a small voice, "I want you to make love to me."

I stare at her, bemused.

What exactly does she mean?

Make love? We do. We have. It's just another term for fucking.

She studies me, her expression grave. *Hell.* Is this her idea of more? All the hearts-and-flowers shit, is that what she means? But we're just talking semantics, surely? This is semantics. "Ana, I—" What does she want from me? "I thought we did."

"I want to touch you."

Fuck. No. I step back as the darkness closes around my ribs.

"Please," she whispers.

No. *No.* Haven't I made it clear?

I can't bear to be touched. I can't.

Ever.

"Oh no, Miss Steele, you've had enough concessions from me this evening. And I'm saying no."

"No?" she queries.

"No."

And for a moment I want to send her home, or upstairs— anywhere away from me. Not here.

Don't touch me.

She's watching me warily and I think about the fact that she's leaving tomorrow and I won't see her for a while. I sigh. I don't have the energy for this. "Look, you're tired, I'm tired. Let's just go to bed."

"So touching is a hard limit for you?"

"Yes. This is old news." I can't keep the exasperation out of my voice.

"Please tell me why."

I don't want to go there. This is not a conversation I want to have. Ever. "Oh, Anastasia, please. Just drop it for now."

Her face falls. "It's important to me," she says, a hesitant plea in her voice.

"Fuck this," I mutter to myself. At the chest of drawers I pull out a T-shirt and throw it to her. "Put that on and get into bed." Why am I even letting her sleep with me? But it's a rhetorical question: deep down I know the answer. It's because I sleep better with her.

She's my dream catcher.

She keeps my nightmares at bay.

She turns away from me and removes her bra, then slips on the T-shirt.

What did I say to her in the playroom this afternoon? She shouldn't hide her body from me.

"I need the bathroom," she says.

"Now you're asking permission?"

"Er . . . no."

"Anastasia, you know where the bathroom is. Today, at this point in our strange arrangement, you don't need my permission to use it." I unbutton my shirt and slip it off, and she dashes past me out of the bedroom as I try to contain my temper.

What's gotten into her?

One evening at my parents' and she's expecting serenades and sunsets and fucking walks in the rain. That's not what I'm about. I've told her this. I don't do romance. I sigh heavily as I remove my pants.

But she wants more. She wants all that romantic shit.

Fuck.

In my closet I throw my pants into the laundry basket and pull on my PJ bottoms, and then wander back into my bedroom.

This isn't going to work, Grey.

But I want it to work.

You should let her go.

No. I can make this work. Somehow.

The radio alarm reads 11:46. Time for bed. I check my phone for any urgent e-mails. There's nothing. I give the bathroom door a brisk knock.

"Come in," Ana garbles. She's brushing her teeth, literally foaming at the mouth—with my toothbrush. She spits into the sink as I stand beside her, and we stare at each other in the mirror. Her eyes are bright with mischief and humor. She rinses off the toothbrush and without a word hands it to me. I put it in my mouth and she looks pleased with herself.

And just like that, all the tension from our previous exchange evaporates.

"Do feel free to borrow my toothbrush," I say sardonically.

"Thank you, Sir." She beams, and for a moment I think she's going to curtsey, but she leaves me to brush my teeth.

When I reenter the bedroom she's stretched out under the covers. She should be stretched out under me. "You know this is not how I saw tonight panning out." I sound sullen.

"Imagine if I said to you that you couldn't touch me," she says, as argumentative as ever.

She's not going to let this go. I sit down on the bed. "Anastasia, I've told you. Fifty shades. I had a rough start in life—you don't want that shit in your head. Why would you?"

No one should have this shit in their head!

"Because I want to know you better."

"You know me well enough."

"How can you say that?" She sits up and kneels facing me, earnest and eager.

Ana. Ana. Ana. Let it go. For fuck's sake.

"You're rolling your eyes," she says. "Last time I did that, I ended up over your knee."

"Oh, I'd like to put you there again." Right now.

Her face brightens. "Tell me, and you can."

"What?"

"You heard me."

"You're bargaining with me?" My voice betrays my disbelief.

She nods. "Negotiating."

I frown. "It doesn't work that way, Anastasia."

"Okay. Tell me, and I'll roll my eyes at you."

I laugh. Now she is being ridiculous, and cute in my T-shirt. Her face shines with longing.

"Always so keen and eager for information," I marvel. And a thought occurs to me: I could spank her. I've wanted to since dinner, but I could make it fun.

I get off the bed. "Don't go away," I warn, and leave the room. From my study I pick up the key to the playroom and head upstairs. In the playroom chest I retrieve the toys I want and contemplate lube as well, but on reflection, and judging from recent experience, I don't think Ana will need any.

She's sitting on the bed when I get back, her expression bright with curiosity.

"When's your first interview tomorrow?" I ask.

"Two."

Excellent. No early morning.

"Good. Get off the bed. Stand over here." I point to a spot in front of me. Ana scrambles off the bed with no hesitation, eager as ever. She's waiting.

"Trust me?"

She nods, and I hold out my hand, revealing two silver kegel balls. She frowns and looks from the balls to me. "These are new. I am going to put these inside you and then I'm going to spank you, not for punishment, but for your pleasure and mine."

H er sharp intake of breath is music to my dick. "Then we'll fuck," I whisper. "And if you're still awake, I'll impart some information about my formative years. Agreed?"

She nods. Her breathing has accelerated, her pupils are larger, darker, with her need and her thirst for knowledge.

"Good girl. Open your mouth."

She hesitates for a moment, bewildered. But she does as she's told before I can reprimand her.

"Wider."

I insert both of the balls into her mouth. They're a little big and heavy but will keep her smart mouth occupied for a moment or two.

"They need lubrication. Suck."

She blinks and tries to suck, her stance changing subtly as she presses her thighs together and squirms.

Oh yes.

"Keep still, Anastasia," I caution, but I'm enjoying the show.

Enough.

"Stop," I order, and tug them from her mouth. At the bed I throw the comforter aside and sit down. "Come here."

She sidles up to me, wanton and sexy.

Oh, Ana, my little freak.

"Now turn around, bend down, and grab your ankles." Her expression tells me it's not what she was expecting to hear. "Don't hesitate," I chide her, and I pop the balls into my mouth. She turns around, and with no effort bends over, presenting her long legs and her fine ass to me, my T-shirt slipping up her back toward her head and her mane of hair.

Well, I could look at this glorious sight for a while and imagine what I'd like to do to it. But right now I want to spank and fuck her. I lay my hand over her backside, enjoying her warmth under my palm as I caress her through her panties.

Oh, this ass is mine, so mine. And it's going to get warmer.

I slide her panties to one side, exposing her labia, and hold them in place with one hand. I resist the urge to run my tongue up and down the length of her sex; besides, my mouth is full. Instead, I trace the line down from her perineum to her clitoris and up again, before easing my finger inside her.

Deep in my throat I hum with approval and slowly circle my finger, stretching her. She moans and I harden. Instantly.

Miss Steele approves. She wants this.

With my finger I circle inside her once more, then withdraw and remove the balls from my mouth. Gently, I insert the first ball into her, then the second, leaving the tag outside, draped against her clitoris. I kiss her bare ass and slide her panties back into place.

"Stand up," I command, and grasp her hips until I know she's steady on her feet. "You okay?"

"Yes." Her voice is rough.

"Turn around."

She complies immediately.

"How does that feel?" I ask.

"Strange."

"Strange good or strange bad?"

"Strange good," she answers.

"Good."

She'll need to get used to them. What better way than to stretch and reach for something?

"I want a glass of water. Go and fetch one for me, please. And when you come back, I shall put you across my knee. Think about that, Anastasia."

She's puzzled, but she turns and walks gingerly, with tentative steps, out of the room. While she's gone I collect a condom from my drawer. I'm running low; I'll need to stock up on these until her pill kicks in. Sitting back down on the bed, I wait with impatience.

When she reenters her walk is more confident, and she has my water.

"Thank you," I say, taking a quick sip and placing the glass on my bedside table. When I look up she's watching me with overt desire.

It's a good look on her.

"Come. Stand beside me. Like last time."

She does, and now her breathing is irregular . . . heavy. Boy, she's really turned on. So different from the last time I spanked her.

Let's rile her up some more, Grey.

"Ask me." My voice is firm.

A mystified look crosses her face.

"Ask me."

Come on, Ana.

Her brow furrows.

"Ask me, Anastasia. I won't say it again." My voice is sharper.

Finally, she realizes what I'm asking for and she blushes. "Spank me, please, Sir," she says quietly.

Those words . . . I close my eyes and let them ring through my head. Grasping her hand, I tug her over my knees so her torso lands on the bed. While stroking her behind with one hand, I smooth her hair off her face with the other, and tuck it behind her ear. Then I grasp her hair at the nape of her neck to hold her in place.

"I want to see your face while I spank you." I caress her behind and push against her vulva, knowing that the action will push the balls deeper inside her.

She hums her approval.

"This is for pleasure, Anastasia, mine and yours."

I lift my hand, then smack her right there.

"Ah!" she mouths, screwing up her face, and I caress her sweet, sweet ass while she adjusts to the sensation. When she relaxes, I smack her again. She groans, and I suppress my response. I begin in earnest, right cheek, left cheek, then the junction of her thighs and ass. Between each smack I fondle and knead her backside, watching her skin turn a delicate shade of pink beneath her lacy underwear.

She moans, absorbing the pleasure, enjoying the experience.

I stop. I want to see her ass in all its rosy glory. Unhurriedly, teasing her, I tug down her panties, skimming my fingertips down her thighs, the backs of her knees, and her calves. She lifts her feet, and I discard her panties on the floor. She squirms, but stops when I place my hand flat against her pink, glowing skin. Grabbing her hair again, I start anew. Gently first, then resuming the pattern.

She's wet; her arousal is on my palm.

I grip her hair harder and she moans, eyes closed, mouth open and slack.

Fuck, she's hot.

"Good girl." My voice is hoarse, my breathing erratic.

I spank her a couple more times until I can bear it no more.

I want her.

Now.

I wrap my fingers around the tab and draw the balls out of her.

She cries out in pleasure. Turning her over, I pause to yank my pants off and put on a wretched condom, then lie down beside her. I grab her hands, lift them over her head, and slowly ease myself onto her and into her as she mewls like a cat.

"Oh, baby." She feels incredible.

"I want you to make love to me." Her words ring in my head.

And gently, oh so gently, I start to move, feeling every precious inch of her beneath and around me. I kiss her, appreciating her mouth and her body at once. She wraps her legs around mine, meeting each gentle thrust, rocking against me until she spirals up and up and up and lets go.

Her orgasm tips me over the edge. "Ana!" I call, pouring myself into her. Letting go. A welcome release that leaves me . . . wanting more. Needing more.

As my equilibrium returns, I push away the strange swell of emotion that gnaws at my insides. It's not like the darkness, but it's something to fear. Something I don't understand.

She flexes her fingers around mine, and I open my eyes and look down into her sleepy, sated gaze.

"I enjoyed that," I whisper, and give her a lingering kiss.

She rewards me with a drowsy smile. I get up, cover her with the comforter, pick up my PJ pants, and pad into the bathroom, where I remove and dispose of the condom. I pull on my pants and find the arnica cream.

Back at the bed, Ana gives me a contented grin.

"Roll over," I order, and for a moment I think she's going to roll her eyes, but she indulges me and moves. "Your ass is a glorious color," I observe, pleased with the results. I squirt some cream on my palm and slowly massage it into her behind.

"Spill the beans, Grey," she says with a yawn.

"Miss Steele, you know how to ruin a moment."

"We had a deal," she insists.

"How do you feel?"

"Shortchanged."

With a heavy sigh I place the arnica cream on the bedside table and slip into bed, pulling Ana into my arms. I kiss her ear. "The woman who brought me into this world was a crack whore, Anastasia. Go to sleep."

She tenses in my arms.

I still. I do not want her sympathy or her pity.

"Was?" she whispers.

"She's dead."

"How long?"

"She died when I was four. I don't really remember her. Carrick has given me some details. I only remember certain things. Please go to sleep."

After a while she relaxes against me. "Good night, Christian." Her voice is sleepy.

"Good night, Ana." I kiss her once more, inhaling her soothing scent and fighting off my memories.

"Don't just pick the apples and throw them away, asshole!"

"Fuck off, you righteous dweeb."

Elliot picks an apple, takes a bite, and throws it at me.

"Maggot," he taunts.

No! Don't call me that.

I jump him. Pounding my fists into his face.

"You fucking pig. This is food. You're just wasting
it. Grandpa sells these. You pig. Pig. Pig."

"ELLIOT. CHRISTIAN."

Dad drags me off Elliot, who is cowering on the ground.

"What is this about?"

"He's insane."

"Elliot!"

"He's destroying the apples." Anger swells in my chest, in my
throat. I think I might explode. "He's taking a bite and then
throwing them away. Throwing them at me."

"Elliot, is this true?"

Elliot turns red under Dad's hard stare.

"I think you'd better come with me. Christian, pick up the
apples. You can help Mom bake a pie."

She's fast asleep when I wake, my nose in her fragrant hair,
my arms cocooning her. I've dreamed about romping through my
grandfather's apple orchard with Elliot; those were happy, angry
days.

It's nearly seven—another lie-in with Miss Steele. It's odd waking up beside her, but odd in a good way. I contemplate waking
her with a morning fuck; my body is more than willing—but she's
practically comatose and she might be sore. I should let her sleep. I
climb out of bed, careful not to wake her, grab a T-shirt, gather her
clothes from the floor, and wander into the living room.

"Good morning, Mr. Grey." Mrs. Jones is busy in the kitchen.

"Good morning, Gail." Stretching, I look out the windows at
the remnants of a vivid dawn.

"You have some laundry there?" she asks.

"Yes. These are Anastasia's."

"Do you want me to wash and press them?"

"Do you have time?"

"I'll put them on the quick cycle."

"Excellent, thank you." I pass her Ana's clothes. "How was your sister?"

"Very well, thanks. The kids are growing. Boys can be rough."

"I know."

She smiles and offers to make me some coffee.

"Please. I'll be in my study." As she watches me her smile changes from pleasant to knowing . . . in the way that's feminine and secretive. Then she hurries out of the kitchen, I assume to the laundry room.

What's her problem?

Okay, this is the first Monday—the first time—in the four years she's worked for me that there's been a woman asleep in my bed. But it's not that big a deal. *Breakfast for two, Mrs. Jones. I think you can manage that.*

I shake my head and wander into my study to start work. I'll shower later . . . maybe with Ana.

I check my e-mails and send one to Andrea and Ros, saying I'll be in this afternoon, not this morning. Then I take a look at Barney's latest schematics.

GAIL KNOCKS AND BRINGS me a second cup of coffee, letting me know it's already 8:15.

That late?

"I'm not going into the office this morning."

"Taylor was asking."

"I'll go this afternoon."

"I'll tell him. I've hung Miss Steele's clothes in your closet."

"Thank you. That was quick. She still asleep?"

"I think so." And there's that little smile again. I arch my brows and her smile broadens as she turns to leave my study. I put my work aside and head off with my coffee to take a shower and have a shave.

ANA IS STILL OUT for the count when I finish dressing.

You've exhausted her, Grey. And it was pleasurable, more than pleasurable. She looks serene, as if she doesn't have a care in the world.

Good.

From the chest I take my watch, and on an impulse open the top drawer and pocket my last condom.

You never know.

I amble back through the living room toward my study.

"Do you want your breakfast yet, sir?"

"I'll have breakfast with Ana. Thanks."

I pick up the phone and call Andrea from my desk. After we've exchanged a few words she puts me through to Ros.

"So when can we expect you?" Ros's tone is sarcastic.

"Good morning, Ros. How are you?" I say sweetly.

"Pissed."

"At me?"

"Yes, at you, and your hands-off work ethic."

"I'll be in later. The reason I'm calling is I've decided to liquidate Woods's company." I've told her this already, but she and Marco are taking too long. I want this done, now. I remind her that this was going to happen if the company's P&L didn't improve. And it hasn't.

"He needs more time."

"I'm not interested, Ros. We're not carrying deadweight."

"Are you sure?"

"I don't want any more lame excuses." Enough, already. I've made up my mind.

"Christian—"

"Have Marco call me, it's shit-or-bust time."

"Okay. Okay. If that's what you really want. Anything else?"

"Yes. Tell Barney that the prototype looks good, though I'm not sure about the interface."

"I thought the interface worked well, once I figured it out. Not that I'm an expert."

"No, it's just missing something."

"Talk to Barney."

"I want to meet him this afternoon to discuss."

"Face-to-face?"

Her sarcasm is irritating. But I ignore her tone and tell her that I want his whole team there to brainstorm.

"He'll be pleased. So I'll see you this afternoon?" She sounds hopeful.

"Okay," I reassure her. "Transfer me back to Andrea."

While I wait for her to pick up the phone I gaze out at the cloudless sky. It's the same shade as Ana's eyes.

Sappy, Grey.

"Andrea—"

A movement distracts me. Looking up, I'm pleased to see Ana standing in the doorway, dressed in nothing but my T-shirt. Her legs, long and shapely, are on display for my eyes only. She has great legs.

"Mr. Grey," Andrea answers.

My eyes lock with Ana's. They *are* the color of a summer sky and just as warm. Good Lord, I could bask in her warmth all day—every day.

Don't be absurd, Grey.

"Clear my schedule this morning, but get Bill to call me. I'll be in at two. I need to talk to Marco this afternoon, that will need at least half an hour."

A soft smile tugs at Ana's lips and I find myself mirroring her.

"Yes, sir," Andrea says.

"Schedule Barney and his team in after Marco or maybe tomorrow, and find time for me to see Claude every day this week."

"Sam wants to talk to you, this morning."

"Tell him to wait."

"It's about Darfur."

"Oh?"

"Apparently he sees the aid convoy as a great personal PR opportunity."

Oh, God. He would, wouldn't he?

"No, I don't want publicity for Darfur." My voice is gruff with exasperation.

"He says there's a journalist from *Forbes* who wants to talk to you about it."

How the hell do they know?

"Tell Sam to deal with it," I snap. That's what he's paid to do.

"Do you want to speak to him directly?" she asks.

"No."

"Will do. I also need to RSVP to the event on Saturday."

"Which event?"

"Chamber of Commerce Gala."

"That's next Saturday?" I ask, as an idea pops into my head.

"Yes, sir."

"Hold on—" I turn to Ana, who's jiggling her left foot but not taking her sky-blue eyes off me. "When will you be back from Georgia?"

"Friday," she says.

"I'll need an extra ticket, because I have a date," I inform Andrea.

"A date?" Andrea squeaks with incredulity.

I sigh. "Yes, Andrea, that's what I said. A date. Miss Anastasia Steele will accompany me."

"Yes, Mr. Grey." She sounds as if I've made her day.

For fuck's sake. What is it with my staff?

"That's all." I hang up. "Good morning, Miss Steele."

"Mr. Grey," Ana says in greeting. I walk around my desk until I'm in front of her, and caress her face.

"I didn't want to wake you, you looked so peaceful. Did you sleep well?"

"I am very well rested, thank you. I just came to say hi before I had a shower." She's smiling and her eyes are shining with delight. It's a pleasure to see her like this. Before I get back to work I lean down to give her a gentle kiss. Suddenly she wraps her arms around my neck and tangles her fingers in my hair, and presses her body along the length of mine.

Whoa.

Her lips are persistent, so I respond, kissing her back, surprised by the intensity of her ardor. With one hand I cup her head, with the other her naked, recently spanked ass, and my body ignites like dry tinder.

"Well, sleep seems to agree with you." My voice is laced with sudden lust. "I suggest you go and have your shower, or shall I lay you across my desk now?"

"I choose the desk," she whispers at the corner of my mouth, grinding her sex against my erection.

Well, this is a surprise.

Her eyes are dark and greedy with want. "You've really got a taste for this, haven't you, Miss Steele? You're becoming insatiable."

"I've only got a taste for you."

"Damn right. *Only me!*" Her words are a siren's call to my libido. Losing all self-restraint, I sweep everything off my desk, sending my papers, phone, and pens all clattering or floating to the floor, but I don't give a damn. I lift Ana and lay her across my desk so her hair spills over the edge and onto the seat of my chair.

"You want it, you got it, baby," I growl, whipping out the condom and unzipping my pants. Making quick work of covering my cock, I stare down at the insatiable Miss Steele. "I sure hope you're ready," I warn her, grabbing hold of her wrists and keeping them at her sides. With one swift move I'm inside her.

"Ah . . . Christ, Ana. You're so ready." I give her a nanosecond to adjust to my presence. Then I start to push. Back and forth. Over and over. Harder and harder. She tips her head back, mouth open in a wordless plea, as her breasts rise and fall in rhythm with each jolt to her body. She wraps her legs around me while I stand, drilling into her.

This what you want, baby?

She meets every thrust, rocking against me and moaning as I possess her. Taking her—higher and higher and higher—until I feel her stiffening around me.

"Come on, baby, give it up for me," I grit through clenched teeth, and she does, spectacularly, crying out and sucking me into my own orgasm.

Fuck. I come as spectacularly as she does, and I slump down on top of her while her body tightens around me with aftershocks.

Damn. That was unexpected.

"What the hell are you doing to me?" I'm breathless, my lips skimming her neck. "You completely beguile me, Ana. You weave some powerful magic."

And you jumped me!

I release her wrists and move to stand, but she tightens her legs around me, her fingers tangling in my hair.

"I'm the one beguiled," she whispers. Our eyes are locked, her scrutiny intense, as if she's seeing through me. Seeing the darkness in my soul.

Shit. Let me go. This is too much.

I cup her face in my hands to kiss her quickly, but as I do the unwelcome thought of her being in this position with someone else pops into my mind. *No. She's not doing this with anyone else. Ever.*

"You. Are. Mine." My words crack between us. "Do you understand?"

"Yes, yours," she says, her expression heartfelt, her words full of conviction, and my irrational jealousy recedes.

"Are you sure you have to go to Georgia?" I ask, smoothing her hair from around her face.

She nods.

Damn.

I pull out of her and she winces.

"Are you sore?"

"A little," she says with a timid smile.

"I like you sore. Reminds you where I've been, and only me." I give her a rough, possessive kiss.

Because I don't want her to go to Georgia.

And no one's jumped me since . . . since Elena.

And even then, it was always calculated, part of a scene.

Standing, I hold out my hand and pull her to a sitting position. As I tug off the condom, she murmurs, "Always prepared."

I give her a confounded look as I fasten my fly. She holds up the empty foil packet by way of explanation.

"A man can hope, Anastasia, dream even, and sometimes his dreams come true." *I had no idea I'd get to use it so soon, and on her terms, not mine. Miss Steele, for such an innocent, you are, as ever, unexpected.*

"So . . . on your desk . . . that's been a dream?" she asks.

Sweetheart. I've had sex on this desk many, many times, but always at my instigation, never at a submissive's.

This is not how it works.

Her face falls as she reads my thoughts.

Shit. What can I say? Ana, unlike you, I have a past.

I run my hand through my hair in frustration; this morning is not going according to plan.

"I'd better go and have a shower," she says, subdued. She stands and takes a few steps toward the door.

"I've got a couple more calls to make. I'll join you for breakfast once you're out of the shower." I gaze after her, wondering what to say to make this right. "I think Mrs. Jones has laundered your clothes from yesterday. They're in the closet."

She looks surprised, and impressed. "Thank you," she says.

"You're most welcome."

Her brow creases as she studies me, baffled.

"What?" I ask.

"What's wrong?"

"What do you mean?"

"Well, you're being more weird than usual."

"You find me weird?" Ana, baby, "weird" is my middle name.

"Sometimes."

Tell her. Tell her no one's pounced on you for a long time.

"As ever, I'm surprised by you, Miss Steele."

"Surprised how?"

"Let's just say that was an unexpected treat."

"We aim to please, Mr. Grey," she teases, still scrutinizing me.

"And please me you do," I acknowledge. *But you disarm me, too.* "I thought you were going to have a shower?"

Her mouth turns down.

Shit.

"Yes, um, I'll see you in a moment." She turns and scampers out of my study, leaving me standing in a maze of confusion. I shake my head to clear it, then begin picking up my scattered belongings from the floor and arranging them on my desk.

How the hell can she just waltz into my study and seduce me? I'm supposed to be in control of this relationship. This is what I was thinking about last night: her unbridled enthusiasm and affection. How the hell am I supposed to deal with that? It's not something I know. I pause as I pick up my phone.

But it's nice.

Yeah.

More than nice.

I chuckle at the thought and remember her "nice" e-mail. Damn, there's a missed call from Bill. He must have phoned during my tryst with Miss Steele. I sit down at my desk, master of my own universe once more—now that she's in the shower—and call him back. I need Bill to tell me about Detroit . . . and I need to get back on my game.

Bill doesn't pick up, so I call Andrea.

"Mr. Grey."

"Is the jet free today and tomorrow?"

"It's not scheduled for use until Thursday, sir."

"Great. Can you try Bill for me?"

"Sure."

My conversation with Bill is lengthy. Ruth has done an excellent job scouting all of the available brownfield sites in Detroit. Two are viable for the tech plant we want to build, and Bill is certain that Detroit has the available labor force we require.

My heart sinks.

Does it have to be Detroit?

I have vague memories of the place: drunks, hobos, and crackheads shouting at us on the streets; the seedy dive we called home; and a young, broken woman, the crack whore I called Mommy, staring into space while she sat in a drab, grimy room filled with stale air and dust motes.

And him.

I shudder. *Don't think about him . . . or her.*

But I can't help it. Ana has said nothing about my nocturnal confession. I've never mentioned the crack whore to anyone. Perhaps that's why Ana attacked me this morning: she thinks I need some TLC.

Fuck that.

Baby. I'll take your body if you offer it up. I'm doing just fine. But even as the thought pops into my head I wonder if I'm "just fine." I ignore my unease; it's something to discuss with Flynn when he's back.

Right now, I'm hungry. I hope she's gotten her sweet butt out of that shower, because I need to eat.

ANA IS STANDING AT the kitchen counter talking to Mrs. Jones, who has set places for our breakfast.

"Would you like something to eat?" asks Mrs. Jones.

"No thank you," Ana says.

Oh no you don't.

"Of course you'll have something to eat," I growl at both of them. "She likes pancakes, bacon, and eggs, Mrs. Jones."

"Yes, Mr. Grey. What would you like, sir?" she replies, without batting an eyelid.

"Omelet, please, and some fruit. Sit," I tell Ana, pointing to one of the barstools. She does, and I take a seat beside her while Mrs. Jones makes our breakfast.

"Have you bought your air ticket?" I ask.

"No, I'll buy it when I get home, over the Internet."

"Do you have the money?"

"Yes," she says, as if I'm five years old, and she tosses her hair over her shoulder, flattening her lips, peeved, I think.

I arch an eyebrow in censure. *I could always spank you again, sweetheart.*

"Yes, I do, thank you," she says quickly, in a more subdued tone.

That's better.

"I have a jet. It's not scheduled to be used for three days; it's at your disposal." This will be a "no." But at least I can offer.

Her lips part in shock and her expression transforms, from stunned to impressed and exasperated in equal measure. "We've already made serious misuse of your company's aviation fleet. I wouldn't want to do it again," she says nonchalantly.

"It's my company, it's my jet."

She shakes her head. "Thank you for the offer. But I'd be happier taking a scheduled flight."

Surely most women would jump at the opportunity of taking a private jet, but it seems material wealth really doesn't impress this girl—or she doesn't like to feel indebted to me. I'm not sure which. Either way, she's a stubborn creature.

"As you wish." I sigh. "Do you have much preparation to do for your interview?"

"No."

"Good." I ask but she still won't tell me which of the publishing houses she's seeing. Instead she gives me a sphinxlike smile. There's no way she's divulging this secret.

"I'm a man of means, Miss Steele."

"I'm fully aware of that, Mr. Grey. Are you going to track my phone?"

Trust her to remember that. "Actually, I'll be quite busy this afternoon, so I'll have to get someone else to do it," I answer, smirking.

"If you can spare someone to do that, you're obviously over-staffed."

Oh, she's sassy today.

"I'll send an e-mail to the head of human resources and have her look into our head count." This is what I like: our banter. It's refreshing and fun, and unlike anything I've known before.

Mrs. Jones serves us breakfast, and I'm pleased to see Ana relishing her food. When Mrs. Jones leaves the kitchen Ana peers up at me.

"What is it, Anastasia?"

"You know, you never did tell me why you don't like to be touched."

Not this again!

"I've told you more than I've ever told anybody." My voice is low to conceal my frustration. Why does she persist with these questions? She eats another couple of mouthfuls of her pancakes.

"Will you think about our arrangement while you're away?" I ask.

"Yes." She's earnest.

"Will you miss me?"

Grey!

She turns to face me, as surprised as I am by the question. "Yes," she says after a moment, her expression open and honest. I was expecting a smart remark, yet I get the truth. And strangely, I find her admission comforting.

"I'll miss you, too," I mutter. "More than you know." My apartment will be a little quieter without her, and a little emptier. I stroke her cheek and kiss her. She gives me a sweet smile before returning to her breakfast.

"I'll brush my teeth, then I should go," she announces, once she's finished.

"So soon. I thought you might stay longer."

She's taken aback. Did she think I'd kick her out?

"I've prevailed upon you and taken up your time for long enough, Mr. Grey. Besides, don't you have an empire to run?"

"I can play hooky." Hope swells in my chest and my voice. And I've just cleared my morning.

"I have to prep for my interviews. And get changed." She eyes me warily.

"You look great."

"Why, thank you, Sir," she says graciously. But her cheeks are coloring their familiar rosy pink, like her ass last night. She's embarrassed. When will she learn to take a compliment?

Rising, she takes her plate to the sink.

"Leave that. Mrs. Jones will do it."

"Okay. I'm just going to brush my teeth."

"Please feel free to use my toothbrush," I offer, with sarcasm.

"I had every intention of doing so," she says, and sashays out of the room. That woman has an answer for everything.

She returns a few moments later with her purse.

"Don't forget to take your BlackBerry, your Mac, and your chargers to Georgia."

"Yes, Sir," she says obediently.

Good girl.

"Come." I lead her to the elevator and step in with her.

"You don't have to come down. I can see myself to my car."

"It's all part of the service," I quip ironically. "Besides, I can kiss you all the way down." I fold her into my arms and do just that, enjoying her taste and her tongue and giving her a proper good-bye.

We're both aroused and breathless by the time the doors open on the garage level. But she's leaving. I take her to her car and open the driver's door for her, ignoring my need.

"Good-bye, for now, Sir," she whispers, and kisses me once more.

"Drive safely, Anastasia. And safe travels." I close her door, stand back, and watch her leave. Then I head upstairs.

I knock on Taylor's study door and let him know that I'd like to go to the office in ten minutes. "I'll have the car waiting, sir."

I CALL WELCH FROM the car.

"Mr. Grey," he rasps.

"Welch. Anastasia Steele is buying an airline ticket today, leaving Seattle tonight for Savannah. I'd like to know which flight she's on."

"Does she have an airline preference?"

"I'm afraid I don't know."

"I'll see what I can do."

I hang up. My cunning plan is falling into place.

"MR. GREY!" ANDREA IS startled at my appearance several hours early. I want to tell her that I do fucking work here, but I decide to behave.

"I thought I'd surprise you."

"Coffee?" she chirps.

"Please."

"With or without milk?"

Good girl.

"With. Steamed milk."

"Yes, Mr. Grey."

"Try Caroline Acton. I'd like to speak to her right away."

"Of course."

"And make an appointment for me to see Flynn, next week." She nods and sits down to work. At my desk, I switch on my computer.

The first e-mail in my inbox is from Elena.

From: Elena Lincoln
Subject: The Weekend
Date: May 30 2011, 10:15
To: Christian Grey

Christian, what gives?
Your mother told me you took a young woman to dinner
yesterday.
I'm intrigued. It's so not your style.
You've found a new submissive?
Call me.
Ex

ELENA LINCOLN
ESCLAVA
For The Beauty That Is You™

That's all I need. I close her e-mail, resolving to ignore it for now. Olivia knocks and enters with my coffee as Andrea buzzes my phone.

"I have Welch for you, and I've left a message for Ms. Acton," Andrea announces.

"Good. Put him through."

Olivia places the latte on my desk and exits flustered. I do my best to ignore her.

"Welch."

"No airline tickets purchased as yet, Mr. Grey. But I'll monitor the situation and inform you, should that change."

"Please do."

He hangs up. I take a sip of coffee and dial Ros.

JUST BEFORE LUNCH ANDREA puts Caroline Acton through. "Mr. Grey, how lovely to hear from you. What can I do for you?"

"Hello, Ms. Acton. I'd like the usual."

"The capsule wardrobe? Do you have a color palette in mind?"

"Blues and greens. Silver maybe, for a formal event." The Chamber of Commerce dinner springs to mind. "Gem colors, I think."

"Nice," Ms. Acton responds with her usual enthusiasm.

"And satin and silk underwear and nightwear. Something glamorous."

"Yes, sir. Do you have a budget in mind?"

"No budget. Go all-out. I want everything high-end."

"Shoes, too?"

"Please."

"Great. Sizes?"

"I'll e-mail you. I have your address from last time."

"When would you like delivery?"

"This Friday."

"I'm sure I can do that. Would you like to see photographs of my choices?"

"Please."

"Great. I'll get on it."

"Thank you." I hang up and Andrea puts Welch through.

"Welch."

"Miss Steele is traveling on DL2610 to Atlanta, departing at 22:25 this evening."

I jot down all the details of her flights and connection into Savannah. I summon Andrea, who enters moments later, carrying her notebook.

"Andrea, Anastasia Steele is traveling on these flights. Upgrade her to first class, check her in, and pay for her to enter the first-class lounge. And buy the seat beside her on all flights, there and back. Use my personal credit card." Andrea's puzzled look tells me that she thinks I've taken leave of my senses, but she recovers quickly and accepts my hand-scribbled note.

"Will do, Mr. Grey." She's trying her best to keep it professional, but I catch her smiling.

This is none of her business.

MY AFTERNOON IS SPENT in meetings. Marco has prepared preliminary reports on the four publishing houses based in Seattle. I set them aside to read later. He's also in agreement with me about Woods and his company. This is going to get ugly, but having looked at the synergies, the only way forward is to absorb Woods's tech division and liquidate the rest of his company. It's going to be expensive, but it's best for GEH.

In the late afternoon I manage to have a quick and strenuous workout with Bastille, so I'm calm and relaxed when I head home.

After a light supper I sit down to read at my desk. First order of the evening is to reply to Elena. But when I open my e-mails, there's one from Ana. She hasn't been far from my thoughts all day.

From: Anastasia Steele
Subject: Interviews
Date: May 30 2011 18:49
To: Christian Grey

Dear Sir,
My interviews went well today.

Thought you might be interested.

How was your day?

Ana

I type my response immediately.

From: Christian Grey
Subject: My Day
Date: May 30 2011 19:03
To: Anastasia Steele

Dear Miss Steele,
Everything you do interests me. You are the most fascinating woman I know.

I'm glad your interviews went well.

My morning was beyond all expectations.

My afternoon was very dull in comparison.

Christian Grey
CEO, Grey Enterprises Holdings, Inc.

I sit back and rub my chin, waiting.

From: Anastasia Steele
Subject: Fine Morning
Date: May 30 2011 19:05
To: Christian Grey

Dear Sir,
The morning was exemplary for me, too, in spite of you

weirding out on me after the impeccable desk sex. Don't
think I didn't notice.

Thank you for breakfast. Or thank Mrs. Jones.

I'd like to ask you questions about her—without you weirding
out on me again.

Ana

Weirding? What on earth does she mean by that? Is she saying
I'm weird? Well, I am, I suppose. Maybe. Perhaps she's realized
how surprised I was when she jumped me—and no one's done that
for a long time.

"Impeccable" . . . I'll take that.

From: Christian Grey
Subject: Publishing and You?
Date: May 30 2011 19:10
To: Anastasia Steele

Anastasia,
"Weirding" is not a verb and should not be used by anyone
who wants to go into publishing. Impeccable? Compared
to what, pray tell? And what do you need to ask about Mrs.
Jones? I'm intrigued.

Christian Grey
CEO, Grey Enterprises Holdings, Inc.

From: Anastasia Steele
Subject: You and Mrs. Jones
Date: May 30 2011 19:17
To: Christian Grey

Dear Sir,
Language evolves and moves on. It is an organic thing. It is not
stuck in an ivory tower, hung with expensive works of art and
overlooking most of Seattle with a helipad stuck on its roof.

Impeccable—compared to the other times we have . . .
what's your word . . . oh yes . . . fucked. Actually, the fucking
has been pretty impeccable, period, in my humble opinion—
but then, as you know, I have very limited experience.

Is Mrs. Jones an ex-sub of yours?

Ana

Her response makes me laugh out loud, then shocks me.
Mrs. Jones! Submissive?
No way.
Ana. Are you jealous? And speaking of language . . . watch yours!

From: Christian Grey
Subject: Language. Watch Your Mouth!
Date: May 30 2011 19:22
To: Anastasia Steele

Anastasia,
Mrs. Jones is a valued employee. I have never had any
relationship with her beyond our professional one. I do
not employ anyone I've had any sexual relations with. I am
shocked that you would think so. The only person I would
make an exception to this rule is you—because you are a

bright young woman with remarkable negotiating skills.
Though, if you continue to use such language, I may have
to reconsider taking you on here. I am glad you have limited
experience. Your experience will continue to be limited—just
to me. I shall take "impeccable" as a compliment—though
with you, I'm never sure if that's what you mean or if your
sense of irony is getting the better of you—as usual.

Christian Grey
CEO, Grey Enterprises Holdings, Inc., from His Ivory
Tower

Though perhaps it might not be a good idea for Ana to work
for me.

From: Anastasia Steele
Subject: Not for All the Tea in China
Date: May 30 2011 19:27
To: Christian Grey

Dear Mr. Grey,
I think I have already expressed my reservations about
working for your company. My views on this have not
changed, are not changing, and will not change, ever. I must
leave you now, as Kate has returned with food. My sense of
irony and I bid you good night.

I will contact you once I'm in Georgia.

Ana

For some reason I'm mildly irritated to hear that she wouldn't
want to work for me. She has an impressive GPA. She's bright,

charming, funny; she'd be an asset to any company. She's also wise
to say no.

From: Christian Grey
Subject: Even Twinings English Breakfast Tea?
Date: May 30 2011 19:29
To: Anastasia Steele

Good night, Anastasia.
I hope you and your sense of irony have a safe flight.

Christian Grey
CEO, Grey Enterprises Holdings, Inc.

I put all thoughts of Miss Steele aside and start on a response
to Elena.

From: Christian Grey
Subject: The Weekend
Date: May 30 2011, 19:47
To: Elena Lincoln

Hello, Elena.
My mother has a big mouth. What can I say?
I met a girl. Brought her to dinner.
It's not a big deal.
How goes it with you?

Best,
Christian

Christian Grey
CEO, Grey Enterprises Holdings, Inc.

From: Elena Lincoln
Subject: The Weekend
Date: May 30 2011, 19:50
To: Christian Grey

Christian, that's bullshit.
Let's do dinner.
Tomorrow?
Ex

ELENA LINCOLN
ESCLAVA
For The Beauty That Is You™

Fuck!

From: Christian Grey
Subject: The Weekend
Date: May 30 2011, 20:01
To: Elena Lincoln

Sure.

Best,
Christian

Christian Grey
CEO, Grey Enterprises Holdings, Inc.

From: Elena Lincoln
Subject: The Weekend
Date: May 30 2011, 20:05
To: Christian Grey

Do you want to meet the girl I mentioned?
Ex

ELENA LINCOLN
ESCLAVA
For The Beauty That Is You™

Not at the moment.

From: Christian Grey
Subject: The Weekend
Date: May 30 2011, 20:11
To: Elena Lincoln

I think I'll let the arrangement I have now run its course.
See you tomorrow.

C.

Christian Grey
CEO, Grey Enterprises Holdings, Inc.

I sit down to read Fred's draft proposal for Eamon Kavanagh, then move on to Marco's summary of the publishing houses in Seattle.

JUST BEFORE 10:00 I'M distracted by a ping from my computer. It's late. I assume it's a message from Ana.

From: Anastasia Steele
Subject: Over-Extravagant Gestures
Date: May 30 2011 21:53
To: Christian Grey

Dear Mr. Grey,
What really alarms me is how you knew which flight I was on.

Your stalking knows no bounds. Let's hope that Dr. Flynn is back from vacation.

I have had a manicure, a back massage, and two glasses of champagne—a very nice start to my vacation.

Thank you.

Ana

She's been upgraded. Well done, Andrea.

From: Christian Grey
Subject: You're Most Welcome
Date: May 30 2011 21:59
To: Anastasia Steele

Dear Miss Steele,
Dr. Flynn is back, and I have an appointment next week.

Who was massaging your back?

Christian Grey
CEO with friends in the right places,
Grey Enterprises Holdings, Inc.

I check the time of her e-mail. She should be on board right now, if her plane is on time. I quickly open Google and check departures from Sea-Tac. Her flight is on schedule.

From: Anastasia Steele
Subject: Strong Able Hands
Date: May 30 2011 22:22
To: Christian Grey

Dear Sir,
A very pleasant young man massaged my back. Yes. Very pleasant indeed. I wouldn't have encountered Jean-Paul in the ordinary departure lounge—so thank you again for that treat.

What the hell?

I'm not sure if I'll be allowed to e-mail once we take off, and I need my beauty sleep since I've not been sleeping so well recently.

Pleasant dreams, Mr. Grey . . . thinking of you.

Ana

Is she trying to make me jealous? Does she have any idea how mad I can get? She's been gone for a few hours, and she's deliberately making me angry. Why does she do this to me?

From: Christian Grey
Subject: Enjoy It While You Can
Date: May 30 2011 22:25
To: Anastasia Steele

Dear Miss Steele,
I know what you're trying to do—and trust me, you've
succeeded. Next time you'll be in the cargo hold, bound and
gagged in a crate. Believe me when I say that attending to
you in that state will give me so much more pleasure than
merely upgrading your ticket.

I look forward to your return.

Christian Grey
Palm-Twitching CEO,
Grey Enterprises Holdings, Inc.

Her response is almost immediate.

From: Anastasia Steele
Subject: Joking?
Date: May 30 2011 22:30
To: Christian Grey

You see—I have no idea if you're joking—and if you're not,
then I think I'll stay in Georgia. Crates are a hard limit for me.
Sorry I made you mad. Tell me you forgive me.

A

Of course I'm joking . . . sort of. At least she knows I'm mad.
Her plane should be taking off. How is she e-mailing?

From: Christian Grey
Subject: Joking
Date: May 30 2011 22:31
To: Anastasia Steele

How can you be e-mailing? Are you risking the life of
everyone on board, including yourself, by using your
BlackBerry? I think that contravenes one of the rules.

Christian Grey
Two-Palms-Twitching CEO,
Grey Enterprises Holdings, Inc.

And we know what happens if you contravene the rules, Miss
Steele. I check the Sea-Tac website for flight departures; her plane
has left. I won't be hearing from her for a while. That thought, as
well as her little e-mail stunt, has put me in a foul mood. Abandoning my work, I head into the kitchen and decide to pour myself a
drink, tonight Armagnac.

Taylor pops his head around the entrance to the living room.

"Not now," I bark.

"Very good, sir," he says, and heads back to wherever he came
from.

Don't take your mood out on the staff, Grey.

Annoyed at myself, I walk toward the windows and stare out at
the Seattle skyline. I wonder how she's gotten under my skin, and
why our relationship is not progressing in the direction I would
like. I'm hoping that once she's had a chance to reflect in Georgia,
she'll make the right decision. Won't she?

Anxiety blooms in my chest. I take another slug of my drink
and sit down at my piano to play.

TUESDAY, MAY 31, 2011

Mommy is gone. I don't know where.

He's here. I hear his boots. They are loud boots.

They have silver buckles. They stomp. Loud.

He stomps. And he shouts.

I am in Mommy's closet.

Hiding.

He won't hear me.

I can be quiet. Very quiet.

Quiet because I'm not here.

"You fucking bitch!" he shouts.

He shouts a lot.

"You fucking bitch!"

He shouts at Mommy.

He shouts at me.

He hits Mommy.

He hits me.

I hear the door close. He's not here anymore.

And Mommy is gone, too.

I stay in the closet. In the dark. I'm very quiet.

I sit for a long time. A long, long, long time.

Where is Mommy?

There's a whisper of dawn in the sky when I open my eyes. The radio alarm says 5:23. I've slept fitfully, plagued by unpleasant dreams, and I'm exhausted, but I decide to go for a run to wake myself up. Once I'm in sweats, I pick up my phone. There's a text from Ana.

> Arrived safely in Savannah. A :)

Good. She's there, and safe. The thought pleases me and I quickly scan my e-mail. The subject of Ana's latest message leaps out at me: "Do you like to scare me?"

No fucking way.

My scalp prickles and I sit down on the bed, scrolling through her words. She must have sent this during her layover in Atlanta, before she sent her text.

From: Anastasia Steele
Subject: Do you like to scare me?
Date: May 31 2011 06:52 EST
To: Christian Grey

You know how much I dislike you spending money on me. Yes, you're very rich, but still it makes me uncomfortable, like you're paying me for sex. However, I like traveling first class, it's so much more civilized than coach. So thank you. I mean it—and I did enjoy the massage from Jean-Paul. He was very gay. I omitted that bit in my e-mail to you to wind you up, because I was annoyed with you, and I'm sorry about that.

But as usual you overreact. You can't write things like that to me—bound and gagged in a crate. (Were you serious or was it a joke?) That scares me . . . you scare me . . . I am completely caught up in your spell, considering a lifestyle with you that I didn't even know existed until last week, and then you write something like that and I want to run screaming into the hills. I won't, of course, because I'd miss you. Really miss you. I want us to work, but I am terrified of the depth of feeling I have for you and the dark path you're leading me down. What you are offering is erotic and sexy, and I'm curious, but I'm also scared you'll hurt me—

physically and emotionally. After three months you could say good-bye, and where will that leave me if you do? But then I suppose that risk is there in any relationship. This just isn't the sort of relationship I ever envisaged having, especially as my first. It's a huge leap of faith for me.

You were right when you said I didn't have a submissive bone in my body . . . and I agree with you now. Having said that, I want to be with you, and if that's what I have to do, I would like to try, but I think I'll suck at it and end up black and blue—and I don't relish that idea at all.

I am so happy that you have said that you will try more. I just need to think about what "more" means to me, and that's one of the reasons why I wanted some distance. You dazzle me so much I find it very difficult to think clearly when we're together.

They are calling my flight. I have to go.

More later.

Your Ana

She's reprimanding me. Again. But she's stunned me with her honesty. It's illuminating. I read her e-mail again and again, and each time I pause at "Your Ana."

My Ana.

She wants us to work.

She wants to be with me.

There's hope, Grey.

I place my phone on my bedside, and decide I need that run, to clear my head so I can think about my response.

I take my usual route up Stewart to Westlake Avenue then around Denny Park a few times, Four Tet's "She Just Likes to Fight" ringing in my ears.

Ana's given me a great deal to process.

Paying her for sex?
Like a whore.

I've never thought of her that way. Just the idea makes me mad. Really fucking mad. I sprint once more around the park, my anger spurring me on. Why does she do this to herself? I'm rich, so what? She just needs to get used to that. I'm reminded of our conversation yesterday about the GEH jet. She wouldn't take that offer.

At least she doesn't want me for my money.

But does she want me at all?

She says I dazzle her. But boy, has she got that the wrong way around. She dazzles me in a way that I've never experienced, yet she's flown across the country to get away from me.

How's that supposed to make me feel?

She's right. It is a dark path I'm leading her down, but one that is far more intimate than any vanilla relationship—or so I've seen. I only have to look at Elliot and his alarmingly casual approach to dating to see the difference.

And I'd never hurt her physically or emotionally—how can she think that? I just want to push her limits, see what she will and won't do. Punish her when she colors outside the lines . . . yeah, it might hurt, but not beyond anything she can take. We can work up to what I'd like to do. We can take it slow.

And here's the rub.

If she's going to do what I want her to do, I'm going to have to reassure her and give her "more." What that might be . . . I don't yet know. I've taken her to meet my parents. That was more, surely. And that wasn't so hard.

I take a slower jog around the park to think about what disturbs me most about her e-mail. It isn't her fear, it's that she's terrified of the depth of feeling she has for me.

What does that mean?

That unfamiliar feeling surfaces in my chest as my lungs burn for air. It scares me. Scares me so much that I push myself harder, so that all I feel is the pain of exertion in my legs and in my chest and the cold sweat that trickles down my back.

Yeah. Don't go there, Grey.

Stay in control.

BACK IN MY APARTMENT I have a quick shower and shave, and then I dress. Gail is in the kitchen when I walk through on the way to my study.

"Good morning, Mr. Grey. Coffee?"

"Please," I say, not stopping. I'm on a mission.

At my desk I fire up my iMac and compose my response to Ana.

From: Christian Grey
Subject: Finally!
Date: May 31 2011 07:30
To: Anastasia Steele

Anastasia,

I am annoyed that as soon as you put some distance between us, you communicate openly and honestly with me. Why can't you do that when we're together?

Yes, I'm rich. Get used to it. Why shouldn't I spend money on you? We've told your father I'm your boyfriend, for heaven's sake. Isn't that what boyfriends do? As your Dom, I would expect you to accept whatever I spend on you with no argument. Incidentally, tell your mother, too.

I don't know how to answer your comment about feeling like a whore. I know that's not what you've written, but it's what you imply. I don't know what I can say or do to eradicate these feelings. I'd like you to have the best of everything. I work exceptionally hard so I can spend my money as I see fit. I could buy you your heart's desire, Anastasia, and I want to. Call it redistribution of wealth, if you will. Or simply know that I would not, could not *ever* think of you in the way you described, and I'm angry that's how you perceive yourself.

For such a bright, witty, beautiful young woman, you have some real self-esteem issues, and I have half a mind to make an appointment for you with Dr. Flynn.

I apologize for frightening you. I find the thought of instilling fear in you abhorrent. Do you really think I'd let you travel in the hold? I offered you my private jet, for heaven's sake. Yes, it was a joke, a poor one obviously. However, the fact is the thought of you bound and gagged turns me on (this is not a joke—it's true). I can lose the crate—crates do nothing for me. I know you have issues with gagging— we've talked about that—and if/when I do gag you, we'll discuss it. What I think you fail to realize is that in Dom/ sub relationships it is the sub who has all the power. That's you. I'll repeat this—you are the one with all the power. Not I. In the boathouse you said no. I can't touch you if you say no—that's why we have an agreement—what you will and won't do. If we try things and you don't like them, we can revise the agreement. It's up to you—not me. And if you don't want to be bound and gagged in a crate, then it won't happen.

I want to share my lifestyle with you. I have never wanted anything so much. Frankly, I'm in awe of you, that one so innocent would be willing to try. That says more to me than you could ever know. You fail to see I am caught in your spell, too, even though I have told you this countless times. I don't want to lose you. I am nervous that you've flown three thousand miles to get away from me for a few days, because you can't think clearly around me. It's the same for me, Anastasia. My reason vanishes when we're together—that's the depth of my feeling for you.

I understand your trepidation. I did try to stay away from you; I knew you were inexperienced, though I would never have pursued you if I had known exactly how innocent you were—and yet you still manage to disarm me completely in a way that nobody has before. Your e-mail, for example: I have read and reread it countless times trying to understand your point of view. Three months is an arbitrary amount of time. We could make it six months, a year? How long do you want it to be? What would make you comfortable? Tell me.

I understand that this is a huge leap of faith for you. I have to earn your trust, but by the same token, you have to communicate with me when I am failing to do this. You seem so strong and self-contained, and then I read what you've written here, and I see another side to you. We have to guide each other, Anastasia, and I can only take my cues from you. You have to be honest with me, and we have to both find a way to make this arrangement work.

You worry about not being submissive. Well, maybe that's true. Having said that, the only time you do assume the correct demeanor for a sub is in the playroom. It seems that's the one place where you let me exercise proper control over you and the only place you do as you're told. "Exemplary" is the term that comes to mind. And I'd never beat you black and blue. I aim for pink. Outside the playroom, I like that you challenge me. It's a very novel and refreshing experience, and I wouldn't want to change that. So, yes, tell me what you want in terms of more. I will endeavor to keep an open mind, and I shall try to give you the space you need and stay away from you while you are in Georgia. I look forward to your next e-mail.

In the meantime, enjoy yourself. But not too much.

Christian Grey
CEO, Grey Enterprises Holdings, Inc.

I press send and take a sip of my cold coffee.

Now you have to wait, Grey. See what she says.

I stomp into the kitchen to see what Gail has prepared for breakfast.

TAYLOR IS WAITING IN the car to whisk me to work.

"What was it you wanted last night?" I ask him.

"It was nothing important, sir."

"Good," I respond, and gaze out the window, trying to put Ana and Georgia out of my mind. I fail miserably, but an idea starts to take shape.

I call Andrea. "Morning."

"Good morning, Mr. Grey."

"I'm on my way in, but can you put me through to Bill?"

"Yes, sir."

A few moments later I have Bill on the line.

"Mr. Grey."

"Did your people look at Georgia as an option to site the tech plant? Savannah, in particular?"

"I believe we did, sir. But I'll need to check."

"Check. Come back to me."

"Will do. Is that all?"

"For now. Thanks."

MY DAY IS FULL of meetings. I look at my e-mail sporadically, but there's nothing from Ana. I wonder if she's daunted by the tone of my e-mail, or if she's busy doing other things.

What other things?

It's impossible to avoid thoughts of her. Throughout the day I exchange texts with Caroline Acton, approving and vetoing outfits she's chosen for Ana. I hope she likes them: she'll look stunning in all of them.

Bill has come back to me with a potential site near Savannah for our plant. Ruth is making inquiries.

At least it's not Detroit.

Elena calls, and we decide to have dinner at Columbia Tower. "Christian, you're being so coy about this girl," she chides. "I'll tell you everything this evening. Right now I'm busy." "You're always busy." She laughs. "See you at eight." "See you then."

Why are the women in my life so nosy? Elena. My mother. Ana . . . I wonder for the hundredth time what she's doing. And behold, there's a response from her, at last.

From: Anastasia Steele
Subject: Verbose?
Date: May 31 2011 19:08 EST
To: Christian Grey

Sir, you are quite the loquacious writer. I have to go to dinner at Bob's golf club, and just so you know, I am rolling my eyes at the thought. But you and your twitchy palm are a long way from me so my behind is safe, for now. I loved your e-mail. Will respond when I can. I miss you already.
Enjoy your afternoon.

Your Ana

It's not a "no," and she misses me. I'm relieved and amused at her tone. I respond.

From: Christian Grey
Subject: Your Behind
Date: May 31 2011 16:10
To: Anastasia Steele

Dear Miss Steele,
I am distracted by the title of this e-mail. Needless to say it *is* safe—for now.

Enjoy your dinner, and I miss you, too, especially your behind
and your smart mouth.

My afternoon will be dull, brightened only by thoughts of you
and your eye rolling. I think it was you who so judiciously
pointed out to me that I, too, suffer from that nasty habit.

Christian Grey
CEO & Eye Roller,
Grey Enterprises Holdings, Inc.

A few minutes later her reply pings into my inbox.

From: Anastasia Steele
Subject: Eye Rolling
Date: May 31 2011 19:14 EST
To: Christian Grey

Dear Mr. Grey,
Stop e-mailing me. I am trying to get ready for dinner. You
are very distracting, even when you are on the other side of
the continent. And yes—who spanks you when you roll your
eyes?

Your Ana

Oh, Ana, you do.
All the time.
I remember her telling me to keep still and tugging my pubic
hair while she was sitting astride me, naked. The thought is
arousing.

From: Christian Grey
Subject: Your Behind
Date: May 31 2011 16:18
To: Anastasia Steele

Dear Miss Steele,
I still prefer my title to yours, in so many different ways. It
is lucky that I am master of my own destiny and no one
castigates me. Except my mother, occasionally, and Dr.
Flynn, of course. And you.

Christian Grey
CEO, Grey Enterprises Holdings, Inc.

I find myself drumming my fingers, waiting for her reply.

From: Anastasia Steele
Subject: Chastising . . . Me?
Date: May 31 2011 19:22 EST
To: Christian Grey

Dear Sir,
When have I ever plucked up the nerve to chastise you, Mr.
Grey? I think you are mixing me up with someone else . . .
which is very worrying. I really do have to get ready.

Your Ana

You. You chastise me via e-mail at every opportunity—and how
could I ever mix you up with anyone else?

From: Christian Grey
Subject: Your Behind
Date: May 31 2011 16:25
To: Anastasia Steele

Dear Miss Steele,
You do it all the time in print. Can I zip up your dress?

Christian Grey
CEO, Grey Enterprises Holdings, Inc.

From: Anastasia Steele
Subject: NC-17
Date: May 31 2011 19:28 EST
To: Christian Grey

I would rather you unzipped it.

Her words travel directly to my dick, passing "Go" on the way.
Fuck.
This calls for—what did she call them? SHOUTY CAPITALS.

From: Christian Grey
Subject: Careful what you wish for . . .
Date: May 31 2011 16:31
To: Anastasia Steele

SO WOULD I.

Christian Grey
CEO, Grey Enterprises Holdings, Inc.

From: Anastasia Steele
Subject: Panting
Date: May 31 2011 19:33 EST
To: Christian Grey

Slowly . . .

From: Christian Grey
Subject: Groaning
Date: May 31 2011 16:35
To: Anastasia Steele

Wish I were there.

Christian Grey
CEO, Grey Enterprises Holdings, Inc.

From: Anastasia Steele
Subject: Moaning
Date: May 31 2011 19:37 EST
To: Christian Grey

SO DO I.

Who else can turn me on via e-mail?

From: Anastasia Steele
Subject: Moaning
Date: May 31 2011 19:39 EST
To: Christian Grey

Gotta go.

Laters, baby.

I smirk at her words.

From: Christian Grey
Subject: Plagiarism
Date: May 31 2011 16:41
To: Anastasia Steele

You stole my line.
And left me hanging.

Enjoy your dinner.

Christian Grey
CEO, Grey Enterprises Holdings, Inc.

Andrea knocks on the door with new schematics from Barney for the solar-power tablet we're developing. She's startled that I'm pleased to see her. "Thanks, Andrea."

"You're most welcome, Mr. Grey." She gives me a curious smile. "Would you like some coffee?"

"Please."

"Milk?"

"No thanks."

MY DAY HAS IMPROVED immensely. I have knocked Bastille on his ass twice in our two rounds of kickboxing. That never happens. As I slip on my jacket after my shower, I feel ready to face Elena and all her questions.

Taylor appears. "Would you like me to drive, sir?"

"No. I'll take the R8."

"Very good, sir."

Before I leave I check my e-mail.

From: Anastasia Steele
Subject: Who are you to cry thief?
Date: May 31 2011 22:18 EST
To: Christian Grey

Sir, I think you'll find it was Elliot's line originally.

Hanging how?

Your Ana

Is she flirting with me? Again?
And she's my Ana. Again.

From: Christian Grey
Subject: Unfinished Business
Date: May 31 2011 19:22
To: Anastasia Steele

Miss Steele,
You're back. You left so suddenly—just when things were getting interesting.

Elliot's not very original. He must have stolen that line from someone.

How was dinner?

Christian Grey
CEO, Grey Enterprises Holdings, Inc.

I press send.

From: Anastasia Steele
Subject: Unfinished Business?
Date: May 31 2011 22:26 EST
To: Christian Grey

Dinner was filling—you'll be very pleased to hear I ate far too much.

Getting interesting? How?

I'm glad she's eating . . .

From: Christian Grey
Subject: Unfinished Business—Definitely
Date: May 31 2011 19:30
To: Anastasia Steele

Are you being deliberately obtuse? I think you'd just asked me to unzip your dress.

And I was looking forward to doing just that. I am also glad to hear you are eating.

Christian Grey
CEO, Grey Enterprises Holdings, Inc.

From: Anastasia Steele
Subject: Well . . . There's Always the Weekend
Date: May 31 2011 22:36 EST
To: Christian Grey

Of course I eat . . . It's only the uncertainty I feel around you that puts me off my food.

And I would never be unwittingly obtuse, Mr. Grey.

Surely you've worked that out by now. ;)

She loses appetite around me? That's not good. And she's making fun of me. *Again.*

From: Christian Grey
Subject: Can't Wait
Date: May 31 2011 19:40
To: Anastasia Steele

I shall remember that, Miss Steele, and no doubt use the knowledge to my advantage.

I'm sorry to hear that I put you off your food. I thought I had a more concupiscent effect on you. That has been my experience, and most pleasurable it has been, too.

I very much look forward to the next time.

Christian Grey
CEO, Grey Enterprises Holdings, Inc.

From: Anastasia Steele
Subject: Gymnastic Linguistics
Date: May 31 2011 22:36 EST
To: Christian Grey

Have you been playing with the thesaurus again?

I hoot with laughter.

From: Christian Grey
Subject: Rumbled
Date: May 31 2011 19:40
To: Anastasia Steele

You know me so well, Miss Steele.

I am having dinner with an old friend now so I will be driving.

Laters, baby©.

Christian Grey
CEO, Grey Enterprises Holdings, Inc.

As much as I'd like to keep up the banter with Ana, I don't want to be late for dinner. If I were, Elena would be displeased. I power down my computer, collect my wallet and phone, and take the elevator to the garage.

THE MILE HIGH CLUB is on the penthouse floor of Columbia Tower. The sun is sinking toward the peaks of Olympic National Park, coloring the sky with an impressive fusion of oranges, pinks, and opals. It's stunning. Ana would love this view. I should bring her here.

Elena is seated at a corner table. She gives me a small wave and a big smile. The maître d' escorts me to her table, and she rises, presenting her cheek to me.

"Hello, Christian," she purrs.

"Good evening, Elena. You're looking great, as usual." I kiss her cheek. She tosses her sleek platinum hair to one side, which she does when she's feeling playful.

"Sit," she says. "What would you like to drink?" Her fingers and her trademark scarlet fingernails are wrapped around a champagne flute.

"I see you've started on the Cristal."

"Well, I think we've got something to celebrate, don't you?"

"We do?"

"Christian. This girl. Spill the beans."

"I'll have a glass of the Mendocino sauvignon blanc," I tell the hovering waiter. He nods and hurries off.

"So, not a cause for celebration?" Elena takes a sip of her champagne, eyebrows raised.

"I don't know why you're making such a big deal of this."

"I'm not making a big deal. I'm curious. How old is she? What does she do?"

"She's just graduated."

"Oh. A little young for you?"

I arch a brow. "Really? You're going to go there?"

Elena laughs.

"How is Isaac?" I ask with a smirk.

She laughs again. "Behaving." Her eyes sparkle with mischief.

"How boring for you." My voice is dry.

She smiles, resigned. "He's a good pet. Shall we order?"

HALFWAY THROUGH THE CRAB chowder I put Elena out of her misery.

"Her name is Anastasia, she studied literature at WSU, and I met her when she came to interview me for the student newspaper. I gave the commencement address this year."

"Is she in the lifestyle?"

"Not yet. But I'm hopeful."

"Wow."

"Yeah. She's escaped to Georgia to think it through."

"That's a long way to go."

"I know." I look down at my chowder, wondering how Ana is and what she's doing; sleeping, I hope . . . alone. When I raise my head Elena is studying me. Intently.

"I haven't seen you like this," she says.

"What do you mean?"

"You're distracted. That's not like you."

"Is it that obvious?"

She nods, her eyes softening. "Obvious to me. I think she's turned your world upside down."

I inhale sharply but hide the fact by raising my glass to my lips.

Perceptive, Mrs. Lincoln.

"You think?" I murmur after my sip.

"I think," she says, her eyes searching mine.

"She's very disarming."

"I'm sure that's novel. And I bet you're worrying about what she's doing in Georgia, what she's thinking. I know how you are."

"Yes. I want her to make the right decision."

"You should go and see her."

"What?"

"Get on a plane."

"Really?"

"If she's undecided. Go use your considerable charm."

My snort is derisive.

"Christian," she scolds, "when you want something badly enough, you go after it and you always win. You know that. You're so negative about yourself. Drives me crazy."

I sigh. "I'm not sure."

"The poor girl is probably bored to tears down there. Go. You'll get your answer. If it's no, you can move on, if it's yes, you can enjoy being yourself with her."

"She's back Friday."

"Seize the day, my dear."

"She did say she missed me."

"There you go." Her eyes flash with certainty.

"I'll think about it. More champagne?"

"Please," she says, and gives me a girlish grin.

DRIVING BACK TO ESCALA, I contemplate Elena's advice. I *could* go to see Ana. She said she's missed me . . . the jet's available.

Back home I read her latest e-mail.

From: Anastasia Steele
Subject: Suitable Dinner Companions
Date: May 31 2011 23:58 EST
To: Christian Grey

I hope you and your friend had a very pleasant dinner.

Ana

P.S. Was it Mrs. Robinson?

Shit.

This is the perfect excuse. This is going to need an answer in person.

I buzz Taylor and tell him I'm going to need Stephan and the Gulfstream in the morning.

"Very good, Mr. Grey. Where are you going?"

"*We're* going to Savannah."

"Yes, sir." And there's a hint of amusement in his voice.

WEDNESDAY, JUNE 1, 2011

It's been an interesting morning. We left Boeing Field at 11:30 PST; Stephan is flying with his first officer, Jill Beighley, and we're due to arrive in Georgia at 19:30 EST.

Bill has managed to arrange a meeting with the Savannah Brownfield Redevelopment Authority tomorrow, and I might be meeting them for a drink this evening. So if Anastasia is otherwise occupied, or doesn't want to see me, the journey won't be a complete waste of time.

Yeah, yeah. Tell yourself that, Grey.

Taylor has joined me for a light lunch and is now sorting through some paperwork, and I have a whole lot of reading to do.

The only part of the equation I've yet to solve is arranging to see Ana. I'll see how that goes once I arrive in Savannah; I'm hoping some inspiration will come to me on the flight.

I run my hand through my hair, and for the first time in a long while I lie back and doze as the G550 cruises at thirty thousand feet, bound for Savannah/Hilton Head International. The drone of the engines is soothing, and I'm tired. So tired.

That would be the nightmares, Grey.

I don't know why they are worse at the moment. I close my eyes.

"This is how you will be with me. Do you understand?"
"Yes, Ma'am."
She runs a scarlet fingernail across my chest.
I flinch and pull against the restraints as the darkness
surfaces, burning my skin in the wake of her touch. But I
don't make a sound.
I don't dare.

"If you behave, I'll let you come. In my mouth."

Fuck.

"But not yet. We've got a long way to go before then."

Her fingernail blazes down my skin, from the top of my sternum to my navel.

I want to scream.

She grabs my face, squeezing open my mouth, and kisses me. Her tongue demanding and wet.

She brandishes the leather flogger.

And I know this will be tough to endure.

But I have my eye on the prize. Her fucking mouth.

As the first lash falls and blisters across my skin, I welcome the pain and the endorphin rush.

"Mr. Grey, we'll be landing in twenty minutes," Taylor informs me, startling me awake. "Are you okay, sir?"

"Yeah. Sure. Thanks."

"Would you like some water?"

"Please." I take a deep breath to bring my heart rate down, and Taylor passes me a glass of cold Evian. I take a welcome sip, glad that it's just Taylor on board. It's not often I dream about my heady days with Mrs. Lincoln.

Out of the window the sky is blue, the sparse clouds pinking with the early-evening sun. The light up here is brilliant. Golden. Tranquil. The sinking sun reflecting off the cumulus clouds. For a moment I wish I were in my sailplane. I bet the thermals are fantastic up here.

Yes!

That's what I should do: take Ana soaring. That would be *more*, wouldn't it?

"Taylor."

"Yes, sir."

"I'd like to take Anastasia soaring in Georgia—at dawn tomorrow, if we can find somewhere to do that. But later would be fine, too." If it's later I'll have to move my meeting.

"I'll get on it."

"Never mind the cost."

"Okay, sir."

"Thanks."

Now I just have to tell Ana.

THERE ARE TWO CARS waiting for us when the G550 comes to a halt on the tarmac near the Signature Flight Support terminal at the airport. Taylor and I step out of the plane and into the suffocating heat.

Hell, it's sticky, even at this time.

The rep hands the keys for both cars to Taylor. I raise a brow at him. "Ford Mustang?"

"It's all I could find in Savannah at short notice." Taylor looks sheepish.

"At least it's a red convertible. Though in this heat I hope it has AC."

"It should have everything, sir."

"Good. Thanks." I take the keys from him and, grabbing my messenger bag, leave him to unload the rest of the luggage from the plane into his Suburban.

I shake hands with Stephan and Beighley and thank them for a smooth flight. In the Mustang, I cruise out of the airport and onward to downtown Savannah, listening to Bruce on my iPod through the car sound system.

ANDREA HAS BOOKED ME into a suite at the Bohemian Hotel, which looks out over the Savannah River. It's dusk and the view from the balcony is impressive: the river is luminous, reflecting the graduated colors of the sky and the lights on the suspension bridge and the docks. The sky is incandescent, the colors shaded from deep purple to a rosy pink.

It's almost as striking as twilight over the Sound.

But I don't have time to stand here and admire the view. I set up my laptop, crank the air-conditioning to full blast, and call Ros for an update.

"Why the sudden interest in Georgia, Christian?"

"It's personal."

She huffs down the phone. "Since when have you let your personal life interfere with business?"

Since I met Anastasia Steele.

"I don't like Detroit," I snap.

"Okay." She backs off.

"I might meet the Savannah Brownfield liaison for a drink later," I add, attempting to placate her.

"Whatever, Christian. There are a few other things we need to talk about. The aid has arrived in Rotterdam. Do you still want to go ahead?"

"Yes. Let's get it done. I made a commitment at the End Global Hunger launch. This needs to happen before I can face that committee again."

"Okay. Any further thoughts on the publishing acquisition?"

"I'm still undecided."

"I think SIP has some potential."

"Yeah. Maybe. Let me think about it for a while longer."

"I'm seeing Marco to discuss the Lucas Woods situation."

"Okay, let me know how that goes. Call me later."

"Will do. Bye for now."

I'm avoiding the inevitable. I know this. But I decide it would be better to tackle Miss Steele—via e-mail or phone, I've yet to decide which—on a full stomach, so I order dinner. While I'm waiting there's a text from Andrea letting me know my drinks appointment is off. I'm fine with that. I'll see them tomorrow morning, provided I'm not soaring with Ana.

Before room service arrives, Taylor calls.

"Mr. Grey."

"Taylor. Are you checked in?"

"Yes, sir. Your luggage will be on its way up in a moment."

"Great."

"The Brunswick Soaring Association has a glider free. I've asked Andrea to fax through your flying credentials to them. Once the paperwork's signed, we're good to go."

"Great."

"They'll do anytime from six a.m."

"Even better. Have them ready from then. Send me the address."

"Will do."

There's a knock on the door—my luggage and room service have arrived simultaneously. The food smells delicious: fried green tomatoes and shrimp and grits. Well, I'm in the South.

While I eat I contemplate my strategy with Ana. I could pay a visit to her mom's tomorrow at breakfast. Bring bagels. Then take her soaring. That's probably the best plan. She hasn't been in touch all day, so I guess she's mad. I reread her last message once I've finished dinner.

What the hell has she got against Elena? She knows nothing about our relationship. What we had happened a long time ago and now we're just friends. What right does Ana have to be mad?

And if it wasn't for Elena, God knows what would have happened to me.

There's a knock on the door. It's Taylor.

"Good evening, sir. Happy with your room?"

"Yes, it's fine."

"I have the paperwork for the Brunswick Soaring Association here."

I scan the hire agreement. It looks fine. I sign it and give it back to him. "I'll drive myself tomorrow. I'll see you there?"

"Yes, sir. I'll be there from six."

"I'll let you know if anything changes."

"Shall I unpack for you, sir?"

"Please. Thanks."

He nods and takes my suitcase into the bedroom.

I'm restless, and I need to get what I'm going to say to Ana clear in my mind. I glance at my watch; it's twenty past nine. I've left this really late. Perhaps I should have a quick drink first. I leave Taylor to unpack and decide to check out the hotel bar before I speak to Ros again and write to Ana.

The rooftop bar is crowded, but I find a seat at the end of the counter and order a beer. It's a hip, contemporary place, with moody lighting and a relaxed vibe. I scan the bar, avoiding eye contact with the two women sitting next to me . . . and a movement captures my attention: a frustrated flip of glossy mahogany hair that catches and refracts the light.

It's Ana. Fuck.

She's facing away from me, seated opposite a woman who could only be her mother. The resemblance is striking.

What are the fucking odds?

In all the gin joints . . . *Jesus*.

I watch them, transfixed. They're drinking cocktails—Cosmopolitans, by the look of them. Her mother is stunning: like Ana, but older; she looks late thirties, with long, dark hair, and eyes that are Ana's shade of blue. She has a bohemian vibe about her . . . not someone I'd automatically associate with the golf club set. Perhaps she's dressed that way because she's out with her young, beautiful daughter.

This is priceless.

Seize the day, Grey.

I fish my phone out of my jeans pocket. It's time to e-mail Ana. This should be interesting. I'll test her mood . . . and I get to watch.

From: Christian Grey
Subject: Dinner Companions
Date: June 1 2011 21:40 EST
To: Anastasia Steele

Yes, I had dinner with Mrs. Robinson. She is just an old friend, Anastasia.

Looking forward to seeing you again. I miss you.

Christian Grey
CEO, Grey Enterprises Holdings, Inc.

Her mother looks earnest; maybe she's concerned for her daughter, or maybe she's trying to extract information from her.

Good luck, Mrs. Adams.

And for a moment I wonder if they're discussing me. Her mother stands; it looks like she's visiting the restroom. Ana checks her purse and pulls out her BlackBerry.

Here we go . . .

She begins to read, her shoulders hunched over, her fingers flexing and drumming on the table. She starts tapping furiously at the keys. I can't see her face, which is frustrating, but I don't think she's impressed with what she's just read. A moment later she abandons the phone on the table in what appears to be disgust.

That's not good.

Her mother returns and signals one of the waiters for another round of drinks. I wonder how many they've had.

I check my phone, and sure enough, there's a response.

From: Anastasia Steele
Subject: OLD Dinner Companions
Date: June 1 2011 21:42 EST
To: Christian Grey

She's not just an old friend.

Has she found another adolescent boy to sink her teeth into?

Did you get too old for her?

Is that the reason your relationship finished?

What the hell? My temper simmers as I read.

Isaac is in his late twenties.

Like me.

How dare she?

Is it the drink talking?

Time to declare yourself, Grey.

From: Christian Grey
Subject: Careful . . .
Date: June 1 2011 21:45 EST
To: Anastasia Steele

This is not something I wish to discuss via e-mail.

How many Cosmopolitans are you going to drink?

Christian Grey
CEO, Grey Enterprises Holdings, Inc.

She studies her phone, sits up suddenly, and looks around the room.

Showtime, Grey.

I deposit ten bucks on the counter and saunter over to them.

Our eyes meet. She blanches—shocked, I think—and I don't know how she'll greet me, or how I'll contain my temper if she says anything else about Elena.

She tucks her hair behind her ears with restless fingers. A sure sign that she's nervous. "Hi," she says, her voice strained and high-pitched.

"Hi." I lean down and kiss her cheek. She smells amazing, even if she does tense as my lips brush her skin. She looks lovely; she's caught some sun, and she's not wearing a bra. Her breasts are straining against the silky material of her top, but hidden by her long hair.

For my eyes only, I hope.

And even though she's mad, I'm glad to see her. I've missed her.

"Christian, this is my mother, Carla." Ana gestures to her mom.

"Mrs. Adams, I am delighted to meet you."

Her mom's eyes are all over me.

Shit! She's checking me out. *Best ignore it, Grey.*

After a longer-than-necessary pause, she reaches out to shake my hand. "Christian."

"What are you doing here?" Ana asks, her tone accusatory.

"I came to see you, of course. I'm staying in this hotel."

"You're staying here?" she squeaks.

Yes. I can't quite believe it, either. "Well, yesterday you said you wished I was here." I'm trying to gauge her reaction. So far there's been: nervous fidgeting, tensing, an accusatory tone, and a strained voice. This is not going well. "We aim to please, Miss Steele," I add, deadpan, hoping to put her in a good mood.

"Won't you join us for a drink, Christian?" Mrs. Adams says graciously, and catches the eye of the waiter.

I need something stronger than beer. "I'll have a gin and tonic," I tell the waiter. "Hendrick's, if you have it, or Bombay Sapphire. Cucumber with the Hendrick's, lime with the Bombay."

"And two more Cosmos, please," Ana adds, with an anxious look at me.

She's right to be anxious. I think she's had enough to drink already.

"Please pull up a chair, Christian."

"Thank you, Mrs. Adams."

I do as she asks, and sit down beside Ana.

"So you just happen to be staying in the hotel where we're drinking?" Ana's tone is tense.

"Or you just happen to be drinking in the hotel where I'm staying. I just finished dinner, came in here, and saw you. I was distracted, thinking about your most recent e-mail"—I give her a pointed look—"and I glance up and there you are. Quite a coincidence, eh?"

Ana looks flustered. "My mother and I were shopping this morning and on the beach this afternoon. We decided on a few cocktails this evening," she says hurriedly, as if she has to justify drinking in a bar with her mother.

"Did you buy that top?" I ask. She really does look stunning. Her camisole is emerald green; I've made the right choices—gem colors—for the clothes Caroline Acton has selected for her. "The color suits you. And you've caught some sun. You look lovely." Her cheeks color and her lips lift at my compliment. "Well, I was going to pay you a visit tomorrow. But here you are." I take her hand, because I want to touch her, and I give it a gentle squeeze. Slowly I caress her knuckles with my thumb, and her breathing alters.

Yes, Ana. Feel it.

Don't be mad at me.

Her eyes meet mine, and I'm rewarded with her coy smile.

"I thought I'd surprise you. But as ever, Anastasia, you surprise me by being here. I don't want to interrupt the time you have with your mother. I'll have a quick drink and then retire. I have work to do." I resist kissing her knuckles. I don't know what she's said to her mother about us, if anything.

"Christian, it's lovely to meet you finally. Ana has spoken very fondly of you," Mrs. Adams says, with a charming smile.

"Really?" I glance at Ana, who's blushing.

Fondly, eh?

This is good news.

The waiter places my gin and tonic in front of me.

"Hendrick's, sir."

"Thank you."

He serves Ana and her mother fresh Cosmopolitans.

"How long are you in Georgia, Christian?" her mom asks.

"Until Friday, Mrs. Adams."

"Will you have dinner with us tomorrow evening? And please, call me Carla."

"I'd be delighted to, Carla."

"Excellent," she says. "If you two will excuse me, I need to visit the restroom."

Hasn't she just been to the restroom?

I stand as she leaves, then sit down again to face the wrath of Miss Steele. I take her hand once more. "So, you're mad at me for having dinner with an old friend." I kiss each knuckle.

"Yes." She's curt.

Is she jealous?

"Our sexual relationship was over long ago, Anastasia. I don't want anyone but you. Haven't you worked that out yet?"

"I think of her as a child molester, Christian."

My scalp tingles in shock. "That's very judgmental. It wasn't like that." I release her hand in frustration.

"Oh, how was it, then?" she snaps, sticking out her stubborn little chin.

Is this the drink talking?

She continues, "She took advantage of a vulnerable fifteen-year-old boy. If you had been a fifteen-year-old girl and Mrs. Robinson was a Mr. Robinson, tempting you into a BDSM lifestyle, that would have been okay? If it was Mia, say?"

Oh, now she's being ridiculous. "Ana, it wasn't like that."

Her eyes flash. She's really angry. Why? This has nothing to do with her. But I don't want a full-blown argument here in the bar. I moderate my voice. "Okay, it didn't feel like that to me. She was a force for good. What I needed." Good God, I'd probably be dead by now if it wasn't for Elena. I'm struggling to control my temper.

Her brow furrows. "I don't understand."

Shut her down, Grey.

"Anastasia, your mother will be back shortly. I'm not comfortable talking about this now. Later, maybe. If you don't want me here, I have a plane on standby at Hilton Head. I can go."

Her expression changes to panic. "No—don't go. Please. I'm thrilled you're here," she adds quickly.

Thrilled? You could have fooled me.

"I'm just trying to make you understand," she says. "I'm angry that as soon as I left, you had dinner with her. Think about how you are when I get anywhere near José. José is a good friend. I have never had a sexual relationship with him. Whereas you and her—"

"You're jealous?"

How can I make her realize that Elena and I are friends? She has nothing to be jealous about.

Clearly, Miss Steele is possessive.

And it takes me a moment to realize that I like that.

"Yes, and angry about what she did to you," she continues.

"Anastasia, she helped me. That's all I'll say about that. And as for your jealousy, put yourself in my shoes. I haven't had to justify my actions to anyone in the last seven years. Not one person. I do as I wish, Anastasia. I like my autonomy. I didn't go and see Mrs. Robinson to upset you. I went because every now and then we have dinner. She's a friend and a business partner."

Her eyes widen.

Oh. Didn't I mention that?

Why would I mention that? It's nothing to do with her.

"Yes, we're business partners. The sex is over between us. It has been for years."

"Why did your relationship end?"

"Her husband found out. Can we talk about this some other time—somewhere more private?"

"I don't think you'll ever convince me that she's not some kind of pedophile."

Fucking hell, Ana! Enough is enough!

"I don't think of her that way. I never have. Now that's enough!" I growl.

"Did you love her?"

What?

"How are you two getting on?" Carla is back. Ana forces a smile that makes my stomach churn.

"Fine, Mom."

Did I love Elena?

I take a sip of my drink. I fucking worshipped her . . . but did I love her? What a ridiculous question. I know nothing about romantic love. That's the hearts-and-flowers shit she wants. The nineteenth-century novels she's read have filled her head with nonsense.

I've had enough.

"Well, ladies, I shall leave you to your evening. Please, put these drinks on my tab, room number 612. I'll call you in the morning, Anastasia. Until tomorrow, Carla."

"Oh, it's so nice to hear someone use your full name."

"Beautiful name for a beautiful girl." I shake Carla's hand, sincere about the compliment but not the smile on my face.

Ana is quiet, imploring me with a look that I ignore. I kiss her cheek. "Laters, baby," I murmur in her ear, then turn and walk through the bar and back down to my room.

That girl provokes me like no one has before.

And she's pissed at me; maybe she has PMS. She said her period was due this week.

I burst into my room, slam the door, and head straight for the balcony. It's warm outside, and I take a deep breath, inhaling the pungent salty scent of the river. Night has fallen, and the river is inky black, like the sky . . . like my mood. I didn't even get to discuss gliding tomorrow. I rest my hands on the balcony rail. The lights on the shore and the bridge improve the view . . . but not my temperament.

Why am I defending a relationship that began when Ana was still in fourth grade? It's none of her business. Yes, it was unconventional. But that's all.

I run both hands through my hair. This trip isn't working out how I expected, at all. Perhaps it was a mistake to come down here. And to think it was Elena who encouraged me to make the trip.

My phone buzzes, and I hope it's Ana. It's Ros.

"Yes," I snap.

"Jeez, Christian. Am I interrupting something?"

"No. Sorry. What's up?" *Calm down, Grey.*

"I thought I'd update you on my conversation with Marco. But if now is a bad time, I'll call back in the morning."

"No, it's fine."

There's a knock on the door. "Hang on, Ros." I open it, expecting Taylor or someone from housekeeping to do turndown—but it's Ana, standing in the corridor, looking bashful and beautiful.

She's here.

Opening the door wider, I motion her in.

"All the redundancy packages concluded?" I ask Ros, without taking my eyes off Ana.

"Yes."

Ana walks into the room, watching me warily, her lips parted and moist, her eyes darkening. *What's this? A change of heart?* I know that look. It's desire. She wants me. And I want her, too, especially after our spat in the bar.

Why else would she be here?

"And the cost?" I question Ros.

"Nearly two million."

I whistle through my teeth. "That was one expensive mistake."

"GEH gets to exploit the fiber-optic division." She's right. This was one of our goals.

"And Lucas?" I ask.

"He reacted badly."

I open the minibar and gesture to Ana to help herself. Leaving her there, I stroll into the bedroom.

"What did he do?"

"He threw a fit."

In the bathroom I turn on the faucet to run water into the huge sunken marble bath and add some scented bath oil. There's room for six people in here.

"The majority of that money is for him," I remind Ros as I check the water temperature. "And he has the buyout price for the company. He can always start again."

I turn to leave, but as an afterthought I decide to light the various candles that are artfully arranged on the stone bench. *Lit candles count as "more," don't they?*

"Well, he's threatening lawyers, though I don't understand why. We're bulletproof on this. Is that water I hear?" Ros asks.

"Yeah, I'm running a bath."

"Oh? Do you want me to go?"

"No. Anything else?"

"Yes, Fred wants to talk to you."

"Really?"

"He's gone over Barney's new design."

As I wander back into the living room, I acknowledge Barney's design solution for the tablet and ask her to have Andrea send me the revised schematics. Ana has retrieved a bottle of orange juice.

"Is this your new management style: not being here?" Ros asks. I laugh out loud, but mainly at Ana's choice of beverage. *Wise woman.* And I tell Ros that I won't be back in the office until Friday.

"Are you seriously going to change your mind about Detroit?"

"There's a plot of land here that I'm interested in."

"Is Bill aware of this?" Ros is snippy.

"Yeah, get Bill to call."

"Will do. Did you get a drink with the Savannah people this evening?"

I tell her that I'll be seeing them tomorrow. I'm more conciliatory and mindful of my tone, as this is a hot button for Ros. "I want to see what Georgia will offer if we move in." I take a glass off the shelf, hand it to Ana, and point to the ice bucket.

"If their incentives are attractive enough," I continue, "I think we should consider it, though I'm not sure about the damned heat here."

Ana pours her drink.

"It's late to be changing your mind on this, Christian. But it might give us some leverage with Detroit," Ros muses.

"I agree, Detroit has its advantages, too, and it's cooler."

But there are too many ghosts there for me.

"Get Bill to call. Tomorrow." It's late now and I have a visitor. "Not too early," I warn. Ros says good night and I hang up.

Ana eyes me with reserve as I drink her in. Her lush hair falls over small shoulders, framing her lovely, pensive face. "You didn't answer my question," she murmurs.

"No. I didn't."

"No, you didn't answer my question, or no, you didn't love her?"

She's not going to let this go. I lean against the wall and fold my arms so I don't pull her into them. "What are you doing here, Anastasia?"

"I've just told you."

Put her out of her misery, Grey.

"No. I didn't love her."

Her shoulders relax and her face softens. It's what she wanted to hear.

"You're quite the green-eyed goddess, Anastasia. Who would have thought?"

But are you my *green-eyed goddess?*

"Are you making fun of me, Mr. Grey?"

"I wouldn't dare," I retort.

"Oh, I think you would, and I think you do—often." She smirks and sinks perfect teeth into her lip.

She's doing that on purpose.

"Please stop biting your lip. You're in my room, I haven't set eyes on you for nearly three days, and I've flown a long way to see you." I need to know that we're okay, the only way I know how. I want to fuck her, hard.

My phone buzzes, but I switch it off without checking the caller. Whoever it is can wait.

I step toward her. "I want you, Anastasia. Now. And you want me. That's why you're here."

"I really did want to know," she says.

"Well, now that you do, are you coming or going?" I ask, standing in front of her.

"Coming," she says, her eyes on mine.

"Oh, I hope so." I stare down at her, marveling as her irises darken.

She wants me.

"You were so mad at me," I whisper.

It's still novel, dealing with her anger, taking her feelings into account.

"Yes."

"I don't remember anyone but my family ever being mad at me.

I like it." Gently I touch her face with the tips of my fingers and run them down to her chin. She closes her eyes and angles her cheek to my touch. Leaning down, I run my nose along her naked shoulder, up to her ear, inhaling her sweet scent as desire floods my body. My fingers move to her nape and into her hair.

"We should talk," she whispers.

"Later."

"There's so much I want to say."

"Me, too." I kiss the spot beneath her ear and tug her hair, pulling back her head to expose her throat. My teeth and lips graze her chin and down her neck as my body hums with need. "I want you," I whisper, as I kiss the spot where her pulse beats beneath her skin. She moans and holds my arms. I tense for a moment, but the darkness stays dormant.

"Are you bleeding?" I ask between kisses.

She stills. "Yes," she says.

"Do you have cramps?"

"No." Her voice is quiet yet vehement with embarrassment.

I stop kissing her and look down into her eyes. Why is she embarrassed? It's her body. "Did you take your pill?"

"Yes," she answers.

Good. "Let's go have a bath."

In the over-the-top bathroom I release Ana's hand. The atmosphere is hot and humid, steam gently rising above the foam. In this heat I'm overdressed, my linen shirt and jeans sticking to my skin.

Ana watches me, her skin dewy from the humidity.

"Do you have a hair tie?" I ask. Her hair will start clinging to her face. She pulls out a hair elastic from her jeans pocket.

"Put your hair up," I tell her, and watch as she follows my command with quick, efficient grace.

Good girl. No more arguing.

A few strands escape from her ponytail, but she looks lovely. I turn off the faucet and, taking her hand, guide her into the other part of the bathroom, where a large gilded mirror hangs over two sinks set in marble. My eyes on hers in the mirror, I stand behind her and ask her to take off her sandals. Hastily she removes them and lets them drop to the floor.

"Lift up your arms," I whisper. Grasping the hem of her pretty top, I peel it off and over her head, freeing her breasts. Reaching around, I undo the top button and the zipper of her jeans.

"I'm going to have you in the bathroom, Anastasia." Her eyes stray to my mouth and she licks her lips. Under the soft light her pupils gleam with excitement. Bending down, I drop tender kisses on her neck, hook my thumbs into the waistband of her jeans, and slowly peel them down over her fine ass, catching her panties in my hands on the way down. Kneeling behind her, I ease them down her legs, to her feet. "Step out of your jeans," I order. Grabbing the edge of the sink, she obliges; now she's naked and I'm face-to-face with her ass. I pop her jeans, panties, and top onto a white stool beneath the sink and contemplate all the things I could do to that ass. I notice a blue string between her legs; her tampon is still in place, so I settle for kissing and nipping her behind gently before standing up. Our eyes connect in the mirror once more and I splay my hand out over her smooth, flat belly.

"Look at you. You are so beautiful. See how you feel." Her breathing quickens as I take both her hands in mine and spread her fingers on her belly beneath my outstretched hands.

"Feel how soft your skin is," I whisper. Gently I guide her hands across her torso in a wide sweeping circle, then travel them up to her breasts.

"Feel how full your breasts are." I hold her hands beneath her breasts so she's cupping them. Gently I tease her nipples with my thumbs. She moans and bows her back, pressing her breasts into our conjoined hands. Trapping her nipples between her thumbs and mine, I tug gently again and again, and take pleasure watching them harden and lengthen in response.

Like a certain part of my anatomy.

She closes her eyes and wriggles against me, brushing her behind over my erection. She moans, her head against my shoulder.

"That's right, baby," I murmur against her neck, enjoying her body coming alive beneath her touch. I guide her hands down her front to her hips, then in toward her pubic hair. I push my leg between hers and with my foot widen her stance as I guide her hands over her vulva, one hand at a time, over and over, pressing her fingers over her clitoris again and again.

She groans and I watch her writhe against me in the mirror.

Lord, she's a goddess.

"Look at you glow, Anastasia." I kiss and nip her neck and her shoulder, then I let go, leaving her hanging, and she opens her eyes as I step back.

"Carry on," I tell her, wondering what she'll do.

She falters for a moment, then rubs herself with one hand, but not nearly as enthusiastically.

Oh, this will never do.

Quickly I strip off my sticky shirt, jeans, and underwear, freeing my erection.

"You'd rather I do this?" I ask, her eyes blazing at mine in the mirror.

"Oh yes, please," she says, a desperate, needy edge to her voice. I wrap my arms around her, my front against her back, my cock resting in the cleft of her fine, fine ass. I take her hands in mine once more, guiding them over her clitoris, one at a time, again and again, pressing, stroking, and arousing her. She whimpers as I suck and nip at her nape. Her legs begin to tremble. Abruptly I spin her around so she's facing me. I grasp her wrists in one of my hands, holding them behind her back, while I tug on her ponytail with the other, bringing her lips up to mine. I kiss her, consuming her mouth, reveling in the taste of her: orange juice and sweet, sweet Ana. Her breathing is harsh, like mine.

"When did you start your period, Anastasia?"

I want to fuck you without a condom.

"Yesterday," she breathes.

"Good." I step back and spin her around. "Hold on to the sink," I command. Grasping her hips, I lift her and pull her backward so she's bent over. My hand glides down her ass to the blue string, and I tug out the tampon, which I toss in the toilet. She gasps, shocked, I think, but I grab my cock and slide into her quickly.

My breath whistles between my teeth.

Fuck. She feels good. So good. Skin against skin.

I edge back, then sink into her once more, slowly, feeling every precious, slick inch of her. She groans and pushes against me.

Oh yes, Ana.

She tightens her grip on the marble as I pick up speed, and I grasp her hips, building . . . building, then hammering into her. Claiming her. Possessing her.

Don't be jealous, Ana. I want only you.

You.

You.

My fingers find her clitoris and I tease her, caress her, and stimulate her so that her legs begin to tremble once more. "That's right, baby," I murmur, my voice hoarse as I pound into her with a punishing I-own-you rhythm.

Don't argue with me. Don't fight with me.

Her legs stiffen as I grind into her and her body starts to quiver. Suddenly she cries out as her orgasm seizes her, taking me with her.

"Oh, Ana," I breathe as I let go, the world blurring, and I come inside her.

Fuck.

"Oh, baby, will I ever get enough of you?" I whisper as I sink onto her.

Slowly I descend to the floor, bringing her with me and wrapping my arms around her. She sits, her head against my shoulder, still panting.

Sweet Lord.

Was it ever like this?

I kiss her hair and she calms, her eyes closed, her breathing slowly returning to normal as I hold her. We're both sweaty and hot in a humid bathroom, but I don't want to be anywhere else.

She shifts. "I'm bleeding," she says.

"Doesn't bother me." I don't want to let her go.

"I noticed." Her tone is dry.

"Does it bother you?" *It shouldn't. It's natural.* I've known only one woman who was squeamish about period sex, but I wouldn't take any of that crap from her.

"No, not at all." Ana peers up at me with clear blue eyes.

"Good. Let's have a bath." I free her and her brows knit for a moment while she stares at my chest. Her rosy face loses some of its color, and clouded eyes meet mine.

"What is it?" I ask, alarmed by her expression.

"Your scars. They're not from chicken pox."

"No, they're not." My tone is arctic.

I do not want to talk about this.

Standing, I hold my hand out to her and pull her to her feet. Her eyes are wide with horror.

It'll be pity next.

"Don't look at me like that," I warn, and release her hand.

I don't want your fucking pity, Ana. Don't go there.

She studies her hand, suitably chastened, I hope.

"Did she do that?" Her voice is almost inaudible.

I scowl at her, saying nothing, as I try to contain my sudden rage. My silence compels her to look at me.

"She?" I snarl. "Mrs. Robinson?"

Ana pales at my tone.

"She's not an animal, Anastasia. Of course she didn't. I don't understand why you feel you have to demonize her."

She bows her head to avoid eye contact, walks briskly past me, and steps into the bath, sinking into the foam so I can no longer see her body. Looking up at me, her face contrite and open, she says, "I just wonder what you would be like if you hadn't met her. If she hadn't introduced you to your, um, lifestyle."

Damn it. We're back to Elena.

I stalk toward the tub, slip into the water, and sit on the underwater shelf out of her reach. She watches me, waiting for an answer. The silence between us swells until all I can hear is the blood pumping through my ears.

Fuck.

She doesn't take her eyes off mine.

Stand down, Ana!

Nope. It's not going to happen.

I shake my head. *Impossible woman.*

"I would probably have gone the way of my birth mother, had it not been for Mrs. Robinson."

She tucks a damp tendril behind her ear, staying quiet.

What can I say about Elena? I think about our relationship: Elena and me. Those heady years. The secrecy. The furtive couplings. The pain. The pleasure. The release . . . The order and calm she brought to my world. "She loved me in a way I found . . . acceptable," I muse, almost to myself.

"Acceptable?" Ana says in disbelief.

"Yes."

Ana's expression is expectant.

She wants more.

Shit.

"She distracted me from the destructive path I found myself following." My voice is low. "It's very hard to grow up in a perfect family when you're not perfect."

She inhales sharply.

Hell. I hate talking about this.

"Does she still love you?"

No! "I don't think so, not like that. I keep telling you, it was a long time ago. It's in the past. I couldn't change it even if I wanted to, which I don't. She saved me from myself. I've never discussed this with anyone.

"Except Dr. Flynn, of course. And the only reason I'm talking about this now, to you, is because I want you to trust me."

"I do trust you," she says, "but I do want to know you better, and whenever I try to talk to you, you distract me. There's so much I want to know."

"Oh, for pity's sake, Anastasia. What do you want to know? What do I have to do?"

She stares at her hands under the surface of the water. "I'm just trying to understand; you're such an enigma. Unlike anyone I've met before. I'm glad you're telling me what I want to know."

Abruptly filled with resolve, she moves through the water to sit beside me, leaning against me so my skin sticks to hers.

"Please don't be angry with me," she says.

"I am not angry with you, Anastasia. I'm just not used to this kind of talking—this probing. I only have this with Dr. Flynn and with—"

Damn.

"With her? Mrs. Robinson? You talk to her," she says, her voice breathy and quiet.

"Yes, I do."

"What about?"

I turn to face her so suddenly that water sloshes out of the bath and onto the floor. "Persistent, aren't you? Life, the universe— business. Anastasia, Mrs. R and I go way back. We can discuss anything."

"Me?" she asks.

"Yes."

"Why do you talk about me?" she asks, and now she sounds sullen.

"I've never met anyone like you, Anastasia."

"What does that mean? Anyone who didn't just automatically sign your paperwork, no questions asked?"

I shake my head. *No.* "I need advice."

"And you take advice from Mrs. Pedo?" she snaps.

"Anastasia—enough," I almost shout. "Or I'll put you across my knee. I have no sexual or romantic interest in her whatsoever. She's a dear, valued friend and a business partner. That's all. We have a past, a shared history, which was monumentally beneficial for me, though it fucked up her marriage—but that side of our relationship is over."

She squares her shoulders. "And your parents never found out?"

"No," I growl. "I've told you this."

She regards me warily, and I think she knows she's pushed me to my limit.

"Are you done?" I ask.

"For now."

Thank God for that. She wasn't lying when she told me there was much she wanted to say. But we're not talking about what I want to talk about. I need to know where I stand. If our arrangement has a chance.

Seize the day, Grey.

"Right—my turn. You haven't responded to my e-mail."

She tucks her hair behind her ear, then shakes her head. "I was going to respond. But now you're here."

"You'd rather I wasn't?" I hold my breath.

"No, I'm pleased," she says.

"Good. I'm pleased I'm here, too—in spite of your interrogation. So, while it's acceptable to grill me, you think you can claim some kind of diplomatic immunity just because I've flown all this way to see you? I'm not buying it, Miss Steele. I want to know how you feel."

Her brows knit together. "I told you. I am pleased you're here. Thank you for coming all this way." She sounds sincere.

"It's my pleasure." I lean down and kiss her, and she opens like a flower, offering and wanting more. I pull back. "No. I think I want some answers first before we do any more."

She sighs, her wary look returning. "What do you want to know?"

"Well, how you feel about our would-be arrangement, for starters."

She makes a moue with her mouth, as if her response will be unpalatable.

Oh dear.

"I don't think I can do it for an extended period of time. A whole weekend being someone I'm not." She looks down, away from me.

That's not a "no." What's more, I think she's right.

Grasping her chin, I tilt her head up so I can see her eyes.

"No, I don't think you could, either."

"Are you laughing at me?"

"Yes, but in a good way." I kiss her again. "You're not a great submissive."

Her mouth drops open. Is she feigning offense? And then she laughs, a sweet, infectious laugh, and I know she's not offended.

"Maybe I don't have a good teacher."

Good point well made, Miss Steele.

I laugh, too. "Maybe. Perhaps I should be stricter with you." I search her face. "Was it that bad when I spanked you the first time?"

"No, not really," she says, her cheeks flushing a little.

"It's more the idea of it?" I ask, pressing her further.

"I suppose. Feeling pleasure when one isn't supposed to."

"I remember feeling the same. Takes a while to get your head around it."

We are finally having the discussion. "You can always use the safe word, Anastasia. Don't forget that. And, as long as you follow the rules, which fulfill a deep need in me for control and to keep you safe, then perhaps we can find a way forward."

"Why do you need to control me?"

"Because it satisfies a need in me that wasn't met in my formative years."

"So it's a form of therapy?"

"I've not thought of it like that, but yes, I suppose it is."

She nods. "But, here's the thing—one moment you say 'don't defy me,' the next you say you like to be challenged. That's a very fine line to tread successfully."

"I can see that. But you seem to be doing fine so far."

"But at what personal cost? I'm tied up in knots here."

"I like you tied up in knots."

"That's not what I meant!" She dashes her hand through the water, soaking me.

"Did you just splash me?"

"Yes," she says.

"Oh, Miss Steele." I wrap my arm around her waist and tug her onto my lap, slopping water onto the floor once again. "I think we've done enough talking for now."

I hold her head between my hands and kiss her, my tongue teasing her lips apart, then delving into her mouth, dominating her. She runs her fingers through my hair, returning my kiss, twisting her tongue around mine. Angling her head with one hand, I shift her with the other so she's astride me.

I pull back to take a breath. Her eyes are dark and carnal, her lust plain to see. I pull her wrists behind her back and grasp them in one hand. "I'm going to have you now," I declare, and I lift her so that my erection is poised beneath her. "Ready?"

"Yes," she breathes, and slowly I lower her onto me, watching her expression as I fill her. She moans and closes her eyes, thrusting her breasts forward into my face.

Oh, sweet Jesus.

I flex my hips, lifting her, burying myself even deeper inside her, and lean forward so our foreheads are touching.

She feels so good.

"Please, let my hands go," she whispers.

I open my eyes and see her mouth open as she drags air into her lungs.

"Don't touch me," I plead, and release her hands and grasp her hips. She grabs the edge of the bath and slowly starts to take me. Up. Then down. Oh so slowly. She opens her eyes to find mine on her face. Watching her. Riding me. Leaning down, she kisses me, her tongue invading my mouth. I close my eyes, reveling in the sensation.

Oh yes, Ana.

Her fingers are in my hair, tugging and pulling as she kisses me, her wet tongue entwining with mine as she moves. I hold her hips and start lifting her higher and faster, vaguely aware that water is cascading out of the bath.

But I don't care. I want her. Like this.

This beautiful woman who moans into my mouth.

Up. Down. Up. Down. Over and over.

Giving herself to me. Taking me.

"Ah." The pleasure catches in her throat.

"That's right, baby," I whisper, as she quickens around me, then cries out as she explodes into her orgasm.

I wrap my arms around her, embracing her, holding her tightly as I lose myself and come inside her. "Ana, baby!" I cry, and I know I never want to let her go.

She kisses my ear.

"That was—" she breathes.

"Yeah." Holding her arms, I urge her back so I can study her. She looks sleepy and sated, and I imagine I must look the same. "Thank you," I whisper.

She looks confused.

"For not touching me," I clarify.

Her face softens and she raises her hand. I tense. But she shakes her head and traces my lips with her finger.

"You said it's a hard limit. I understand." And she leans forward and kisses me. The unfamiliar feeling surfaces, swelling in my chest, unnamed and dangerous.

"Let's get you to bed. Unless you have to go home?" I'm alarmed at where my emotions are going.

"No. I don't have to go."

"Good. Stay."

I stand her up and climb out of the bath to fetch us both towels, and dismiss my unsettling feelings.

I wrap her in a towel, drape one around my waist, and drop another on the floor in a vain attempt to clean up the water sloshed on the floor. Ana wanders over to the sinks as I drain the bath.

Well. That was an interesting evening.

And she was right. It was good to talk, though I'm not sure we've resolved anything.

She's brushing her teeth with my toothbrush when I walk through the bathroom to the bedroom. It makes me smile. I pick up my phone and see that the missed call was from Taylor.

I text him.

> Everything okay?
> I'll be leaving to go gliding at 6 a.m.

He responds immediately.

> That's why I was calling.
> Weather looks good.
> I'll see you there.
> Good night, sir.

I'm taking Miss Steele soaring! My delight bubbles up into a broad grin that widens when she comes out of the bathroom wrapped in the towel.

"I need my purse," she says, looking a little shy.

"I think you left it in the living room."

She scampers off to fetch it, and I brush my teeth, knowing that the toothbrush has just been in her mouth.

In the bedroom I discard the towel, pull back the sheets, and lie down, waiting for Ana. She's disappeared into the bathroom again and closed the door.

Moments later she returns. She drops her towel and lies down beside me, naked except for a shy smile. We lie in bed facing each other, hugging our pillows. "Do you want to sleep?" I ask. I know we have to get up early, and it's nearly eleven.

"No. I'm not tired," she says, her eyes shining.

"What do you want to do?" *More sex?*

"Talk."

More talking. Oh Lord. I smile, resigned. "About what?"

"Stuff."

"What stuff?"

"You."

"What about me?"

"What's your favorite film?"

I like her quick-fire questions. "Today, it's *The Piano*."

She beams back at me. "Of course. Silly me. Such a sad, excit-

ing score, which no doubt you can play. So many accomplish-
ments, Mr. Grey."

"And the greatest one is you, Miss Steele."

Her grin broadens. "So I am number seventeen."

"Seventeen?"

"Number of women you've, um . . . had sex with."

Oh, shit. "Not exactly."

Her smile vanishes. "You said fifteen."

"I was referring to the number of women in my playroom.
I thought that's what you meant. You didn't ask me how many
women I'd had sex with."

"Oh." Her eyes widen. "Vanilla?" she asks.

"No. You are my one vanilla conquest." And for some strange
reason, I feel insanely pleased with myself. "I can't give you a number. I didn't put notches in the bedpost or anything."

"What are we talking—tens, hundreds . . . thousands?"

"Tens. We're in the tens, for pity's sake." I feign outrage.

"All submissives?"

"Yes."

"Stop grinning at me," she says haughtily, trying and failing to
stifle hers.

"I can't. You're funny." And I feel a little light-headed as we
beam at each other.

"Funny peculiar or funny ha-ha?"

"A bit of both, I think."

"That's damned cheeky, coming from you," she says.

I kiss her nose to prepare her. "This will shock you, Anastasia.
Ready?"

Her eyes are wide and eager, full of delight.

Tell her.

"All submissives in training, when I was training. There are
places in and around Seattle that one can go and practice. Learn
to do what I do."

"Oh," she exclaims.

"Yep, I've paid for sex, Anastasia."

"That's nothing to be proud of," she scolds me. "And you're right, I am deeply shocked. And cross that I can't shock you."

"You wore my underwear."

"Did that shock you?"

"Yes. You didn't wear your panties to meet my parents."

Her delight is restored. "Did that shock you?"

"Yes."

"It seems I can only shock you in the underwear department."

"You told me you were a virgin. That's the biggest shock I've ever had."

"Yes, your face was a picture, a Kodak moment." She giggles, and her face lights up.

"You let me work you over with a riding crop." I'm grinning like the fucking Cheshire cat. When have I ever stretched out naked beside a woman and just talked?

"Did that shock you?"

"Yep."

"Well, I may let you do it again."

"Oh, I do hope so, Miss Steele. This weekend?"

"Okay," she says.

"Okay?"

"Yes. I'll go to the Red Room of Pain again."

"You say my name."

"That shocks you?"

"The fact that I like it shocks me."

"Christian," she whispers, and the sound of my name from her lips spreads warmth through my body.

Ana.

"I want to do something tomorrow."

"What?"

"A surprise. For you."

She yawns.

Enough. She's tired.

"Am I boring you, Miss Steele?"

"Never," she confesses. I lean across and give her a quick kiss.

"Sleep," I order, and switch off the bedside light.

And a few moments later I hear her even breathing; she's fast asleep. I pull a sheet over her, roll onto my back, and stare up at the whirring ceiling fan.

Well, talking isn't so bad.

Today worked out after all.

Thank you, Elena . . .

And with a sated smile, I close my eyes.

No. Don't leave me." The whispered words penetrate my slumber, and I stir and wake.

What was that?

I look around the room. Where the hell am I?

Oh yes, Savannah.

"No. Please. Don't leave me."

What? It's Ana. "I'm not going anywhere," I mutter, bemused. Turning, I prop myself up on my elbow. She's huddled beside me and she looks like she's asleep.

"I won't leave you," she mumbles.

My scalp prickles. "I'm very glad to hear that."

She sighs.

"Ana?" I whisper. But she doesn't react. Her eyes are closed. She's fast asleep. She must be dreaming . . . what is she dreaming about?

"Christian," she says.

"Yes," I respond automatically.

But she says nothing; she's definitely asleep, but I've never heard her talk in her sleep before.

I watch her, fascinated. Her face is illuminated by ambient light from the living area. Her brow crinkles for a moment, as if an unpleasant thought is plaguing her, then it's smooth once more. With her lips parted as she breathes, her face soft in sleep, she's beautiful.

And she doesn't want me to go, and she won't leave me. The candor of her subconscious admission sweeps through me like a summer breeze, leaving warmth and hope in its wake.

She's not going to leave me.

Well, you have your answer, Grey.

I smile down at her. She seems to have settled and stopped talking. I check the time on the radio alarm: 4:57.

It's time to get up anyway, and I'm elated. I'm going soaring. *With Ana.* I love soaring. I place a quick kiss on her temple, rise, and head into the main room of the suite, where I order breakfast and check the local weather report.

Another hot day with high humidity. No rain.

I shower quickly, dry myself, then gather Ana's clothes from the bathroom and lay them out on a chair near the bed. As I pick up her panties I remember how my devious plan to confiscate her underwear backfired.

Oh, Miss Steele.

And after our first night together . . .

"Oh, by the way, I'm wearing your underwear." And she yanks the waistband up, so I can see the words "Polo" and "Ralph" peeking over her jeans.

I shake my head, and from the armoire I take a pair of my boxer briefs and deposit them on the chair. I like it when she wears my clothes.

She mumbles again, and I think she said "cage," but I'm not sure.

What the hell is that about?

She doesn't stir, but remains blissfully asleep while I dress. As I pull on my T-shirt there's a knock on the door. Breakfast has arrived: pastries, a coffee for me, and Twinings English Breakfast tea for Ana. Fortunately the hotel stocks her favorite blend.

It's time to wake Miss Steele.

"Strawberry," she mutters, as I sit down beside her on the bed.

What's with the fruit?

"Anastasia," I summon her gently.

"I want more."

I know you do, and so do I. "Come on, baby." I continue to coax her awake.

She gripes. "No. I want to touch you."

Shit. "Wake up." I lean down and gently tug her earlobe with my teeth.

"No." She screws her eyes tight.

"Wake up, baby."

"Oh no," she protests.

"Time to get up, baby. I'm going to switch on the side light." I reach across and switch it on, bathing her in a pool of dim light. She squints.

"No," she whines. Her reluctance to wake is amusing and different. In my previous relationships a sleepy submissive could expect to be disciplined.

I nuzzle her ear and whisper, "I want to chase the dawn with you." I kiss her cheek, kiss each eyelid in turn, kiss the tip of her nose, and kiss her lips.

Her eyes flicker open.

"Good morning, beautiful."

And they close again. She grumbles, and I grin down at her. "You are not a morning person."

She opens one unfocused eye, studying me. "I thought you wanted sex," she says, her relief obvious.

I suppress my laugh. "Anastasia, I always want sex with you. It's heartwarming to know that you feel the same."

"Of course I do, just not when it's so late." She hugs her pillow.

"It's not late, it's early. Come on—up you go. We're going out. I'll take a rain check on the sex."

"I was having such a nice dream." She sighs, peering up at me.

"Dream about what?"

"You." Her face warms.

"What was I doing this time?"

"Trying to feed me strawberries," she says with a small voice.

That accounts for her babbling. "Dr. Flynn could have a field day with that. Up—get dressed. Don't bother to shower, we can do that later."

She protests but sits up, ignoring the sheet that slips down to her waist and exposes her body. My cock stirs. With her hair mussed, cascading over her shoulders and curling around her naked breasts, she looks gorgeous. Ignoring my arousal, I stand up to give her some room.

"What time is it?" she asks, her voice sleepy.

"Five thirty in the morning."

"Feels like three a.m."

"We don't have much time. I let you sleep as long as possible. Come." I want to drag her out of bed and dress her myself. I can't wait to get her airborne.

"Can't I have a shower?"

"If you have a shower, I'll want one with you, and you and I know what will happen then—the day will just go. Come."

She gives me a patient look. "What are we doing?"

"It's a surprise. I told you."

She shakes her head and beams, very much amused. "Okay." She climbs out of bed, oblivious to her nudity, and notices her clothes on the chair. I'm delighted that she's not her usual shy self; maybe it's because she's sleepy. She slides on my underwear and gives me a broad smile.

"I'll give you some room now that you're up." Leaving her to dress, I wander back into the main room, sit down at the small dining table, and help myself to some coffee.

She joins me a few minutes later.

"Eat," I order, motioning for her to take a seat. She stares at me, transfixed, her eyes glazed. "Anastasia," I say, interrupting her daydream. Her eyelashes flutter as she comes back from wherever she's been.

"I'll have some tea. Can I take a croissant for later?" she asks hopefully.

She's not going to eat.

"Don't rain on my parade, Anastasia."

"I'll eat later, when my stomach's woken up. About seven thirty, okay?"

"Okay." I can't force her.

She looks defiant and stubborn. "I want to roll my eyes at you," she says.

Oh, Ana, bring it on.

"By all means, do, and you will make my day."

She looks up at the fire sprinkler on the ceiling. "Well, a spanking would wake me up, I suppose," she says, as if she's weighing the option.

She's considering it? It doesn't work that way, Anastasia!

"On the other hand, I don't want you to be all hot and bothered; the climate here is warm enough." She gives me a saccharine smile.

"You are, as ever, challenging, Miss Steele." My voice is droll. "Drink your tea."

She sits down and takes a couple of sips.

"Drink up. We should go." I'm keen to get on the road—it's quite a drive.

"Where are we going?"

"You'll see."

Stop with the grinning, Grey.

She pouts with frustration. Miss Steele, as ever, is curious. But all she's wearing is her camisole and jeans; she'll be cold once we're airborne. "Finish your tea," I order, and leave the table. In the bedroom I rifle through the armoire and pull out a sweatshirt. This should do. I call the valet and tell him to bring the car out front.

"I'm ready," she says as I return to the main room.

"You'll need this." I toss the sweatshirt to her as she gives me a bewildered look.

"Trust me." I plant a swift kiss on her lips. Taking her hand, I open the door to the suite and we head for the elevators. There's a hotel employee standing there—Brian, according to his name tag—also waiting for the elevator.

"Good morning," he says, giving us both a cheerful salute as the doors open. I glance at Ana and smirk as we enter.

No shenanigans in elevators this morning.

She hides her smile and peers at the floor, her cheeks coloring. She knows exactly what's going through my mind. Brian wishes us a good day as we exit.

Outside, the valet is waiting with the Mustang. Ana arches a brow, impressed by the GT500. Yeah, it's a fun drive, even if it's only a Mustang. "You know, sometimes it's great being me," I tease her, and with a polite bow I open her door.

"Where are we going?"

"You'll see." I get behind the wheel and ease the car into drive. At the stoplight I quickly program the address of the airfield into the GPS. It directs us out of Savannah toward I-95. I switch on my iPod via the steering wheel, and the car is filled with a sublime melody.

"What's this?" Ana asks.

"It's from *La Traviata*. An opera by Verdi."

"*La Traviata*? I've heard of that. I can't think where. What does it mean?"

I give her a knowing look. "Well, literally, 'the woman led astray.' It's based on Alexandre Dumas's book *La Dame aux Camélias*."

"Ah. I've read it."

"I thought you might have."

"The doomed courtesan," she recounts, her voice tinged with melancholy. "Hmm, it's a depressing story," she says.

"Too depressing?" We can't have that, Miss Steele, especially when I'm in such a good mood. "Do you want to choose some music? This is on my iPod."

I tap the navigation screen and bring up the playlist.

"You choose," I offer, wondering if she'll like anything I have in iTunes. She studies the list and scrolls through it, concentrating hard. She taps on a song, and Verdi's dulcet strings are replaced by a pounding beat and Britney Spears.

" 'Toxic,' eh?" I observe, with wry humor.

Is she trying to tell me something?

Is she referring to me?

"I don't know what you mean," she says innocently.

Does she think I should wear a warning?

Miss Steele wants to play games.

So be it.

I turn the music down a tad. It's a little early for this remix, and for the reminder.

"Sir, this submissive respectfully requests Master's iPod."

I glance away from the spreadsheet I'm reading and study her as she kneels beside me, her eyes cast down.

She's been exceptional this weekend. How can I refuse?

"Sure, Leila, take it. I think it's in the dock."

"Thank you, Master," she says, and stands with her usual grace, without looking at me.

Good girl.

And wearing only red high heels, she teeters over to the iPod dock and collects her reward.

"I didn't put that song on my iPod," I tell her breezily, and floor the gas, throwing us both into the back of our seats, but I hear Ana's small, exasperated huff above the roar of the engine.

As Britney continues at her sultry best, Ana drums her fingers on her thigh, radiating disquiet as she stares out the car window. The Mustang eats up the miles on the freeway; there's no traffic, and dawn's first light is chasing us down I-95.

Ana sighs as Damien Rice begins.

Put her out of her misery, Grey.

And I don't know if it's my good mood, our talk last night, or the fact that I'm about to go soaring—but I want to tell her who put the song on the iPod. "It was Leila."

"Leila?"

"An ex, who put the song on my iPod."

"One of the fifteen?" She turns her full attention to me, hungry for information.

"Yes."

"What happened to her?"

"We finished."

"Why?"

"She wanted more."

"And you didn't?"

I glance at her and shake my head. "I've never wanted more, until I met you." She rewards me with her bashful smile.

Yes, Ana. It's not just you who wants more.

"What happened to the other fourteen?" she asks.

"You want a list? Divorced, beheaded, died?"

"You're not Henry the Eighth," she scolds me.

"Okay. In no particular order, I've only had long-term relationships with four women, apart from Elena."

"Elena?"

"Mrs. Robinson to you."

She pauses for a moment, and I know she's scrutinizing me. I keep my eyes on the road.

"What happened to the four?" she asks.

"So inquisitive, so eager for information, Miss Steele," I tease.

"Oh, Mr. When Is Your Period Due?"

"Anastasia, a man needs to know these things."

"Does he?"

"I do."

"Why?"

"Because I don't want you to get pregnant."

"Neither do I. Well, not for a few years yet," she says a little wistfully.

Of course, that would be with someone else . . . the thought is disquieting . . . She's mine.

"So the other four, what happened?" she persists.

"One met someone else. The other three wanted—more. I wasn't in the market for more then." *Why did I open this can of worms?*

"And the others?"

"Just didn't work out."

She nods and stares out the window as Aaron Neville sings "Tell It Like It Is."

"Where are we headed?" she asks again.

We're close now. "An airfield."

"We're not going back to Seattle, are we?" She sounds panicked.

"No, Anastasia." I chuckle at her reaction. "We're going to indulge in my second favorite pastime."

"Second?"

"Yep. I told you my favorite this morning." Her expression tells me she's completely perplexed. "Indulging in you, Miss Steele. That's got to be top of my list. Any way I can get you."

She looks down at her lap, her lips twitching. "Well, that's quite high up on my list of diverting, kinky priorities, too," she says.

"I'm pleased to hear it."

"So, airfield?"

I beam at her. "Soaring. We're going to chase the dawn, Anastasia." I take a left into the airfield and drive up to the Brunswick Soaring Association hangar, where I stop the car.

"You up for this?" I ask.

"You're flying?"

"Yes."

Her face glows with excitement. "Yes, please!" I love how fearless and enthusiastic she is with any new experience. Leaning over, I kiss her quickly. "Another first, Miss Steele."

Outside it's cool but not cold, and the sky is lighter now, pearl and bright at the horizon. I walk around the car and open Ana's door. With her hand in mine we make our way to the front of the hangar.

Taylor is waiting there with a young bearded man in shorts and sandals.

"Mr. Grey, this is your tow pilot, Mr. Mark Benson," says Taylor. I release Ana so I can shake hands with Benson, who has a wild glint in his eye.

"You've got a great morning for it, Mr. Grey," Benson says. "The wind is at ten knots from the northeast, which means the convergence along the shore should keep you up for a wee while."

Benson is British, with a firm handshake.

"Sounds great," I answer, and watch Ana as she shares a private joke with Taylor. "Anastasia. Come."

"See you later," she says to Taylor.

Ignoring her familiarity with my staff, I introduce her to Benson.

"Mr. Benson, this is my girlfriend, Anastasia Steele."

"Pleased to meet you," she says, and Benson gives her a bright smile as they shake hands.

"Likewise," he says. "If you'd like to follow me."

"Lead the way." I take Ana's hand as we fall into step beside Benson.

"I have a Blaník L23 set up and ready. She's old school. But she handles well."

"Great. I learned to fly in a Blaník. An L13," I tell Benson.

"Can't go wrong with a Blaník. I'm a big fan." He gives me a thumbs-up. "Though I prefer the L23 for the aerobatics."

I nod in agreement.

"You're hooked up to my Piper Pawnee," he continues. "I'll take her up to three thousand feet, then set you guys free. That should give you some flying time."

"I hope so. The cloud cover looks promising."

"It's a bit early in the day for much lift. But you never know. Dave, my mate, will spot the wing. He's in the jakes."

"Okay." I think "jakes" means restroom. "You've been flying long?"

"Since my days in the RAF. But I've been flying these tail-draggers for five years now. We're on CTAF 122.3, so you know."

"Got it."

The L23 looks to be in fine shape, and I make a note of her FAA registration: November. Papa. Three. Alpha.

"First we need to strap on your parachute." Benson reaches into the cockpit and pulls out a parachute for Ana.

"I'll do that," I offer, taking the bundle from Benson before he has a chance to put it or his hands on Ana.

"I'll fetch some ballast," Benson says with a cheery smile, and he heads toward the plane.

"You like strapping me into things," Ana says with a raised brow.

"Miss Steele, you have no idea. Here, step into the straps." I hold open the leg fastenings for her. Leaning over, she puts her hand on my shoulder. I stiffen instinctively, expecting the darkness to wake and choke me, but it doesn't. It's weird. I don't know how I'm going to react where her touch is concerned. She lets go once the loops are around her thighs, and I hoist the shoulder straps up over her arms and fasten the parachute.

Boy, she looks good in a harness.

Briefly, I wonder how she'd look spread-eagled and hanging from the karabiners in the playroom, her mouth and her sex at my disposal. But alas, she's set suspension as a hard limit. "There, you'll do," I mutter, trying to banish the image from my mind. "Do you have your hair tie from yesterday?"

"You want me to put my hair up?" she asks.

"Yes."

She does as she's told. For a change.

"In you go." I steady her with my hand and she starts to climb into the back.

"No, front. The pilot sits in the back."

"But you won't be able to see."

"I'll see plenty." I'll see her enjoying herself, I hope.

She climbs in and I bend over into the cockpit to fasten her into her seat, locking the harness and tightening the straps. "Hmm, twice in one morning. I am a lucky man," I whisper, and kiss her. She beams up at me, her anticipation palpable.

"This won't take long—twenty, thirty minutes at most. Thermals aren't great this time of the morning, but it's so breathtaking up there at this hour. I hope you're not nervous."

"Excited," she says, still grinning.

"Good." I stroke her cheek with my index finger, then put on my own parachute and climb into the pilot seat.

Benson comes back carrying ballast for Ana, and he checks her straps.

"Yep, that's secure. First time?" he asks her.

"Yes."

"You'll love it."

"Thanks, Mr. Benson," Ana says.

"Call me Mark," he replies, *fucking twinkling* at her. I narrow my eyes at him. "Okay?" he asks me.

"Yep. Let's go," I say, impatient to be airborne and to get him away from my girl. Benson nods, shuts the canopy, and ambles over to the Piper. Off to the right I notice Dave, Benson's mate, has appeared, propping up the wingtip. Quickly I test the equipment: pedals (I hear the rudder move behind me); control stick—side to side (a quick glance at the wings and I can see the ailerons moving); and control stick—front to back (I hear the elevator respond).

Right. We're ready.

Benson climbs into the Piper and almost immediately the single propeller starts up, loud and throaty in the morning quiet. A few moments later his plane is rolling forward, taking up the slack of the towrope, and we're off. I balance the ailerons and the rudder as the Piper picks up speed, then I ease back on the control stick, and we sail into the air before Benson does.

"Here we go, baby," I shout to Ana as we gain height.

"Brunswick Traffic, Delta Victor, heading two-seven-zero." It's Benson on the radio. I ignore him as we climb higher and higher. The L23 handles well, and I watch Ana; her head whips from side to side as she tries to take in the view. I wish I could see her smile.

We head west, the newborn sun behind us, and I note when we cross I-95. I love the serenity up here, away from everything and everyone, just me and the glider looking for lift . . . and to think I've never shared this experience with anyone before. The light is beautiful, lambent, all I had hoped it would be . . . for Ana and for me.

When I check the altimeter we're nearing three thousand feet and coasting at 105 knots. Benson's voice crackles over the radio, informing me that we're at three thousand feet and we can release.

"Affirmative. Release," I radio back, and pull the release knob. The Piper disappears and I roll us into a slow dip, until we're heading southwest and riding the wind. Ana laughs out loud. Encouraged by her reaction, I continue to spiral, hoping we might find some convergence lift near the coastline or thermals beneath pale pink clouds—the shallow cumulus might mean lift, even this early.

Suddenly filled with a heady combination of mischief and joy, I shout at Ana, "Hold on tight!" And I take us into a full roll. She squeals, her hands shooting up and bracing against the canopy. When I right us once more she's laughing. It is the most gratifying response a man could want, and it makes me laugh, too.

"I'm glad I didn't have breakfast!" she shouts.

"Yes, in hindsight it's good you didn't, because I'm going to do that again."

This time she holds on to the harness and stares directly down at the ground as she's suspended over it. She giggles, the noise mixing with the whistle of the wind.

"Beautiful, isn't it?" I shout.

"Yes."

I know we haven't got long, as there's not much lift out here—but I don't care. Ana is enjoying herself . . . and so am I.

"See the joystick in front of you? Grab hold."

She tries to turn her head, but she's buckled in too tight.

"Go on, Anastasia. Grab it," I urge her.

My joystick moves in my hands, and I know she's holding hers.

"Hold tight. Keep it steady. See the middle dial in front? Keep the needle dead center."

We continue to fly in a straight line, the yaw string staying perpendicular to the canopy.

"Good girl."

My Ana. Never backs down from a challenge. And for some bizarre reason I feel immensely proud of her.

"I am amazed you let me take control," she shouts.

"You'd be amazed what I'd let you do, Miss Steele. Back to me now."

In command of the joystick once more, I turn us in the direction of the airfield as we begin to lose altitude. I think I can land us there. I call over the radio to inform Benson and whoever might be listening that we're going to land, and then I execute another circle to bring us closer to the ground.

"Hang on, baby. This can get bumpy."

I dip again and bring the L23 into line with the runway as we descend toward the grass. We land with a bump, and I manage to

keep both wings up until we reach a teeth-jarring stop near the end
of the runway. I unclip the canopy, open it, release my harness,
and clamber out.

I stretch my limbs, undo my parachute, and smile down at the
rosy-cheeked Miss Steele. "How was that?" I ask, reaching down to
unbuckle her from the seat and the parachute.

"That was extraordinary. Thank you," she says, her eyes sparkling with joy.

"Was it more?" I pray she can't hear the hope in my voice.

"Much more." She beams, and I feel ten feet tall.

"Come." I hold out my hand and help her out of the cockpit.
As she jumps down I fold her into my arms, pulling her against
me. Filled with adrenaline, my body responds immediately to her
softness. In a nanosecond my hands are in her hair, and I'm tipping
her head back so I can kiss her. My hand skims down to the base
of her spine, pressing her against my growing erection, and my
mouth takes hers in a long, lingering, possessive kiss.

I want her.

Here.

Now.

On the grass.

She responds in kind, her fingers twisting in my hair, tugging,
begging for more, as she opens up for me like a morning glory.

I break away for air and rationality.

Not in a field!

Benson and Taylor are nearby.

Her eyes are luminous, pleading for more.

Don't look at me like that, Ana.

"Breakfast," I whisper, before I do something I'll regret. Turning, I clasp her hand and walk back toward the car.

"What about the glider?" she asks as she tries to keep up
with me.

"Someone will take care of that." It's what I pay Taylor to do.
"We'll eat now. Come."

She bounces along beside me, brimming with happiness; I

don't know if I've ever seen her so buoyant. Her mood is infectious and I don't remember if I've ever felt this upbeat, either. I can't help my big, fat grin as I hold open the car door for her.

With Kings of Leon belting from the sound system I ease the Mustang out of the airfield toward I-95.

As we cruise along the freeway, Ana's BlackBerry starts beeping.

"What's that?" I ask.

"Alarm for my pill," she mutters.

"Good, well done. I hate condoms."

From the sideways look I give her, I think she's rolling her eyes, but I'm not sure.

"I like that you introduced me to Mark as your girlfriend," she says, changing the subject.

"Isn't that what you are?"

"Am I? I thought you wanted a submissive."

"So did I, Anastasia, and I do. But I've told you, I want more, too."

"I'm very happy that you want more," she says.

"We aim to please, Miss Steele," I tease as I pull into the International House of Pancakes—my father's guilty pleasure.

"IHOP?" she says in disbelief.

The Mustang rumbles to a stop. "I hope you're hungry."

"I would never have pictured you here."

"My dad used to bring us to one of these whenever my mom went away to a medical conference." We shuffle into a booth, facing each other. "It was our secret." I pick up a menu, watching Ana as she tucks her hair behind her ears and examines what IHOP has to offer for breakfast. She licks her lips in anticipation. And I'm forced to suppress my physical reaction. "I know what I want," I whisper, and wonder how she would feel visiting the restroom with me. Her eyes meet mine, and her pupils expand.

"I want what you want," she murmurs. As ever, Miss Steele does not back away from a challenge.

"Here?" *Are you sure, Ana?* Her eyes dart around the quiet restaurant, then come to rest on me, darkening and full of carnal promise. "Don't bite your lip," I warn. Much as I'd like to, I'm not going to fuck her in the restroom at IHOP. She deserves better than that, and frankly, so do I. "Not here, not now. If I can't have you here, don't tempt me."

We're interrupted.

"Hi, my name's Leandra. What can I get for you . . . er . . . folks . . . er . . . today, this mornin'?"

Oh, God. I ignore the redheaded server.

"Anastasia?" I prompt her.

"I told you, I want what you want."

Hell. She might as well be addressing my groin.

"Shall I give you folks another minute to decide?" the waitress asks.

"No. We know what we want." I cannot tear my gaze from Ana's. "We'll have two portions of the original buttermilk pancakes with maple syrup and bacon on the side, two glasses of orange juice, one black coffee with skim milk, and one English Breakfast tea, if you have it."

Ana smiles.

"Thank you, sir. Will that be all?" the waitress exclaims, all breathy and embarrassed. Tearing my attention away from Ana, I dismiss the waitress with a look and she scurries away.

"You know, it's really not fair," Ana says, her voice quiet as her finger traces a figure eight on the table.

"What's not fair?"

"How you disarm people. Women. Me."

"Do I disarm you?" I'm stunned.

"All the time."

"It's just looks, Anastasia."

"No, Christian, it's much more than that."

She has this the wrong way around, and once again I tell her how disarming I find her.

Her brow furrows. "Is that why you've changed your mind?"

"Changed my mind?"

"Yes—about . . . er . . . us?"

Have I changed my mind? I think I've just relaxed my boundaries a little, that's all. "I don't think I've changed my mind per se. We just need to redefine our parameters, redraw our battle lines, if you will. We can make this work, I'm sure. I want you submissive in my playroom. I will punish you if you digress from the rules. Other than that . . . well, I think it's all up for discussion. Those are my requirements, Miss Steele. What say you to that?"

"So I get to sleep with you? In your bed?"

"Is that what you want?"

"Yes."

"I agree, then. Besides, I sleep very well when you're in my bed. I had no idea."

"I was frightened you'd leave me if I didn't agree to all of it," she says, her face a little pale.

"I'm not going anywhere, Anastasia. Besides—" *How can she think that?* I need to reassure her. "We're following your advice, your definition: compromise. You e-mailed it to me. And so far, it's working for me."

"I love that you want more."

"I know." My tone is warm.

"How do you know?"

"Trust me. I just do." *You told me in your sleep.*

The waitress returns with our breakfast and I watch Ana devour it. "More" seems to be working for her.

"This is delicious," she says.

"I like that you're hungry."

"Must have been all the exercise last night and the thrill this morning."

"It was a thrill, wasn't it?"

"It was mighty fine, Mr. Grey," she says as she pops the final piece of pancake into her mouth. "Can I treat you?" she adds.

"Treat me how?"

"Pay for this meal."

I snort. "I don't think so."

"Please. I want to."

"Are you trying to completely emasculate me?" I raise an eyebrow in warning.

"This is probably the only place that I'll be able to afford to pay."

"Anastasia, I appreciate the thought. I do. But no."

She purses her lips with irritation when I ask the redhead for the check. "Don't scowl," I warn, and check the time: it's 8:30. I have a meeting at 11:15 with the Savannah Brownfield Redevelopment Authority, so unfortunately we have to get back to the city. I contemplate canceling the meeting, because I'd like to spend the day with Ana, but no, that's too much. I'm running after this girl when I should be concentrating on my business.

Priorities, Grey.

With her hand in mine, we head to the car looking like any other couple. She's swamped in my sweatshirt, looking casual, relaxed, beautiful—and yes, she's with me. Three guys strolling into IHOP check her out; she's oblivious even when I put my arm around her to stake my claim. She really has no idea how lovely she is. I open her car door and she gives me a sunny smile.

I could get used to this.

I program her mother's address into the GPS and we set off north on I-95, listening to the Foo Fighters. Ana's feet tap to the beat. This is the sort of music she likes—all-American rock. The traffic on the freeway is heavier now, with commuters heading into the city. But I don't care: I like being here with her, spending time. Holding her hand, touching her knee, watching her smile. She tells me about previous visits to Savannah; she's not keen on the heat, either, but her eyes light up when she talks about her mother. It'll be interesting to see her interacting with her mother and stepfather this evening.

I pull up outside her mother's home with some regret. I wish we could play hooky all day; the last twelve hours have been . . . nice.

More than nice, Grey. Sublime.

"Do you want to come in?" she asks.

"I need to work, Anastasia, but I'll be back this evening. What time?"

She suggests seven, then looks from her hands to me, her eyes bright and joyful. "Thank you . . . for the more."

"My pleasure, Anastasia." I lean over and kiss her, inhaling her sweet, sweet scent.

"I'll see you later."

"Try to stop me," I whisper.

She climbs out of the car, still in my sweatshirt, and waves good-bye. I head back to the hotel, feeling a little emptier now that she's not with me.

IN MY ROOM, I call Taylor.

"Mr. Grey."

"Yeah . . . thanks for organizing this morning."

"You're most welcome, sir." He sounds surprised.

"I'll be ready to leave at ten forty-five for the meeting."

"I'll have the Suburban waiting outside."

"Thanks."

I change out of my jeans and into my suit but leave my favorite tie beside my laptop as I order up coffee from room service.

I work through my e-mails, drink coffee, and consider calling Ros; however, it's too early for her. I read through all the paperwork that Bill has sent: Savannah does make a good case for siting the plant here. I check my inbox, and there's a new message from Ana.

From: Anastasia Steele
Subject: Soaring as Opposed to Sore-ing
Date: June 2 2011 10:20 EST
To: Christian Grey

Sometimes, you really know how to show a girl a good time.

Thank you

Ana x

The title makes me laugh and the kiss makes me feel ten feet tall. I type up my response.

From: Christian Grey
Subject: Soaring vs Sore-ing
Date: June 2 2011 10:24 EST
To: Anastasia Steele

I'll take either of those over your snoring. I had a good time, too.

But I always do when I'm with you.

Christian Grey
CEO, Grey Enterprises Holdings, Inc.

Her answer is almost immediate.

From: Anastasia Steele
Subject: SNORING
Date: June 2 2011 10:26 EST
To: Christian Grey

I DO NOT SNORE. And if I do, it's very ungallant of you to point it out.

You are no gentleman, Mr. Grey! And you are in the Deep South, too!

Ana

I chuckle.

From: Christian Grey
Subject: Somniloquy
Date: June 2 2011 10:28 EST
To: Anastasia Steele

I have never claimed to be a gentleman, Anastasia, and I think I have demonstrated that point to you on numerous occasions. I am not intimidated by your SHOUTY capitals. But I will confess to a small white lie: no—you don't snore, but you do talk. And it's fascinating.

What happened to my kiss?

Christian Grey
Cad & CEO, Grey Enterprises Holdings, Inc.

This will drive her crazy.

From: Anastasia Steele
Subject: Spill the Beans
Date: June 2 2011 10:32 EST
To: Christian Grey

You are a cad and a scoundrel—definitely no gentleman.

So, what did I say? No kisses for you until you talk!

Oh, this could run and run . . .

From: Christian Grey
Subject: Sleeping Talking Beauty
Date: June 2 2011 10:35 EST
To: Anastasia Steele

It would be most ungallant of me to say, and I have already
been chastised for that.

But if you behave yourself, I may tell you this evening. I do
have to go into a meeting now.

Laters, baby.

Christian Grey
CEO, Cad & Scoundrel, Grey Enterprises Holdings, Inc.

With a broad grin I slip on my tie, grab my jacket, and head
downstairs to find Taylor.

JUST OVER AN HOUR later, I'm winding up my meeting with the
Savannah Brownfield Redevelopment Authority. Georgia has a
great deal to offer, and the team has promised GEH some serious
tax incentives. There's a knock at the door and Taylor enters the
small conference room. His face looks grim, but what's more worrying is that he never, ever interrupts my meetings. My scalp prickles.

Ana? Is she okay?

"Excuse me, ladies and gentlemen," he says to all of us.

"Yes, Taylor," I ask, and he approaches and speaks discreetly in
my ear.

"We have a situation at home concerning Miss Leila Williams."

Leila? What the hell? And part of me is relieved that it's not
Ana.

"Would you excuse me, please?" I ask the two men and two
women from the SBRA.

In the hallway, Taylor's tone is grave as he apologizes once more for interrupting my meeting.

"Don't worry. Tell me what's happened."

"Miss Williams is in an ambulance on the way to the ER at Seattle Free Hope."

"Ambulance?"

"Yes, sir. She broke into the apartment and made a suicide attempt in front of Mrs. Jones."

Fuck. "Suicide?" *Leila? In my apartment?*

"She slashed her wrist. Gail went with her in the ambulance. She's informed me that the EMTs arrived in time and Miss Williams is not in any immediate danger."

"Why Escala? Why in front of Gail?" I'm shocked.

Taylor shakes his head. "I don't know, sir. Neither does Gail. She can't get any sense out of Miss Williams. Apparently, she only wants to talk to you."

"Fuck."

"Exactly, sir," Taylor says without judgment. I scrape my hands through my hair, trying to grasp the magnitude of what Leila has done. What the hell am I supposed to do? Why did she come to me? Was she expecting to see me? Where's her husband? What's happened to him?

"How's Gail?"

"A little shaken."

"I'm not surprised."

"I thought you should know, sir."

"Yes. Sure. Thanks," I mumble, distracted. I can't believe it; Leila seemed happy when she last e-mailed, what, six or seven months ago. But there are no answers for me here in Georgia—I have to go back and talk to her. Find out why. "Tell Stephan to ready the jet. I need to go home."

"Will do."

"Let's leave as soon as we can."

"I'll be in the car."

"Thank you."

Taylor heads toward the exit, raising the phone to his ear.

I'm reeling.

Leila. What the hell?

She's been out of my life for a couple of years. We've shared the occasional e-mail. She got married. She seemed happy. What's happened?

I head back into the boardroom and make my apologies before stepping outside into the stifling heat, where Taylor is waiting in the Suburban.

"The plane will be ready in forty-five minutes. We can head back to the hotel, pack, and go," he informs me.

"Good," I respond, grateful for the car's air-conditioning. "I should call Gail."

"I've tried, but her phone goes to voice mail. I think she's still at the hospital."

"Okay, I'll call her later." This is not what Gail needs on a Thursday morning. "How did Leila get into the apartment?"

"I don't know, sir." Taylor makes eye contact with me in the rearview mirror, his face apologetic and grim at once. "I'll make it a priority to find out."

OUR BAGS ARE PACKED and we're on our way to Savannah/Hilton Head International when I call Ana, but frustratingly, she doesn't answer. I brood, staring out the window as we cruise toward the airport. I don't have to wait long for her to return my call.

"Anastasia."

"Hi," she says, her voice breathy, and it's such a pleasure to hear her.

"I have to return to Seattle. Something's come up. I am on my way to the airport now. Please apologize to your mother—I can't make dinner."

"Nothing serious, I hope?"

"I have a situation that I have to deal with. I'll see you tomorrow. I'll send Taylor to meet you at Sea-Tac if I can't come myself."

"Okay." She sighs. "I hope you sort out your situation. Have a safe flight."

I wish I didn't have to go.

"You, too, baby," I whisper, and hang up before I change my mind and stay.

I CALL ROS AS we taxi toward the runway.

"Christian, how's Savannah?"

"I'm on the plane coming home. I have a problem I have to deal with."

"Something at GEH?" Ros asks, alarmed.

"No. It's personal."

"Anything I can do?"

"No. I'll see you tomorrow."

"How did your meeting go?"

"Positive. But I had to cut it short. Let's see what they put in writing. I might prefer Detroit just because it's cooler."

"The heat's that bad?"

"Suffocating. I've got to go. I'll call for an update later."

"Safe travels, Christian."

ON THE FLIGHT I throw myself into work to distract me from the problem waiting at home. By the time we've touched down I've read three reports and written fifteen e-mails. Our car is waiting, and Taylor drives through the pouring rain straight to Seattle Free Hope. I have to see Leila and find out what the hell is going on. As we near the hospital my anger surfaces.

Why would she do this to me?

The rain is lashing down as I climb out of the car; the day is as bleak as my mood. I take a deep breath to control my fury and head through the front doors. At the reception desk I ask for Leila Reed.

"Are you family?" The nurse on duty glowers at me, her mouth pinched and sour.

"No." I sigh. This is going to be difficult.

"Well, I'm sorry, I can't help you."

"She tried to open a vein in my apartment. I think I'm entitled to know where the hell she is," I hiss through my teeth.

"Don't take that tone with me!" she snaps. I glare at her. I'm not going to get anywhere with this woman.

"Where is your ER department?"

"Sir, there's nothing we can do if you're not family."

"Don't worry, I'll find it myself," I growl, and storm over to the double doors. I know I could call my mother, who would expedite this for me, but then I'd have to explain what's happened.

The ER is bustling with doctors and nurses, and triage is full of patients. I accost a young nurse and give her my brightest smile. "Hello, I'm looking for Leila Reed—she was admitted earlier today. Can you tell me where she might be?"

"And you are?" she asks, a flush creeping over her face.

"I'm her brother," I lie smoothly, ignoring her reaction.

"This way, Mr. Reed." She bustles over to the nurses' station and checks her computer. "She's on the second floor; Behavioral Health ward. Take the elevators at the end of the corridor."

"Thanks." I reward her with a wink and she pushes a stray lock behind her ear, giving me a flirtatious smile that reminds me of a certain girl I left in Georgia.

As I step out of the elevator on the second floor I know something is wrong. On the other side of what look like locked doors, two security guards and a nurse are combing the corridor, checking each room. My scalp prickles, but I walk over to the reception area, pretending not to notice the commotion.

"Can I help you?" asks a young man with a ring through his nose.

"I'm looking for Leila Reed. I'm her brother."

He pales. "Oh. Mr. Reed. Can you come with me?"

I follow him to a waiting room and sit down on the plastic chair that he points to; I note it's bolted to the floor. "The doctor will be with you shortly."

"Why can't I see her?" I ask.

"The doctor will explain," he says, his expression guarded, and he exits before I can ask any further questions.

Shit. Perhaps I'm too late.

The thought nauseates me. I get up and pace the small room, contemplating a call to Gail, but I don't have to wait long. A young man with short dreads and dark, intelligent eyes enters. Is he her doctor?

"Mr. Reed?" he asks.

"Where's Leila?"

He assesses me for a moment, then sighs and steels himself. "I'm afraid I don't know," he says. "She's managed to give us the slip."

"What?"

"She's gone. How she got out I don't know."

"Got out?" I exclaim in disbelief, and sink onto one of the chairs. He sits down opposite me.

"Yes. She's disappeared. We're doing a search for her now."

"She's still here?"

"We don't know."

"And who are you?" I ask.

"I'm Dr. Azikiwe, the on-call psychiatrist."

He looks too young to be a psychiatrist. "What can you tell me about Leila?" I ask.

"Well, she was admitted after a failed suicide attempt. She tried to slash one of her wrists at an ex-boyfriend's house. His housekeeper brought her here."

I feel the blood draining from my face. "And?" I ask. I need more information.

"That's about as much as we know. She said it was an error of judgment, that she was fine, but we wanted to keep her here under observation and ask her further questions."

"Did you talk to her?"

"I did."

"Why did she do this?"

"She said it was a cry for help. Nothing more. And, having made such a spectacle of herself, she was embarrassed and wanted to go home. She said she didn't want to kill herself. I believed her. I suspect it was just suicidal ideation on her part."

"How could you let her escape?" I run my hand through my hair, trying to contain my frustration.

"I don't know how she's gotten away. There'll be an internal investigation. If she contacts you, I suggest you urge her to come back. She needs help. Can I ask you some questions?"

"Sure," I agree, distracted.

"Is there any history of mental illness in your family?" I frown, then remember that he's talking about Leila's family.

"I don't know. My family is very private about such matters."

He looks concerned. "Do you know anything about this ex-boyfriend?"

"No," I state, a little too quickly. "Have you contacted her husband?"

The doctor's eyes widen. "She's married?"

"Yes."

"That's not what she told us."

"Oh. Well, I'll call him. I won't waste any more of your time."

"But I have more questions for you—"

"I'd rather spend my time looking for her. She's obviously in a bad way." I rise.

"But, this husband—"

"I'll get in touch with him." This is getting me nowhere.

"But we should do that—" Dr. Azikiwe stands.

"I can't help you. I need to find her." I head to the door.

"Mr. Reed—"

"Good-bye," I mutter, hurrying out of the waiting room and not bothering with the elevator. I take the fire escape stairs two at a time. I loathe hospitals. A memory from my childhood surfaces: I'm small and scared and mute, and the smell of disinfectant and blood clouds my nostrils.

I shudder.

As I step out of the hospital I stand for a moment and let the torrential rain wash that memory away. It's been a stressful afternoon, but at least the rain is a refreshing relief from the heat in Savannah. Taylor swings around to pick me up in the SUV.

"Home," I direct him, as I get back in the car. Once I've buckled my seatbelt I call Welch from my cell.

"Mr. Grey," he growls.

"Welch, I have a problem. I need you to locate Leila Reed, née Williams."

GAIL IS PALE AND quiet as she studies me with concern. "You're not going to finish, sir?" she asks.

I shake my head.

"Was the food okay?"

"Yes, of course." I give her a small smile. "After today's events, I'm not hungry. How are you bearing up?"

"I'm good, Mr. Grey. It was a total shock. I just want to keep busy."

"I hear you. Thanks for making dinner. If you remember anything, let me know."

"Of course. But like I said, she only wanted to speak to you."

Why? What is she expecting me to do?

"Thanks for not involving the police."

"The police are not what that girl needs. She needs help."

"She does. I wish I knew where she was."

"You'll find her," she says with quiet confidence, surprising me.

"Do you need anything?" I ask.

"No, Mr. Grey. I'm fine." She takes the plate with my half-eaten meal to the sink.

The news from Welch about Leila is frustrating. The trail has gone cold. She's not at the hospital, and they're still mystified as to how she escaped. A small part of me admires that; she was always resourceful. But what could have made her so unhappy? I rest my head in my hands. What a day—from the sublime to the ridiculous. Soaring with Ana, and now this mess to deal with. Taylor is at a loss as to how Leila got into the apartment, and Gail has no idea, either. Apparently, Leila marched into the kitchen demanding to know where I was. And when Gail said I wasn't there, she cried out "He's gone," then slashed her wrist with a box cutter. Fortunately, the cut wasn't deep.

I glance at Gail cleaning up in the kitchen. My blood runs cold. Leila could have hurt her. Perhaps Leila's objective was to hurt me. *But why?* I scrunch my eyes, trying to remember if anything in our last correspondence might give me a clue as to why she's gone off the rails. I draw a blank, exasperated, and with a sigh I head into my study.

As I sit down my phone buzzes with a text.

Ana?

It's Elliot.

> Hey Hotshot. Wanna shoot some pool?

Shooting pool with Elliot means him coming here and drinking all my beer. Frankly, I'm not in the mood.

> Working. Next week?

> Sure. Before I hit the beach.
> I'll thrash you.
> Laters.

I toss my phone onto the desk and pore over Leila's file, looking for anything that might give me a clue as to where she is. I find her parents' address and phone number, but nothing for her husband. Where is he? Why isn't she with him?

I don't want to call her parents and alarm them. I call Welch and give him their number; he can find out if she's been in touch with them.

When I switch on my iMac there's an e-mail from Ana.

From: Anastasia Steele
Subject: Safe Arrival?
Date: June 2 2011 22:32 EST
To: Christian Grey

Dear Sir,
Please let me know that you have arrived safely. I am starting
to worry. Thinking of you.

Your Ana x

Before I know it, my finger is on the little kiss she's sent me.
Ana.
Sappy, Grey. Sappy. Get a grip.

From: Christian Grey
Subject: Sorry
Date: June 2 2011 19:36
To: Anastasia Steele

Dear Miss Steele,
I have arrived safely, and please accept my apologies for not
letting you know. I don't want to cause you any worry. It's
heartwarming to know that you care for me. I am thinking of
you, too, and as ever looking forward to seeing you tomorrow.

Christian Grey
CEO, Grey Enterprises Holdings, Inc.

I press send and wish that she was here with me. She brightens up my home, my life . . . me. I shake my head at my fanciful
thoughts and look through the rest of my e-mails.

A ping tells me there's a new one from Ana.

From: Anastasia Steele
Subject: The Situation
Date: June 2 2011 22:40 EST
To: Christian Grey

Dear Mr. Grey,
I think it is very evident that I care for you deeply. How could you doubt that?

I hope your "situation" is under control.

Your Ana x

P.S.: Are you going to tell me what I said in my sleep?

She cares for me deeply? That's nice. All at once that foreign feeling, absent all day, stirs and expands in my chest. Beneath it is a well of pain I don't want to acknowledge or deal with. It tugs at a lost memory of a young woman brushing out her long, dark hair . . .

Fuck.

Don't go there, Grey.

I respond to Ana's e-mail—and as a distraction decide to tease her.

From: Christian Grey
Subject: Pleading the Fifth
Date: June 2 2011 19:45
To: Anastasia Steele

Dear Miss Steele,
I like very much that you care for me. The "situation" here is not yet resolved.

With regard to your P.S., the answer is no.

Christian Grey
CEO, Grey Enterprises Holdings, Inc.

From: Anastasia Steele
Subject: Pleading Insanity
Date: June 2 2011 22:48 EST
To: Christian Grey

I hope it was amusing. But you should know I cannot accept
any responsibility for what comes out of my mouth when I
am unconscious. In fact—you probably misheard me.

A man of your advanced years is surely a little deaf.

For the first time since I got back to Seattle, I laugh. What a
welcome distraction she is.

From: Christian Grey
Subject: Pleading Guilty
Date: June 2 2011 19:52
To: Anastasia Steele

Dear Miss Steele,
Sorry, could you speak up? I can't hear you.

Christian Grey
CEO, Grey Enterprises Holdings, Inc.

Her response is swift.

From: Anastasia Steele
Subject: Pleading Insanity Again
Date: June 2 2011 22:54 EST
To: Christian Grey

You are driving me crazy.

From: Christian Grey
Subject: I Hope So . . .
Date: June 2 2011 19:59
To: Anastasia Steele

Dear Miss Steele,
I intend to do exactly that on Friday evening. Looking forward
to it.

;)

Christian Grey
CEO, Grey Enterprises Holdings, Inc.

I'll have to think of something extra-special for my little freak.

From: Anastasia Steele
Subject: Grrrrrr
Date: June 2 2011 23:02 EST
To: Christian Grey

I am officially pissed at you.

Good night.

Miss A. R. Steele

Whoa. Would I tolerate this from anyone else?

From: Christian Grey
Subject: Wild Cat
Date: June 2 2011 20:05
To: Anastasia Steele

Are you growling at me, Miss Steele?

I possess a cat of my own for growlers.

Christian Grey
CEO, Grey Enterprises Holdings, Inc.

She doesn't respond. Five minutes go by and nothing. Six . . . Seven.

Damn. She means it. How can I tell her that while she slept she said she wouldn't leave me? She'll think I'm crazy.

From: Christian Grey
Subject: What You Said in Your Sleep
Date: June 2 2011 20:20
To: Anastasia Steele

Anastasia,
I'd rather hear you say the words that you uttered in your
sleep when you're conscious, that's why I won't tell you. Go

to sleep. You'll need to be rested, with what I have in mind
for you tomorrow.

Christian Grey
CEO, Grey Enterprises Holdings, Inc.

She doesn't respond; I hope for once she's doing what she's told
and she's asleep. Briefly I think of what we could do tomorrow, but
it's too arousing, so I push the thought aside and concentrate on
my e-mails.

But I have to confess I feel a little lighter after some e-mail banter with Miss Steele. She's good for my dark, dark soul.

FRIDAY, JUNE 3, 2011

I can't sleep. It's after two and I've been staring at the ceiling for an hour. Tonight it's not my sleeping nightmares that are keeping me awake. It's a waking one.

Leila Williams.

The smoke detector on my ceiling is winking at me, its flashing green light mocking me.

Hell!

I close my eyes and let my thoughts run free.

Why was Leila suicidal? What possessed her? Her desperate unhappiness resonates with a younger, miserable me. I'm trying to quash my memories, but the anger and desolation of my solitary teen years resurfaces and it won't go away. It reminds me of my pain and of how I lashed out at everyone during my youth. Suicide crossed my mind often, but I always held back. I resisted for Grace. I knew she'd be devastated. I knew she would blame herself if I took my life, and she'd done so much for me—how could I hurt her like that? And after I met Elena . . . everything changed.

Rising from the bed, I push these disquieting thoughts to the back of my mind. I need the piano.

I need Ana.

If she'd signed the contract and everything had gone according to plan, she would be with me, upstairs, asleep. I could wake her, and lose myself in her . . . or, under our new arrangement, she would be beside me, and I could fuck her and then watch her sleep.

What would she make of Leila?

As I sit down on the piano bench I know that Ana will never

meet Leila, which is a good thing. I know how she feels about Elena. Lord knows how she'd feel about an ex . . . a wayward ex.

This is what I can't reconcile: Leila was happy, mischievous, and bright when I knew her. She was an excellent submissive; I thought she'd settled down and was happily married. Her e-mails never indicated that anything was awry. What went wrong?

I start to play . . . and my troubled thoughts recede until it's just the music and me.

Leila is servicing my cock with her mouth.
Her skilled mouth.
Her hands are tied behind her back.
Her hair braided.
She's on her knees.
Eyes cast down. Modest. Alluring.
Not seeing me.
And suddenly she's Ana.
Ana on her knees before me. Naked. Beautiful.
My cock in her mouth.
But Ana's eyes are on mine.
Her blazing blue eyes see everything.
See me. My soul.
She sees the darkness and the monster beneath.
Her eyes widen in horror and suddenly she disappears.

Shit! I wake with a start, and a painful erection that wanes as soon as I recall Ana's wounded look in my dream.

What the hell?

I rarely have erotic dreams. *Why now?* I check my alarm; I've beaten it by a few minutes. The morning sunlight is creeping between the buildings as I rise. Already I'm restless, no doubt as a result of my disturbing dream, so I decide to go for a run to burn off some energy. There are no new e-mails, no messages, no updates on Leila. The apartment is quiet as I leave. There's no sign of Gail yet. I hope she's recovered from yesterday's ordeal.

I open the glass doors in the lobby, step outside into a balmy, sunny morning, and carefully scan the street. As I start my run I check down the alleys and in the doorways I pass, and behind the parked cars, to see if Leila is there.

Where are you, Leila Williams?

I turn the volume up on the Foo Fighters and my feet pound the sidewalk.

OLIVIA IS EXCEPTIONALLY IRRITATING today. She's spilled my coffee, dropped an important call, and keeps mooning at me with her big brown eyes.

"Get Ros back on the line," I bark at her. "Better still, get her up here." I shut my office door and go back to my desk; I must try not to take my temper out on my staff.

Welch has no news, except that Leila's parents think their daughter is still in Portland with her husband. There's a knock on my door.

"Come in." I hope to God it's not Olivia. Ros pokes her head around.

"You wanted to see me?"

"Yes. Sure. Come in. Where are we with Woods?"

ROS EXITS JUST BEFORE ten. All is on track: Woods has decided to accept the deal, and the aid for Darfur will soon be on the road to Munich in preparation for the airlift. There's no news yet from Savannah about their offer.

I check my inbox and find a welcome e-mail from Ana.

From: Anastasia Steele
Subject: Homeward Bound
Date: June 3 2011 12:53 EST
To: Christian Grey

Dear Mr. Grey,
I am once again ensconced in first class, for which I thank

you. I am counting the minutes until I see you this evening
and perhaps torturing the truth out of you about my
nocturnal admissions.

Your Ana x

Torturing me? *Oh, Miss Steele, I think it will be the other way
around.* As I have a great deal to do, I keep my reply short.

From: Christian Grey
Subject: Homeward Bound
Date: June 3 2011 09:58
To: Anastasia Steele

Anastasia, I look forward to seeing you.

Christian Grey
CEO, Grey Enterprises Holdings, Inc.

But Ana is not satisfied.

From: Anastasia Steele
Subject: Homeward Bound
Date: June 3 2011 13:01 EST
To: Christian Grey

Dearest Mr. Grey,
I hope everything is okay re "the situation." The tone of your
e-mail is worrying.

Ana x

At least I still earned a kiss. Surely she should be airborne by now?

From: Christian Grey
Subject: Homeward Bound
Date: June 3 2011 10:04
To: Anastasia Steele

Anastasia,
The situation could be better. Have you taken off yet? If so, you should not be e-mailing. You are putting yourself at risk, in direct contravention of the rule regarding your personal safety. I meant what I said about punishments.

Christian Grey
CEO, Grey Enterprises Holdings, Inc.

I'm about to call Welch for an update, but there's a ping—Ana again.

From: Anastasia Steele
Subject: Overreaction
Date: June 3 2011 13:06 EST
To: Christian Grey

Dear Mr. Grumpy,
The aircraft doors are still open. We are delayed but only by ten minutes. My welfare and that of the passengers around me is vouchsafed. You may stow your twitchy palm for now.

Miss Steele

A reluctant smile tugs at my lips. *Mr. Grumpy, eh?* And no kiss. *Oh dear.*

From: Christian Grey
Subject: Apologies—Twitchy Palm Stowed
Date: June 3 2011 10:08
To: Anastasia Steele

I miss you and your smart mouth, Miss Steele.

I want you safely home.

Christian Grey
CEO, Grey Enterprises Holdings, Inc.

From: Anastasia Steele
Subject: Apology Accepted
Date: June 3 2011 13:10 EST
To: Christian Grey

They are shutting the doors. You won't hear another peep from me, especially given your deafness.

Laters.

Ana x

My kiss is back. *Well, that's a relief.* Grudgingly, I drag myself away from the computer screen and pick up my phone to call Welch.

AT ONE O'CLOCK I decline Andrea's offer of lunch at my desk. I need to get out. The walls of my office are closing in on me, and I think it's because there's been no news about Leila.

I'm worried about her. *Hell, she came to see me.* She decided to use my home as her stage. How could I not take this personally? Why didn't she e-mail me or phone? If she was in trouble, I could have helped. I would have helped—I've done it before.

I need some fresh air. I march past Olivia and Andrea, who both look busy, though I catch Andrea's puzzled look as I step into the elevator.

Outside, it's a bright, bustling afternoon. I take a deep breath and detect the soothing tang of salt water from the Sound. Perhaps I should take the rest of the day off? But I can't. I have a meeting with the mayor this afternoon. It's irritating—I'm seeing him tomorrow at the Chamber of Commerce gala.

The gala!

Suddenly I have an idea, and with a renewed sense of purpose I head toward a small store I know.

AFTER MY MEETING AT the mayor's office, I walk the ten or so blocks back to Escala; Taylor has gone to collect Ana from the airport. Gail is in the kitchen when I enter the living room.

"Good evening, Mr. Grey."

"Hi, Gail. How was your day?"

"Good, thank you, sir."

"Feeling better?"

"Yes, sir. The clothes arrived for Miss Steele—I unpacked them and hung them in the closet in her room."

"Great. No sign of Leila?" Dumb question: Gail would have called me.

"No, sir. This also arrived." She holds up a small red store bag.

"Good." I take the bag from her, ignoring the delighted twinkle in her eye.

"How many for supper this evening?"

"Two, thanks. And Gail—"

"Sir?"

"Can you put the satin sheets on the playroom bed?"

I really hope to get Ana in there at some point over the weekend. "Yes, Mr. Grey," she says, her tone a little surprised. She turns back to whatever she's conjuring in the kitchen, leaving me a little baffled by her behavior.

Maybe Gail doesn't approve, but it's what I want from Ana.

In my study I take the Cartier box from its bag. It's a present for Ana, which I'll give to her tomorrow in time for the gala: a pair of earrings. Simple. Elegant. Beautiful. Just like her. I smile; even in her chucks and jeans she has a certain gamine charm.

I hope she accepts my gift. As my submissive, she'd have no choice, but under our alternative arrangement, I don't know what her reaction will be. Whatever the outcome, it will be interesting. She always surprises me. As I put the box in my desk drawer a ping on my computer distracts me. Barney's latest tablet designs are in my inbox, and I'm eager to see them.

Five minutes later, Welch calls.

"Mr. Grey," he wheezes.

"Yes. What news?"

"I spoke with Russell Reed, Mrs. Reed's husband."

"And?" Immediately I'm agitated. I storm out of my study and across the living room to the windows.

"He says his wife is away visiting her parents," Welch reports.

"What?"

"Precisely." Welch sounds as pissed as I am.

Seeing Seattle at my feet, knowing Mrs. Reed aka Leila Williams is out there somewhere, increases my irritation. I rake my fingers through my hair.

"Maybe that's what she told him."

"Maybe," he says. "But we've found nothing so far."

"No trace?" I can't believe she could just disappear.

"Nothing. But if she so much as uses an ATM, cashes a check, or logs in to her social media, we'll find her."

"Okay."

"We'd like to scour the CCTV footage from around the hospital. It's going to cost money and take a little longer. Is that acceptable?"

"Yes." A tingle prickles my scalp—not from the call. For some unknown reason I sense I'm being watched. Turning, I see Ana standing on the threshold of the room, scrutinizing me, her brow furrowed and her lips pensive, and she's wearing a short, short skirt. She's all eyes and legs . . . especially legs. I imagine them wrapped around my waist.

Desire, raw and real, fires my blood as I stare.

"We'll get right on it," Welch says.

I finish up with him, my eyes fixed on Ana's, and I prowl toward her, stripping off my jacket and tie and tossing them onto the sofa. *Ana.*

I wrap my arms around her, tugging at her ponytail, lifting her eager lips to mine. She tastes of heaven and home and fall and Ana. Her scent invades my nostrils as I take everything her warm, sweet mouth has to offer. My body hardens with expectation and hunger as our tongues entwine. I want to lose myself in her, to forget about the shitty end to my week, forget about everything but her.

My lips feverish against hers, I tug the hair tie from her ponytail as her fingers knot in mine. I'm suddenly overwhelmed by my need, desperate for her. And I pull away, staring down into a face that's dazed with passion.

I feel the same way. *What is she doing to me?*

"What's wrong?" she whispers.

And the answer is clear, ringing in my head.

I've missed you.

"I'm so glad you're back. Shower with me. Now."

"Yes," she responds, her voice hoarse. I take her hand and we head to my bathroom. I turn on the shower, then face her. She's gorgeous, her eyes bright and gleaming with anticipation, as she watches me. My gaze rakes down her body to her naked legs. I've never seen her in such a short skirt, with so much of her flesh on display, and I'm not sure I approve. *She's for my eyes only.*

"I like your skirt. It's very short." *Too short.* "You have great legs." Stepping out of my shoes, I take off my socks, and without breaking eye contact, she, too, slips off her shoes.

Fuck the shower. I want her now.

Stepping toward her, I clasp her head, and we step back so she's against the tiled wall, her lips parting as she inhales. Holding her face and lacing my fingers into her hair, I kiss her: her cheek, her throat, her mouth. She's nectar and I can't get enough. Her breath catches in her throat and she grasps my arms, but at her touch there's no protest from the darkness within. There's just Ana, in all her beauty and innocence, kissing me back with a fervor that matches mine.

My blood is thick with desire, my erection painful. "I want you now. Here . . . fast, hard," I murmur, as my hand runs up her naked thigh beneath her skirt. "Are you still bleeding?"

"No."

"Good." I push her skirt up over her hips, hook both thumbs into her cotton panties and drop to the floor, kneeling, slipping the panties down her legs.

She gasps when I grab her hips and kiss the sweet junction beneath her pubic hair. Moving my hands to the backs of her thighs, I part her legs, exposing her clitoris to my tongue. When I start my sensual assault her fingers dive into my hair. My tongue torments her, and she moans and tips her head back against the wall.

She smells exquisite. She tastes better.

As she purrs she tilts her pelvis toward my invading, insistent tongue, and her legs begin to tremble.

Enough. I want to come inside her.

It will be my skin against her skin again, like in Savannah. Releasing her, I stand and grasp her face, capturing her surprised and disappointed mouth with mine, kissing her hard. I unzip my fly and lift her, clutching her under her thighs. "Wrap your legs around me, baby." My voice is rough and urgent. As soon as she does, I thrust forward, sliding into her.

She's mine. She's heaven.

Clinging to me, she whimpers as I plunge into her—slowly at first, then building as my body takes control, driving me forward, driving me into her, faster and faster, harder and harder, my face at her throat. She moans and I feel her quicken around me, and I'm lost, in her, in us, as she climaxes, crying out her release. The feel of her pulsing around me tips me over the edge and I come deep and hard inside her, growling out a garbled version of her name.

I kiss her throat, not wanting to withdraw, waiting for her to calm. We're in a cloud of steam from the shower, and my shirt and pants are sticking to my body, but I don't care. Ana's breathing slows, and she feels weightier in my arms as she relaxes. Her expression is wanton and dazed as I pull out of her, so I hold her fast while she finds her feet. Her lips rise in a winsome smile. "You seem pleased to see me," she says.

"Yes, Miss Steele, I think my pleasure is pretty self-evident. Come—let me get you in the shower."

I undress quickly, and when I'm naked I begin undoing the buttons on Ana's blouse. Her eyes move from my fingers to my face.

"How was your journey?" I ask.

"Fine, thank you," she says, her voice a little throaty. "Thanks once again for first class. It really is a much nicer way to travel." She takes a quick breath, as if she's steeling herself. "I have some news," she says.

"Oh?" What now? I remove her blouse and deposit it on top of my clothes.

"I have a job." She sounds reticent.

Why? Did she think I'd be angry? Of course she's found a job. Pride swells in my chest. "Congratulations, Miss Steele. Now will you tell me where?" I ask with a smile.

"You don't know?"

"Why would I know?"

"With your stalking capabilities, I thought you might have—" She stops to study my face.

"Anastasia, I wouldn't dream of interfering in your career. Unless you ask me to, of course."

"So you have no idea which company?"

"No. I know there are four publishing companies in Seattle—so I am assuming it's one of them."

"SIP," she announces.

"Oh, the small one, good. Well done." It's the company that Ros identified as ripe for takeover. This will be easy.

I kiss Ana's forehead. "Clever girl. When do you start?"

"Monday."

"That soon, eh? I'd better take advantage of you while I still can. Turn around."

She obeys immediately. I remove her bra and skirt, then cup her behind and kiss her shoulder. Leaning against her, I nuzzle her hair. Her scent lingers in my nostrils, soothing, familiar, and uniquely Ana. The feel of her body against mine is both calming and enticing. She really is the whole package.

"You intoxicate me, Miss Steele, and you calm me. Such a heady combination." Grateful that she's here, I kiss her hair, then take her hand and pull her into the hot shower.

"Ow," she squeaks and closes her eyes, flinching under the steamy cascade.

"It's only a little hot water." I grin down at her. Opening one eye, she lifts her chin and slowly surrenders to the heat.

"Turn around," I order. "I want to wash you." She complies, and I squeeze some shower gel on my hand, work up a lather, and begin to massage her shoulders.

"I have something else to tell you," she says, her shoulders tensing.

"Oh yes?" I keep my voice mild. *Why is she tense?* My hands glide over her chest to her beautiful breasts.

"My friend José's photography show is opening Thursday in Portland."

"Yes, what about it?" *The photographer again?*

"I said I would go. Do you want to come with me?" The words come in a rush, as if she's anxious to get them out.

An invitation? I'm stunned. I only get invitations from my family, from work, and from Elena.

"What time?"

"The opening is at seven thirty."

This will count as *more*, surely. I kiss her ear and whisper, "Okay." Her shoulders soften as she leans back against me. She seems relieved and I'm not sure whether to be amused or annoyed. Am I really that unapproachable?

"Were you nervous about asking me?"

"Yes. How can you tell?"

"Anastasia, your whole body's just relaxed." I mask my irritation.

"Well, you just seem to be, um . . . on the jealous side."

Yes. I'm jealous. The thought of Ana with anyone else is . . . unsettling. Very unsettling. "Yes, I am. And you'd do well to remember that. But thank you for asking. We'll take *Charlie Tango.*"

She flashes me a quick grin as my hands slide down her body, the body she's given to me and no one else.

"Can I wash you?" she asks, diverting me.

"I don't think so." I kiss her neck as I rinse her back.

"Will you ever let me touch you?" Her voice is a gentle entreaty, but it doesn't stop the darkness that's swirling suddenly from nowhere and tightening around my throat.

No.

I will it away, cupping and concentrating on Ana's ass, her fucking glorious behind. My body responds on a primal level—at war with the darkness. I need her. I need her to chase my fear away.

"Put your hands on the wall, Anastasia. I'm going to take you again," I whisper, and with a startled glance at me, she splays her hands on the tiles. I grab her hips, pulling her back from the wall. "Hold fast, Anastasia," I warn, as the water streams over her back.

She bends her head and braces herself as my hands sweep through her pubic hair. She squirms, her behind brushing my arousal.

Fuck! And like that, my residual fear melts away.

"Do you want this?" I ask as my fingers tease her. In answer she wiggles her butt against my erection, making me smile. "Tell me," I demand, my voice strained.

"Yes." Her agreement slices through the pouring water, keeping the darkness at bay.

Oh, baby.

She's still wet from earlier—from me, from her—I don't know. In the moment I give a silent word of thanks to Dr. Greene: no more condoms. I ease into Ana and slowly, deliberately make her mine again.

I WRAP HER IN a bathrobe and kiss her soundly. "Dry your hair," I order, handing her a hair dryer I never use. "Are you hungry?"

"Famished," she admits, and I don't know if she means it or if she's said it merely to please me. But pleased I am.

"Great. Me, too. I'll check where Mrs. Jones is with dinner. You have ten minutes. Don't get dressed." I kiss her once more and pad out to the kitchen.

Gail is washing something at the sink. She looks up as I peer over her shoulder.

"Clams, Mr. Grey," she says.

Delicious. Pasta alle Vongole, one of my favorites.

"Ten minutes?" I ask.

"Twelve," she says.

"Great."

She gives me a look as I head into my study. I ignore it. She's seen me in less than my bathrobe before—what the hell is her problem?

I check through some e-mails and my phone to see if there's any news about Leila. Nothing—but since Ana's arrival, I don't feel as hopeless as I did earlier.

Ana enters the kitchen at the same time that I do, lured no doubt by the tantalizing smell of our dinner. When she sees Mrs. Jones she clutches the neck of her bathrobe.

"Just in time," Gail says, serving our meal in two large bowls at the place settings on the counter.

"Sit." I point to one of the barstools. Ana's anxious eyes pass from me to Mrs. Jones.

She's self-conscious.

Baby, I have staff. Get over it.

"Wine?" I offer, to distract her.

"Please," she says, sounding reserved as she takes her seat.

I open a bottle of Sancerre and pour two small glasses.

"There's cheese in the fridge if you'd like, sir," Gail says. I nod, and she exits the room, much to Ana's relief. I take my seat.

"Cheers." I raise my glass.

"Cheers," Ana replies, and the crystal glasses sing as we clink. She takes a bite of her food and makes an appreciative noise in the back of her throat. Perhaps she *is* famished.

"Are you going to tell me?" she asks.

"Tell you what?" Mrs. Jones has outdone herself; the pasta tastes delicious.

"What I said in my sleep."

I shake my head. "Eat up. You know I like watching you eat."

She pouts with mock exasperation. "You are so pervy," she exclaims under her breath.

Oh, baby, you have no idea. And a thought springs to mind: maybe we should explore something new in the playroom tonight. Something fun.

"Tell me about this friend of yours," I ask.

"My friend?"

"The photographer." I keep my voice light, but she regards me with a fleeting frown.

"Well, we met the first day of college. He's an engineering major, but his passion is photography."

"And?"

"That's it." Her evasive answers are irritating.

"Nothing else?"

She tosses her hair over her shoulder. "We've become good friends. It turns out my dad and José's dad served together in the military before I was born. They've gotten back in touch, and they're now best buds."

Oh. "Your dad and his dad?"

"Yeah." She twirls more pasta around her fork.

"I see."

"This tastes delicious." She gives me a contented smile, and her robe gapes a little, revealing the swell of her breast. The sight stirs my cock.

"How are you feeling?" I ask.

"Fine," she says.

"Up for more?"

"More?"

"More wine?" *More sex? In the playroom?*

"A small glass, please."

I pour her a little more Sancerre. I don't want either of us to drink too much if we're going to play.

"How's the, um . . . situation that brought you to Seattle?"

Leila. Shit. This I do not want to discuss. "Out of hand. But nothing for you to worry about, Anastasia. I have plans for you this evening."

I want to see if we can play this so-called arrangement of ours both ways.

"Oh?"

"Yes. I want you ready and waiting in my playroom in fifteen minutes." I stand up, watching her closely to gauge her reaction. She takes a quick sip of her wine, her pupils widening. "You can get ready in your room. Incidentally, the walk-in closet is now full of clothes for you. I don't want any arguments about them."

Her mouth sets in a surprised *o*. And I give her a stern look, daring her to argue with me. Remarkably, she says nothing, and I head off to my study to send a quick e-mail to Ros telling her I want to start the process to acquire SIP as soon as possible.

I scan a couple of work e-mails, but see nothing in my inbox about Mrs. Reed. I put thoughts of Leila out of my mind; she's preoccupied me for the last twenty-four hours. Tonight I'm going to focus on Ana—and have some fun.

When I return to the kitchen Ana's disappeared; I presume she's getting ready upstairs.

In my closet I remove my robe and slip on my favorite jeans. As I do, images of Ana in my bathroom come to mind—her flawless back, then her hands pressed against the tiles while I fucked her.

Boy, the girl has stamina.

Let's see how much.

With a sense of exhilaration I collect my iPod from the living room and bolt upstairs to the playroom.

When I find Ana kneeling as she should be at the entrance facing the room—eyes down, legs parted, and wearing only her panties—my first feeling is one of relief.

She's still here; she's game.

My second is pride: she has followed my instructions to the letter. My smile is hard to hide.

Miss Steele does not back down from a challenge.

Closing the door behind me, I note that her bathrobe has been hung up on the peg. I walk past her barefoot and deposit my iPod on the chest. I've decided that I'm going to deprive her of all her senses but touch, and see how she fares with that. The bed has been made up with satin sheets.

And the leather shackles are in place.

At the chest I take out a hair tie, a blindfold, a fur glove, earbuds, and the handy transmitter that Barney designed for my iPod. I lay out the items in a neat row, plugging the transmitter into the top of the iPod, letting Ana wait. Anticipation is half the buildup to a scene. Once I'm satisfied I go and stand over her. Ana's head is bowed, the ambient light burnishing her hair. She looks modest and beautiful, the epitome of a submissive.

"You look lovely." I cup her face and tilt her head up until blue eyes meet gray. "You are one beautiful woman, Anastasia. And you're all mine," I whisper. "Stand up."

She's a little stiff as she gets to her feet. "Look at me," I order, and when I look into her eyes I know I could drown in her serious, rapt expression. I've got her full attention. "We don't have a signed contract, Anastasia. But we've discussed limits. And I want to re-iterate we have safe words, okay?"

She blinks a couple of times, but remains mute.

"What are they?" I demand.

She hesitates.

Oh, this will never do.

"What are the safe words, Anastasia?"

"Yellow."

"And?"

"Red."

"Remember those."

She raises an eyebrow in obvious scorn, and is about to say something.

Oh no. Not in my playroom.

"Don't start with your smart mouth in here, Miss Steele. Or I will fuck it with you on your knees. Do you understand?"

As pleasing as that thought is, her obedience is what I want right now.

She swallows her chagrin.

"Well?"

"Yes, Sir," she says quickly.

"Good girl. My intention is not that you should use the safe word because you're in pain. What I intend to do to you will be intense. Very intense, and you have to guide me. Do you understand?"

Her face remains impassive, giving nothing away.

"This is about touch, Anastasia. You will not be able to see me or hear me. But you'll be able to feel me." Ignoring her confounded look, I turn to the audio player above the chest and switch it to auxiliary mode.

I just have to choose a song; and in that moment I recall our conversation in the car after she'd slept in my bed at The Heathman. Let's see if she likes some Tudor choral music.

"I am going to tie you to that bed, Anastasia. But I'm going to blindfold you first and"—I show her the iPod—"you will not be able to hear me. All you will hear is the music I'm going to play for you."

I think it's surprise I see registering on her face, but I'm not sure.

"Come." I lead her to the foot of the bed. "Stand here." Leaning down, I breathe in her sweet scent and whisper in her ear,

"Wait here. Keep your eyes on the bed. Picture yourself lying here, bound and totally at my mercy."

She sucks in her breath.

Yes, baby. Think about it. I resist the temptation to plant a soft kiss on her shoulder. I need to braid her hair first and fetch a flogger. From the top of the chest I grab the hair tie, and from the rack I select my favorite flogger, which I stuff into the back pocket of my jeans.

When I return to stand behind her, I gently take her hair and braid it. "While I like your pigtails, Anastasia, I am impatient to have you right now. So one will have to do." I fasten and tug on the braid so she's forced to step back against me. Winding the end around my wrist, I pull to the right, bending her head to expose her neck. I run my nose from her earlobe to her shoulder, sucking and biting gently.

Hmm . . . She smells so good.

She shivers and hums deep in her throat.

"Hush, now," I caution, and taking the flogger from my pocket, I reach around her, my arms brushing hers, and show it to her.

I hear her catch her breath and see her fingers twitch.

"Touch it," I whisper, knowing that's what she wants. She raises her hand, pauses, then runs her fingers through the soft suede tails. It's arousing. "I will use this. It will not hurt, but it will bring your blood to the surface of your skin and make you very sensitive. What are the safe words, Anastasia?"

"Um . . . 'yellow' and 'red,' Sir," she murmurs, transfixed by the flogger.

"Good girl. Remember, most of your fear is in your mind." I drop the flogger on the bed and brush my fingers down her sides, past the soft swell of her hips, and slip them into her panties. "You won't be needing these." I drag them down her legs and kneel behind her. She grabs hold of the pillar to shuffle awkwardly out of her underwear.

"Stand still," I command, and kiss her behind, gently nipping each cheek. "Now lie down. Faceup." I spank her once, and she jumps, startled, and scurries onto the bed. She lies down facing me, her eyes on mine, glowing with excitement—and a little trepidation, I think.

"Hands above your head."

She does as she's told. I retrieve the earbuds, blindfold, iPod, and the remote from atop the chest of drawers. Sitting beside her on the bed, I show her the iPod with the transmitter. Her look darts from my face to the devices and back again.

"This sends what's playing on the iPod to the system in the room. I can hear what you're hearing, and I have a remote control unit for it."

Once she's seen everything, I insert the earbuds into her ears and place the iPod on the pillow. "Lift your head." She obeys, and I slip the blindfold over her eyes. Rising, I take her left hand and cuff her wrist to the leather shackle at the top corner of the bed. I let my fingers linger down her outstretched arm and she wriggles in response. As I walk slowly around the bed, her head follows the sound of my footsteps; I repeat the process with her right hand, cuffing her wrist.

Ana's breathing alters, becoming erratic and fast through parted lips. A flush creeps up her chest, and she squirms and lifts her hips in anticipation.

Good.

At the bottom of the bed I grab both her ankles. "Lift your head again," I order. She does so immediately, and I drag her down the bed so that her arms are fully extended.

She lets out a quiet moan and lifts her hips once more.

I cuff each of her ankles to the corresponding corner of the bed so that she's spread-eagled before me and I step back to admire the view.

Fuck.

Has she ever looked this hot?

She's totally and willingly at my mercy. The knowledge is intoxicating, and I stand for a moment to marvel at her generosity and courage.

I drag myself away from the spellbinding sight and from the chest of drawers collect the rabbit-fur glove. Before I put it on I press play on the remote; there's a brief hiss, and then the forty-part motet begins, the singer's angelic voice ringing through the playroom and over the delectable Miss Steele.

She stills as she listens.

And I walk around the bed, drinking her in.

Reaching out, I caress her neck with the glove. She inhales sharply and pulls at her shackles, but she doesn't cry out or tell me to stop. Slowly I run my gloved hand down her throat, over her sternum, then over her breasts, enjoying her restrained squirm. Circling her breasts, I gently tug on each of her nipples, and her moan of appreciation encourages me to head south. At a leisurely, deliberate pace I explore her body: her belly, her hips, the apex of her thighs, and down each leg. The music swells, more voices joining the choir in perfect counterpoint to my moving hand. I watch her mouth to determine how she's feeling; now she gapes in pleasure, now she bites her lip. When I run my hand over her sex she clenches her behind, pushing herself into my hand.

Though I normally like her to keep still, the movement pleases me.

Miss Steele is enjoying this. She's greedy.

When I brush her breasts again her nipples harden in the wake of the glove.

Yes.

Now that her skin is sensitized I remove the glove and pick up the flogger. With great care I trail the beaded ends over her skin, following the same pattern: over her chest, her breasts, her belly, through her pubic hair, and down her legs. As more choristers lend their voices to the motet I lift the handle of the flogger and flick the tresses across her belly. She cries out, I think in surprise, but she doesn't safe-word. I give her a moment to absorb the sensation, then do it again—a little harder this time.

She pulls at her shackles and calls out once more, a garbled cry—but it's not the safe word. I lash the flogger over her breasts, and she tilts her head back and lets out a soundless cry, her mouth slack as she writhes on the red satin.

Still no safe word. Ana is embracing her inner freak.

I feel giddy with delight as I rain the tails up and down her body, watching her skin warm under their bite. When the choristers pause, so do I.

Christ. She looks stunning.

I begin again as the music crescendoes, all the voices singing together; I flick the flogger over her, again and again, and she writhes beneath each blow.

When the last note rings through the room I stop, dropping the flogger on the floor. I'm breathless, panting with want and need.

Fuck.

She lays on the bed, helpless, her skin pretty in pink, and she's panting, too.

Oh, baby.

I climb onto the bed between her legs and crawl over her, holding myself above her. When the music starts again, the lone voice singing a sweet seraphic note, I follow the same pattern as the glove and the flogger—but this time with my mouth, kissing and sucking and worshipping every inch of her body. I tease each of her nipples until they are glistening with my saliva and standing at attention. She writhes as much as the restraints allow and groans beneath me. My tongue trails down to her belly, around her navel, laving her. Tasting her. Venerating her. Moving down, through her pubic hair to her sweet, exposed clitoris that's begging for the touch of my tongue. Around and around I swirl, drinking in her scent, drinking in her reaction, until I feel her tremble beneath me.

Oh no. Not yet, Ana. Not yet.

I stop and she huffs her voiceless disappointment.

I kneel up between her legs and pull open my fly, freeing my erection. Then, leaning over, I gently undo the left shackle around her ankle. She curls her leg around me in a long-limbed caress while I release her other ankle. Once she's free I massage and knead the life back into her legs, from her calves up to her thighs. She wriggles beneath me, raising her hips in perfect rhythm to the Tallis motet, as my thumbs work their way up her inner thighs, which are dewy from her arousal.

I stifle a growl and grasp her hips, lifting her from the bed, and in one swift, rough move I bury myself inside her.

Fuck.

She's slick and hot and wet and her body pulses around me, on the edge.

No. Too soon. Way too soon.

I stop, holding myself still over her and in her, while sweat beads on my brow.

"Please," she calls out, and I tighten my hold on her as I quell the urge to move and lose myself in her. Closing my eyes so I can't see her laid out beneath me in all her wonder, I concentrate on the music; and once I'm in control again, slowly I start to move. As the intensity of the choral piece builds I slowly increase my pace, matching the power and rhythm of the music, cherishing every tight inch inside her.

She fists her hands and tilts her head back and moans.

Yes.

"Please," she pleads between gritted teeth.

I hear you, baby.

Laying her back down on the bed, I stretch out over her, supporting my weight on my elbows, and I follow the rhythm, thrusting into her and losing myself in her and the music.

Sweet, brave Ana.

Sweat glides down my back.

Come on, baby.

Please.

And finally she explodes around me, shouting out her release and pushing me into an intense, draining climax where I lose all sense of self. I collapse on top of her as my world shifts and realigns, leaving that unfamiliar emotion swirling in my chest, consuming me.

I shake my head, trying to chase away the ominous and confusing feeling. Reaching up, I grab the remote and switch off the music.

No more Tallis.

The music definitely contributed to what was almost a religious experience. I frown, attempting but failing to get a handle on my feelings. I slide out of Ana and stretch to release her from each cuff.

She sighs as she flexes her fingers, and gently I remove the blindfold and the earbuds.

Big blue eyes blink up at me.

"Hi," I whisper.

"Hi, yourself," she says, playful and bashful. Her response is delightful and, leaning down, I plant a tender kiss on her lips.

"Well done, you." My voice is filled with pride.

She did it. She took it. She took it all.

"Turn over."

Her eyes widen in alarm.

"I'm just going to rub your shoulders."

"Oh, okay."

She rolls over and flops down on the bed with her eyes closed. I sit astride her and massage her shoulders.

A pleasurable rumble resonates deep in her throat.

"What was that music?" she asks.

"It's called *Spem in Alium*, a forty-part motet by Thomas Tallis."

"It was . . . overwhelming."

"I've always wanted to fuck to it."

"Not another first, Mr. Grey?"

I grin. "Indeed, Miss Steele."

"Well, it's the first time I've fucked to it, too," she says, her voice betraying her fatigue.

"You and I, we're giving each other many firsts."

"What did I say to you in my sleep, Chris—er, Sir?"

Not this again. *Put her out of her misery, Grey.*

"You said lots of things, Anastasia. You talked about cages and strawberries. That you wanted more, and that you missed me."

"Is that all?" She sounds relieved.

Why would she be relieved?

I stretch out beside her so I can see her face.

"What did you think you'd said?"

She opens her eyes for a brief moment, and shuts them again quickly.

"That I thought you were ugly, conceited, and that you were hopeless in bed." One blue eye peeks open and watches me warily.

Oh . . . she's lying.

"Well, naturally I am all those things, and now you've got me really intrigued. What are you hiding from me, Miss Steele?"

"I'm not hiding anything."

"Anastasia, you're a hopeless liar."

"I thought you were going to make me giggle after sex; this isn't doing it for me."

Her answer is unexpected, and I give her a reluctant smile. "I can't tell jokes," I confess.

"Mr. Grey! Something you can't do?" She rewards me with a broad, infectious grin.

"No, hopeless joke teller," I say, as if it's a badge of honor.

She giggles. "I'm a hopeless joke teller, too."

"That is such a lovely sound," I whisper, and kiss her. But I still want to know why she's relieved. "And you are hiding something, Anastasia. I may have to torture it out of you."

"Ha!" The space between us is filled with her laughter. "I think you've done enough torturing."

Her response wipes the smile off my face, and her expression softens immediately. "Maybe I'll let you torture me like that again," she says coyly.

Relief sweeps through me. "I'd like that very much, Miss Steele."

"We aim to please, Mr. Grey."

"You're okay?" I ask, humbled and anxious at once.

"More than okay." She gives me her timid smile.

"You're amazing." I kiss her forehead, then climb off the bed as that ominous feeling ripples through me once more. Shaking it off, I button my fly and hold out my hand to help her off the bed.

When she's standing I pull her into my arms and kiss her, savoring her taste.

"Bed," I mutter, and lead her to the door. There I wrap her in the bathrobe she's left hanging on the peg, and before she can protest I pick her up and carry her downstairs to my bedroom.

"I'm so tired," she mumbles once she's in my bed.

"Sleep now," I whisper, and wrap her in my arms. I close my eyes, fighting the disquieting sensation that surges and fills my chest once more. It's like homesickness and a homecoming rolled into one . . . and it's terrifying.

The summer breeze teases my hair, its caress the nimble fingers of a lover.

My lover.

Ana.

I wake suddenly, confused. My bedroom is shrouded in darkness, and beside me Ana sleeps, her breathing gentle and even. I prop myself up on one elbow and run my hand through my hair, with the uncanny feeling that someone has just done exactly that. I glance around the room, peering into the shadowy corners, but Ana and I are alone.

Strange. I could swear someone was here. Someone touched me.

It was just a dream.

I shake off the disturbing thought and check the time. It's after 4:30 in the morning. As I flop back down onto my pillow, Ana mumbles an incoherent word and turns over to face me, still fast asleep. She looks serene and beautiful.

I stare at the ceiling, the flashing light of the smoke alarm taunting me once more. We have no contract. Yet Ana's here. Beside me. *What does this mean?* How am I supposed to deal with her? Will she abide by my rules? I need to know that she's safe. I rub my face. This is uncharted territory for me; it's out of my control, and it's unsettling.

Leila pops into my mind.

Shit.

My mind races: Leila, work, Ana . . . and I know I won't get back to sleep. Getting up, I pull on some PJ pants, close the bedroom door, and head into the living room to my piano.

Chopin is my solace; the somber notes match my mood and I play them over and over. A small movement at the edge of my vision catches my attention, and looking up, I see it's Ana coming toward me, her footsteps hesitant. "You should be asleep," I mutter, but continue playing.

"So should you," she volleys back. Her face is firm with resolve, yet she looks small and vulnerable dressed only in my oversized bathrobe. I hide my smile.

"Are you scolding me, Miss Steele?"

"Yes, Mr. Grey, I am."

"Well, I can't sleep."

I have too much weighing on my mind, and I'd rather she went back to bed and slept. She must be tired from yesterday. She disregards my mood and sits down beside me on the piano bench, leaning her head on my shoulder.

It's such a tender and intimate gesture that for a moment I lose my place in the prelude, but I continue playing, feeling more at peace because she's with me.

"What was that?" she asks when I finish.

"Chopin. A prelude. Opus twenty-eight, number four. In E minor, if you're interested."

"I'm always interested in what you do."

Sweet Ana. I kiss her hair. "I didn't mean to wake you."

"You didn't," she says, not moving her head. "Play the other one."

"Other one?"

"The Bach piece that you played the first night I stayed."

"Oh, the Marcello."

I can't remember when I last played for someone upon request. For me the piano is a solitary instrument, for my ears only. My family hasn't heard me play for years. But since she's asked, I'll play for my sweet Ana. My fingers caress the keys and the haunting melody echoes through the living room.

"Why do you only play such sad music?" she asks.

Is it sad?

"So you were just six when you started to play?" She continues her questions, lifting her head and studying me. Her face is open and eager for information, as usual; and after last night, who am I to deny her anything?

"I threw myself into learning the piano to please my new mother."

"To fit into the perfect family?" My words from our candid night in Savannah echo in her soft voice.

"Yes, so to speak." I don't want to talk about this and I'm surprised how much of my personal information she's retained. "Why are you awake? Don't you need to recover from yesterday's exertions?"

"It's eight in the morning for me. And I need to take my pill."

"Well remembered," I muse. "Only you would start a course of time-specific birth control pills in a different time zone. Perhaps you should wait half an hour, and then another half hour tomorrow morning. So eventually you can take them at a reasonable time."

"Good plan," she says. "So what shall we do for half an hour?"

Well, I could fuck you over this piano.

"I can think of a few things." My voice is seductive.

"On the other hand, we could talk." She smiles, provocative.

I'm not in the mood for talking. "I prefer what I have in mind." I snake my arm around her waist, pull her into my lap, and nuzzle her hair.

"You'd always rather have sex than talk." She laughs.

"True. Especially with you." Her hands curl around my biceps, yet the darkness stays still and quiet. I trail kisses from the base of her ear to her throat. "Maybe on my piano," I murmur, as my body responds to a mental image of her sprawled naked on the top, her hair spilling down over the side.

"I want to get something straight." She speaks quietly in my ear.

"Always so eager for information, Miss Steele. What needs straightening out?" Her skin is soft and warm against my lips as I nudge her bathrobe off her shoulder with my nose.

"Us," she says, and the simple word sounds like a prayer.

"Hmm. What about us?" I pause. *Where is she going with this?*
"The contract."

I stop and stare down into her shrewd gaze. *Why is she doing this now?* My fingers glide down her cheek.

"Well, I think the contract is moot, don't you?"

"Moot?" she says, and her lips soften with the hint of a smile.

"Moot." I mirror her expression.

"But you were so keen." Uncertainty clouds Ana's eyes.

"Well, that was before. Anyway, the rules aren't moot, they still stand." I need to know you're safe.

"Before? Before what?"

"Before—" Before all this. Before you turned my world upside down, before you sleeping with me. Before you laid your head on my shoulder at the piano. It's all . . . "More," I murmur, driving away the now-familiar unease in my gut.

"Oh," she says, and I think she's pleased.

"Besides, we've been in the playroom twice now, and you haven't run screaming for the hills."

"Do you expect me to?"

"Nothing you do is expected, Anastasia."

The *v* between her brows is back. "So, let me be clear. You just want me to follow the rules element of the contract all the time, but not the rest of the contract?"

"Except in the playroom. I want you to follow the spirit of the contract in the playroom, and yes, I want you to follow the rules—all the time. Then I'll know you're safe. And I'll be able to have you anytime I wish," I add flippantly.

"And if I break one of the rules?" she asks.

"Then I'll punish you."

"But won't you need my permission?"

"Yes, I will."

"And if I say no?" she persists.

Why is she being so willful?

"If you say no, you'll say no. I'll have to find a way to persuade you." She should know this. She didn't let me spank her in the boathouse, and I wanted to. But I got to do it later that evening . . . with her approval.

She stands and walks toward the entrance of the living room, and for a moment I think she's storming off, but she turns, her expression perplexed. "So the punishment aspect remains."

"Yes, but only if you break the rules." This is clear to me. Why not to her?

"I'll need to reread them," she says, suddenly all businesslike.

She wants to do this now?

"I'll fetch them for you."

In my study I fire up my computer and print out the rules, wondering why we are discussing this at five in the morning.

She's at the sink, drinking a glass of water, when I return with the printout. I sit down on a stool and wait, watching her. Her back is stiff and tense; this does not bode well. When she turns around I slide the sheet of paper toward her across the kitchen island.

"Here you go."

She scans the rules quickly. "So the obedience thing still stands?"

"Oh yes."

She shakes her head, and an ironic smile tugs at the corner of her mouth as her eyes dart to the heavens.

Oh joy.

My spirits suddenly lift.

"Did you just roll your eyes at me, Anastasia?"

"Possibly. Depends what your reaction is." She looks wary and amused at once.

"Same as always." If she'll let me . . .

She swallows and her eyes widen with anticipation. "So . . ."

"Yes?"

"You want to spank me now?"

"Yes. And I will."

"Oh, really, Mr. Grey?" She folds her arms, her chin thrust upward in a challenge.

"Are you going to stop me?"

"You're going to have to catch me first." She wears a coquettish smile, which addresses my dick directly.

She wants to play.

I ease myself off the stool, watching her carefully. "Oh, really, Miss Steele?" The air almost crackles between us.

Which way will she run?

Her eyes are on mine, brimming with excitement. Her teeth tease her lower lip.

"And you're biting your lip." *Is she doing it on purpose?* I move slowly to my left.

"You wouldn't," she taunts. "After all, you roll your eyes." With her eyes fixed on me, she, too, moves to her left.

"Yes, but you've just raised the bar on the excitement stakes with this game."

"I'm quite fast, you know," she teases.

"So am I."

How does she make everything so thrilling?

"Are you going to come quietly?"

"Do I ever?" She grins, taking the bait.

"Miss Steele, what do you mean?" I stalk her around the kitchen island. "It'll be worse for you if I have to come and get you."

"That's only if you catch me, Christian. And right now, I have no intention of letting you catch me."

Is she serious?

"Anastasia, you may fall and hurt yourself. Which will put you in direct contravention of rule number seven, now six."

"I have been in danger since I met you, Mr. Grey, rules or no rules."

"Yes, you have."

Perhaps this is not a game. Is she trying to tell me something? She hesitates, and I make a sudden lunge to grab her. She squeals and dashes around the island, to the relative safety of the opposite side of the dining table. With her lips parted, her expression both wary and daring at once, the bathrobe slips off one shoulder. She looks hot. Really fucking hot.

Slowly I prowl toward her, and she backs away.

"You certainly know how to distract a man, Anastasia."

"We aim to please, Mr. Grey. Distract you from what?"

"Life. The universe." *Ex-subs who've gone missing. Work. Our arrangement. Everything.*

"You did seem very preoccupied as you were playing."

She's not backing down. I stop and fold my arms, reassessing my strategy. "We can do this all day, baby, but I will get you, and it will just be worse for you when I do."

"No, you won't," she says, with absolute certainty.

I frown. "Anyone would think you didn't want me to catch you."

"I don't. That's the point. I feel about punishment the way you feel about me touching you."

And from nowhere the darkness crawls over me, shrouding my skin, leaving an icy trail of despair in its wake.

No. No. I can't bear to be touched. Ever.

"That's how you feel?" It's like she's touched me, her nails leaving white tracks over my chest.

She blinks several times, assessing my reaction, and when she speaks her voice is gentle. "No. It doesn't affect me quite as much as that, but it gives you an idea." Her expression is anxious.

Well, hell! This shines a whole different light on our relationship. "Oh," I mutter, because I can't think of anything else to say.

She takes a deep breath and approaches me, and when she's standing in front of me she looks up, her eyes burning with apprehension.

"You hate it that much?" I whisper.

This is it. We are really incompatible.

No. I don't want to believe that.

"Well . . . no," she says, and relief washes through me. "No," she continues. "I feel ambivalent about it. I don't like it, but I don't hate it."

"But last night, in the playroom, you—"

"I do it for you, Christian, because you need it. I don't. You didn't hurt me last night. That was in a different context, and I can rationalize that internally, and I trust you. But when you want to punish me, I worry that you'll hurt me."

Fuck. Tell her.

It's truth-or-dare time, Grey.

"I want to hurt you. But not beyond anything that you couldn't take." I'd never go too far.

"Why?"

"I just need it," I whisper. "I can't tell you."

"Can't or won't?"

"Won't."

"So you know why?"

"Yes."

"But you won't tell me."

"If I do, you will run screaming from this room, and you'll never want to return. I can't risk that, Anastasia."

"You want me to stay."

"More than you know. I couldn't bear to lose you."

I can no longer stomach the distance between us. I grab her to stop her from running, and I pull her into my arms, my lips seeking hers. She answers my need, her mouth molding to mine, kissing me back with the same passion and hope and longing. The hovering darkness recedes and I find my solace.

"Don't leave me," I whisper against her lips. "You said you wouldn't leave me, and you begged me not to leave you, in your sleep."

"I don't want to go," she says, but her eyes are searching mine, looking for answers. And I'm exposed—my ugly, torn soul on display.

"Show me," she says.

And I don't know what she means.

"Show you?"

"Show me how much it can hurt."

"What?" I lean back and stare at her in disbelief.

"Punish me. I want to know how bad it can get."

Oh no. I release her and step out of her reach.

She gazes at me: open, honest, serious. She's offering herself to me once more; mine for the taking, to do with as I wish. I'm stunned. She'd fulfill this need for me? I can't believe it. "You would try?"

"Yes. I said I would." Her expression is full of resolve.

"Ana, you're so confusing."

"I'm confused, too. I'm trying to work this out. And you and I will know, once and for all, if I can do this. If I can handle this, then maybe you—"

She stops, and I take a further step back. She wants to touch me.
No.

But if we do this, then I'll know. She'll know.

We're here much sooner than I thought we'd be.

Can I do this?

And in that moment I know there's nothing I want more . . . There's nothing that will satisfy the monster within me more.

Before I can change my mind I grasp her arm and lead her upstairs to the playroom. At the door I stop. "I'll show you how bad it can be, and you can make your own mind up. Are you ready for this?"

She nods, her face set with the stubborn determination that I've come to know so well.

So be it.

I open the door, quickly grab a belt from the rack before she changes her mind, and lead her to the bench in the corner of the room.

"Bend over the bench," I order quietly.

She does as she's told, saying nothing.

"We're here because you said yes, Anastasia. And you ran from me. I am going to hit you six times, and you will count with me."

Still she says nothing.

I fold the hem of her bathrobe over her back, revealing her beautiful naked behind. I run my palm over her buttocks and the top of her thighs, and a frisson runs through me.

This is it. What I want. What I've been working toward.

"I am doing this so that you remember not to run from me,

and as exciting as it is, I never want you to run from me. And you rolled your eyes at me. You know how I feel about that." I take a deep breath, savoring this moment, trying to steady my thundering heartbeat.

I need this. This is what I do. And we're finally here.

She can do it.

She's never let me down yet.

Holding her in place with one hand at the small of her back, I shake out the belt. I take another deep breath, focusing on the task in hand.

She won't run. She's asked me.

Then I wield it, striking her across both cheeks, hard.

She cries out, in shock.

But she's not called out the number . . . or the safe word.

"Count, Anastasia!" I demand.

"One!" she shouts.

Okay . . . no safe word.

I hit her again.

"Two!" she screams.

That's right, let it out, baby.

I hit her once more.

"Three!" She winces.

There are three stripes across her backside.

I make it four.

She shouts the number, loud and clear.

There's no one to hear you, baby. Shout all you need.

I belt her again.

"Five," she sobs, and I pause, waiting for her to safe-word.

She doesn't.

And one for luck.

"Six," Ana whispers, her voice forced and hoarse.

I drop the belt, savoring my sweet, euphoric release. I'm punch-drunk, breathless, and finally replete. Oh, this beautiful girl, my beautiful girl. I want to kiss every inch of her body. We're here. Where I want to be. I reach for her, pulling her into my arms.

"Let go. No—" She struggles out of my grasp, scrambling away from me, pushing and shoving and finally turning on me like a seething wildcat. "Don't touch me!" she hisses. Her face is blotchy and smeared with tears, her nose is running, and her hair is a dark, tangled mess, but she has never looked so magnificent . . . and at the same time so angry.

Her anger crashes over me like a tidal wave.

She's mad. Really mad.

Okay, I hadn't figured on anger.

Give her a moment. Wait for the endorphins to kick in.

She dashes away her tears with the back of her hand. "This is what you really like? Me, like this?" She wipes her nose with the sleeve of the bathrobe.

My euphoria vanishes. I'm stunned, completely helpless and paralyzed by her anger. The crying I know and understand, but this rage . . . somewhere deep inside it resonates with me and I don't want to think about that.

Don't go there, Grey.

Why didn't she ask me to stop? She didn't safe-word. She deserved to be punished. She ran from me. She rolled her eyes. *This is what happens when you defy me, baby.*

She scowls. Blue eyes wide and bright, filled with hurt and rage and sudden, chilling insight.

Shit. What have I done?

It's sobering.

I'm unbalanced, teetering at the edge of a dangerous precipice, desperately searching for the words to make this right, but my mind is blank.

"Well, you are one fucked-up son of a bitch," she snarls.

All the breath leaves my body, and it's like she's whipped *me* with a belt . . . *Fuck!*

She's recognized me for what I am.

She's seen the monster.

"Ana," I whisper, pleading with her. I want her to stop. I want to hold her and make the pain go away. I want her to sob in my arms.

"Don't you dare Ana me! You need to sort your shit out, Grey!"

she snaps, and walks out of the playroom, quietly shutting the door behind her. Stunned, I stare at the closed door, her words ringing in my ears.

You are one fucked-up son of a bitch.

No one has ever walked out on me. *What the hell?* Mechanically, I run my hand through my hair, trying to rationalize her reaction, and mine. I just let her go. I'm not mad . . . *I'm . . . what?* I stoop to pick up the belt, walk to the wall, and hang it on its peg. That was, without doubt, one of the most satisfying moments of my life. A moment ago I felt lighter, the weight of uncertainty between us gone.

It's done. We're there.

Now that she knows what's involved, we can move on.

I told her. People like me like inflicting pain.

But only on women who like it.

My sense of unease grows.

Her reaction—the image of her injured, haunted look is back, unwelcome, in my mind's eye. It's unsettling. I am used to making women cry—it's what I do.

But Ana?

I sink to the floor and lean my head against the wall, my arms on my bent knees. Just let her cry. She'll feel better for crying. Women do, in my experience. Give her a moment, then go and offer her aftercare. She didn't safe-word. She asked me. She wanted to know, curious as ever. It's just been a rude awakening, that's all.

You are one fucked-up son of a bitch.

Closing my eyes, I smile without humor. *Yes, Ana, yes I am, and now you know.* Now we can move forward with our relationship . . . arrangement. Whatever this is.

My thoughts don't comfort me and my sense of unease grows. Her wounded eyes glaring at me, outraged, accusatory, pitying . . . she can see me for what I am. *A monster.*

Flynn springs to mind: *Don't dwell on the negative, Christian.*

I close my eyes once more and see Ana's anguished face.

What a fool I am.

This was too soon.

Way, way too soon.

Fuck.

I'll reassure her.

Yes—let her cry, then reassure her.

I was angry with her for running from me. *Why did she do that?*

Hell. She's so different from any other woman I've known. Of course she wouldn't react in the same way.

I need to face her, hold her. We'll get through this. I wonder where she is.

Shit!

Panic seizes me. Suppose she's gone? No, she wouldn't do that. Not without saying good-bye. I stand and race out of the room and down the stairs. She's not in the living room—she must be in bed. I dash to my bedroom.

The bed is empty.

Full-blown anxiety erupts in the pit of my belly. No, she can't have gone! Upstairs—she must be in her room. I take the stairs three at a time and pause, breathless, outside her bedroom door. She's in there, crying.

Oh, thank God.

I lean my head against the door, overwhelmed by my relief.

Don't leave. The thought is awful.

Of course she just needs to cry.

Taking a steadying breath, I head to the bathroom beside the playroom to fetch some arnica cream, Advil, and a glass of water, and I return to her room.

Inside it's still dark, though dawn is a pale streak on the horizon, and it takes me a moment to find my beautiful girl. She's curled up in the middle of the bed, small and vulnerable, sobbing quietly. The sound of her grief rips through me, leaving me winded. My subs never affected me like this—even when they were bawling. I don't get it. Why do I feel so lost? Putting down the arnica, water, and tablets, I lift the comforter, slide in beside her, and reach for her. She stiffens, her whole body screaming, *Don't touch me!* The irony is not lost on me.

"Hush," I whisper, in a vain attempt to halt her tears and calm her. She doesn't respond. She remains frozen, unyielding.

"Don't fight me, Ana, please." She relaxes a fraction, allowing me to pull her into my arms, and I bury my nose in her wonderfully fragrant hair. She smells as sweet as ever, her scent a soothing balm to my nerves. And I plant a tender kiss on her neck.

"Don't hate me," I murmur, as I press my lips to her throat, tasting her. She says nothing, but slowly her crying dissipates into soft sniffling sobs. At last she's quiet. I think she might have fallen asleep, but I cannot bring myself to check, in case I disturb her. At least she's calmer now.

Dawn comes and goes, and the ambient light gets brighter, intruding into the room as morning moves on. And still we lie quietly. My mind drifts as I hold my girl in my arms, and I observe the changing quality of the light. I can't remember an instance when I just lay down and let time creep by and my thoughts wander. It's relaxing, imagining what we could do for the rest of the day. Maybe I should take her to see *The Grace*.

Yes. We could go sailing this afternoon.

If she's still talking to you, Grey.

She moves, a slight twitch in her foot, and I know she's awake.

"I brought you some Advil and some arnica cream."

Finally she responds, slowly turning in my arms to face me. Pain-riven eyes focus on mine, her look intense, questioning. She takes her time to scrutinize me, as if seeing me for the first time. It's unnerving because, as usual, I have no idea what she's thinking, what she's seeing. But she's definitely calmer, and I welcome the small spark of relief this brings. Today might be a good day after all.

She caresses my cheek and runs her fingers along my jaw, tickling my stubble. I close my eyes, savoring her touch. It's still so new, this sensation, being touched and enjoying her innocent fingers gently stroking my face, the darkness quiet. I don't mind her touching my face . . . or her fingers in my hair.

"I'm sorry," she says.

Her soft-spoken words are a surprise. She's apologizing to me?

"What for?"

"What I said."

Relief courses unchecked through my body. She's forgiven me. Besides, what she said in anger was right—I am a fucked-up son of a bitch.

"You didn't tell me anything I didn't know." And for the first time in so many years I find myself apologizing. "I'm sorry I hurt you."

Her shoulders lift a little and she gives me a slight smile. I've won a reprieve. We're safe. We're okay. I'm relieved.

"I asked for it," she says.

You sure did, baby.

She swallows nervously. "I don't think I can be everything you want me to be," she concedes, her eyes wide with heartfelt sincerity.

The world stops.

Fuck.

We're not safe at all.

Grey, make this right.

"You are everything I want you to be."

She frowns. Her eyes are red-rimmed and she's so pale, the palest I've ever seen her. It's oddly stirring. "I don't understand," she says. "I'm not obedient, and you can be as sure as hell I'm not going to let you do *that* to me again. And that's what you need—you said so."

And there it is—her coup de grace. I pushed too far. Now she knows—and all the arguments I had with myself before I embarked on the pursuit of this girl flood back to me. She's not into the lifestyle. How can I corrupt her this way? She's too young, too innocent—too . . . *Ana.*

My dreams are just that . . . dreams. This isn't going to work.

I close my eyes; I can't bear to look at her. It's true, she would be better off without me. Now that she's seen the monster, she knows she can't contend with him. I have to free her—let her go her own way. This won't work between us.

Focus, Grey.

"You're right. I should let you go. I'm no good for you."

Her eyes widen. "I don't want to go," she whispers. Tears pool in her eyes, glistening on long dark lashes.

"I don't want you to go, either," I answer, because it's the truth, and that feeling—that ominous, frightening feeling—is back, over-whelming me. The tears trickle down her cheeks once more. Gently I wipe away a falling tear with my thumb, and before I know it the words tumble out. "I've come alive since I met you." I trace my thumb along her bottom lip. I want to kiss her, hard. Make her forget. Dazzle her. Arouse her—I know I can. But something holds me back—her wary, injured look. Why would she want to be kissed by a monster? She might push me away, and I don't know if I could deal with any more rejection. Her words haunt me, pulling at some dark and repressed memory.

You are one fucked-up son of a bitch.

"Me, too," she whispers. "I've fallen in love with you, Christian."

I remember Carrick teaching me to dive. My toes gripping the pool edge as I fell arching into the water—and now I'm falling once more, into the abyss, in slow motion.

There's no way she can feel that about me.

Not me. *No!*

And I'm choking for air, strangled by her words pressing their momentous weight on my chest. I plunge down and down, the darkness welcoming me. I can't hear them. I can't deal with them. She doesn't know what she's saying, who she's dealing with—*what* she's dealing with.

"No." My voice is raw with pained disbelief. "You can't love me, Ana. No. That's wrong."

I need to set her right on this. She cannot love a monster. She cannot love a fucked-up son of a bitch. She needs to go. She needs out—and in an instant, everything becomes crystal clear. This is my eureka moment; I can't make her happy. I can't be what she needs. I can't let this go on. This has to finish. It should never have started.

"Wrong? Why's it wrong?"

"Well, look at you. I can't make you happy." The anguish is plain in my voice as I sink deeper and deeper into the abyss, shrouded in despair.

No one can love me.

"But you do make me happy," she says, not comprehending.

Anastasia Steele, look at yourself. I have to be honest with her. "Not at the moment. Not doing what I want to do."

She blinks, her lashes fluttering over her large, wounded eyes, studying me intently as she searches for the truth. "We'll never get past that, will we?"

I shake my head, because I can't think of anything to say. It comes down to incompatibility, again. She closes her eyes, as if in pain, and when she opens them again, they are clearer, full of resolve. Her tears have stopped. And the blood starts pounding through my head as my heart hammers. I know what she's going to say. I dread what she's going to say.

"Well, I'd better go, then." She winces as she sits up.

Now? She can't go now.

"No, don't go." I'm free-falling, deeper and deeper. Her leaving feels like a monumental mistake. My mistake. But she can't stay if she feels this way about me, she just can't.

"There's no point in me staying," she says, and gingerly climbs out of the bed still wrapped in her bathrobe. She's really leaving. I can't believe it. I scramble out of bed to stop her, but her look pins me to the floor—her expression so bleak, so cold, so distant—not my Ana at all.

"I'm going to get dressed. I'd like some privacy," she says. How flat and empty her voice sounds as she turns and leaves, closing the door behind her. I stare at the closed door.

This is the second time in one day that she's walked out on me.

I sit up and cradle my head in my hands, trying to calm down, trying to rationalize my feelings.

She loves me?

How did this happen? How?

Grey, you fucking fool.

Wasn't this always a risk, with someone like her? Someone

good and innocent and courageous. A risk that she'd not see the real me until it was too late. That I would make her suffer like this?

Why is this so painful? I feel like I've punctured a lung. I follow her out of the room. She might want privacy, but if she's leaving me I need clothes.

When I reach my bedroom, she's showering, so I quickly change into jeans and a T-shirt, I've chosen black—suitable for my mood. Grabbing my phone, I wander through the apartment, tempted to sit at the piano and hammer out some woeful lament. But instead I stand in the middle of the room, feeling nothing.

Vacant.

Focus, Grey! This is the right decision. Let her go.

My phone buzzes. It's Welch. Has he found Leila?

"Welch."

"Mr. Grey, I have news." His voice grates over the phone. This guy should stop smoking. He sounds like Deep Throat.

"You found her?" My spirits lift a little.

"No, sir."

"What is it, then?" *Why the hell have you called?*

"Leila left her husband. He finally admitted it to me. He's washed his hands of her."

This is news.

"I see."

"He has an idea where she might be, but he wants his palm greased. Wants to know who's so interested in his wife. Though that's not what he called her."

I fight my surging anger. "How much does he want?"

"He said two thousand."

"He said what?" I shout, losing it. Why didn't he just admit earlier that Leila had walked out on him? "Well, he could have told us the fucking truth. What's his number? I need to call him. Welch, this is a real fuckup."

I glance up, and Ana is standing awkwardly at the entrance to the living room, dressed in jeans and an ugly sweatshirt. She's all big eyes and tight, pinched face, her suitcase beside her.

"Find her," I snap, hanging up. I'll deal with Welch later.

Ana walks over to the sofa, and from her backpack removes the Mac, her phone, and the key to her car. Taking a deep breath, she marches to the kitchen and lays all three items on the counter.

What the hell? She's returning her things?

She turns to face me, determination clear on her small ashen face. It's her stubborn look, the one I know so well.

"I need the money that Taylor got for my Beetle." Her voice is calm but monotone.

"Ana, I don't want those things—they're yours." She can't do this to me. "Please, take them."

"No, Christian. I only accepted them under sufferance, and I don't want them anymore."

"Ana, be reasonable!"

"I don't want anything that will remind me of you. I just need the money that Taylor got for my car." Her voice is devoid of emotion.

She wants to forget me.

"Are you really trying to wound me?"

"No, I'm not. I'm trying to protect myself."

Of course—she's trying to protect herself from the monster.

"Please Ana, take that stuff."

Her lips are so pale.

"Christian, I don't want to fight—I just need that money."

Money. It always comes down to the fucking money.

"Will you take a check?" I snarl.

"Yes. I think you're good for it."

She wants money, I'll give her money. I storm into my study, barely holding on to my temper. Sitting at my desk I call Taylor.

"Good morning, Mr. Grey."

I ignore his greeting. "How much did you get for Ana's VW?"

"Twelve thousand dollars, sir."

"That much?" In spite of my bleak mood, I'm surprised.

"It's a classic," he says by way of explanation.

"Thanks. Can you take Miss Steele home now?"

"Of course. I'll be right down."

I hang up and take out my checkbook from my desk drawer. As I do, I remember my conversation with Welch about Leila's fucking asshole of a husband.

It's always about fucking money!

In my anger I double the amount that Taylor got for the death trap and stuff the check into an envelope.

When I return she's still standing by the kitchen island, lost, almost childlike. I hand her the envelope, my anger evaporating at the sight of her.

"Taylor got a good price . . . it's a classic car," I mumble in apology. "You can ask him. He'll take you home." I nod to where Taylor is waiting at the entrance of the living room.

"That's fine, I can get myself home, thank you."

No! Accept the ride, Ana. Why does she do this?

"Are you going to defy me at every turn?"

"Why change a habit of a lifetime?" She gives me a blank look.

That's it in a nutshell—why our arrangement was doomed from the start. She's just not cut out for this, and deep down, I always knew it. I close my eyes.

I am such a fool.

I try a softer approach, pleading with her.

"Please, Ana. Let Taylor take you home."

"I'll get the car, Miss Steele," Taylor announces with quiet authority and leaves. Maybe she'll listen to him. She glances around, but he's already gone down to the basement to fetch the car.

She turns back to me, her eyes wider all of a sudden. And I hold my breath. I really can't believe she's going. This is the last time I'll see her, and she looks so sad. It cuts deep that I'm the one responsible for that look. I take a hesitant step forward; I want to hold her one more time and beg her to stay.

She steps back, and it's a move that signals all too clearly that she doesn't want me. I've driven her away.

I freeze. "I don't want you to go."

"I can't stay. I know what I want, and you can't give it to me, and I can't give you what you need."

Oh, please, Ana—let me hold you one more time. Smell your

sweet, sweet scent. Feel you in my arms. I step toward her again, but she holds up her hands, halting me.

"Don't—please." She recoils, panic etched on her face. "I can't do this." And she grabs her suitcase and backpack and heads for the foyer. I follow, meek and helpless in her wake, my eyes fixed on her small frame.

In the foyer I call the elevator. I can't take my eyes off her . . . her delicate, elfin face, those lips, the way her dark lashes fan out and cast a shadow over her pale, pale cheeks. Words fail me as I try to memorize every detail. I have no dazzling lines, no quick wit, no arrogant commands. I have nothing—nothing but a yawning void inside my chest.

The elevator doors open and Ana heads straight in. She looks around at me—and for a moment her mask slips, and there it is: my pain reflected on her beautiful face.

No . . . Ana. Don't go.

"Good-bye, Christian."

"Ana . . . good-bye."

The doors close, and she's gone.

I sink slowly to the floor and put my head in my hands. The void is now cavernous and aching, overwhelming me.

Grey, what the hell have you done?

WHEN I LOOK UP again, the paintings in my foyer, my Madonnas, bring a mirthless smile to my lips. The idealization of motherhood. All of them gazing at their infants, or staring inauspiciously down at me.

They're right to look at me that way. She's gone. She's really gone. The best thing that ever happened to me. After she said she'd never leave. She promised me she'd never leave. I close my eyes, shutting out those lifeless, pitying stares, and tip my head back against the wall. Okay, she said it in her sleep—and like the fool I am, I believed her. I've always known deep down I was no good for her, and she was too good for me. This is how it should be.

Then why do I feel like shit? Why is this so painful?

The chime announcing the arrival of the elevator forces my eyes open again, and my heart leaps into my mouth. She's back. I sit paralyzed, waiting, and the doors pull back—and Taylor steps out and momentarily freezes.

Hell. How long have I been sitting here?

"Miss Steele is home, Mr. Grey," he says, as if he addresses me while I'm prostrate on the floor every day.

"How was she?" I ask, as dispassionately as I can, though I really want to know.

"Upset, sir," he says, showing no emotion whatsoever.

I nod, dismissing him. But he doesn't leave.

"Can I get you anything, sir?" he asks, much too kindly for my liking.

"No." *Go. Leave me alone.*

"Sir," he says, and he exits, leaving me slouched on the foyer floor.

Much as I'd like to sit here all day and wallow in my despair, I can't. I want an update from Welch, and I need to call Leila's poor excuse for a husband.

And I need a shower. Perhaps this agony will wash away in the shower.

As I stand I touch the wooden table that dominates the foyer, my fingers absentmindedly tracing its delicate marquetry. I'd have liked to fuck Miss Steele over this. I close my eyes, imagining her sprawled across this table, her head held back, chin up, mouth open in ecstasy, and her luscious hair pooling over the edge. Shit, it makes me hard just thinking about it.

Fuck.

The pain in my gut twists and tightens.

She's gone, Grey. Get used to it.

And drawing on years of enforced control, I bring my body to heel.

THE SHOWER IS BLISTERING, the temperature just a notch below painful, the way I like it. I stand beneath the cascade, trying to forget her, hoping this heat will scorch her out of my head and wash her scent off my body.

If she's going to leave, there's no coming back.

Never.

I scrub my hair with grim determination.

Good riddance.

And I suck in a breath.

No. Not good riddance.

I raise my face to the streaming water. It's not good riddance at all—I am going to miss her. I lean my forehead against the tiles. Just last night she was in here with me. I stare at my hands, my fingers caressing the line of grout in the tiles where only yesterday her hands were braced against the wall.

Fuck this.

Switching off the water, I step out of the shower cubicle. As I wrap a towel around my waist, it sinks in: each day will be darker and emptier, because she's no longer in it.

No more facetious, witty e-mails.

No more of her smart mouth.

No more curiosity.

Her bright blue eyes will no longer regard me in thinly veiled amusement . . . or shock . . . or lust. I stare at the brooding morose jerk staring back at me in the bathroom mirror.

"What the hell have you done, asshole?" I sneer at him. He mouths the words back at me with vitriolic contempt. And the bastard blinks at me, big gray eyes raw with misery.

"She's better off without you. You can't be what she wants. You can't give her what she needs. She wants hearts and flowers. She deserves better than you, you fucked-up prick." Repulsed by the image glowering back at me, I turn away from the mirror.

To hell with shaving for today.

I dry off at my chest of drawers and grab some underwear and a clean T-shirt. As I turn I notice a small box on my pillow. The rug is pulled from under me again, revealing once more the abyss beneath, its jaws open, waiting for me, and my anger turns to fear.

It's something from her. What would she give me? I drop my

clothes and, taking a deep breath, sit on the bed and pick up the box.

It's a glider. A model-making kit for a Blaník L23. A scribbled note falls from the top of the box and wafts onto the bed.

This reminded me of a happy time.
Thank you.

Ana

It's the perfect present from the perfect girl.

Pain lances through me.

Why is this so painful? *Why?*

Some long-lost, ugly memory stirs, trying to sink its teeth into the here and now. No. That is not a place I want my mind to return to. I get up, tossing the box onto the bed, and dress hurriedly. When I'm finished I grab the box and the note and head for my study. I will handle this better from my seat of power.

MY CONVERSATION WITH WELCH is brief. My conversation with Russell Reed—the miserable lying bastard who married Leila—is briefer. I didn't know that they'd wed during one drunken weekend in Vegas. No wonder their marriage failed after just eighteen months. She left him twelve weeks ago. *So where are you now, Leila Williams? What have you been doing?*

I focus my mind on Leila, trying to think of some clue from our past that might tell me where she is. I need to know. I need to know she's safe. And why she came here. Why me?

She wanted more, and I didn't, but that was long ago. It was easy when she left—our arrangement was terminated by mutual consent. In fact, our whole arrangement had been exemplary: just how it should be. She was mischievous when she was with me, deliberately so, and not the broken creature that Gail described.

I recall how much she enjoyed our sessions in the playroom. Leila loved the kink. A memory surfaces—I'm tying her big toes together, turning her feet in so she can't clench her backside and avoid the pain. Yeah, she loved all that shit, and so did I. She was a great submissive. But she never captured my attention like Anastasia Steele.

She never drove me to distraction like Ana.

I gaze at the glider kit on my desk and trace the edges of the box with my finger, knowing that Ana's fingers have touched it.

My sweet Anastasia.

What a contrast you are to all the women I've known. The only woman I've ever chased, and the one woman who can't give me what I want.

I don't understand.

I've come alive since I've known her. These last few weeks have been the most exciting, the most unpredictable, the most fascinating in my life. I've been enticed from my monochrome world into one rich with color—and yet she can't be what I need.

I put my head in my hands. She will never like what I do. I tried to convince myself that we could work up to the rougher shit, but that's not going to happen, ever. She's better off without me. What would she want with a fucked-up monster who can't bear to be touched?

And yet she bought me this thoughtful gift. Who does that for me, apart from my family? I study the box once more and open it. All the plastic parts of the craft are stuck on one grid, swathed in cellophane. Memories of her squealing in the glider during the wingover come to mind—her hands up, braced against the Perspex canopy. I can't help but smile.

Lord, that was so much fun—the equivalent of pulling her pigtails in the playground. Ana in pigtails . . . I shut down that thought immediately. I don't want to go there, our first bath. And all I'm left with is the thought that I won't see her again.

The abyss yawns open.

No. Not again.

I need to make this plane. It will be a distraction. Ripping open the cellophane, I scan the instructions. I need glue, modeling glue. I search through my desk drawers.

Shit. Nestled at the back of one drawer I find the red leather box containing the Cartier earrings. I never got the chance to give them to her—and now I never will.

I call Andrea and leave a message on her cell, asking her to cancel tonight. I can't face the gala, not without my date.

I open the red leather box and examine the earrings. They are beautiful: simple yet elegant, just like the enchanting Miss Steele . . . who left me this morning because I punished her . . . because I pushed her too hard. I cradle my head once again. But she let me. She didn't stop me. She let me because she *loves* me. The thought is horrifying, and I dismiss it immediately. She can't. It's simple: no one can feel like that about me. Not if they know me.

Move on, Grey. Focus.

Where's the damned glue? I stash the earrings back in the drawer and continue my search. Nothing.

I buzz Taylor.

"Mr. Grey?"

"I need some modeling glue."

He pauses for a moment. "For what sort of model, sir?"

"A model glider."

"Balsa wood or plastic?"

"Plastic."

"I have some. I'll bring it down now, sir."

I thank him, a little stunned that he has modeling glue. Moments later he knocks on the door.

"Come in."

He paces into my study and places the small plastic container on my desk. He doesn't leave and I have to ask.

"Why do you have this?"

"I build the odd plane." His face reddens.

"Oh?" My curiosity is piqued.

"Flying was my first love, sir."

I don't understand.

"Color blind," he explains flatly.

"So you became a Marine?"

"Yes, sir."

"Thank you for this."

"No problem, Mr. Grey. Have you eaten?"

His question takes me by surprise.

"I'm not hungry, Taylor. Please, go, enjoy the afternoon with your daughter, and I'll see you tomorrow. I won't bother you again."

He pauses for a moment, and my irritation builds. *Go.*

"I'm good." *Hell,* my voice is choked.

"Sir." He nods. "I'll return tomorrow evening."

I give him a quick dismissive nod, and he's gone.

When was the last time Taylor offered me anything to eat? I must look more fucked up than I thought. Sulking, I grab the glue.

THE GLIDER IS IN the palm of my hand. I marvel at it with a sense of achievement, memories of that flight nudging my consciousness. Anastasia was impossible to wake—I smile as I recall—and once up she was difficult, disarming and beautiful, and funny.

Christ, that was fun: her girlish excitement during the flight, the squealing, and afterward, our kiss.

It was my first attempt at *more.* It's extraordinary that over such a short time I have collected so many happy memories.

The pain surfaces once more—nagging, aching, reminding me of all that I've lost.

Focus on the glider, Grey.

Now I have to stick the transfers in place; they're fiddly little suckers.

FINALLY THE LAST ONE is on and drying. My glider has its own FAA registration. November. Nine. Five. Two. Echo. Charlie.

Echo Charlie.

I look up and the light is fading. It's late. My first thought is that I can show this to Ana.

No more Ana.

I clench my teeth and stretch my stiff shoulders. Standing

slowly, I realize I haven't eaten all day or had anything to drink, and my head is throbbing.

I feel like shit.

I check my phone in the hope that she's called, but there's only a text from Andrea.

> CC Gala canx.
> Hope all well.
> A

While I'm reading Andrea's message the phone buzzes. My heart rate immediately spikes, then falls when I recognize it's Elena.

"Hello." I don't bother to disguise my disappointment.

"Christian, is that any way to say hi? What's eating you?" she scolds, but her voice is full of humor.

I stare out the window. It's dusk over Seattle. I wonder briefly what Ana is doing. I don't want to tell Elena what's happened; I don't want to say the words out loud and make them a reality.

"Christian? What gives? Tell me." Her tone shifts to brusque and annoyed.

"She left me," I mutter, sounding morose.

"Oh." Elena sounds surprised. "Want me to come over?"

"No."

She takes a deep breath. "This life isn't for everyone."

"I know."

"Hell, Christian, you sound like shit. Do you want to go out to dinner?"

"No."

"I'm coming over."

"No, Elena. I'm not good company. I'm tired and I want to be alone. I'll call you during the week."

"Christian . . . it's for the best."

"I know. Good-bye."

I hang up. I don't want to talk to her; she encouraged me to fly down to Savannah. Perhaps she knew this day would come. I scowl at the phone, toss it onto my desk, and go in search of something to drink and eat.

I EXAMINE THE CONTENTS of my fridge.

Nothing appeals.

In the cupboard I find a bag of pretzels. I open them and eat one after the other as I walk to the window. Outside, night has fallen; lights twinkle and wink through the pouring rain. The world moves on.

Move on, Grey.

Move on.

SUNDAY, JUNE 5, 2011

I gaze up at the bedroom ceiling. Sleep eludes me. I'm tormented by Ana's fragrance, which still clings to my bedsheets. I pull her pillow over my face to breathe in her scent. It's torture, it's heaven, and for a moment I contemplate death by suffocation.

Get a grip, Grey.

I rerun the morning's events in my head. Could they have unfolded any differently? As a rule I never do this, because it's a waste of energy, but today I'm looking for clues as to where I went wrong. And no matter how I play it out, I know in my bones we would have reached this impasse, whether it was this morning, or in a week, or a month, or a year. Better that it happened now, before I inflicted any further pain on Anastasia.

I think of her huddled in her little white bed. I can't picture her in the new apartment—I've not been there—but I imagine her in that room in Vancouver where I once slept with her. I shake my head; that was the best night's sleep I'd had in years. The radio alarm reads 2:00 in the morning. I have lain here for two hours, my mind churning. I take a deep breath, inhaling her scent once more, and I close my eyes.

Mommy can't see me. I stand in front of her. She can't see me. She's asleep with her eyes open. Or sick.

I hear a rattle. His keys. He's back.

I run and hide and make myself small under the table in the kitchen. My cars are here with me.

Bang. The door slams shut, making me jump.

Through my fingers I see Mommy. She turns her head to see him. Then she's asleep on the couch. He's wearing his

big boots with the shiny buckles and standing over Mommy
shouting. He hits Mommy with a belt. *Get Up! Get Up! You
are one fucked-up bitch. You are one fucked-up bitch.* Mommy
makes a noise. A wailing noise.
Stop. Stop hitting Mommy. Stop hitting Mommy.
I run at him and hit him and I hit him and I hit him.
But he laughs and smacks me across the face.
No! Mommy shouts.
You are one fucked-up bitch.
Mommy makes herself small. Small like me. And then she's
quiet. *You are one fucked-up bitch. You are one fucked-up
bitch. You are one fucked-up bitch.*
I am under the table. I have my fingers in my ears and I
close my eyes. The sound stops. He turns and I can see
his boots as he stomps into the kitchen. He carries the
belt, slapping it against his leg. He is trying to find me. He
stoops down and grins. He smells nasty. Of smoking and
drinking and bad smells. *There you are, you little shit.*

A chilling wail wakes me. I'm drenched in sweat and my heart
is pounding. I sit bolt upright in bed.
Fuck.
The eerie noise was from me.
I take a deep steadying breath, trying to rid my memory of the
smell of body odor and cheap bourbon and stale Camel cigarettes.
You are one fucked-up son of a bitch.
Ana's words ring in my head.
Like his.
Fuck.
I couldn't help the crack whore.
I tried. Good God, I tried.
There you are, you little shit.
But I could help Ana.
I let her go.
I had to let her go.

She didn't need all this shit.

I glance at the clock: it's 3:30. I head into the kitchen and after drinking a large glass of water I make my way to the piano.

I WAKE AGAIN WITH a jolt and it's light—early-morning sunshine fills the room. I was dreaming of Ana: Ana kissing me, her tongue in my mouth, my fingers in her hair; pressing her delectable body against me, her hands tethered above her head.

Where is she?

For one sweet moment I forget all that transpired yesterday— then it floods back.

She's gone.

Fuck.

The evidence of my desire presses into the mattress—but the memory of her bright eyes, clouded with hurt and humiliation as she left, soon solves that problem.

Feeling like shit, I lie on my back and stare at the ceiling, arms behind my head. The day stretches out before me, and for the first time in years, I don't know what to do with myself. I check the time again: 5:58.

Hell, I might as well go for a run.

PROKOFIEV'S "ARRIVAL OF THE Montagues and Capulets" blares in my ears as I pound the sidewalk through the early morning quiet of Fourth Avenue. I ache everywhere—my lungs are bursting, my head is throbbing, and the yawning, dull ache of loss eats away at my insides. I cannot run from this pain, though I'm trying. I stop to change the music and drag precious air into my lungs. I want something . . . violent. "Pump It," by the Black Eyed Peas, yeah. I pick up the pace.

I find myself running down Vine Street, and I know it's insane, but I hope to see her. As I near her street my heart races still harder and my anxiety escalates. I'm not desperate to see her—I just want to check that she's okay. No, that's not true. I want to see her. Finally on her street, I pace past her apartment building.

All is quiet—an Oldsmobile trundles up the road, two dog walkers are out—but there's no sign of life from inside her apartment. Crossing the street, I pause on the sidewalk opposite, then duck into the doorway of an apartment building to catch my breath.

The curtains of one room are closed, the others open. Perhaps that's her room. Maybe she's still asleep—if she's there at all. A nightmare scenario forms in my mind: she went out last night, got drunk, met someone . . .

No.

Bile rises in my throat. The thought of her body in someone else's hands, some asshole basking in the warmth of her smile, making her giggle, making her laugh—making her come. It takes all my self-control not to go barging through the front door of her apartment to check that she's there and on her own.

You brought this on yourself, Grey.

Forget her. She's not for you.

I tug my Seahawks cap low over my face and sprint on down Western Avenue.

My jealousy is raw and angry; it fills the gaping hole. I hate it—it stirs something deep in my psyche that I really don't want to examine. I run harder, away from that memory, away from the pain, away from Anastasia Steele.

IT'S DUSK OVER SEATTLE. I stand up and stretch. I've been at my desk in my study all day, and it's been productive. Ros has worked hard, too. She's prepared and sent me a first draft business plan and letter of intent for SIP.

At least I'll be able to keep an eye on Ana.

The thought is painful and appealing in equal measure.

I've read and commented on two patent applications, a few contracts, and a new design spec, and while lost in the detail of those, I have not thought about her. The little glider is still on my desk, taunting me, reminding me of happier times, like she said. I picture her standing in the doorway of my study, wearing one of my T-shirts, all long legs and blue eyes, just before she seduced me.

Another first.

I miss her.

There—I admit it. I check my phone, hoping in vain, and there's a text from Elliot.

Beer, hotshot?

I respond:

No. Busy.

Elliot's response is immediate.

Fuck you, then.

Yeah. Fuck me.

Nothing from Ana: no missed call. No e-mail. The nagging pain in my gut intensifies. She's not going to call. She wanted out. She wanted to get away from me, and I can't blame her.

It's for the best.

I head to the kitchen for a change of scenery.

Gail is back. The kitchen has been cleaned, and there's a pot bubbling on the stove. Smells good . . . but I'm not hungry. She walks in while I'm eyeing what's cooking.

"Good evening, sir."

"Gail."

She pauses—surprised by something. Surprised by me? *Shit, I must look bad.*

"Chicken Chasseur?" she asks, her voice uncertain.

"Sure," I mutter.

"For two?" she asks.

I stare at her, and she looks embarrassed.

"For one."

"Ten minutes?" she says, her voice wavering.

"Fine." My voice is frigid.

I turn to leave.

"Mr. Grey?" She stops me.

"What, Gail?"

"It's nothing. Sorry to disturb you." She turns to the stove to stir the chicken, and I head off to have another shower.

Christ, even my staff have noticed that something's rotten in the state of fucking Denmark.

MONDAY, JUNE 6, 2011

I dread going to bed. It's after midnight, and I'm tired, but I sit at my piano, playing the Bach Marcello piece over and over again. Remembering her head resting on my shoulder, I can almost smell her sweet fragrance.

For fuck's sake, she said she'd try!

I stop playing and clutch my head in both hands, my elbows hammering out two discordant chords as I lean on the keys. She said she'd try, but she fell at the first hurdle.

Then she ran.

Why did I hit her so hard?

Deep inside I know the answer—because she asked me to, and I was too impetuous and selfish to resist the temptation. Seduced by her challenge, I seized the opportunity to move us on to where I wanted us to be. And she didn't safe-word, and I hurt her more than she could take—when I promised her I'd never do that.

What a fucking fool I am.

How could she trust me after that? It's right that she's gone. Why the hell would she want to be with me, anyway?

I contemplate getting drunk. I have not been drunk since I was fifteen—well, once, when I was twenty-one. I loathe the loss of control: I know what alcohol can do to a man. I shudder and snap my mind shut to those memories, and decide to call it a night.

Lying in my bed, I pray for a dreamless sleep . . . but if I am to dream, I want to dream of her.

Mommy is pretty today. She sits down and lets me brush her hair. She looks at me in the mirror and she smiles her special smile. Her special smile for me. There is a loud

noise. A crash. He's back. No! *Where the fuck are you, bitch?*
Got a friend in need here. A friend with dough. Mommy
stands and takes my hand and pushes me into her closet. I
sit on her shoes and try to be quiet and cover my ears and
close my eyes tight. The clothes smell of Mommy. I like
the smell. I like being here. Away from him. He is shouting.
Where is the little fucking runt? He has my hair and he pulls
me out of the closet. *Don't want you spoiling the party, you
little shit.* He slaps Mommy hard on her face. *Make it good
for my friend and you get your fix, bitch.* Mommy looks at
me and she has tears. Don't cry, Mommy. Another man
comes into the room. A big man with dirty hair. The big
man smiles at Mommy. I am pulled into the other room.
He pushes me onto the floor and I hurt my knees. *Now,
what am I going to do with you, you piece of shit?* He smells
nasty. He smells of beer and he is smoking a cigarette.

I wake. My heart is hammering like I've run forty blocks chased
by the hounds of hell. I vault out of bed, pushing the nightmare
back into the recesses of my consciousness, and hurry to the
kitchen to fetch a glass of water.

I need to see Flynn. The nightmares are worse than ever. I
didn't have nightmares when I slept with Ana beside me.

Hell.

It never occurred to me to sleep with any of my subs. Well, I
never felt the inclination. Was I worried that they might touch me
in the night? I don't know. It took an inebriated innocent to show
me how restful it could be.

I'd watched my subs sleep before, but it was always as a prelude
to waking them for some sexual relief.

I remember gazing at Ana for hours when she slept at The
Heathman. The longer I watched her the more beautiful she
became: her flawless skin luminous in the soft light, her dark
hair fanning out on the white pillow, and her eyelashes fluttering
while she slept. Her lips were parted, and I could see her teeth,
and her tongue when she licked her lips. It was a most arousing

experience—just watching her. And when I finally went to sleep beside her, listening to her even breathing, watching her breasts rise and fall with each breath, I slept well . . . so well.

I wander into my study and pick up the glider. The sight of it elicits a fond smile and comforts me. I feel both proud to have made it and ridiculous for what I am about to do. It was her last gift to me. Her first gift being . . . what?

Of course. *Herself.*

She sacrificed herself to my need. My greed. My lust. My ego . . . my fucking damaged ego.

Damn, will this pain ever just stop?

Feeling a little foolish, I take the glider with me to bed.

"**WHAT WOULD YOU LIKE** for breakfast, sir?"

"Just coffee, Gail."

She hesitates. "Sir, you didn't eat your dinner."

"And?"

"Maybe you're coming down with something."

"Gail, just coffee. Please." I shut her down—this is none of her business. Her lips thin, but she nods and turns to the Gaggia. I head in to the study to collect my papers for the office and look for a padded envelope.

I CALL ROS FROM the car.

"Great work on the SIP material, but the business plan needs some revision. Let's offer."

"Christian, this is fast."

"I want to move quickly. I've e-mailed you my thoughts on the offering price. I'll be in the office from seven thirty. Let's meet."

"If you're sure."

"I'm sure."

"Okay. I'll call Andrea to schedule. I have the stats on Detroit v. Savannah."

"Bottom line?"

"Detroit."

"I see."

Shit . . . not Savannah.

"Let's talk later." I hang up.

I sit, brooding in the back of the Audi, as Taylor speeds through the traffic. I wonder how Anastasia will be getting to work this morning. Perhaps she bought a car yesterday, though somehow I doubt it. I wonder if she feels as miserable as I do . . . I hope not. Maybe she's realized that I was a ridiculous infatuation.

She can't love me.

And certainly not now—not after all I've done to her. No one's ever said they loved me, except Mom and Dad, of course, but even then it was out of their sense of duty. Flynn's nagging words about unconditional parental love—even for kids who are adopted—ring in my head. But I've never been convinced; I've been nothing but a disappointment to them.

"Mr. Grey?"

"Sorry, what is it?" Taylor has caught me unawares. He's holding the car door open, waiting for me with a look of concern.

"We're here, sir."

Shit . . . how long have we been here? "Thanks. I'll let you know what time this evening."

Focus, Grey.

ANDREA AND OLIVIA BOTH look up as I come out of the elevator. Olivia flutters her eyelashes and tucks a strand of hair behind her ear. *Christ—I'm done with this silly girl.* I need HR to move her to another department.

"Coffee, please, Olivia—and get me a croissant." She leaps up to follow my orders.

"Andrea—get me Welch, Barney, then Flynn, then Claude Bastille on the phone. I don't want to be disturbed at all, not even by my mother . . . unless . . . unless Anastasia Steele calls. Okay?"

"Yes, sir. Do you want to go through your schedule now?"

"No. I need coffee and something to eat first." I scowl at Olivia, who is moving at a snail's pace toward the elevator.

"Yes, Mr. Grey," Andrea calls after me as I open the door to my office.

From my briefcase I take the padded envelope that holds my most precious possession—the glider. I place it on my desk, and my mind drifts to Miss Steele.

She'll be starting her new job this morning, meeting new people . . . new men. The thought is depressing. She'll forget me.

No, she won't forget me. Women always remember the first man they fucked, don't they? I'll always hold a place in her memory, for that alone. But I don't want to be a memory: I want to stay in her mind. I need to stay in her mind. What can I do?

There's a knock at the door and Andrea appears. "Coffee and croissants for you, Mr. Grey."

"Come in."

As she scurries over to my desk her eyes dart to the glider, but wisely she holds her tongue. She places breakfast on my desk.

Black coffee. *Well done, Andrea.* "Thanks."

"I've left messages for Welch, Barney, and Bastille. Flynn is calling back in five."

"Good. I want you to cancel any social engagements I have this week. No lunches, nothing in the evening. Get Barney on the phone and find me the number of a good florist."

She scribbles furiously on her notepad.

"Sir, we use Arcadia's Roses. Would you like me to send flowers for you?"

"No, give me the number. I'll do it myself. That's all."

She nods and leaves promptly, as if she can't get out of my office fast enough. A few moments later the phone buzzes. It's Barney.

"Barney, I need you to make me a stand for a model glider."

BETWEEN MEETINGS I CALL the florist and order two dozen white roses for Ana, to be delivered to her home this evening. That way she won't be embarrassed or inconvenienced at work.

And she won't be able to forget me.

"Would you like a message with the flowers, sir?" the florist asks.

A message for Ana?

What to say?

Come back. I'm sorry. I won't hit you again.

The words pop unbidden into my head, making me frown.

"Um . . . something like, 'Congratulations on your first day at work. I hope it went well.' " I spy the glider on my desk. " 'And thank you for the glider. That was very thoughtful. It has pride of place on my desk. Christian.' "

The florist reads it back to me.

Damn, it doesn't express what I want to say to her at all.

"Will that be all, Mr. Grey?"

"Yes. Thank you."

"You're welcome, sir, and have a nice day."

I look daggers at the phone. *Nice day my ass.*

"HEY, MAN, WHAT'S EATING you?" Claude gets up from the floor, where I've just knocked him flat on his lean, mean rear end. "You're on fire this afternoon, Grey." He rises slowly, with the grace of a big cat reassessing its prey. We are sparring alone in the basement gym at Grey House.

"I'm pissed off," I hiss.

His expression is cool as we circle each other.

"Not a good idea to enter the ring if your thoughts are elsewhere," Claude says, amused, but not taking his eyes off me.

"I'm finding it helps."

"More on your left. Protect your right. Hand up, Grey."

He swings and hits me on my shoulder, almost knocking me off balance.

"Concentrate, Grey. None of your boardroom bullshit in here. Or is it a girl? Some fine piece of ass finally cramping your cool." He sneers, goading me. It works: I middle-kick to his side and drop-punch once, then twice, and he staggers back, dreadlocks flying.

"Mind your own fucking business, Bastille."

"Whoa, we have found the source of the pain," Claude crows in triumph. He swings suddenly, but I anticipate his action and block him, thrusting up with a punch and a swift kick. He jumps back this time, impressed.

"Whatever shit's happening in your privileged little world, Grey, it's working. Bring it on."

Oh, he is going down. I lunge at him.

THE TRAFFIC IS LIGHT on the way home.

"Taylor, can we make a detour?"

"Where to, sir?"

"Can you drive past Miss Steele's apartment?"

"Yes, sir."

I've got used to this ache. It seems to be ever-present, like tinnitus. In meetings it's muted and less obtrusive; it's only when I'm alone with my thoughts that it flares up and rages inside me. How long does this last?

As we approach her apartment, my heartbeat spikes.

Perhaps I'll see her.

The possibility is thrilling and unsettling. And I realize that I have thought of nothing but her since she left. Her absence is my constant companion.

"Drive slow," I instruct Taylor as we near her building.

The lights are on.

She's home!

I hope she's alone, and missing me.

Has she received my flowers?

I want to check my phone to see if she's sent me a message, but I can't drag my gaze away from her apartment; I don't want to miss seeing her. Is she well? Is she thinking about me? I wonder how her first day at work went.

"Again, sir?" Taylor asks, as we slowly cruise past, and the apartment disappears from view.

"No." I exhale; I hadn't realized I'd stopped breathing. As we head back to Escala I sift through my e-mails and texts, hoping for something from her . . . but there's nothing. There's a text from Elena.

> You okay?

I ignore it.

IT'S QUIET IN MY apartment; I'd not really noticed before. Anastasia's absence has accentuated the silence.

Taking a sip of cognac, I wander listlessly into my library. It's ironic I never showed her this room, given her love of literature. I expect to find some solace in here because the room holds no memories of us. I survey all my books, neatly shelved and cataloged, and my eyes stray to the billiard table. Does she play billiards? I don't suppose she does.

An image of her spread-eagled over the green baize springs to my mind. There may not be any memories in here, but my mind is more than capable, and more than willing, to create vivid erotic images of the lovely Miss Steele.

I can't bear it.

I take another swig of cognac and head out of the room.

TUESDAY, JUNE 7, 2011

We're fucking. Fucking hard. Against the bathroom door. She's mine. I bury myself in her, again and again. Glorying in her: the feel of her, her smell, her taste. Fisting my hand in her hair, holding her in place. Holding her ass. Her legs wrapped around my waist. She cannot move; she's pinioned by me. Wrapped around me like silk. Her hands pulling my hair. Oh yes. I'm home, she's home. This is the place I want to be . . . inside her . . .

She. Is. Mine. Her muscles are tightening as she comes, clenching around me, her head back. Come for me! She cries out and I follow . . . oh yes, my sweet, sweet Anastasia. She smiles, sleepy, sated—and oh so sexy. She stands and gazes at me, that playful smile on her lips, then pushes me away and walks backward, saying nothing. I grab her and we're in the playroom. I'm holding her down over the bench. I raise my arm to punish her, belt in hand . . . and she disappears. She's by the door. Her face white, shocked and sad, and she's silently drifting away . . . The door has disappeared, and she won't stop. She holds out her hands in entreaty. *Join me*, she whispers, but she's moving backward, getting fainter . . . disappearing before my eyes . . . vanishing . . . she's gone. *No!* I shout. *No!* But I have no voice. I have nothing. I'm mute. Mute . . . again.

I wake, confused.
Shit—it's a dream. Another vivid dream.
Different, though.

Hell! I'm a sticky mess. Briefly I feel that long-forgotten but familiar sense of fear and exhilaration—but Elena doesn't own me now.

Jesus H. Christ, I've come for Team USA. This hasn't happened to me since I was, what? Fifteen, sixteen?

I lie back in the darkness, disgusted with myself. I drag my T-shirt off and wipe myself down. There's semen everywhere. I find myself smirking in the darkness, despite the dull ache of loss. The erotic dream was worth it. The rest of it . . . fucking hell. I turn over and go back to sleep.

He is gone. Mommy is sitting on the couch. She is quiet. She looks at the wall and blinks sometimes. I stand in front of her, but she doesn't see me. I wave and she sees me, but she waves me away. No, Maggot, not now. He hurts Mommy. He hurts me. I hate him. He makes me so mad. It's best when it's just Mommy and me. She is mine then. My Mommy. My tummy hurts. It is hungry again. I am in the kitchen, looking for cookies. I pull the chair to the cupboard and climb up. I find a box of crackers. It is the only thing in the cupboard. I sit down on the chair and open the box. There are two left. I eat them. They taste good. I hear him. He's back. I jump down and I run to my bedroom and climb into bed. I pretend to be asleep. He pokes me with his finger. *Stay here, you little shit. I'm going to fuck your bitch of a mother. I don't want to see your fuck-ugly face for the rest of the evening. Understand?* He slaps my face when I don't reply. *Or you get the burn, you little prick.* No. No. I don't like that. I don't like the burn. It hurts. *Got it, retard?* I know he wants me to cry. But it's hard. I can't make the noise. He hits me with his fist—

Startled awake again, I lie panting in the pale dawn light, waiting for my heart rate to slow, trying to lose the acrid taste of fear in my mouth.

She saved you from this shit, Grey.

You didn't relive the pain of these memories when she was with you. Why did you let her leave?

I glance at the clock: 5:15. Time for a run.

HER BUILDING LOOKS GLOOMY; it's still in shadow, untouched by the early-morning sun. Fitting. It reflects my mood. Her apartment is dark inside, yet the curtains to the room I watched before are drawn. It must be her room.

I hope to God that she's sleeping alone up there. I envisage her curled up on her white iron bed, a small ball of Ana. Is she dreaming of me? Do I give her nightmares? Has she forgotten me?

I've never felt this miserable, not even as a teenager. Maybe before I was a Grey . . . my memory spirals back. No, no—not awake as well. This is too much. Pulling my hood up and leaning against the granite wall, I'm hidden in the doorway of the building opposite. The awful thought crosses my mind that I might be standing here in a week, a month . . . a year? Watching, waiting, just to catch a glimpse of the girl who used to be mine. It's painful. I've become what she's always accused me of being—her stalker.

I can't go on like this. I have to see her. See that she's okay. I need to erase the last image I have of her: hurt, humiliated, defeated . . . and leaving me.

I have to think of a way.

BACK AT ESCALA, GAIL watches me impassively.

"I didn't ask for this." I stare at the omelet she's placed in front of me.

"I'll throw it away, then, Mr. Grey," she says, and reaches for the plate. She knows I hate waste, but she doesn't quail at my hard stare.

"You did this on purpose, Mrs. Jones." Interfering woman.

And she smiles, a small victorious smile. I scowl, but she's unfazed, and with the memory of last night's nightmare lingering, I devour my breakfast.

COULD I JUST CALL Ana and say hi? Would she take my call? My eyes wander to the glider on my desk. She asked for a clean break. I should honor that and leave her alone. But I want to hear her voice. For a moment I contemplate calling her and hanging up, just to hear her speak.

"Christian? Christian, are you okay?"

"Sorry, Ros, what was that?"

"You're so distracted. I've never seen you like this."

"I'm fine," I snap.

Shit—concentrate, Grey. "What were you saying?"

Ros eyes me suspiciously. "I was saying that SIP is in more financial difficulty than we thought. Are you sure you want to go ahead?"

"Yes." My voice is vehement. "I am."

"Their team will be here this afternoon to sign the heads of agreement."

"Good. Now, what's the latest on our proposal for Eamon Kavanagh?"

I STAND BROODING, STARING down through the slatted wooden blinds at Taylor, who is parked outside Flynn's office. It's late afternoon and I'm still thinking about Ana.

"Christian, I'm more than happy to take your money and watch you stare out the window, but I don't think the view is the reason you're here," Flynn says.

When I turn to face him he's regarding me with an air of polite anticipation. I sigh and make my way to his couch.

"The nightmares are back. Like never before."

Flynn lifts a brow. "The same ones?"

"Yes."

"What's changed?" He cocks his head to one side, waiting for my response. When I remain mute, he adds, "Christian, you look as miserable as sin. Something's happened."

I feel like I did with Elena; part of me doesn't want to tell him, because then it's real.

"I met a girl."

"And?"

"She left me."

He looks surprised. "Women have left you before. Why is this different?"

I stare at him blankly.

Why is it different? *Because Ana was different.*

My thoughts blur together in a colorful tangled tapestry: she wasn't a submissive. We had no contract. She was sexually inexperienced. She was the first woman I wanted more from than just sex. Christ—all the firsts I experienced with her: the first girl I'd slept beside, the first virgin, the first to meet my family, the first to fly in *Charlie Tango*, the first I took soaring.

Yeah . . . Different.

Flynn interrupts my thoughts. "It's a simple question, Christian."

"I miss her."

His face remains kind and concerned, but he gives nothing away.

"You've never missed any of the women you were involved with previously?"

"No."

"So there was something different about her," he prompts.

I shrug, but he persists.

"Did you have a contractual relationship with her? Was she a submissive?"

"I'd hoped she would be. But it wasn't for her."

Flynn frowns. "I don't understand."

"I broke one of my rules. I chased this girl, thinking that she'd be interested, and it turned out it wasn't for her."

"Tell me what happened."

The floodgates open and I recount the past month's events, from the moment Ana fell into my office to when she left last Saturday morning.

"I see. You've certainly packed a lot in since we last spoke." He rubs his chin as he studies me. "There are many issues here, Christian. But right now the one I want to focus on is how you felt when she said she loved you."

I inhale sharply, my gut tightening with fear.

"Horrified," I whisper.

"Of course you did." He shakes his head. "You're not the monster you think you are. You're more than worthy of affection, Christian. You know that. I've told you often enough. It's only in your mind that you're not."

I give him a level gaze, ignoring his platitude.

"And how do you feel now?" he asks.

Lost. I feel lost.

"I miss her. I want to see her." I'm in the confessional once more, owning up to my sins: the dark, dark need that I have for her, as if she were an addiction.

"So in spite of the fact that, as you perceive it, she couldn't fulfill your needs, you miss her?"

"Yes. It's not just my perception, John. She can't be what I want her to be, and I can't be what she wants me to be."

"Are you sure?"

"She walked out."

"She walked out because you belted her. If she doesn't share your tastes, can you blame her?"

"No."

"Have you thought about trying a relationship her way?"

What? I stare at him, shocked. He continues, "Did you find sexual relations with her satisfying?"

"Yes, of course," I snap, irritated. He ignores my tone.

"Did you find beating her satisfying?"

"Very."

"Would you like to do it again?"

Do that to her again? And watch her walk out—again?

"No."

"And why's that?"

"Because it's not her scene. I hurt her. Really hurt her . . . and she can't . . . she won't . . ." I pause. "She doesn't enjoy it. She was angry. Really fucking angry." Her expression, her wounded eyes, will haunt me for a long time . . . and I never want to be the cause of that look again.

"Are you surprised?"

I shake my head. "She was mad," I whisper. "I'd never seen her so angry."

"How did that make you feel?"

"Helpless."

"And that's a familiar feeling," he prompts.

"Familiar, how?" *What does he mean?*

"Don't you recognize yourself at all? Your past?" His question knocks me off balance.

Fuck, we've been over and over this.

"No, I don't. It's different. The relationship I had with Mrs. Lincoln was completely different."

"I wasn't referring to Mrs. Lincoln."

"What were you referring to?" My voice is pin-drop quiet, because suddenly I see where he's going with this.

"You know."

I gulp for air, swamped by the impotence and rage of a defenseless child. Yes. The rage. The deep infuriating rage . . . and fear. The darkness swirls angrily inside me.

"It's not the same," I hiss through gritted teeth, as I strain to hold my temper.

"No, it's not," Flynn concedes.

But the image of her rage comes unwelcome to my mind.

"This is what you really like? Me, like this?"

It dampens my anger.

"I know what you're trying to do here, Doctor, but it's an unfair comparison. She asked me to show her. She's a consenting adult, for fuck's sake. She could have safe-worded. She could have told me to stop. She didn't."

"I know. I know." He holds his hand up. "I'm just callously illustrating a point, Christian. You're an angry man, and you have every reason to be. I'm not going to rehash all that right now—you're obviously suffering, and the whole point of these sessions is to move you to a place where you are more accepting and comfortable with yourself." He pauses. "This girl . . ."

"Anastasia," I mutter petulantly.

"Anastasia. She's obviously had a profound effect on you. Her leaving has triggered your abandonment issues and your PTSD. She clearly means much more to you than you're willing to admit to yourself."

I take a sharp breath. *Is that why this is so painful? Because she means more, so much more?*

"You need to focus on where you want to be," Flynn continues. "And it sounds to me like you want to be with this girl. You miss her. Do you want to be with her?"

Be with Ana?

"Yes," I whisper.

"Then you have to focus on that goal. This goes back to what I've been banging on about for our last few sessions—the SFBT. If she's in love with you, as she told you she is, she must be suffering, too. So I repeat my question: have you considered a more conventional relationship with this girl?"

"No, I haven't."

"Why not?"

"Because it's never occurred to me that I could."

"Well if she's not prepared to be your submissive, you can't play the role of dominant."

I glare at him. It's not a role—it's who I am. And from nowhere, I recall an earlier e-mail to Anastasia. My words: *What I think you fail to realize is that in Dom/sub relationships it is the sub who has all the power. That's you. I'll repeat this—you are the one with all the power. Not I. If she doesn't want to do this . . . then neither can I.*

Hope stirs in my chest.

Could I?

Could I have a vanilla relationship with Anastasia?

My scalp prickles.

Fuck. Possibly.

If I could, would she want me back?

"Christian, you have demonstrated that you are an extraordinarily capable person, in spite of your problems. You're a rare individual. Once you focus on a goal, you drive ahead and achieve it—usually surpassing all your own expectations. Listening to you today, it's clear you were focused on getting Anastasia to where you wanted her to be, but you didn't take into account her inexperience or her feelings. It seems to me that you've been so focused on reaching your goal that you missed the journey that you were taking together."

The last month flashes before me: her tripping into my office, her acute embarrassment at Clayton's, her witty, snarky e-mails, her smart mouth . . . her giggle . . . her quiet fortitude and defiance, her courage—and it occurs to me that I have enjoyed every single minute. Every infuriating, distracting, humorous, sensual, carnal second of her—yes, I have. We've been on an extraordinary journey, both of us—well, I certainly have.

My thoughts take a darker turn.

She doesn't know the depths of my depravity, the darkness in my soul, the monster beneath—maybe I should leave her alone.

I'm not worthy of her. She can't love me.

But even as I think the words, I know that I don't have the strength to stay away from her . . . if she'll have me.

Flynn summons my attention. "Christian, think about it. Our time is up now. I want to see you in a few days and talk through some of the other issues you mentioned. I'll have Janet call Andrea and arrange an appointment." He stands, and I know it's time to leave.

"You've given me a lot to think about," I tell him.

"I wouldn't be doing my job if I didn't. Just a few days, Christian. We have so much more to talk about." He shakes my hand and gives me a reassuring smile, and I leave with a small blossom of hope.

STANDING ON THE BALCONY, I survey Seattle at night. Up here I'm at one remove, away from it all. What did she call it?

My ivory tower.

Normally I find it peaceful—but lately my peace of mind has been shattered by a certain blue-eyed young woman.

"Have you thought about trying a relationship her way?" Flynn's words taunt me, suggesting so many possibilities.

Could I win her back? The thought terrifies me.

I take a sip of my cognac. Why would she want me back? Could I ever be what she wants me to be? I won't let go of my hope. I need to find a way.

I need her.

Something startles me—a movement, a shadow at the periphery of my vision. I frown. What the . . . ? I turn toward the shadow, but find nothing. I'm seeing things now. I slug the cognac and head back into the living room.

WEDNESDAY, JUNE 8, 2011

Mommy! Mommy! Mommy is asleep on the floor. She has
been asleep for a long time. I shake her. She doesn't wake
up. I call her. She doesn't wake up. He isn't here and still
Mommy doesn't wake up.

I am thirsty. In the kitchen I pull a chair to the sink and I
have a drink. The water splashes over my sweater. My sweater
is dirty. Mommy is still asleep. Mommy, wake up! She lies
still. She is cold. I fetch my blankie and I cover Mommy and
I lie down on the sticky green rug beside her.

My tummy hurts. It is hungry, but Mommy is still asleep.
I have two toy cars. One red. One yellow. My green car is
gone. They race by the floor where Mommy is sleeping. I
think Mommy is sick. I search for something to eat. In the
icebox I find peas. They are cold. I eat them slowly. They
make my tummy hurt. I sleep beside Mommy. The peas
are gone. In the icebox is something. It smells funny. I lick
it and my tongue sticks. I eat it slowly. It tastes nasty. I drink
some water. I play with my cars and I sleep beside Mommy.
Mommy is so cold and she won't wake up. The door crashes
open. I cover Mommy with my blankie. *Fuck. What the fuck
happened here? Oh, the crazy fucked-up bitch. Shit. Fuck.
Get out of my way, you little shit.* He kicks me and I hit my
head on the floor. My head hurts. He calls somebody and he
goes. He locks the door. I lay down beside Mommy. My head
hurts. The lady policeman is here. No. No. No. Don't touch
me. Don't touch me. Don't touch me. I stay by Mommy. No.
Stay away from me. The lady policeman has my blankie and

she grabs me. I scream. *Mommy. Mommy.* The words are
gone. I can't say the words. Mommy can't hear me. I have no
words.

I wake breathing hard, taking huge gulps of air, checking my
surroundings. Oh, thank God—I'm in my bed. Slowly the fear
recedes. I'm twenty-seven, not four. This shit has to stop.

I used to have my nightmares under control. Maybe one every
couple of weeks, but nothing like this—night after night.

Since she left.

I turn over and lie flat on my back, staring at the ceiling. When
she slept beside me, I slept well. I need her in my life, in my bed.
She was the day to my night. I'm going to get her back.

How?

"Have you thought about trying a relationship her way?"

She wants hearts and flowers. Can I give her that? I frown,
trying to recall the romantic moments in my life . . . And there's
nothing . . . except with Ana. The "more." The gliding, and IHOP,
and taking her up in *Charlie Tango.*

Maybe I *can* do this. I drift back to sleep, the mantra in my
head: *She's mine. She's mine* . . . and I smell her, feel her soft skin,
taste her lips, and hear her moans. Exhausted, I fall into an erotic,
Ana-filled dream.

I wake suddenly. My scalp tingles, and for a moment I think
whatever's disturbed me is external rather than internal. I sit up
and rub my head and slowly scan the room.

In spite of the carnal dream, my body has behaved. Elena
would be pleased. She texted yesterday, but Elena's the last person
I want to talk to—there's only one thing I want to do right now. I
get up and pull on my running gear.

I'm going to check on Ana.

HER STREET IS QUIET except for the rumble of a delivery truck
and the out-of-tune whistling of a solitary dog walker. Her apartment is in darkness, the curtains to her room closed. I keep a silent

vigil from my stalker's hide, staring up at the windows and thinking. I need a plan—a plan to win her back.

As dawn's light brightens her window, I turn my iPod up loud,
and with Moby blaring in my ears I run back to Escala.

"I'LL HAVE A CROISSANT, Mrs. Jones."

She stills in surprise and I raise a brow.

"Apricot preserves?" she asks, recovering.

"Please."

"I'll heat up a couple for you, Mr. Grey. Here's your coffee."

"Thank you, Gail."

She smiles. Is it just because I'm having croissants? If it makes
her that happy, I should have them more often.

IN THE BACK OF the Audi, I plot. I need to get up close and personal with Ana Steele, to begin my campaign to win her back. I
call Andrea, knowing that at 7:15 she won't be at her desk yet, and
I leave a voice mail. "Andrea, as soon as you're in, I want to run
through my schedule for the next few days." There—step one in
my offensive is to make time in my schedule for Ana. What the
hell am I supposed to be doing this week? Currently, I don't have
a clue. Normally I'm on this shit, but lately I've been all over the
place. Now I have a mission to focus on. *You can do this, Grey.*

But deep down I wish I had the courage of my convictions.
Anxiety unfurls in my gut. Can I convince Ana to take me back?
Will she listen? I hope so. This has to work. I miss her.

"MR. GREY, I CANCELED all your social events this week, apart
from the one for tomorrow—I don't know what the occasion is.
Your calendar says Portland, that's it."

Yes! The fucking photographer!

I beam at Andrea, and her eyebrows shoot up in surprise.
"Thanks, Andrea. That's all for now. Send in Sam."

"Sure, Mr. Grey. Would you like some more coffee?"

"Please."

"With milk?"

"Yes. Latte. Thank you."

She smiles politely and leaves.

This is it! My in! The photographer! Now . . . what to do?

MY MORNING HAS BEEN back-to-back meetings, and my staff have been watching me nervously, waiting for me to explode. Okay, that's been my modus operandi for the last few days—but today I feel clearer, calmer, and present; able to deal with everything.

It's now lunchtime; my workout with Claude has gone well. The only fly in the ointment is that there's no more news about Leila. All we know is that she's split up with her husband and she could be anywhere. If she surfaces, Welch will find her.

I'm famished. Olivia sets a plate down on my desk.

"Your sandwich, Mr. Grey."

"Chicken and mayonnaise?"

"Um . . ."

I stare at her. She just doesn't get it.

Olivia offers an inept apology.

"I said chicken *with mayonnaise*, Olivia. It's not that hard."

"I'm sorry, Mr. Grey."

"It's fine. Just go." She looks relieved but scrambles to leave the room.

I buzz Andrea.

"Sir?"

"Come in here."

Andrea appears at the doorway, looking calm and efficient.

"Get rid of that girl."

Andrea pulls herself up straight.

"Sir, Olivia is Senator Blandino's daughter."

"I don't care if she's the Queen of fucking England. Get her out of my office."

"Yes, sir." Andrea flushes.

"Get someone else to help you," I offer in a gentler tone. I don't want to alienate Andrea.

"Yes, Mr. Grey."

"Thank you. That's all."

She smiles and I know she's back on board. She's a good PA; I don't want her to quit because I'm being an asshole. She exits, leaving me to my chicken sandwich—no mayo—and my campaign plan.

Portland.

I know the form of e-mail address for employees at SIP. I think Anastasia will respond better in writing; she always has. How to begin?

~~Dear Ana~~

No.

~~Dear Anastasia~~

No.

~~Dear Miss Steele~~

Shit!

HALF AN HOUR LATER I'm still staring at a blank computer screen. What the hell do I say?

Come back . . . please?
~~Forgive me.~~
~~I miss you.~~
~~Let's try it your way.~~

I put my head in my hands. Why is this so difficult?

Keep it simple, Grey. Just cut the crap.

I take a deep breath and tap out an e-mail. *Yes . . . this will do.* Andrea buzzes me.

"Ms. Bailey is here to see you, sir."

"Tell her to wait."

I hang up and take a moment, and with my heart pounding, I press send.

From: Christian Grey
Subject: Tomorrow
Date: June 8 2011 14:05
To: Anastasia Steele

Dear Anastasia

Forgive this intrusion at work. I hope that it's going well. Did you get my flowers?

I note that tomorrow is the gallery opening for your friend's show, and I'm sure you've not had time to purchase a car, and it's a long drive. I would be more than happy to take you—should you wish.

Let me know.

Christian Grey
CEO, Grey Enterprises Holdings, Inc.

I watch my inbox.

And watch.

And watch . . . my anxiety growing with every second that crawls by.

Getting up, I pace the office—but that takes me away from my computer. Back at my desk, I check my e-mail yet again.

Nothing.

To distract myself, I trace my finger along the wings of my glider.

For fuck's sake, Grey, get a grip.

Come on, Anastasia, answer me. She's always been so prompt. I check my watch . . . 14:09.

Four minutes!

Still nothing.

Getting up, I pace around my office once more, peering at my watch every three seconds, or so it feels.

By 2:20 I'm in despair. She's not going to reply. She really does hate me . . . who could blame her?

Then I hear the ping of an e-mail. My heart leaps into my throat.

Hell! It's from Ros, telling me she's gone back to her office.

And then it's there, in my inbox, the magical line:

From: Anastasia Steele.

From: Anastasia Steele
Subject: Tomorrow
Date: June 8 2011 14:25
To: Christian Grey

Hi Christian

Thank you for the flowers; they are lovely.

Yes, I would appreciate a lift.

Thank you.

Anastasia Steele
Assistant to Jack Hyde, Editor, SIP

Relief floods through me; I close my eyes, savoring the feeling. *YES!*

I pore over her e-mail looking for clues, but as usual I have no idea what the thoughts are behind her words. The tone is friendly enough, but that's it. Just friendly.

Carpe Diem, Grey.

From: Christian Grey
Subject: Tomorrow
Date: June 8 2011 14:27
To: Anastasia Steele

Dear Anastasia

What time shall I pick you up?

Christian Grey
CEO, Grey Enterprises Holdings, Inc.

I don't have to wait quite so long.

From: Anastasia Steele
Subject: Tomorrow
Date: June 8 2011 14:32
To: Christian Grey

José's show starts at 7:30. What time would you suggest?

Anastasia Steele
Assistant to Jack Hyde, Editor, SIP

We can take *Charlie Tango*.

From: Christian Grey
Subject: Tomorrow
Date: June 8 2011 14:34
To: Anastasia Steele

Dear Anastasia

Portland is some distance away. I shall pick you up at 5:45.

I look forward to seeing you.

Christian Grey
CEO, Grey Enterprises Holdings, Inc.

From: Anastasia Steele
Subject: Tomorrow
Date: June 8 2011 14:38
To: Christian Grey

See you then.

Anastasia Steele
Assistant to Jack Hyde, Editor, SIP

My campaign to win her back is under way. I feel elated; the small blossom of hope is now a Japanese flowering cherry.

I buzz Andrea.

"Miss Bailey went back to her office, Mr. Grey."

"I know, she e-mailed me. I need Taylor here in an hour."

"Yes, sir."

I hang up. Anastasia is working for a guy named Jack Hyde. I want to know more about him. I call Ros.

"Christian." She sounds pissed. *Tough.*

"Do we have access to the employee files from SIP?"

"Not yet. But I can get them."

"Please. Today if you can. I want everything they have on Jack Hyde, and anyone who's worked for him."

"Can I ask why?"

"No."

She's silent for a moment.

"Christian, I don't know what's got into you recently."

"Ros, just do it, okay?"

She sighs. "Okay. Now can we have our meeting about the Taiwan shipyard proposal?"

"Yes. I had an important call to make. It took longer than I thought."

"I'll be right up."

WHEN ROS LEAVES I follow her out of the office.

"WSU next Friday," I tell Andrea, who scribbles a reminder in her notebook.

"And I get to fly in the company chopper?" Ros bubbles with enthusiasm.

"Helicopter," I correct her.

"Whatever, Christian." She rolls her eyes as she enters the elevator, and it makes me smile.

Andrea watches Ros leave, then gives me an expectant look.

"Call Stephan—I'll be flying *Charlie Tango* to Portland tomorrow evening, and I'll need him to fly her back to Boeing Field," I tell Andrea.

"Yes, Mr. Grey."

I see no sign of Olivia. "Has she gone?"

"Olivia?" Andrea asks.

I nod.

"Yes." She seems relieved.

"Where to?"

"Finance."

"Good thinking. It'll keep Senator Blandino off my back."

Andrea looks pleased at the compliment.

"You're getting someone else to help out here?" I ask.

"Yes, sir. I'm seeing three candidates tomorrow morning."

"Good. Is Taylor here?"

"Yes, sir."

"Cancel the rest of my meetings today. I'm going out."

"Out?" she squeaks in surprise.

"Yes." I grin. "Out."

"WHERE TO, SIR?" TAYLOR asks, as I stretch out in the back of the SUV.

"The Mac store."

"On Northeast Forty-Fifth?"

"Yes." I'm going to buy Ana an iPad. Leaning back in my seat, I close my eyes and contemplate which apps and songs I'm going to download and install for her. I could choose "Toxic." I smirk at the thought. No, I don't think that would be popular with her. She'd be mad as hell—and for the first time in a while the thought of her mad makes me smile. Mad like she was in Georgia, not like last Saturday. I shift in my seat; I don't want to be reminded of that. I turn my thoughts back to potential song choices, feeling more buoyant than I have in days. My phone buzzes, and my heart rate spikes.

Dare I hope?

> Hey. Asshole. Beer?

Hell. A text from my brother.

> No. Busy.

> You're always busy.
> Going to Barbados tomorrow.
> To, you know, RELAX.
> See you when I get back.
> And we will have that beer!!!

> Laters, Lelliot. Safe Travels.

IT'S BEEN A DIVERTING evening, filled with music—a nostalgic journey through my iTunes, making a playlist for Anastasia. I remember her dancing in my kitchen; I wish I knew what she'd been listening to. She looked totally ridiculous, and utterly adorable. That was after I fucked her for the first time.

No. After I made love to her the first time?

Neither term feels right.

I recall her impassioned plea the night I introduced her to my parents. *"I want you to make love to me."* How shocked I was by her simple statement—and yet all she wanted was to touch me. I shudder at the thought. I have to make her understand that this is a hard limit for me—I cannot tolerate being touched.

I shake my head. *You're getting way ahead of yourself, Grey—* you have to close this deal first. I check the inscription on the iPad.

> Anastasia—this is for you.
> I know what you want to hear.
> This music on here says it for me.
> Christian

Perhaps this will do it. She wants hearts and flowers; perhaps this will come close. But I shake my head, because I have no idea. There's so much I want to say to her, if she'll listen. And if she won't, the songs will say it for me. I just hope she allows me the opportunity to give them to her.

But if she doesn't like my proposition, if she doesn't like the thought of being with me—what will I do? I might just be a convenient ride to Portland. The thought depresses me, as I head toward my bedroom for some much-needed sleep.

Do I dare to hope?

Damn it. Yes, I do.

The doctor holds up her hands. *I'm not going to hurt you. I need to check your tummy. Here.* She gives me a cold, round sucky thing and she lets me play with it. *You put it on your tummy, and I won't touch you and I can hear your tummy.* The doctor is good . . . the doctor is Mommy.

My new mommy is pretty. She's like an angel. A doctor angel. She strokes my hair. I like it when she strokes my hair. She lets me eat ice cream and cake. She doesn't shout when she finds the bread and apples hidden in my shoes. Or under my bed. Or under my pillow. *Darling, the food is in the kitchen. Just find me or Daddy when you're hungry. Point with your finger. Can you do that?* There is another boy. Lelliot. He is mean. So I punch him. But my new mommy doesn't like the fighting. There is a piano. I like the noise. I stand at the piano and press the white and the black. The noise from the black is strange. Miss Kathie sits at the piano with me. She teaches the black and the white notes. She has long brown hair and she looks like someone I know. She smells of flowers and apple pie baking. She smells of good. She makes the piano sound pretty. She is kind to me. She smiles and I play. She smiles and I am happy. She smiles and she's Ana. Beautiful Ana, sitting with me as I play a fugue, a prelude, an adagio, a sonata. She sighs, resting her head on my shoulder, and she smiles. *I love listening to you play, Christian. I love you, Christian.* Ana. Stay with me. You're mine. I love you, too.

I wake, with a start.
Today, I win her back.

E L James

GREY

After twenty-five years working in TV, E L James decided to pursue her childhood dream, and set out to write stories that readers would fall in love with. The result was the sensuous romance *Fifty Shades of Grey* and its two sequels, *Fifty Shades Darker* and *Fifty Shades Freed*, a trilogy that went on to sell more than 125 million copies worldwide in 52 languages.

In 2012 E L James was named one of Barbara Walters's "Ten Most Fascinating People of the Year," one of *Time* magazine's "Most Influential People in the World," and *Publishers Weekly's* "Person of the Year." *Fifty Shades of Grey* stayed on the *New York Times* Best Seller List for 133 consecutive weeks, and in 2015 the film adaptation—on which James worked as producer—broke box-office records all over the world for Universal Pictures.

E L James lives in West London with her husband, the novelist and screenwriter Niall Leonard, and their two sons. She continues to write novels while acting as producer on the upcoming movie versions of *Fifty Shades Darker* and *Fifty Shades Freed*.

The Fifty Shades Trilogy

Romantic, liberating and totally addictive, the Fifty Shades trilogy will obsess you, possess you and stay with you forever.